MW01002716

THE
PROMISE

THE PROMISE

Book #1 of The Piecer Chronicles

Maxx Powr

Fairalon Books

The Promise

Editing by:
Sarah Liu

Cover design by Maxx Powr

Created in the United States of America

DEDICATION

The Promise is dedicated to the love of my life and best
friend, Elizabeth.

Contents

Chapter One

Graduation Day

Chase pushed his way through to his designated spot on the stadium field for the ceremony. Graduation was being held in the outdoor Piecer Academy Stadium. It was an enormous field, larger than a standard football field, rebuilt from the ground up after the Great War. It was specifically designed for Piecer Corp cadet training and doubled as a sports arena.

Today it was packed with Corp families anxious to see their foster sons graduate. For twenty-two-year-old Chase 523 and his twenty-one-year-old brother, Loose 524, it was the end of their training and the only life they had ever known.

Tripp 523 stood in formation behind Chase in the 523 section. Tripp was the foster son of Adrian Mckinnis, a veteran and victim of the Great Klix War. Mckinnis adopted Tripp after being medically discharged from the war for losing half his foot.

Twenty years ago, the Earth had been caught completely by surprise when the Klix attacked without mercy. The Klix were from the planet Kattar in the Tork system of the Shephard's Galaxy. They were a bipedal species, like humans, but larger and stronger. They had gray-blue leathery skin, retractable claws, and small bones protruding from the top of their head like a crown.

Four cricket-leg-like appendages, called scrapers, grew

directly out of the back of their heads. When rubbed against one another, these scrapers would make the clicking sound the Klix used to communicate and from which they got their familiar name.

"Did I miss anything?" he asked Tripp.

"Yeah, Cha-Cha, you missed it all," said Tripp in a dead serious tone. "You missed your own graduation."

Cha-Cha was Tripp's bastardized version of Chase Chambers, his first name and his foster parents' last name.

"You're shittin' me. I'm not that late."

Tripp looked serious, but couldn't hold it in, then started laughing.

"Nah, you didn't miss a thing, just a bunch of sweaty people bakin' in the sun."

Chase laughed.

"For a second there...I didn't think you were gonna make it," said Tripp.

"Had to, my parents are here."

"Had to? You didn't wanna come?"

"Fuck no. Disband the Corp? It's bullshit, total bullshit."

"Well, it's been twenty years since we had any trouble, and there are plenty of normies now that can take over."

Unlike the Piecers, created in a lab from superior DNA, "normies" were biologically conceived humans.

"Twenty years is nothing," Chase replied. "It's an eyeblink. You always have to be ready and—I saw something."

"What?"

"A shy-sighting."

On Earth, before the Great War, it wasn't unusual to see a light in the night sky appear and then disappear, seemingly out of nowhere—like a twinkling star. The event was so common it was given a name: "shy-sightings." People presumed these were worm-drive ships visiting our world, much like the Earth's starships had visited their worlds. It was thought that these beings were shy, popping in, then changing their minds, and popping out to return to their own star systems. The night sky twinkled with shy-sightings. The public humanized these beings, thinking them timid, cute, and cuddly, and likened them to tiny space aliens from Earth's holographic cartoons.

"Shylien" plush toys were created: fuzzy, teddy-bear-like soft toys about the size of a soccer ball, with oversized eyes and tiny antennae. They came in different colors, green and gray being the most popular. Every little boy and girl slept with their Shylien and often gazed out the window hoping to see a shy sighting, making a wish when they did. They soon became highly prized collectibles, and most children had more than one.

Everyone was eager and ready to meet these cute aliens and few suspected the shy-sightings were anything more than a friendly curiosity. No one knew they were being watched, analyzed, and recorded. Only a few suspected that these sightings were scout ships, observing and planning, but they were dismissed as crackpots.

"You saw a shy-sighting," Tripp asked, "when?"

"Last night. I couldn't sleep. I was lying in my bed and I saw it."

"Anyone else see it?"

"No."

"So you're lying in bed, looking up, and you saw something?" asked Tripp with one eyebrow raised.

"Y'know, you're kinda slow," said Chase, half annoyed, half joking, "but I think you're getting it."

Tripp laughed.

"Ha, Cha-Cha, that's called dreaming. People do that, at night, in bed. Geez, you've always been such a worrywart, and you fell asleep worrying. That's all. Don't need a shrink to interpret that dream. You wanna drill twenty more years... stupidly waiting for something to happen? For what?"

"You have to be ready," said Chase.

Tripp looked at him skeptically.

"Umm...I suppose, but let the normies be ready. I'm done with it," said Tripp. "No more drills. No more orders. No more shitty Corp food. No more four a.m. rousts to run thirty

3

miles. Dang, I won't miss that. I don't know what I'm going to do, but I won't miss that."

"I guess," said Chase, "it's still a big mistake."

"You are so gung-ho-Charlie about the Corp. I don't get it."

"I wouldn't be here without the Corp. You either, bone-head!"

"True, but now that I'm here, I'd kinda like to run my own life," said Tripp, "if you don't mind."

"Well, that oughta be a train wreck," Chase said, laughing. "You seen my brother?"

"Probably," Tripp replied, "but it's *my* train to wreck, and he's twelve rows up on the right in the 524 section, day-dreaming as usual."

The air was hot and deathly still, the trees behind the stadium unmoving, as if painted on the sky. The Piecer pennants surrounding the stadium hung limp like wet rags in the stifling, breezeless heat. It was one of those muggy days so humid you could rub your fingers together in the air and feel them wet on your fingertips.

Chase stared out at the crowd, hoping to catch a glimpse of his parents. Ivory white hand fans—one for each person—flittered rapidly back and forth across the blurry faces in the bleachers. From where Chase stood, they looked like a field of thousands of white butterflies flapping their wings.

A cheer grew louder and louder as General Gilbert Tupi, a large man with a weathered, noticeably scarred face and buzz-cut gray-white hair, stepped up to the wooden lectern placed in the center of the stadium. Clenched in his bionic right hand was a heavy satchel filled with silver and gold Piecer Stars for the graduating cadets.

The ultimate goal for any cadet was the Piecer Star, a gold double helix on a silver star badge with a small sword, said to symbolize the Sword of Damocles, centered through the DNA strand. The badge doubled as a communicator and was the Corp's symbol of achievement and initiation into the broth-erhood of Piecers. *Sacrificium Pro Victoria*, a Latin phrase lettered in gold and silver, each word on a separate spiral of the DNA strand, meaning "Sacrifice for Victory," was the Corp motto.

Five tiny bronze stars, indicating rank, stood out on General Tupi's shoulders against his black uniform, sparkling when the sun hit them just right. Though unnecessary, Tupi had the habit of turning his head toward the Piecer Star communicator attached to his chest whenever he used it. He had never gotten used to having a Star badge communicator, having always worn an older tech ear piece.

Tupi smiled and waved until the crowd quieted down. Most people used the older tech ear piece, but the Star badge worked just as well broadcasting to these devices.

"Hello, everyone," he said, and the sound was relayed to the receivers in each crowd member's ears. The chattering crowd hushed, waiting for him to speak.

"Welcome, everyone—cadets, friends, and families," he said, smiling. "Thank you all for coming. I'll try not to drone on too long in this horrendous heat."

A smattering of applause rippled through the stands as Tupi wiped his brow with his sleeve. Being a "normie," a non-engineered human, in a dress black Piecer uniform, he was not immune to the dreadful heat, and sweat trickled down his face. Normies were often of high rank, as they had the luxury of a normal life span and had miraculously survived the war.

"As you all know," he began, "many years ago, we fought a great war against the Klix."

As he said the words, he looked down at his prosthetic arm and made a fist. It was a perfect replacement, and though he had full use of it, hand and fingers, it was not his arm. He winced with recalled pain of the searing explosion that changed him forever. Then he returned to his speech.

"Earth incurred massive casualties. Many brave soldiers on both sides suffered greatly."

Chase mumbled under his breath, "Brave soldiers on both sides, my ass! Politically correct bullshit."

Tripp laughed as General Tupi continued. "We are here today to honor the brave men of the Piecer Corp, thank them and their families, and bid farewell to a once useful, and now, thankfully, unnecessary program."

"Bullshit," said Chase under a covered cough.

General Tupi paused and glared in his direction. Some of the 524 graduates turned and looked disapprovingly at him. His foster brother, Loose, laughed and pointed at him. Chase gave Loose the middle finger salute, mouthing the words *fuck you*, which only made Loose laugh more.

In the Corp, batches were addressed by their last three digits, so the 19524s were simply the 524s. It was easier and sounded more like a platoon number than a batch ID. General Tupi, however, preferred using the surname of the cadets' foster parents as their last name. He disapproved of the numbering system for anything other than military records and emphasized that the cadets were human beings—not machines.

"Gage and Hector are here, right?" asked Chase.

"Yep, Hector's two rows up, and Gage is bringing up the rear."

"Shit, I must have run right past him."

"Yep, you did...not too observant for a guy who sees tiny things in the sky," Tripp said, laughing.

"Very funny. You see the *Promise*?" Chase asked, changing the subject. "Are they letting us take her out for a spin?"

"Yep, she's over there," answered Tripp, pointing to the back of the stadium. "No one's gone in her yet, maybe after."

The *Promise* was Earth's first worm-drive starship, and she was enormous, taking up most of the field in the back of the stadium. Her dull gray hull and angular lines made her look cold, almost dead. Two rotary guns protruded from the bow ahead of dark, almost black-tinted windows. Aft sections of the engines were darker, almost a gunmetal blue from the heat of repeated engine burns. On both sides of the front of the ship, the *Promise*'s name could still be seen above the somewhat faded "Explore and Protect" logo painted on the sides of the cockpit.

"God, I loved that ship," said Chase. "You could go anywhere in that thing."

"Isn't 'going anywhere' how all this shit started?" asked Tripp sarcastically.

"Yeah, yeah, woulda happened anyway. They didn't use our ships to attack us. They had the tech too."

"I guess," said Tripp, "but maybe they wouldn't have found us…and I'm okay with no more visitors to Earth…*and* I'm not interested in visiting them either. I think I'm going to lie on a beach somewhere until I get sunburned, heal, then get sunburned again."

"Trained on that ship," said Chase angrily. "Can't believe they're going to mothball her, in a fucking museum. She can still serve."

"They did that to all of the worm-drive ships, Cha-Cha, only a few still around, scrapped the rest. The *Promise* is last because they were still using her for training."

"I know, but it's the stupidest thing they could ever do—next to the stupider thing they're about to do by disbanding the Corp."

"Oh, I don't know," said Tripp, "flying around all over the place advertising Earth didn't work out so well the first time. Klix almost wiped us out."

"I guess we're just a bunch of pussies hiding under the covers now," said Chase.

"Geez, what is with you?" asked Tripp, now seeing Chase's skinned knuckles. "You punch out the wall again?"

"It's nothing," he said, pulling his hand back. "I don't know. Something's wrong; I can feel it. Disbanding the Corp, mothballing the *Promise*. It's fucked up!"

"Everything's fine. Shit, when this is over, I'll buy you a beer to calm your ass down."

"Yeah, yeah. Where they takin' her?"

"I heard she's going to the space museum in New San Diego."

"Sucks," said Chase. "That's all I'm sayin'."

"At least they're not scrappin' her. Being the first worm-drive ship, she probably should be in a museum anyway."

"I guess."

"Hey, they flew her here for our graduation. That's pretty cool, right? It's an honor. So gimme a smile, Chasey-wasey. Come on. You can do it!"

"God, you're so defective," said Chase, laughing. "You shoulda been recovered." Chase smiled.

"There it is!" Tripp grinned. "You know you're beautiful when you smile," he said, blowing him a kiss.

Chase feigned vomiting, and then changed the subject. "Can you see my parents?" he asked, craning his neck over the other cadets.

Tripp scanned the crowd, searching. "Section three," Tripp said. "Good seats...front row, on the right. Your family got connections?"

"Very funny."

"Your mom is smiling, and your dad's chatting up the guy next to him, pointing in our direction, probably bragging on you. Hey, he's wearing Scout Specs and waving his fan."

"Hi, Chase's dad," Tripp mouthed, waving. "You give him those?" he asked.

"Yeah, for his birthday."

"How'd you get 'em?"

"I borrowed them from supply. They won't miss 'em."

"Common thievery; I like it. You might be part Quargg."

The Quargg were an alien species known for stealing anything they came across that wasn't locked down.

"How can you see all that? I can see people there, but... you can see all that?"

"I'm special," said Tripp, laughing. "I gots the bird eyes!" He flapped his arms.

"You got the bird brain to go with it too," added Chase.

Tripp made some funny bird call noises while Chase looked out over the bleachers, trying to make out familiar faces. Chase called out to Jack 523, who was scanning the crowd with his own Scout Specs.

Jack 523 was the "little brother" of the batch. Though the same age, he was much shorter than the other 523s but just as fast. He could also heal quickly and could hear better than any of them. He was nicknamed "Batman" by the other 523s because of his bat-like extraordinary hearing. Jack had been scheduled to be recovered because of his small size, but anytime the New San Diego Institute for Conception evaluator or SDIC came to remove him, Jack heard him coming and was out the door, unable to be found. After multiple "surprise" visits hoping to catch him off guard, they simply gave up. Jack would come home after they left, laughing and saying, "Jack be nimble, Jack be quick," and he and his foster parents would laugh at the SDIC car heading down the road without him. His foster parents loved him and had no intention of turning him in to be recovered.

"Hey, Jack, can I borrow those?" asked Chase.

"Sure, Chase," he said, tossing the specs to him. "I want 'em back, though. I'm checkin' out the babes."

"Just for a sec," replied Chase.

Chase immediately zeroed in on the crowd where his parents were sitting. He smiled, waving at his dad and mom in the stands. Then he tossed the specs back to Jack with a "thanks."

"Your old man here?" Chase asked Tripp.

"Yeah...said he wouldn't miss it."

"Hey, well, that's something, ain't it?" said Chase, patting him on the shoulder.

"I guess...if he's sober. You're lucky; your foster p's are great."

"Yeah, but your dad is okay. We both could have been recovered; at least he saved your ass."

"I guess, but he drinks too much. He's different when he drinks—mean."

"I don't blame him," said Chase. "If I lost my wife, half my foot, and my career to a Klix bomb blast, I'd drink too."

"Maybe," said Tripp, "but I wouldn't have taken on a kid to raise. It didn't help me any, growing up with an angry drunk. If it wasn't for Hector and his mom living next door, I would've run away."

"I'm glad you stuck it out...and I *do* know I'm lucky."

Chase thought about his foster parents for a moment and just how lucky he had been. He could have been assigned to anyone, to foster parents who might have had him "recovered" for his initial small size. Chase remembered when the SDIC came for him and how his parents saved him from certain death.

"But your father is here," Chase said. "He came for you, and it ain't the talk—it's the do."

"Yeah, it's the *do*," Tripp repeated. "I guess he does care, in his own screwed up way. When he wasn't drunk, he was great."

Tripp shook off his sadness, forcing a grin. "Hey, we're on our own after we graduate. Once we get our Stars, I'm gonna get my own place. I guess the 524s get their Stars today too. You and Loose going to stay with the Chambers?"

"Fuck Loose," said Chase. "Why do the 524s get to graduate anyway?"

"Whaddya mean?"

"They didn't finish their training. They didn't earn a Star."

"Why do you care? Won't *be* a Corp tomorrow anyway."

"It's not right," said Chase. "You put in the work, you get your Star. That's how it's done. Piecers don't take shortcuts. And for the millionth time, disbanding the Corp is just stupid."

"You're kinda bitchy today, aintcha? That time of the month?"

"Oh, fuck you. It's not right. You have to *earn* it. Means nothin' if they give them out for no reason."

Tripp cocked his head, looking surprised. Then he laughed, and that made Chase laugh.

"Okayyyy...well, you better pay attention, butthead, or you're gonna get us kicked outta here...and we won't get *our* Stars."

"Before I go on," Tupi continued. "I ask for a moment of silence for the valiant Sixers—those brave men who came before you, whose short and painful lives were given willingly in our defense and in defense of our home, Mother Earth."

The crowd fell silent, and every cadet in the 523s and 524s bowed their heads. Sobbing could be heard from the families in the stands. It was not often they were asked to recall the horror. Having lived in peace for so long, most had forgotten the bad days, the death, the war, and the suffering. New "normie" families grew up not knowing how bad it had been, how close to annihilation they had come. They forgot quickly. They *wanted* to forget.

The Piecer Corp project, creating soldiers from specially designed DNA, was a good plan with one major flaw: it took too long. Earth couldn't wait for cadets to mature to normal adults. By necessity, scientists went further with the Piecer Sixer program, altering the aging gene to accelerate growth, creating an adult recruit in as little as two years. They were fast, strong, smart, and deadly, but at a heavy cost.

For these Piecers, there was a horrible downside to the accelerated aging process. It didn't stop. A recruit had about two years of fighting ability before they were considered elderly and unfit for duty. These original Piecers became known as the "Sixers" because few lived beyond six years.

Growing at that rate was extremely painful, and the recruits had to take large quantities of powerful synthetic opiates, or "soaps" as they came to call them, to simply function. The pain of their accelerated growth increased with age, and those who weren't already addicted to the "soaps" soon could not live without them. Some found the pain so excruciating that they killed themselves, overdosing on soaps with the help of the scientists who created them and now pitied them. Unofficially, the men coined the term "Sixer Heaven" for those Sixers taking their final dose of soaps, with many joking about how many soaps it would take to get to "Sixer Heaven."

Those addicted to the soaps were dazed, often euphoric;

others had to take so many soaps to kill the pain that they were actively hallucinating on the battlefield. It turned out that these were often their best soldiers, charging into the Klix forces without care or fear—feeling no pain and often smiling while laughing—as they continued firing their weapons with their legs blown off by alien shrapnel bombs or mines. Among the Corp the mantra was, "As long as I can hold my weapon, my enemies will fear me."

And the Klix *did* fear the Sixers. They gained a reputation for their courage and their savagery. Living through the carnage and the drugs, some of the Sixers became barbaric, taking souvenirs of their kills. Chunks of alien skulls hung around their necks as trophies. Body parts, alien medals, and belt buckles—anything that caught their eye was used to adorn their uniforms, proof of their kills.

Most human survivors, having suffered greatly at the hands of the Klix, cheered the tactic. However, the government tried to quash this behavior as being too savage. They wanted to do something to stop it and still appease the troops, so they decided to add an alien skull emblem to the Piecer uniforms, hoping to placate them.

Government officials felt the optics were better in what was left of the underground Earth media. The uniforms were less offensive to the few loud public critics than alien body parts dangling around the Sixers' necks. It appeased most of the men, some actually preferring the new uniform over the uniforms covered in smelly and decaying body parts. After implementation of the new uniforms, most stopped collecting souvenirs, but no one dared challenge those who continued the practice.

Talk of halting the Piecer Corp plan increased. Criticism grew, watching the Sixers come home from the war wounded and suffering, already too old to fight at the age of five. The Piecer program was questioned for its worth, as many felt it was immoral to sacrifice these brave men and inflict so much pain on them. The Sixers were heroes and didn't deserve to be forced to suffer in this manner.

But the military was worried they would lose their most valuable resource, the genetically superior fighting men, and would only agree to a compromise. As the outcry grew and the Sixers aged, the military finally relented, agreeing to use only "normal" growth Piecers, once there were enough of them to fill the ranks. Then the Sixer program would be discontinued.

Sadly, the Sixer program went on for years, using full divisions of ten to fifteen thousand of the disposable Sixers. Thousands upon thousands of age-accelerated recruits were sacrificed to allow for the normal aging process of the new Piecer force to grow into adulthood.

General Tupi looked up from his lectern, signaling that the moment of silence had passed. "For many of you, today is a bittersweet graduation day," he said. "You have succeeded in your training and have also brought honor to yourselves and your families, but you will soon be saying goodbye to lifelong friends. I know *I* will miss you all. You will miss each other. Our leaders have worked tirelessly, and they have succeeded beyond our wildest dreams. We have lived in peace with the Klix Supremacy for the last twenty years. Our treaty has stood the test of time."

"Fucking idiots," Chase grumbled. "Every last one of 'em."

Tripp pushed Chase from behind again, laughing.

General Tupi continued. "We would like to thank your foster families for the selfless job of raising and guiding you to the fine men you have become. We honor your foster mothers and foster sisters. We thank them for the courage to stay home, the courage to rebuild humanity, the courage to live. Without them, there would be no us, no future, no humanity."

"Go, Mom!" screamed one of the cadets.

"Please...let's have all our beloved mothers, sisters and daughters, stand up and take a bow," said Tupi.

General Tupi paused as everyone applauded, the men turning to the women, the cadets turning to their foster families. The women stood, smiled, and then sat back down. General Tupi waited until everyone was seated, smiling before speaking again.

"But today, we are here to pay tribute and bid farewell to the last classes of a long line of heroes, the Piecer Corp graduates of 2173."

The crowd broke into cheers, hoots and whistles. Tupi waited for them to die down. Then his smile melted away and he looked serious and sad.

"I know many of you were troubled by the morality of the Piecer Corp—creating people, soldiers, and sending them to their deaths. We all were. We loved the Sixers, our heroes, and felt their pain. We grieved when they died, when they suffered. We love our Piecers and have felt their loss too, our foster sons, all my sons."

Tupi's eyes teared up, and he took a deep breath to compose himself.

"But they have saved us, our Sixers, our Piecer Corp. Their sacrifice allowed us the time to rebuild. Humanity has been replenished, and the creation of soldiers is no longer a necessity." Tupi paused and smiled. "I am very happy to say that from this day forward, our foster sons—our Piecers—you too can live in peace. So go home to your families. Live out your lives without war. Get married. Have children. Raise a family of your own."

He paused and stared at the 523 section and with a gleam in his eye said, "But *not* with my granddaughter."

General Tupi was known to have a gorgeous granddaughter, raising her after her parents were killed in the war. But he was very protective of her and kept her away from the military and the Corp as much as possible.

The stadium grew silent, save for a few chuckles from the cadets. Finally, a slow and building *OOHHH* drifted through the crowd.

Then the crowd went completely silent, thinking the general had slighted the 523 cadets or the "bad batch," as they had come to be called. The bad batch was renowned—the best the Corp had to offer. The 19,523rd batch had special abilities the other batches (before and after) did not possess. They could heal faster, see better, hear better, smell better and run faster than any other batch. They excelled at the academy and were revered by their superiors—including Tupi.

General Tupi exaggerated a head nod and winked extra-long to make sure everyone knew he was kidding. The crowd burst into laughter and hoots, and they began chanting, "Tupi, Tupi."

He bent over, laughing along with them, and then held up his hand for silence. When everyone quieted down, he scanned the graduates from left to right, looking into their eyes, smiling and showing his approval. His eyes watered, and a look of admiration came over him.

"Please forgive my awkward jest. These things can get so boring and we should laugh more...now that our future is secure. Really," said Tupi. "I love all our cadets and would be proud to have any of the 523s date my granddaughter."

He glanced in the direction of the 523s, making eye contact with Chase for a moment, and then moved on.

"To the Piecer Corp graduating class of 2173, I could not be prouder of you—even if you were my own sons. I thank you, *we* thank you, for your devotion to your duties, and I am happy to say you are hereby released from further military obligation!"

The thundering sound of the crowd and the cadets cheering and stamping their feet filled the stadium.

Chase grumbled and looked at his foster brother, Loose, who appeared bored by the whole spectacle. Loose glanced skyward and then checked the time on the stadium scoreboard against his wrist display, as if anxious for the ceremony to end. Chase looked around at his 523 brothers, smiling and recalling the fun they had during training.

I wonder if we'll stay in touch, he thought. *I wonder if...*

Tripp pushed him from behind, laughing. "Shit, pay attention," he said. "You're just like your idiot brother."

Chase laughed, and when he turned back, he looked again for Loose but couldn't find him.

"And now," General Tupi said. "It is time. I know our beloved Drill Sergeant Grant has pounded this adage into you: 'always…always have a way out.' Today, *this* is your way out."

Tupi gave a nod in Sergeant Grant's direction. Sergeant Grant smiled, gave him the thumbs up sign, and looked left and right with his hand shielding his eyes, as if looking for a way out. Tupi mimicked Grant with his hand over his eyes, turning right and left looking for *his* way out. Then he turned back to the cadets.

He paused, staring out over the crowd and the cadets in formation in front of him. He thought about the field they were on, and what the field had looked like when he was their age, pockmarked with bomb craters and stained with blood. He blinked in the bright sun, and in that moment, he remembered all that had happened to him and those he loved, now gone. He remembered how hopeful mankind was at the invention of the first worm drive—and the horror it wrought.

This is a joyous occasion, you old fool, he thought, shaking his head. *No time for sad thoughts.*

He opened his eyes and forced a smile.

Clearing his throat, he then addressed the crowd. "Please come up as we call your name to receive your Star and your diploma…"

As he spoke, a sudden explosion lit up the sky. Tupi looked up while the Piecer cadets instinctively hit the ground, drawing their laser rifles and searching for the source. Everyone was momentarily blinded, and their ears rang from the sound. The crowd screamed to each other to run, yet no one could hear anyone else. With blurred vision, people stumbled around stunned and disoriented as they fled the stadium in a daze, as if feeling their way through the air. Bombers overhead began to unload their deadly cargo.

A follow-up fireball blast hit the lectern, sending bits and pieces of the lectern flying everywhere. Exploded Piecer Stars littered the field and sparkled under the light of each additional bomb burst. All that was left of General Tupi was the smoldering tritanium frame of his artificial arm, its metal fingers still twitching.

"We're under attack!" one of the remaining officers screamed. "Return fire. Defend yourselves!"

Families of the cadets ran screaming from the stadium as blast after blast hit the field and bleacher seats. The cadets tried to fire on the ships, but their weapons proved useless. The initial blinding blast had been an electromagnetic pulse explosion, or EMP, in the atmosphere. It created a shock wave that disabled electronics, including communications and the Piecers' laser weapons. They were helpless.

"Take cover!" ordered a lieutenant, just before another blast blew him to pieces.

"Chase, what the fuck is going on?" Hector shouted from the bottom of a crater blown out by a bomb.

"They're back."

"*Who's* back?"

"The fucking Klix."

"But we have a treaty."

"They never gave a shit about the treaty," said Chase. "They just used the time to regroup and rebuild."

"What do we do?"

"You seen Gage?"

Nearby, a pile of exploded bleachers spread apart from below. Gage was pushing broken seats aside like cardboard. He looked at his shoulder and winced. A large piece of wood about the size of a tent spike was sticking out and through his shoulder.

"Those fuckers, they bled me!" he shouted, grabbing the stake and yanking.

Blood sprayed from the wound, spurting in time with his heartbeat.

"Damn, that hurts! I thought the good lookin' guy's not supposed to get hit."

He examined the wood chunk closely, still dripping with his blood.

"Now that's a fucking splinter!" he said. "Somebody's gonna pay for that shit."

He tossed the stake over his shoulder and put his hand up to the wound to slow the flow of blood.

A scream from the sky intensified and Chase yelled, "Hit the deck!" Everyone dropped to the ground as another Klix bomb exploded nearby, sending dirt and debris flying everywhere. After waiting while listening, not hearing another bomb drop, they climbed to their feet.

"You okay?" Chase asked Gage.

"Yeah," Gage replied. "Just a scratch. See?" He pulled his hand away from his wound, revealing a now-narrow slit where the stake had entered. The skin around the slit was bright red—almost glowing—and engorged with blood.

"Better already."

He put his hand back on the wound, and in mere moments, the blood had stopped gushing. When he pulled his hand away again, the hole had completely closed and stopped bleeding. The skin around the wound was pink and turning darker, but no evidence of an entry wound could be found, only a bruise on the skin.

"See any other 523s?" Chase asked. "Where's Batman? Where's Grant?"

"Jack didn't make it," said Gage. "Nothin' left of him to heal. Grant's dead, too."

"And Tripp...where's Tripp? He was right behind me, a second ago."

"Ran for cover. That boy knows how to cover his ass," Gage replied.

"Here," Tripp called, running from the back of the last standing set of bleachers. "Hid under the bleachers."

"Way to hide in the bullseye, dumbass. Only bleachers not hit," said Gage. "You are one lucky mother."

Tripp smiled. "Who hit us? I couldn't see shit under the bleachers."

"Klix," answered Chase. "I saw one of their transport ships."

"You were right, Cha-Cha, about the shy-sighting. I should've believed you. Sorry."

"I didn't want to believe it either," replied Chase. "Anyone seen my parents, or my brother?"

"Or my father?" asked Tripp.

"Negative," replied Gage. "Anyone seen my mom?"

"Haven't seen anybody's family," Tripp said sadly. "Not since the EMP went off. Everyone ran for cover. You see anyone, Hector?"

Hector ran up from in front of them, looking left and right for any survivors.

"I was a little busy stayin' alive," he said, "but I *did* see your brother break rank just before the Klix hit; probably had to take a leak. 524s got hit pretty bad. He may be the only one left. What now?"

Gage turned and pointed at the stadium field. "Who's that?" he asked.

"Where?" asked Hector.

"There, out on the field...limping."

Another Klix ship was headed in their direction, ready to unload more bombs.

"Scatter called Chase; he's targeting us."

The squad ran in different directions, diving into any cover they could find.

Out on the field, the limping older soldier in dated fatigues hollered at the sky and waved his arms, attracting the attention of the Klix ship hovering over them. Readying a bomb drop, the ship spotted Mckinnis, turned and headed toward him in the center of the field.

"Holy shit, that's my dad," said Tripp. "What the fuck's he doing?"

"He's trying to draw the ship away from us by trying to shoot at the Klix with our fucked-up weapons," said Gage. "He doesn't know the EMP made 'em useless. He keeps picking them up off the ground and aiming them at the Klix, but

19

they're not firing."

"Shit! He's drunk again. He doesn't know they won't work. I gotta stop him."

"Come down, you gray fuckers," his father yelled, picking up and throwing down one felled soldier's weapon after another. "This is for Marie, cocksuckers!" he hollered, aiming again and then pulling the useless trigger.

McInnis limped forward to the center of the field, to the edge of the crater where Tupi had been giving his address.

"Fucking cheap-ass weapons," he shrieked. "We had *real* weapons in the Great War."

Tripp took off like a rabbit, heading right for his dad.

"Wait, Tripp!" Chase yelled. "They've seen him."

His father shouted at the Klix ship hovering above him and threw his weapon at the ship. The ship targeted him, and released a bomb. Mckinnis looked over at his son, smiled, and then gave the Klix the finger, screaming, "Fuck you!"

As Tripp ran toward the field's center, he saw the bomb drop and his father disappear in a smoky red mist. The blast blew Tripp backwards, and he landed against what was left of the fence that surrounded the stadium.

Hector ran to him and helped him sit up. Dazed, Tripp struggled to his feet, scanning the field, trying to find his father. There was nothing left of him; he was gone. He started to yell at the Klix ship, but Hector pulled him away.

"I'm sorry," said Hector. "He's gone. We have to go. There will be another time."

"They killed him," Tripp screamed angrily. "He was a harmless old man, and they fuckin' killed him."

Tripp yelled again at the Klix—cursing and shaking his fist—but Hector wrapped his arm around him and yanked him away. The Klix ships spread out and away from the stadium, continuing their bombing campaign while heading into the Piecer family neighborhood.

"I know," said Hector, still pulling on Tripp. "We'll get 'em...just not now, not without weapons."

Tripp started crying, cursing at the sky as Hector led him

back to Chase and the others.

"I'm sorry," said Chase. "He was a brave man to face the Klix like that. He probably saved all our lives."

Tripp wiped his eyes and took a deep breath.

"I'm gonna kill those motherfuckers," he seethed, "if it's the last thing that I do, I'm gonna kill 'em all. They killed my dad. They just blew him away as if he was nothin'."

"And we're going to help you," said Hector, turning to Chase. "What's the plan, Chief?"

Chase called out orders, "Help any survivors. Try to find your families and secure them. I'm going to look for my family. Then, we rendezvous at Alpha-Seven!"

Alpha-Seven was code for the Pwyll crater station on Europa, one of Jupiter's largest moons. In the event of an emergency, they had agreed to meet at the station to plan their next move.

"Rendezvous at Alpha-Seven? How? And what about *you*?" Gage asked Chase. "How will we find you?"

"Find other worm-drive ships if you can. We'll need as many as possible. Check the museums. If you can't find one, meet me back here at the *Promise*. I'll wait as long as I can. Stay alive!"

His team saluted as he turned away and he ran through the blown-out stadium bleachers, frantically searching for his parents.

"Section three...they were in section three," Chase mumbled, orienting himself in the rubble.

He found a burnt and broken section four sign and knew he was close. Scanning the area, his heart sank. Where section three should have been was a crater blast, smoke, body parts, and bloodied hand fans. Chase searched the rubble frantically for any signs of his parents. They had always protected him and now he'd have to protect them, if they were still alive.

Home, he thought. *If they got away, they'd go home.*

Chapter Two

Home

After searching the rubble at the destroyed stadium, Chase ran like a madman, following the burned-out road home, not wanting to pass his parents and miss them. He hopped over debris from the Klix blasts and dodged crater holes where the road used to be.

The Klix were everywhere, landing and unloading troops while ships aloft bombed fleeing humans wherever they were found. The smell of death, burning wood and flesh, was overwhelming. The Klix were back, and their weapons were deadlier than ever.

Using the remaining walls of bombed-out buildings as cover, Chase dodged the Klix troops patrolling along the way.

"No time to engage, no time to fight...control yourself," he said to himself. "Breathe. I need to get home, need to make sure my parents are safe."

He followed the road, passing row upon row of destroyed and burning buildings. It looked like a giant had smashed each house with his fist, flattening most to the ground and burning the rest. He could smell smoke from the incendiary bombs the Klix were using to burn their Piecer homes. He heard distant screams as bomb blasts rained down from above.

Along the way, he recognized homes of friends and neighbors completely destroyed, still ablaze. Bodies lay strewn on both sides of the road like so many rag dolls tossed into a closet. He recognized a few of them and hesitated—wanting to stop and help—but they were gone. There was nothing he could do.

Chase stopped running to get his bearings, leaning up against a back wall of the remains of a house. The usual landmarks were gone, most blown away entirely. His pulse pounded in his ear.

My friends, their families...gone, he thought, feeling the hate and anger building inside him.

Chase's only working weapon was his tritanium combat knife in his boot sheath. These knives were favored by Piecer troops because they were practically indestructible. Once sharpened at the factory, they never lost their razor's edge. A tritanium knife could pierce steel with enough force behind it, and it would remain as sharp as the day it was made.

He took a deep breath and closed his eyes, trying to focus and breathe. Suddenly he felt hot acrid breath near his face. He remained motionless, his eyes still closed. He felt a push to his shoulder with a rifle butt nudging him to see if he was alive or dead, and then he heard a faint click.

His father's words came back to him. *Breathe. Are you ready? Breathe. Are you prepared? Breathe. Calm yourself, focus, complete your mission.*

Martin Chambers, Chase's foster father was a normie. He was only seventeen when he met and fell in love with Chase's foster mother, fifteen-year-old Gwendolyn Christensen. They had been dating for only a year but were already planning their future together. The universe seemed so open then, those moments of innocence so promising before the war. They were deeply in love and never expected to be apart, until the attack.

At the start of the Great War, Martin was called to duty. This was the same week Gwendolyn informed him she was pregnant. They arranged a quickie wedding ceremony so their child would have their father's surname, and Robert Chambers was born eight months later. Gwen transmitted his picture to Martin on the front lines, and they both wept—

praying the war would end soon—but it was not to be.

Gwendolyn was seventeen when she gave birth and had to raise Robert alone. Home became an underground subway system abandoned long ago. The entrance was almost entirely caved in from Klix bombs and concealed from their patrols.

Martin was needed on the front and could rarely be spared for leave. He quickly rose to the rank of captain and tried desperately to keep in touch with Gwen using military communicators. Their transmissions were necessarily kept short fearing their communications would be traced and Gwen and the baby's hiding place exposed.

Gwen did her best to raise Robert in hiding, in the shadow of war. Shell-shocked soldiers sometimes wandered into the subway looking for food, first aid, or a brief respite from the horror above ground. Gwen fed them, tended their wounds, and listened to their stories, hoping to glean any information she could about Martin's division. Food was scarce, and she'd leave Robert in their care to scavenge for any food she could find in the blown-out stores or homes.

As he got older, Robert would wait anxiously for Gwen's safe return, hoping to hear a story about Martin's exploits in the war. He grew up worshiping his father, and wanting to be a soldier just like him. At sixteen, he volunteered for the military, the minimum age for any recruit.

Naturally, Martin and Gwendolyn were very proud of him, and Martin was able to finagle leave to come home for Robert's induction into the military. They placed Robert's military photo on the desk of the ticket counter in the underground subway station, displaying it like any proud parent of any soldier. But the war raged on above, and Martin returned to the front while Robert left home for basic training, training alongside a mix of Sixers and normie recruits.

He was a good soldier and earned the rank of corporal within one year and a battlefield promotion to sergeant at a year and six months for heroism and outstanding leadership at the Battle of Joshua Tree Park. Robert fought alongside the Sixers as a sergeant until the Spring of Tears battle in Palm Springs cost him his life and the lives of twenty thousand Sixers and normie soldiers alike.

When the news came back to Gwendolyn and Martin, it was a punch to the gut like no other; they could not catch their breath, they could not think, they could not believe he was gone. They had always understood the cost of war, having lost so many friends and family, but the loss of their only son was too much to bear.

Martin came back from the front for Robert's burial and never went back. The military was in disarray, and no one came looking for him, either by omission or perhaps in sympathy. He and Gwen worked to support the troops and the war effort in any way they could—the war effort that was finally seeing some victories.

The new Piecer program—for the most part—was a success; the soldiers who were allowed to grow at least to their teen years were exceptional killing machines. They had more time to learn from the Sixers and were brave, fast, cunning, and deadly without the pain and the drugs. Earth scientists equipped the Piecer recruits with newer and deadlier laser weapons and the Klix were dying in great numbers. The Earth was finally winning.

Certain areas aboveground were considered safe areas, or Klix-free zones, and humans returned to the surface in these zones. They began to take back what was left of their cities and rural towns using more and more Sixers and normal-growth Piecers.

In the year 2151, Chase 523 was created at the New San Diego Institute for Conception, or SDIC station. He wasn't the first Piecer child created, nor would he be the last, but there was talk of ending the program, now that we had returned to the surface. He was, in fact, part of the nineteen thousand, five hundred and twenty-third batch of normal growth Piecer recruits.

As soon as they were old enough to leave their incubator, the government assigned foster parents to raise the boys and give them a sense of family and belonging. These were special families—usually former military or their relatives—chosen to raise these amazing babies to adulthood. Their job was to guide them and report back anything unusual about their wards, as well as any problems the child might exhibit.

All cadets were male in the Piecer Corp, simply because women were too valuable to risk as soldiers. Birth control was unthinkable, unpatriotic, and anti-Earth, and the surviving government rewarded couples who had more than one child, with an extra food ration bonus paid for female children.

When Martin and Gwendolyn heard that the Piecer program was looking for foster parents, they jumped at the chance. Gwen wanted a Piecer baby badly, but they had no illusions that this was going to be easy or a normal parenting situation.

They went to the incubation terminal to meet their new ward, and everything progressed normally. The first stop was a trip to the registration office to check in and finalize all the official papers sent in months in advance.

"When do we get to see him?" Gwen asked, pacing behind Martin, who was seated in front of the clerk's desk.

"Soon...very soon," said the clerk. "Just one more paper to sign. We must follow protocol."

"We sent all our forms in already," said Martin, "months ago. More forms?"

"Just one," replied the clerk. "Just the one."

"What is this?" Martin asked, holding up the paper.

"This is the Recovery Agreement," replied the clerk. "It's merely a formality—rarely happens, really."

"Sounds like government bullshit to me," said Martin, growing frustrated.

"Martin," said Gwen, holding his arm. "He's just doing his job."

"I understand, Mr. Chambers," said the clerk, looking over his glasses. "And I'm sorry. We're almost done."

The clerk pressed a button on his desk.

"So if we notice anything unusual about the boy, we have to return him...to you?" Martin asked, reading the paper.

"Yes; that is the agreement."

"And then what happens to him?"

The clerk pretended not to hear him.

"What happens to him?" Martin repeated louder.

"I assure you, Mr. Chambers, we will follow all the required procedures to evaluate the boy. He will be tested regularly. If he is defective, he'll need to be returned, and you can have another. That is what you are agreeing to."

"And the boy?"

The clerk glanced around the room, and his plastic smile disappeared.

"He will be recovered..." he whispered. "Recycled, if you will."

"You mean *murdered*, don't you?" Martin snapped.

The clerk bristled. "We don't murder people here, Mr. Chambers. We have few resources left to us, and we create fighting men to defend us from the Klix. We cannot waste resources on defective units."

The clerk took a deep breath and relaxed into another fake smile. "I'm sure he will be fine, but if you have changed your mind, there are others waiting."

Gwendolyn bent over and whispered into his ear, "Just sign the damn paper, Martin."

Martin looked into Gwen's eyes, scribbled his signature on the form, and shoved it at the clerk.

"This is wrong," he whispered to Gwen.

"Thank you, Mr. and Mrs. Chambers," said the clerk as a nurse dressed in all white entered the room holding a baby in a light blue camouflage blanket. "Ah! Here's the boy now."

The baby was quiet while looking around the room at his surroundings.

"Oh my God," said Gwen, shaking his tiny hand with her index finger. "He's perfect. Does he have a name?"

"We've been calling him Chase. He keeps crawling out of his crib, and we have to chase him down. He's from batch

523, and it looks like a good batch. You're lucky. And you can call him anything you want, though. At this age, they don't really know anything."

"No, I like it," said Gwen, cuddling him close. "Hello, little Chase, Chase Chambers. I'm your mommy. He seems to respond to it, to his name. Hi, Chase."

"Uh, well, could be...unlikely."

He stamped the Recovery Agreement and scanned it into the incubation computer system.

"We're all done here," said the clerk. "This is your new address. The government will supply you with housing—as you are raising one of their own. It's a nice neighborhood, in a safe zone, all Piecer foster parents, and pretty close to the Piecer Academy. You can take your son home now. We'll be in touch. You can expect your first inspection in a year's time."

The clerk held out his hand to shake, and Martin turned away abruptly.

"Come on, Gwen, let's get out of here."

They collected their meager belongings from their subway station home and were driven to their new home in a government ATV. Finally, they were dropped at the doorstep of a modest two-story home.

"It's nice," said Gwen. "Bigger than I expected."

"The least they could do," said Martin, opening the door for her.

Gwen cooed at the baby. "We're home, Chase...this is your new home."

Martin placed Robert's military induction picture on the mantel of the fireplace, centering it perfectly and rubbing off the fingerprints on the glass.

"I think he would have liked it here," he said, his voice breaking.

Gwen put Chase on the floor, then reached out and hugged Martin, who was now visibly shaking.

"He died a hero, doing what he wanted to do. He was his father's son."

Chase skittered across the floor in a flash, out of his diaper and out of the room.

"There he goes," Gwen said while running after him, the first of many times during that first year.

The Chambers settled in, and in no time, it felt like their home. Chase was given one of the rooms upstairs where a crib had been placed, and they took the room next door.

The first year went by quickly. Twelve months later to the day, the SDIC evaluator came to their door, unannounced. Mrs. Chambers opened the door, surprised. A tall, thin, balding man in a beige government suit, stood at the doorway with a narrow briefcase.

"Hello, my name is Mr. Talbot, Frank Talbot. You can call me Frank."

"We weren't expecting you, Frank," said Gwen, answering the door. "You might have called first, so we could've cleaned up a little."

Frank laughed. "It's not necessary, really. Didn't the clerk at the SDIC tell you I'd be coming? I'm just here to see if the child is proceeding normally with his development. Have you noticed any problems?"

"Problems? Like what?" Martin asked, entering the room.

"Oh, anything noticeable, any tics, spasms, uneven body parts, underweight, or overweight?"

"What?" said Gwen. "No, he's perfect, and really smart."

"That's great then...glad to hear it. Here are your report forms for the child. It is required that you fill these out annually, sooner if you notice anything unusual."

He placed a set of forms on the table.

"Just protocol," he said, smiling, "you understand. I'm sure it will be easy."

Frank leaned forward, whispering, "I probably shouldn't be telling you this, but if everything is okay, you can just copy the first one and hand it in. Nobody ever reads these things anyway."

"Thank you," said Martin. "I think we can handle it."

Martin moved to open the door for Frank to leave.

"Thank you for coming," said Gwen. "Be sure to put in your report that everything is fine."

"Oh, I will," he said. "Sacrificium Pro Victoria."

"Sacrificium Pro Victoria," she replied while closing and locking the door.

An almost-normal life resumed, and the Chambers happily adapted to their new life with their new son.

When Chase was two years old, the war ended. The Klix could barely land a ship without being swarmed by Piecers. They were lucky if they made it back to their mother ships. Finally, as the Earth built ships to send against the Klix in orbit, the Klix retreated, removing all their ships from orbit and returning to their home world. A truce was called and the Earth began to rebuild.

The years went by quickly, and Chase proved to be a handful. They marveled at his strength and dexterity at such a young age. He seemed to grasp things faster than Robert ever had, and they wondered what kind of child this was.

Martin dutifully filled out the status reports on Chase, copying from the first.

"Normal height, check," he mumbled to himself. "Normal weight, check, intelligence, check, dexterity, check. Anything unusual about him, Gwenny?"

"He's a freaking genius," she replied, laughing. "But don't put that in there. Just check the boxes."

This went on for several years, with Martin checking the appropriate boxes and transmitting the completed form to the SDIC.

When Chase turned ten, there was a knock at the door, and Martin went to answer it.

"Can I help you?" Martin asked.

"Do you remember me, Mr. Chambers? I was here a while back; about nine years ago or so. Frank? Frank Talbot, from the SDIC?"

"Oh, the man with the forms? Yes, I remember you."

"Umm, yes, the forms...about that."

"We sent the last one in only a month ago? You did get it,

didn't you?"

"We did, yes. We got it, but…" Frank paused and took a deep breath. "Well, I'm afraid I have some bad news."

"Bad news? What do you mean?"

Gwen walked in from the kitchen and stood in the back of the room.

"What is it, Mr. Talbot, what's wrong?" she asked.

"It seems there was a problem with batch 523. Have you noticed any issues with the boy?"

"Issues? No, he's perfect. Super smart," Gwen replied.

Martin looked on with a raised eyebrow. "The boy has no issues," he said sternly. "He's fine. He'll make a damn good Piecer soldier, and I oughta know."

"Good. I'm glad to hear that, it's just…"

"It's just what?" asked Martin, his voice raised.

"Some of the 523s have already been recovered."

Gwen moved closer. "What does he mean, Martin? What do you mean, Mr. Talbot?"

"Now, please, it's just that…you have to remember your agreement—the Recovery Agreement you signed."

Martin moved closer to him, inches from his face. His jaw clenched, and his eyes narrowed. "What about it?"

"I've been sent here to return the boy to the SDIC."

"The boy has a name," said Martin. "He's Chase. My *son*, Chase."

Mr. Talbot adjusted his glasses and took a step back from Martin. He wiped his brow now beading up with sweat.

"It's not my decision," he said. "It's just that some of the boys of batch 523, well, they're smaller."

"He hasn't hit his growth spurt yet," replied Martin. "That's all."

"Well, yes, and well…some of them are different. I can't explain it. We're not sure what happened, but we think there was an accident with batch 523."

"What kind of accident?"

"We're still investigating the matter."

"So you guys fuck up, and you want to take back my son?"

Martin got louder with each word.

Gwen had left the room as Martin moved in closer to Mr. Talbot, now steadily wiping his brow.

"Look, it's not me, it's the SDIC—the paper you signed. I just work there! It's the government, not me."

The high-pitched whine of a charging laser rifle could be heard in the background.

"Where's your wife? What, what is she doing?" he asked, his hands trembling as he tried to see past Martin.

"Gwenny? Oh, it sounds like she turned on her laser rifle. She hasn't been quite right since we lost our only other son to the war."

"I...I'm sure he was a great man," said Mr. Talbot. "But I have my orders."

Gwen entered the room with her laser rifle and pointed it at Mr. Talbot.

"You touch my son, and you'll never make it to the door," she said calmly.

Chase came downstairs, stopping and watching.

"Mom?" he said. "What's wrong? Why is Dad shouting? Why is your laser rifle turned on?"

"Oh, we're just pretending, hon...nothing is wrong. Go back upstairs; I'll be right up."

Chase went back upstairs and listened from the top of the stairs, just out of sight.

"Look, I'm sorry. Please don't kill me. I'm just doing my job."

"Gwen, don't shoot the nice man. He's only doing his job. Unless he touches my son. Then you can vaporize him."

Mr. Talbots's eyes went wide, and he tried to swallow but couldn't.

"Maybe...maybe we can make a deal?" he suggested.

"A deal? What kind of a deal?"

"You could agree to take in another cadet, and we could just forget I was ever here."

"And why would you do that? Why should I believe you?"

"I don't want to do this. They make me. But if you could

take on another cadet, they would look the other way."

"Why...what *aren't* you telling me?" asked Martin.

"It's just that this cadet has had behavioral problems. He's one of the 524s and has been moved around a few times. Do—do you have any daughters?"

"Daughters, no, why?"

"That's good, that's good...should be fine, then."

"What are you not telling me?"

"It seems this cadet has issues with girls. His last foster father beat him for spying on his daughter from her closet and then threw him out. It was his third placement."

"We'll take him," said Gwen. "Provided we never see you again."

Gwen lowered her laser rifle and turned it off, a reverse whine indicating it was powering down. Mr. Talbot relaxed, exhaling deeply.

"I'm glad we could resolve this," he said. "I promise you won't see me again after I drop the boy off."

"What's his name?"

"His name is Loose, Loose 524."

Chapter Three

Chase and Loose

After getting nudged with the rifle butt a second time, Chase heard another click. His hand instinctively moved to his combat knife. Pulling it in a blur, he plunged it deep into the source of the hot breath: the Klix soldier's mouth. The soldier grabbed his throat, gagging and gurgling as Chase pulled him down and behind the wall. He then pulled the knife from the Klix's mouth and cut off his head-scrapers so he couldn't call out. It was over in seconds. Chase exhaled, and stabbed his knife into the soil, wiping the Klix's black blood from his blade.

Replacing his knife in its sheath, he looked up to see if he'd been spotted. He grabbed the Klix laser rifle, examined it closely, and pulled the trigger, testing it. Nothing happened.

"Piece of shit," he said, throwing the weapon to the ground.

Klix weapons could only be fired by the Klix, a smart weapons design to prevent other species from stealing their weapons and using them against them. Chase covered the rifle and the dead scout with rocks, rubble, and pieces of wall to prevent discovery.

Keep moving, he thought. *Have to hurry.*

He noticed a broken picture frame with a half-burnt picture inside. It was the house of one of the 522 families he had known since he was a boy.

Maybe they got out in time, he thought, searching the rubble for signs of life and finding nothing.

He looked down the left side of the street and recognized the remains of his own home. The front porch, where he and Loose had first heard about "shy sightings" and the Great War, had been blown away. The top floor, Chase's room, had collapsed onto the first floor, but the first floor appeared to be mostly intact. Fortunately, it hadn't been hit by incendiary bombs. He scanned the area for Klix troops. It was clear.

Slowly and carefully, he made his way toward his house, staying deep inside craters until he was sure it was safe to hop into the next crater closer to home. He slipped around the back of the house so as not to be seen by anyone passing on what was left of the road. The back door was ajar but stuck by pieces of the top walls resting on it. Chase pulled the door open, with enough space to allow entry, and slid inside. Dust and plaster chunks fell from the top floor onto his head and in his eyes. He blinked repeatedly, trying to clear the stinging plaster dust.

It was quiet. He looked down at the floor and saw two sets of footprints in the plaster dust. Someone had been there before him. Chase inched his way to what was left of his parents' room. The furniture was strewn about, and his father's dresser lay face down on the floor. On the bed, he found a small note:

Dear Chase & Loose,

If you find this, your mother and I are okay and have gone into hiding. We will try to contact you when we can.

In my closet, you will find my foot-locker. Take whatever will help you. My old guns should work.

Save yourself, and don't worry about us. Your mission now is more important than any one family. You must

save humanity from the Klix.
  We love you both very much.

Go with God,
Mom and Dad

Chase wiped his eyes, folded the note, and put it in his pocket. He closed his eyes for a moment, remembering his early years at the house, his family eating together at the dinner table, and his father telling the boys the story of the Great War.

Chase was ten years old when his new nine-year-old brother, Loose, entered the family. It was strange to have a new person in the house, but Chase was thrilled to have a brother, especially a Piecer brother. Loose kept to himself initially, but Martin insisted the boys play together and train together and that helped them become close quickly. They were happy together and Loose enjoyed being part of his new family. Gwen insisted on a family portrait for the mantel, and Martin obliged—speedily setting a timer on his camera drone. The family grouped together in front of the fireplace all smiling, happy, and at the last second, Loose made bunny ears over Chase's head. Everyone laughed at the image and decided it depicted their family accurately. It was placed proudly on the mantel next to Robert's induction picture.

As Chase developed, his parents could see he was indeed different from the other Piecer children, different even from Loose. Chase was shorter than the rest and easily excited. There were nights he could not sleep. He was quicker to anger and at times unable to control his rage. Martin taught him to meditate, hoping to lessen the problem. Whenever Chase was losing control, he would close his eyes, take three deep breaths, and pause.

"Think about your mission," his father would to say to him. "Think about your weapon. Breathe. Are you ready? Breathe. Are you prepared? Breathe. Calm yourself, focus, complete your mission."

Randomly and without notice, his father would try to catch him off guard and lightly slap him in the face, often after he closed his eyes and took one or more of his deep meditation breaths.

"Don't ever be caught napping," he'd say to a stunned and angry Chase. "That's how they get ya. Now calm yourself. Breathe. Focus."

Chase learned quickly. He was ready, prepared, calm, and focused. After being slapped several times unprepared, his father tried to slap him again, this time just after he had closed his eyes to catch him off guard. Chase's arm moved in a blur, stopping his father's hand before it could come near his face. His eyes were still closed, and he was grinning from ear to ear.

"You're ready," his father had said. "Always be ready."

Using this breathing technique, Chase could calm himself and focus. For the most part, the meditation trick helped him to control his temper. The exception came when someone hurt him or hurt someone he cared about. Then blind rage swept over him, and he was unstoppable, almost killing a man who had pushed his father during an argument over the Piecer program and the "little bastards the government created in a lab." His father had to pull him off the bloodied, unconscious man before he beat him to death.

After the fight, Martin pulled Chase aside. "Just because you're able to kill doesn't mean you have to kill," he said. "Remember, without mercy, without restraint, you are no different than the Klix."

Chase didn't like being compared to the Klix. The Klix were scum. The Klix were the enemy. He thought about his father's words often.

Loose was more devious than Chase and quicker to lie than own up to even the most minor infraction. The Chambers assumed this was due to his fear of being moved yet again to another foster home and they overlooked it.

As boys, Chase and Loose often played together in the rubble from the Great War. Though Earth was rebuilding, there were still entire city blocks of buildings reduced to brick or concrete chips, twisted metal, and broken glass. Martin frowned upon them playing in the debris, as many of the remaining structures were unsafe and could give way at any time. But it was in the rubble where Chase found his first pet, an orphaned kitten he named Spot. He found the starving kit wandering in the debris, softly mewing. Spot was black except for a large blotch of white on his head. There was a good chance his mother had been eaten, as food was still scarce following the war. By necessity, cats and dogs were butchered to feed a starving population. Meat was meat, and nobody asked where it came from—or even what it was. After the war, only human-shy feral animals had a chance to survive, and only if they stayed well-hidden.

The kitten was weak when Chase found him, and he knew it would die on its own. He couldn't just leave it; it was against his Piecer code of protecting the weak and the innocent from harm. The code was drilled into them, it was bred into them. His parents were not surprised at all when Chase brought the kitten home, and they allowed him to keep it.

He nursed the kitten back to health with an eyedropper and powdered milk, feeding him every three hours until he was strong enough to eat on his own. The kitten was growing stronger every day, hopping and playing in his room and Chase quickly grew attached to his new friend. He would run home from field drills to feed him or just to check on him, then run back before he was missed. The kitten would jump up on his lap and roll over, allowing Chase to feed him more easily, initially from the eyedropper, and later from an improvised baby bottle with a balloon for a nipple on the end. Spot followed Chase everywhere, and Chase had to make sure he shut the door to his room or Spot would try to follow him to the Piecer Academy.

Loose preferred the urban rubble to the natural woods. He liked damaged things and reveled in breaking things, as long as he knew he wouldn't get in trouble. That was part of the thrill of playing in the wreckage; it was the risk, the unknown, and it was exciting. They were preparing for war, and war wasn't fought on a level playing field and it was never without risk. At times, he'd step out on a floor, testing it to see if it would give way. Hearing it creak, he would step out farther, testing himself, just to see if he could save himself if the floor did give way. The risk was too tantalizing to ignore.

The city rubble made Chase angry. He imagined the buildings, the families, and the storefronts before they were blown to bits. He imagined his parents and their friends running, fleeing from the bombs. He imagined the shock and surprise on their faces as terror rained down from the sky. The anger would build until he had to force himself to focus on his breathing and distract himself; otherwise, he'd get too angry and start smashing things or punch the wall.

But as much as it made him mad, there was value in exploring the rubble. Sometimes Chase would find unexploded alien ordnance in the bombed-out buildings and would bring them home to show his father. At first, his father's face would turn ashen white. Chase would laugh, carrying the unexploded bomb gently, and then pretend to trip and drop it.

"Don't worry, Dad...I defused them," he would say, laughing.

His father was not pleased, clutching his chest as if having a heart attack. Eventually, Chase could not pull off his ruse, and his father would simply say, "That's nice, son."

Chase hammed it up further, even going so far as restarting the timer on the bombs, with a clicking sound and blinking lights. But his father didn't show the slightest bit of worry. He knew Chase had become quite adept at defusing bombs and that doing so gave him a thorough understanding of the aliens' weapons technology. He knew it was good training for him.

After a short time, Chase got bored with the city rubble and preferred "running the woods" as his father called it. These were the woods of old Earth before the war. Though fire had swept through major sections, some of it was untouched and pristine, and he loved the sounds and smells of a living forest. When Chase ran the woods, he thought of nothing other than the run, the next hop, the next hurdle, and how to defeat it.

Martin felt it was safer running the woods than playing in an abandoned building, frequently taking the boys to the woods to run them out. They had more energy than normie boys, and he had to wear them out or they'd take that energy home. That unspent energy is how most of the furniture in their home had been damaged or destroyed completely.

He was always amazed by the boys' speed and agility. They were more like deer than boys as they ran through the woods jumping, hopping, and running up the sides of the trees to avoid obstacles. They could run faster through the woods than most boys could run on a level track, and once they started competing against each other, nothing could stop them. Though one year older, Chase was smaller than Loose, but faster, and more agile. He was always waiting at the end of the woods for Loose to catch up. He'd pretend he had been waiting a long time, often lying on a log or leaning up against a tree, looking bored.

"What took ya?" he'd always say, teasing Loose.

"Screw you. I can see your chest moving; you're still panting. You just got here."

Loose was not a good loser, and usually, after he caught his breath, he'd hit Chase hard, from behind. Chase would just laugh because he knew he had beaten him. He shrugged off the hit as the price of victory, and it made Loose even madder when he acted like he didn't feel it.

Loose was not a good winner either. Before Chase reached puberty, Loose's size was a huge advantage. Loose not only had a longer reach on him in boxing, but he also used his size and weight when wrestling to pin Chase to the ground. During one impromptu match in the woods, Loose pinned Chase by kneeling on his shoulders and arms. Chase couldn't move, and even with his unusual strength, he couldn't lift Loose off of him. When Martin went to find them to go home, he found Loose on top of Chase with his hands around

Chase's throat, choking him and laughing. Chase was laughing too, for a while, and Martin thought nothing of it initially.

Then the laughing stopped, and he could hear Chase gasping. Loose was laughing harder as Chase struggled for air, and his father could see Chase was turning blue. Loose's eyes were wide and vacant—as if watching from afar—and he was getting excited.

"Let him up, Loose," Martin called. "That's enough for one day; time to go home."

Loose ignored him.

"Loose," he called louder, hurrying toward them, "let him up!"

Loose pretended not to hear and squeezed harder. Chase's eyes went wide and then rolled back in his head. His body went limp. But Loose kept squeezing.

"I said let him up now!" his father screamed, pulling Loose backward off of Chase.

Loose let go and lunged at his father, raising his fist to hit him, stopping just short of a full swing. Then he smiled awkwardly.

"We're just playin', Dad...he's fine."

Chase gasped and took a deep breath. His face pinked up in seconds, and he jumped to his feet. He grabbed Loose from behind with his arm around his throat in a choke hold. He pulled hard as Loose jabbed at him with both elbows trying to get him off. But Chase had locked on like a vise, and nothing was going to pull him off. Loose looked at his father in disbelief as he was pulled back down to the ground with Chase firmly attached to his neck.

"Okay, Chase, that's enough," his father said.

Chase pulled harder and Loose struggled for air. "He was trying to kill me," Chase screamed, half crying, trying to fight the tears. "I said I give, and he wouldn't stop."

"Enough!" his father screamed, and Chase relaxed his grip.

Loose coughed and stumbled forward. "I'll get you, you little fucker!" he yelled. "I'll get you."

"Loose, goddammit, that's enough," Martin screamed. "Go home and get ready for supper."

Loose took off running home through the woods, while Martin stayed behind to talk to Chase.

"What is wrong with you two?" his father shouted. "You're supposed to be brothers."

Chase looked down at the ground.

"C'mon, let's go home and get cleaned up for dinner; no more fighting. Save it for your sparring partners."

"Yes, sir," Chase replied meekly. "But he was trying to strangle me."

Martin did not respond, sighing heavily.

The family got ready for dinner while Chase ran to his room to check on Spot. With the rest of the family seated around the dinner table, Martin called out to Chase, but there was no reply. It wasn't like Chase to ignore his father or be late for dinner. Finally, after shouting up the stairs, Martin went up to look for him and found him sobbing in the middle of the floor of his room. His kitten was dead, and he was clutching its lifeless body close to his chest.

"Oh, Son, what happened?" his father asked.

"I don't know, Dad. He was fine this morning. He's still warm."

"I'm so sorry," he said, sitting down next to Chase and putting his arm around him.

"Why did he have to die, Dad...why?"

"I don't know, Son—but I'm really sorry. I liked Spot. It's very sad."

"He must have fallen. His neck is all floppy."

His father looked closely and could see that the kitten's neck was broken. His brow furrowed as he looked toward the door.

"He was lucky you found him, Chase," his father said, turning back to him. "You gave him a good life for weeks, a chance he would not have had on his own. You saved him, you loved him, and he loved you."

"But Dad, he was so little. I was supposed to protect him."

"I know, I know, it hurts. And you did the best you could."

Martin reached out and patted his shoulder. "We need to give him a proper burial, Son. Do you have a box or something we can put him in?"

"Yes. I still have the box I used to bring him home."

"Perfect. We'll put some cloth in the bottom so it's soft, okay?"

"Yeah, he'd like that," said Chase.

"Martin, are you coming to dinner?" Chase's mother called.

"We'll be along shortly, Gwenny. Chase's cat passed away, and we're going to give him a proper burial in the back yard first."

"Oh no, he must be crushed," she said. "I'll meet you out back."

"What?" asked Loose. "What about dinner?"

"Dinner can wait," she replied. "Your brother's kitten died."

"So?" Loose said, half smiling. "I'm hungry. Can we eat it?"

"No, we're not eating it," she yelled. "It was your brother's friend."

"But it's just a cat, and I'm hungry."

"You will have to wait. Life is not something to take for granted. Lord knows we've seen too much death already. Now, we are all going out there to support your brother, and you will too."

"What? No way. I'm gonna eat."

"No, you are coming with me or you are not going to eat at all."

"Why? That's bullshi—"

He stopped, not finishing his word. Mrs. Chambers glared at him.

"Don't talk like that to me, or you won't be getting any dinner today or tomorrow."

Loose grimaced and bit his lip.

"I'm sorry," he said. "I'll go."

"That's better," she said. "And you will be nice to your brother."

They went out back as Chase and his father placed the box in the ground and covered it with dirt.

"Want to say anything, Son?"

Chase sniffled and put his hand on the tiny mound of dirt and patted it.

"G'bye, Spot," he whispered. "I'll miss you."

"Loose," his father said loudly, "you have anything to say?"

Loose looked at his staring father.

"What? Me? No. I don't have anything to say. It's just an f-ing cat...sir."

His father glared at him. Loose looked back, gave a quick glance, and then looked away. Everyone was quiet for a moment.

"Spot was a good kitten," his mother said in a soft but breaking voice. "He was sweet and kind, which is all we can ask of anyone in this world."

She put her arm around Chase and squeezed him. "He's up in heaven, playing with Robert and the other kittens, honey. Robert will take care of him now."

"You think so?" Chase asked.

"I'm sure of it. Robert loved kittens, and Spot was an innocent. All innocents go to heaven."

Her eyes welled with tears as she thought of her lost son, and Chase leaned in to her.

"Time to go inside for dinner, everyone," Martin said. "Loose, wait. I want a word with you."

Chase and his mother went inside, his mother still holding him, both crying.

"Did you have anything to do with this?" his father asked quietly.

"What? Me? No. Hell no...sir."

"I noticed you smiling before."

"Well, it's sad and all, but Chase looks funny cryin', that's all. I was laughing at Chase. Stupid kitten must'a just fallen or something and broke his neck. Shit happens, Dad, ya know?"

"How did you know his neck was broken? You didn't see him."

"I don't know...I mean, I just guessed."

"Get inside, Son. We'll talk more later."

"Yes, sir. I'm starving," said Loose, hurrying inside.

Martin never brought it up again. He mentioned it to Loose's Piecer handlers, but most shrugged it off as an isolated incident.

A staccato of clicking jarred him from his thoughts and back to the matter at hand. He popped up and glanced out the bedroom window. On the road, directly across the street, he saw a Klix officer and two Klix soldiers. The officer gestured toward the house with his laser rifle. He would have to hurry and get out before he was discovered.

He crawled over to his father's closet and pulled open the closet door. The capsule-shaped footlocker was in the back of the closet. He reached in, pulling it across the floor into the bedroom. A large padlock kept the lid from opening.

Grabbing his knife from his boot sheath, he shoved the blade into the lock. Pushing down and away, he cut through the steel hasp like it was butter.

Inside the footlocker resting on top were two long trench coats—one black cloth, one dark black leather—and two western-style hats. The coats were full length with large pockets on the inside of the coats as well as pockets on the outside. Chase smiled. These were his foster parents' long coats from Halloween, when they had dressed up as an old-fashioned Earth cowboy and cowgirl. The house shook as another bomb blast hit nearby. Plaster dust fell on his head again, and he spat out the dust he inhaled.

Well, this hat will come in handy anyway, he thought, placing it on his head. *At least it'll keep the shit out of my eyes.*

He pulled out the other hat and the coats, setting them on

the floor quietly and peeked out the window again. The Klix officer and two of his men were headed his way.

Below the coats and hats were two western style gun belts, double gun holsters in each belt. His father had shown him these guns a long time ago: a pair of .357 magnum revolvers with mini-scopes, and a pair of .45 caliber semi-automatic pistols. The antique guns had been handed down generation after generation in his father's family. They used chemical combustion to propel a lead bullet. They were primitive, but that meant they were immune to EMP blasts. They appeared to be in near perfect condition, each one carefully wrapped in an oily rag.

He remembered the nights he watched his father carefully reloading spent cartridges with smokeless gunpowder and lead bullet heads, and telling Chase to always keep his weapons in good working order. Chase pulled one of the gun belts around him and buckled it as he'd seen his father do so many times. He tied down the two holsters, one to each leg.

I guess this is how you wear these things, he thought, flexing his legs. *Feels right.*

He pulled one of the .357s out of the oily rag and examined it closely. He wondered how effective they were or would be against the Klix.

Chase pushed the release on the cylinder, and it flopped out of the side of the gun frame. He spun it slowly with his thumb, checking each chamber to make sure it was fully loaded. The bullets appeared to be in pristine condition.

He snapped the cylinder back in the gun gently and checked the other revolver. Then, he slid each gun into the holsters on his legs and flexed his knees. *Not bad. Not heavy. Feels balanced,* he thought.

He grabbed the gun belt of .45 caliber semi-automatics and slung it over his shoulder. He pulled the .45s out of their rags and pressed the tiny button on the side, releasing the magazines.

"Shit...Dad kept 'em all loaded," he said out loud, slapping the clip back into the gun. "He said to always be ready, and he wasn't kidding."

He shoved the loaded guns into the holster slung over his shoulder and slipped a tiny rawhide loop over the hammers to keep the guns from falling out. He reached into the bottom of the footlocker, checking for anything else that might help, and felt several bags of coins. He pulled the tie string from one of them and spilled the coins into his hand. They were pure silver. Silver had become the prized currency of the galaxy due to its ability to fuse with bitanium to make tritanium, the strongest metal known.

These might come in handy, he thought. *Thanks, Dad.*

Glancing out of the window, he searched frantically for the Klix. He couldn't see them or hear them.

Fuck! Where are they? He crouched to the floor and duckwalked to the other window on the opposite side of the house. Suddenly, he could hear the Klix communicating.

As he scrambled crab-like back to the other window, he could hear the Klix prying the back door to open it wider to enter. Chase drew his .357s—one in each hand—and held his breath so as not to make a sound. With a loud crash and the thud of plaster chunks from above, the Klix were in the house now, with their weapons drawn while making their way through the house in a search and destroy pattern Chase knew all too well.

I hope these suckers work, he thought, *or I'm already dead.*

Chapter Four

Stealing the *Promise*

The Klix officer was first to make his way into the bedroom and spot Chase. Loud clicking followed, and the officer raised his weapon to fire. Chase pulled the trigger on the gun in his right hand as fast as he could, sending lead flying with a loud boom-boom-boom at the Klix. It hit the Klix's body armor with a deafening crack, and he clicked a kind of scream as it penetrated the armor and sunk into him. The armor had been designed to stop laser weapons by dispersing the concentrated light beam. It wasn't designed to stop lead.

All six shots hit the Klix squarely in the chest, and he was blown backwards—out the door and into the hall. The other Klix started clicking back and forth until everything went silent.

"Damn, these are loud!" he said, staring at the fired pistol. "No secret I'm here now."

Through the ringing in his ears from the rounds fired, he listened intently, trying to determine where the two remaining Klix were. It was quiet. Nobody moved. No clicking.

Shit, I don't like quiet, Chase thought. Quiet was death. He couldn't stay there.

He put on his father's black trench coat, stuffing the pockets with the boxes of ammo and bags of silver. Reloading the one now-empty gun, he noted it was warm to the touch.

Crude, he thought, glancing at the dead alien lying in a pool of black blood, *but effective.*

He grabbed up the other coat and hat, stuffed it into a pillowcase, and threw it over his shoulder. Seeing his reflection in a cracked mirror on the wall, he stopped momentarily, almost not recognizing himself. He pushed his chin-length black hair up under his hat and noticed his eyes were reddened from the stinging plaster dust that had fallen into them. Patches of white plaster clung to his beard stubble in streaks and flecks of powder.

I look ridiculous, he thought, wiping the dust from his face. He blinked quickly to try to flush the dust from his eyes. His eyes cleared, and he stared again into the mirror.

I kinda like the hat though.

He pulled it down tightly to keep it from falling off. *Breathe. Focus.*

Two guns, two Klix, and they were not going to let him leave there alive.

Where are they?

As Chase closed his eyes, time seemed to stop. He took a deep breath to calm himself. The ringing in his ears subsided. He listened carefully. His heart beat in his ears, and he could hear his breaths, in and out. Then he heard it: two more breathers on the opposite sides of the doorway, right behind the wall.

He smiled and then ran for the door. Diving through the doorway, he spun and fell backward, firing. The Klix hesitated for one brief second, not wanting to shoot each other as he passed between them. That was all he needed. With a gun in each hand, he unloaded six shots from each revolver into the stunned Klix. They were both blown back into the wall they had been hiding behind, each shot throwing them against the wall until they fell dead to the floor.

That noise is going to bring more trouble, he thought. *I gotta get outta here.*

He looked around his house again, grabbing a photo of his family from a picture frame that had fallen off the fireplace mantel onto the floor. It was the rabbit ears picture with Loose holding up his fingers behind Chase's head, with everyone smiling. Chase sighed while remembering that day—when they were all happy.

Lying next to it was the military induction picture of Robert Chambers in his uniform. Chase removed the picture from its frame and placed it on top of his family picture.

This was probably the last time he'd be here, and it might be the last thing he had to remember them by.

He folded the pictures carefully and put them into his pocket, patting his pocket to make sure they were safely tucked inside.

Time to scoot, he thought, checking right and left for any more Klix.

Chase knew he'd be spotted on the road, so he decided to take the detour through the woods. It was a more direct route, and it was unlikely the Klix would be in the uninhabited forest. He could make it back to the stadium and to the *Promise* in little time.

Running full bore, he lost himself in his thoughts. He pushed himself to run faster, worried he wouldn't get back to the stadium in time to meet his team. The deer was back in his element. The faster he went, the faster he wanted to go. He lost himself within the run. There was nothing but the path ahead, a trajectory and forward momentum—a falling forward without falling. When he ran, he was focused. He became the deer. Even the long coat and pistols strapped to his legs didn't slow him down. Adrenaline fueled him, and he made it back to the outskirts of the stadium in minutes, stopping at the edge of the woods to analyze his next move.

The *Promise* was guarded by a half-dozen Klix amidst the rubble of the stadium: two at the nose, two aft at the cargo ramp, and two at the center-forward ladder used to board the ship. The ship appeared only slightly damaged from the earlier barrage—a few blast marks, but no actual damage to the hull. The tritanium plating could withstand even a direct hit from most conventional bombs or weapons.

Fortunately, the *Promise* would have been unaffected by the EMP blast. Wormholes created great fields of electromagnetic energy, and the *Promise* had been built to shield it from any electromagnetic waves it would encounter.

The ship was the oldest working worm-drive starship in the fleet and had been refurbished for training purposes. The weapons were still usable, though somewhat dated by current standards. Only the updated pulse laser, added after the *Promise* was built, showed any modernization of equipment. It was built like a flying tank, and in its day, it was the pride of the fleet.

Chase searched the stadium perimeter, hoping to see any of his 523 brothers. There were none to be found. He was on his own, and he'd have to steal the *Promise* alone. In his mind, six adversaries were not a problem, if he could use his weapons. But blasting them with his .357s would certainly bring more Klix running. This would have to be quiet—close-up and personal, two at a time.

He inched his way to the rear of the *Promise*, circling behind the two aft guards. The two Klix were distracted, clicking back and forth as if arguing. They were thumping their chests and pointing at the *Promise*, as if they were taking possession of the ship for themselves. Chase had other plans. He slipped behind them and tapped them on the shoulders. As they turned around, startled, he slit both of their throats with one full swipe of his combat knife. They grabbed their throats and crumpled to the ground silently like deflated balloons, without so much as a chance to click for help. He pulled them out of sight and pushed them into a crater blown out of the stadium dirt.

Two down, four to go, he thought. *Time to get creative.*

Chase climbed up the aft cargo bay ramp to the *Promise* and entered. Keeping low, not knowing if there were any Klix aboard, he reached the inside of the center-forward ladder in little time. Then he started clicking, almost clucking with his tongue, changing the pitch in an attempt to resemble what he had heard back home. It was a crude imitation of the Klix language, but it didn't matter. He had no idea what he was saying, if he was saying anything at all. At first, the two Klix at the bottom of the ladder didn't hear him, so he clicked louder. Finally, one of the Klix motioned to the other that he was going up, and climbed the ladder to the hatch. Once his head popped up to floor level, Chase stabbed him through the top of his head and down through his jaw, silencing him forever. He quickly pulled him up all the way into the ship and laid his dead body on the floor. All was quiet.

The other Klix soldier looked up and then started clicking louder and louder at the open hatch. Not hearing a response, he mounted the ladder to see what was happening. Chase lay in wait and dispatched him as soon as he entered.

Four down, two to go.

The two forward guards turned and saw that they were alone. They raised their weapons and began frantically clicking back and forth, searching the area for the other guards. One turned his head, placing his scrapers close to his communicator as if Klix whispering. The Klix communicator was about the size of a deck of cards: a small screen device that glowed green when active and was attached to their chest armor. Getting no response, he kept his head turned and clicked loudly into it.

"Jig's up," said Chase out loud, no longer worried about being discovered.

Chase ran to the cockpit and scanned the controls. The cockpit of the *Promise* was loaded with buttons of all colors, panels filled with switches, levers, joysticks, and display screens. All Piecer cadets were trained in air and space vehicles, and Chase had completed his training on the *Promise*.

But it had been awhile since he had trained, and the array of switches were suddenly overwhelming. He took a deep breath, whispering to himself, "Focus. Breathe."

In an instant, his training came back to him, and his fingers flew over the controls in a blur. The cargo bay ramp and ladders retracted, and the Klix started running toward the hatches, firing their laser rifles. Chase punched the red ignition button, and the *Promise*'s engines burst into life.

"C'mon, baby, let's get Daddy outta here," he said aloud.

The Klix were firing repeatedly at the hatch doors and anything else they could hit, but the tritanium hull held easily against their trivial laser blasts. It would take a lot more than rifle blasts to even scratch her.

Chase transferred gun control from the weapons station to his pilot's seat. He jumped into the seat and flipped the switch on the twin rotary guns mounted in front of the *Promise*. The multi barrels began to rotate to a blur.

"Okay, you fuckers...you wanna play? Let's play!" he said loudly.

Hope they didn't disable these suckers, he thought.

Chase located the ammo gauge on the instrument panel.

"Not much, but better than nothing," he mumbled. "Let's see how you like being shot at."

The ship lifted a few feet in the air, and Chase spun it around at the surprised Klix now running from the center of the ship—and away as fast as they could.

"Invade *this*, assholes," he said, holding up his middle finger at the Klix.

He let loose with two quick trigger pulls, tracing a path from the ship to the fleeing Klix and cutting them in half. A warning siren indicating incoming ships blared from the cockpit.

"Okay; let's see what you got," Chase said out loud.

He pushed the throttle all the way, and the ship took off vertically in a shower of flame and dust. The *Promise* reached space in seconds.

Not bad, Chase thought. But he wasn't going to lose those ships with these engines. He needed the worm drive.

Chase evaded the incoming ships, fending off the ship-to-ship missiles fired at the *Promise*.

I can't keep this up forever, he thought as he dodged and swerved, their shots barely missing. He flipped the toggles for the worm drive.

Nothing happened.

"*Reactor core offline,*" the female voice of the onboard computer announced. "*Worm drive initiation cannot be completed.*"

"Fuck! I need that reactor."

Chase began the reactor sequence as the ship was rocked by one of the ship-to-ship shots that found its mark.

"*Nuclear reactor at forty percent,*" the ship's computer reported.

"Shit, a few more like that, and I'm stardust."

Chase turned and swiveled in his seat, trying to engage the ships firing at him. He reached over and armed the pulse laser cannons. He waited for the green light, indicating the cannons were armed. Nothing happened.

"What the fuck!" he screamed, still whirling frantically, dodging more and more shots from the Klix ships.

He reached over and tapped the light, flicking his finger at the plastic capsule covering the "enabled" indicator. The light flickered and then glowed green.

Oh, for crap's sake, he thought. *Green light...here we go.*

He swiveled the pilot's chair, lining up his shot with the lead attacking Klix ship, and pulled the trigger on the pulse laser.

"Bye bye, bad guy," he said, smiling.

"*Nuclear reactor at eighty percent,*" the ship's computer reported.

The laser cannon shot twin green laser beams through the Klix ship, drilling perfect round holes in the ship's hull. For a moment, he could see stars through the holes he had just made. The Klix ship seemed to tremble, and then he saw it spinning off to the right just before it exploded.

"*Reactor core online,*" the computer reported.

"Time to go," Chase said.

"*Warning,*" said the computer voice, "*two percent nuclear fuel remaining. Three percent fuel capacity recommended for wormhole creation. Worm drive initiation at current levels may be unstable.*"

Three more Klix ships zeroed in on him.

"Hmm, certain death or uncertain death; no choice there."

Chase hit the wormhole generator switch and the entire bridge of the *Promise* glowed red.

"Initiating wormhole. Warning, two percent nuclear fuel remaining. Three percent fuel capacity recommended for wormhole creation. Recommend abort procedure."

Nag, nag, nag, thought Chase. "Sorry, no time to argue," he said as he flipped the audio off on the ship's computer. The bridge continued to pulse a glowing red. Ahead of the *Promise,* a swirl of white mist and a bubble appeared: the wormhole was forming. Chase continued to swerve left and right to throw off the Klix and avoid getting hit. The Klix split up their formation, coming at him from three directions.

They're not all gonna miss this time, he thought.

"C'mon, baby...it's now or never," he said.

The mist grew into a large swirling ball, and Chase smashed the throttle forward into the center of the white vortex in front of him. The *Promise* bucked momentarily and then shot forward into the spinning whirlpool of stars.

Chapter Five

Betrayed

While the Klix bombed the graduation ceremony, Loose slipped away, watching from afar. He snuck out of the stadium, making sure to stay well behind the Klix bombing runs. He surveyed the damage to the Piecer neighborhoods and then ran through the woods to a predesignated remote spot. He dug deep into the soil, retrieving a cigar-sized tritanium box which held a small electronic device, a stinger pistol, and a translator inside. He pressed the button on the device, and it began to flash. Soon, a ship hovered over the area and descended. The ramp from the door of the ship deployed, and General Klume, the leader of the Klix Supremacy, descended with three of his guards behind him.

General Klume was the emperor of Kattar, a planet about eighty thousand light years from Earth. Klume was a bloodthirsty madman intent on conquering the universe. Kattar was the home world inhabited by the Klix, larger and stronger than humans with small bones protruding from the top of their head like a crown. As they aged, the bones became longer and more prominent and were perceived as a sign of wisdom. Klix often lived to three hundred Earth years or longer, and some elderly Klix had head bones the length of antelope horns.

Sixty Earth years ago, the emperor, Kalar Ku, ruled the entire Klix world. At the age of 270, he had consolidated the various Klix factions into one, becoming the emperor of all of Kattar. There were no nations, no boundaries, just the dominion of Kalar Ku.

Kattar, once rich in resources, became depleted over time. In search of new resources, the Klix found several nearby planets that could be mined and began a space mining operation that lasted for decades. Mining became their primary industry, with the ore being transported back to Kattar for smelting and refining.

Nearby planets reached by traditional rocketry were soon depleted as well. The emperor knew his power was directly connected to his ability to supply more raw material and resources to his planet. He had to "feed the furnace," a common Klix expression. He issued a decree stating that the first scientist to create a new trans-galactic engine that could reach other planets would be given a position in his court as his second in command.

His current second in command, General Klume of the Royal Guard, assumed it was impossible to create a trans-galactic drive and the emperor would expire from old age before anyone succeeded him, turning command over to Klume. He had been groomed his entire life to take over one day and had dedicated himself to the emperor and his military. He had risked his life many times exploring nearby planets for resources to quarry, for the benefit of his emperor and his world. The throne was destined to be his, but that was soon to change.

Kar Tekka, a technician in the emperor's interplanetary exploration division, or I-PED, proved that trans-warping—covering great distances of space through wormholes—could be done, and he created the first Klix trans-warp portal.

Emperor Ku called Kar Tekka to the Great Hall to bestow his prize upon him. A grand ceremony and feast was to be held for the emperor's court and distinguished citizens of the realm. The emperor was in his chamber preparing for the event and was feeling upbeat, happy, when General Klume came in to see him.

"Ah, Klume, it is good to see you," he said. "Is it not wonderful?"

"Is what not wonderful, your majesty?"

"Kar Tekka, he's done it. He has created a trans-warp portal and a prototype for a trans-warp drive. Soon, we will be able to travel anywhere and reap untold riches across our galaxy and beyond. We can feed the furnace forever."

"Yes, wonderful, wonderful," he clicked, "untold riches."

"As leader of my military, you will be sent out to explore and harvest these worlds."

"Why not simply attack the Quargg world? It is within our rocket engine range when our orbits align, and our scans indicate they have many riches, ripe for the taking."

"We do not need to make enemies, Klume, my friend."

"But they steal from our mining operations whenever they can."

"Yes, that is true, but we do not want war; war is bad for our people. Production would be stopped. No, we must search for other planets—with our new trans-warp capabilities."

"Yes, my liege...and these other planets, what if they are inhabited?"

"Oh, Klume, you lust for a fight, don't you? There are billions of planets in our galaxy alone, most uninhabited. You will search those. There is no need to create conflict with other beings if we find them. Besides, you are too valuable to me to risk."

"Conflict is what I do, sire. I am a soldier. I have always been a soldier. I live for battle. And the risk of death excites me. It is the only thing that makes me feel alive."

Kalar Ku click-laughed.

"Can you not find a woman on all of Kattar to excite you, Klume, my friend? Have a child—a son perhaps—an heir to your estate?"

"Bah! I have no interest in family life. Domestication is for pets."

"But Klume, you don't *have* to fight. You can choose other

worlds. The universe is unlimited. Why risk yourself or our men in a needless squabble when there are so many other options?"

Klume pursed his lips and frowned.

"Perhaps we could enslave those planets," clicked Klume, "and use them to process our precious metals and minerals. Is not labor a precious resource too?"

The emperor paused, considering it.

"What would our people do, then?" he asked. "They need work to fill their lives, to give them purpose."

"I do not think our people share your views on working in the smelter or the mines. It is dreadful work."

"That is why I am emperor," he clicked, smiling. "I know what's best for my people. They need work to feel useful, productive. Work is necessary for fulfillment."

Klume grunted while the emperor pulled his cloak around his back, getting ready for the festivities.

"Damn this stupid thing; the braid keeps getting caught on my armor."

"Let me help you, sire," clicked the general, stepping behind the emperor and adjusting his cape.

"Thank you, Klume. I don't know what I would do without—"

Klume plunged his dagger into the emperor's back and pulled it up toward his heart. The emperor gasped, pulling away from Klume with horror in his eyes, clicking madly, black blood pouring from his gaping wound.

"What? Why, Klume? You are my General...my friend. What have you done?" he clicked, falling to the floor. "My people, they will avenge me."

"Your people—bah. When I tell them they no longer have to work, that slaves will do their jobs, do you think they will even remember you?"

The emperor clicked once more and was silent, bleeding out on the floor.

"I was never your friend. I am a soldier. Killing is what I do. Do you think you can replace me, or change me into your errand boy, your plunder puppet? It is time for Klume to rule. It is the era of the Klume Dynasty."

Klume looked around the room for a way to dispose of the emperor's body. Inside the chamber was a stone crypt created for the emperor to be used upon his death.

"This will do," he clicked to himself, laughing. "It is almost poetic."

The lid was easily four inches thick, carved from solid stone. Even General Klume, the largest Klix in the entire army, had a difficult time sliding the lid to one side far enough to dump the emperor's body into it.

"Rest peacefully, old one. The people need a new leader."

Klume wiped up the blood with the emperor's cape and then tossed it in with the emperor's body. He shoved the lid over and sealed the dead emperor beneath the airtight slab.

The time for the ceremony was at hand, and Klume strode into the room exuberantly, flanked by ten of his best soldiers. Everyone looked for the emperor, assuming he would arrive shortly.

"Attention, everyone," Klume clicked from the front of the room, by the emperor's throne. "I have some historic news. The emperor has abdicated his throne and left me in charge of the empire."

The room burst into loud click-shouting and click-yelling.

"Silence!" Klume shouted. "It was not my idea. Our dear emperor thought it best that a soldier should lead you—a soldier to take the reins of power and use the new discovery of our loyal subject, Kar Tekka, to rule the galaxy and then the universe."

Louder click-shouting followed, with several Klix loyal to the emperor moving toward Klume. His guards stepped in front of him, and one of Kalar Ku's guards shouted, "Treachery!" He drew his ceremonial sword and was immediately shot by one of Klume's guards.

"Does anyone else wish to object to our emperor's own wishes?" clicked Klume. "Who dares defy the emperor?"

"Where is the emperor?" someone clicked. "Why can't he

tell us?"

"The emperor has retired and gone into seclusion. The crown has become too heavy for him. He has trusted me to reveal his plan. He trusts you to follow his decree."

Clicking chattered throughout the crowd nonstop.

"Enough," clicked Klume angrily. "The emperor has more news for you."

The crowd went silent. Finally, after an awkward long pause, one in the crowd spoke up. "What? What did the emperor say?"

"The emperor no longer wants you to work in the smelter or the mines," said Klume. "No longer will you sweat and toil all the days of your lives for meager earnings. As your new emperor, I will have slaves do your work, and you will live like emperors yourself."

Klume paused, watching their faces turn from shock and anger to unimaginable relief as they considered the possibility of never having to work again.

"And we will start with the Quargg world," he added.

The crowd clicked back and forth excitedly.

"How can this be?" one click-shouted.

"The Quargg will surely fight us," clicked another. "They have armies. Many will die."

"Yes, many will die to feed the furnace," said Klume. "But that is what we must do. Besides, our technology is superior to the Quargg; our weapons are superior. They stand little chance of defending themselves."

"What if they defeat us?" clicked a skeptic in the crowd.

Klume grew enraged, grabbed a pistol from one of his guards, and shot the questioner dead.

"Anyone else wish to speak of defeat? No one will stand against the Klix, and if they do, they will meet the same fate. We will attack the Quargg while Kar Tekka completes his work on our trans-warp drive ships. Then the Quargg will do our labor for us, and the Klix will rule the universe."

The crowd grew quiet, no one daring to object.

"We owe everything to Kar Tekka!" Klume click-shouted.

"Kar Tekka, please come forward," clicked Klume.

Kar Tekka moved forward—his hands shaking—unsure what would happen. Klume threw his arm around his shoulders.

"Kar Tekka is the one who will make you all rich," Klume clicked. "He will build great ships. We will, what do you call it, Kar Tekka, 'trans-warp'? We will trans-warp to the very stars themselves!"

"Yes, General Klume, it is called 'trans-warping.' What we do is create a wormhole in space and—"

He was soon interrupted by Klume pulling him closer to him hard and click-laughing loudly.

"Hahaha, scientists...they think we care how it works."

Kar Tekka laughed along nervously.

"Everyone, this is our new Chief of I-PED, Kar Tekka."

Kar Tekka looked at him, amazed and scared.

"He will be in charge of intergalactic exploration, and all our resources will be redirected to the conquest of space."

There was an awkward silence in the ceremonial chamber.

"All hail, Kar Tekka, Chief of I-PED and savior of Kattar," Klume click-shouted.

Klume's guards started chanting, "All hail, Kar Tekka!" and the crowd soon took up the cheer.

Plans did not go as Klume intended. The Quargg fought them off with ease.

Back on Kattar, inside the Great Hall where the emperor would meet with his counselors and high-ranking military advisors, Klume spoke aloud to his sergeant at arms, Kot Kik. Along both sides of the hall, royal guards stood at the ready.

"It is as if they knew we were coming," he screamed. "There is treachery in our empire."

The guards nervously fingered their ornamental swords, while their eyes darted left and right, searching for signs of the traitor.

"Kot Kik, bring me the scientist, Kar Tekka."

Kot Kik left the room and returned, pulling Kar Tekka

into the Great Hall by his arm and throwing him to the ground in front of Klume. Kar Tekka trembled, kneeling on the floor and bowing to his king.

"Kar Tekka," clicked Klume. "The Quargg knew of our arrival. They have our weapons, our shields. How can this be? It's like we were fighting ourselves."

"I do not know, sire."

"And our trans-warp drive, do you think they have that too?"

"I have said nothing to anyone, sire. Only our secret factory has the design for our trans-warp ship."

"It is complete, yes?"

"Yes; I have worked day and night to create a working drive for the ship."

"And we can duplicate this technology for all our ships?"

"Yes, sire. It is easily copied."

"The Quargg seem to know everything about us," said Klume, rubbing his scrapers. "How do you think this is possible?"

"I don't know, truly I do not. Perhaps there is a traitor amongst us."

"Ah, exactly what I was thinking," said Klume.

Klume raised his pistol and shot Kar Tekka dead on the spot.

"Bring me our next best scientist," he click-shouted to his guards. "And get this traitor out of my sight."

The guards eagerly dragged Kar Tekka's body out of the room and went to fetch the new Chief of I-PED.

"We will deal with the Quargg another day," Klume said aloud to himself. "Our losses were severe; first, we must rebuild."

Klume concentrated all his resources on building trans-warp ships, copying Kar Tekka's design exactly. Now that they had a wormhole drive, there were other worlds with resources—worlds not as well guarded as the Quargg.

"Find me a new planet to pillage!" screamed Klume. "Make it an easy target."

"Sire, we have been monitoring intergalactic space transmissions and have found two planets to consider, both rich in minerals."

"Well, what are they? Do they have defenses? A military?"

"There is Soren in the Kaleda Galaxy, the second planet from the star Kelous-7. They are rich in technology, but have little silver."

"And weapons? Do they have sophisticated weapons?"

"No, sire. They appear to be a pacifist society. We could not locate weapons of any significance or a military of any kind."

"Excellent. And the other?"

"It is the third planet from their star, in the galaxy 'Ketala-9.' They call it Earth."

"Does it have silver? Technology? A military?"

"Yes, sire, the Earth planet is rich in silver. Their technology is advanced, but their defenses are weak. Their military, though sizeable, is no match for our troops or weapons."

"This Earth planet sounds like the riper plum," said Klume. "But I do not want a repeat of the fiasco with the Quargg. We will attack the weaker target first, Soren. Our troops need a victory to build up their confidence. We will take their technology for our own and use it to our advantage."

"What if they resist, my liege?"

"You say they are a pacifist planet?"

"Yes, my lord."

"If they resist, kill them all."

"Yes, my lord...and the Earth planet?"

"Do nothing for now. Send ships to scout the planet, but do not linger. I don't want them to suspect anything."

"Yes, Emperor Klume; our first trans-warp ships will be ready soon. They won't even know we are there. They will see us as the twinkle in the stars."

***

General Klume stood on the ramp, looking down at

Loose. He stood nearly three meters tall, the largest Klix Loose had ever seen. His head bones were very large and it appeared he had sharpened the tips to use as weapons.

Loose approached him with the Klix bent arm salute, a fist to the chest and then an arm straight out in a fist like a punch.

"General Klume," he clicked in his best Klix imitation.

The general flipped the switch on his translator and clicked back, saying, "Use the communicator we gave you, mouth talker. You are disgusting, talking from the same orifice you eat with. And your pathetic attempt at our language insults me."

The general moved closer to him. "Have you taken possession of all the Piecer territory?" he clicked.

Loose pressed his communicator and began to speak, the translated results clicking in response. "Most of the Piecer homes were destroyed, general."

"Most? Then you failed. Our survey indicates only eighty percent of Piecer homes were destroyed. Eighty percent is not most."

"Okay, eighty percent of their homes were destroyed, and the rest were damaged. Demolition teams are mopping them up now."

"And the Piecers and their families?"

"Most are dead. They died in the first volley. The rest have gone into hiding underground."

"Most? Eighty percent? Is this what humans call success? Klix call it failure."

"I call it a damn good start, General. I know all their hiding places underground. We will round them up, but we have to be cautious. We don't want to lose any more of *your* men."

"My men? Who dares defy the Klix?"

"Only a few, Your Excellency; a few Piecers who escaped. We should have them in custody by morning. They will offer little resistance once we have their families."

"Do not fail me, human. The Klix reward failure with death."

"I *never* fail," said Loose.

"And your family? Have you captured them?"

"I haven't found their bodies, but..."

"And your Piecer brother—is he dead?"

"Not sure. A patrol found a few of your men dead at my old house. It might have been him. Could've been blown up in the stadium blast, but the *Promise* is missing from the stadium, and that sounds like Chase to me."

"You are pathetic, human. You come to me with excuses and promises of future deeds."

"With all due respect, fuck you, General. I gave you the coordinates to the stadium, so you could get all the Piecers at once. I gave you the coordinates for all the Piecer districts, and your fucking shitty pilots missed. They fucking missed! So don't hang this on me. It is *your* failure, not mine."

"You dare speak to me that way? I will peel your skin from your body and watch you slowly fry under your own star, your own Sun."

"We had a deal. I govern the Earth. All humans become my property. You get the resources and the slave labor until you harvest all the silver. Then I repopulate the Earth with my progeny only. Earth will be *my* domain, like Kattar is yours."

General Klume's face flushed so black with disgust his features were barely visible. "Do not compare yourself to me...and what makes you think I need you now?"

"Humans will fight you to their very last breath. You will win a dead planet. Who will you have to mine Earth's silver? Your men?"

Klume paused, deliberating, and took a deep breath.

"Very well, but do not fail me again."

"I never do. Oh, and general, if you ever threaten me again, I will kill you before you ever reach your communicator. My weapon was shielded from your EMP, and I never fucking miss."

"I will keep my bargain, Piecer Loose, but you must guarantee all your soldiers will be wiped out—including your brother—if you can even find him."

Loose handed him a piece of paper. "I can find him. These are the coordinates where my parents would hide underground if they could. Send your troops there, round them up, and take them back to your planet. We might need them later. As for my brother, if he's not with my parents, I know where he's going. You have my word."

"Hah! Your word is shit. Only your lust for power can be trusted. My troops will find your parents if they are there. Find your Piecer brother and any other Piecers who survived and bring them to me," said the general. "I will make an example of them to anyone who would dare oppose the Klix Supremacy."

"I will need a Klix trans-warp ship, some men, and one of your engineers."

"For what? Starships are needed for our war effort as are my men."

"*I* need them for *our* war effort, if you want to win."

Klume looked away angrily before turning back to Loose. "Very well, but if you fail..."

"I told you, I never fail."

General Klume hesitated and then clicked orders to his men. Moments later, a trans-warp scout ship with a complement of men landed in the clearing.

"Do you have an engineer among your crew?" Klume clicked to the captain of the vessel.

The captain clicked his response.

"You have your ship and your men, human," said Klume. "If you fail, you will not get another chance."

"Yeah, yeah, you're scarin' me. Don't worry. I'm not doing this for you; I'm doing this for me."

The general turned to the captain of the scout ship.

"You will take your orders from this human, Loose 524," the general clicked to the captain.

"Yes, general."

Loose handed a paper to the captain.

"These are your coordinates, but we'll need to pick up

some bait along the way. Where's your engineer? I want to speak with him. We're goin' fishin'."

The captain barked out the coordinates to his first officer while Loose was seen talking to the engineer. They took off in the Klix ship and disappeared into the Klix-generated worm-hole.

Chapter Six

Evelyn

After searching in vain for their families, Gage, Tripp, and Hector slipped into the woods and headed back to the stadium. When they reached the edge of the forest, they could see the bombed-out remains of the athletic field.

"Tripp," said Gage, "use those eyes of yours and scan for Klix."

"Yes, sir," he replied, scanning the area.

"Hector, you smell anything?"

"Death," replied Hector. "I smell death."

"Any Klix?"

"They're here...somewhere."

"Stay down and out of sight."

When batch 19523 reached puberty, their unusual abilities and size increased, surpassing the other Piecer cadets. They shared these same remarkable abilities, but in different proportions.

After an injury, they all could heal fairly quickly, but Gage 523 could heal within moments of the injury. During one training exercise, he stepped on a nail, and it went through his boot and his foot, poking out through the top. His superiors rushed him to the Piecer infirmary—fearing infection or tetanus—but by the time they got him there, his foot had completely healed. Only his boot and sock showed a hole where the nail had penetrated. They couldn't explain it and took numerous blood samples hoping to find out how he did it. They also noted yellow spots on his lower back and neck which defied explanation.

Gage was self-conscious of the spots and rarely removed his shirt for anything. The yellow spots were a stark contrast against his dark ebony skin. His foster mother, Karen Bielinski, tried to make him feel better, explaining the spots were a divine gift.

"You have been marked by God," she told him. "You are special."

"Well, I don't feel so special," he replied. "Kids laugh at me if I take my shirt off."

"They're ignorant, and you shouldn't listen to them."

"It still bothers me. Why am I the only 523 with spots?"

"You never get sick. If you get cut, you heal almost instantly. That's God's work."

"That's fucked up is what it is."

"Gage! We don't talk like that around here."

"I'm sorry. It's just so embarrassing."

"You have nothing to feel ashamed about. Those spots could be where God's fingertips touched you."

"Well, God got into the finger paints, then," he said, half kidding, half angry. "And he only likes yellow."

Karen made the sign of the cross.

"Yellow is the color of the sun. Your spots are beautiful."

"Well, he coulda used brown paint that day, is all I'm saying."

Karen reached out, hugged him, and he smiled.

"Gage baby, God has a plan for you," she said. "You are very, very lucky."

"I don't feel lucky. Well, sometimes. I'm glad you're my mom. That's lucky."

"You'll see," she said, cradling him in her arms. "Someday you will shine like the sun."

She always knew how to make him feel better, and he eventually overcame his shyness, often taking the lead at the academy.

Hector 523 also had a special talent. He could smell as well as a dog. When his fellow cadets would hide in ambush in war games, they were unable to fool him, even if they tried to cover their scent. He could even tell who was hiding in which bush, without ever seeing them. On overnight maneuvers, he would tell everyone what they would be having for dinner in the mess hall, even while they were more than a mile away.

"The nose knows," he would say when coming up behind his quarry. "You can't fool the nose."

Tripp 523 had the sight of a hawk or eagle during the day and an owl at night. He could see what others could only see using Scout Specs. At night, his vision was equal to a normal cadet in the daylight, and he was their best point man by far.

Hector and Tripp lived next door to each other, which wasn't unusual, as all Piecers lived near each other in government housing. Living next door, they shared back yards, giving them plenty of space to play and improve their skills.

Tripp practically lived at Hector's house. His foster father, Adrian McInnis, had dedicated his life to the military and fought valiantly beside his wife, Marie, until she was killed, both of them hit by the same Klix bomb. He always blamed himself for not taking the brunt of the explosion, but he survived and was medically discharged due to losing half his foot.

He lost more than his wife and half his foot to the blast. The explosion left an all-encompassing pain in his soul, and he tried to drown his anguish by drinking, usually until he passed out. The only recourse left to him to stay involved with the military was to become a Piecer Corp foster father. Unfortunately, his drinking did not disqualify him from taking on a Piecer child, and he adopted Tripp.

He drank to forget and to numb his pain, but there were days when he was so drunk, he'd beat Tripp for any minor infraction. For the most part, Tripp took the beatings thinking he deserved it, until he got older. Then, he would run next door to Hector's house and stay there until his father sobered up. It was not uncommon for Tripp to run over to Hector's house in the middle of the night in his underwear, seeking refuge. Hector's mother, Catherine O'Rourke, always let him come inside and gave him some clothes to wear and a late-night supper, knowing he probably hadn't been fed.

Catherine always said grace prior to any meal, thanking God that they had any food at all to eat. Tripp did not understand the ritual, but he found comfort in it nonetheless. Often while Catherine and Tripp were seated at the table, Hector would wake up and join them for a late-night snack if there was food. The boys sat around the table, eyeing the silverware and hoping to "borrow" a knife or two to take outside to play the next day.

Hector loved playing with knives. He would steal his mother's paring knives and challenge Tripp to throwing contests. The paring knife blade was heavier than the hilt, and it flew straighter and farther than her other knives. The knife was coveted, and sometimes they had to share just the one blade.

The boys had become fairly accurate and would often challenge themselves by hunting in the woods for squirrels. Tripp could spot a squirrel climbing a tree from one hundred yards away, while Hector used his nose to find them closer and could smell them hiding behind a limb of a tree.

"Not much good if they're so far away," said Hector. "Maybe if we had a crossbow or something."

"Yeah, I guess so," said Tripp. "I'll keep looking."

"Wait, there's one up there..." Hector whispered. "Hiding."

"I don't see anything," Tripp whispered back, searching the trees. "Where?"

"Two trees over—three quarters up—behind the big branch on the right."

"Oh, I see his little shitty paws clinging to this side of the branch. You got a shot at him?"

"No, but..."

Hector whirled around and let his knife fly. Behind him, a

squirrel had climbed up the side of a tree and paused, momentarily watching them as the knife hit him.

"Dinner!" said Hector, retrieving his blade and stuffing the dead squirrel in a sack.

"Nice shot," said Tripp. "How the hell do you do that?"

"The nose knows," Hector replied, grinning. "We'll have meat tonight. You should come by."

"Yeah, yeah," said Tripp. "Wait...don't move. Hand me the knife."

Hector froze and handed it to him gently. Tripp slowly and carefully aimed at a tree twenty yards away and let the knife fly. There was a squeak and a plop sound.

"Got him," Tripp shouted. "That's two."

"You could see that?" asked Hector, surprised.

"Hell yeah; I think he was giving me the finger," said Tripp. "The little bastard... that'll teach him to flip off armed strangers."

Hector laughed. "Let's get a few more and bring 'em home. My mom makes a mean stew."

"Sounds good; I'm hungry already."

"Knife," Hector whispered.

Tripp was a few feet away and tossed the blade gently to Hector, hilt first. Hector caught the blade and whirled around, throwing in one smooth motion. Another squirrel fell victim to his blade.

"That was awesome," said Tripp. "You gotta teach me how you do that."

"It was a perfect toss. We should do that more...you know, practice that shit."

"The tossing part?"

"Yeah, I think it helps."

"You're shittin' me."

"No, for some reason, I was able to zero in on the squirrel while catching the blade, and it just flew out of my hand. I didn't even have to think about it."

"I didn't even see the damn thing."

"You just have to smell 'em." Hector laughed. "They smell

a little like dogs, but much worse."

As they grew older, they would challenge each other in the woods, throwing kitchen knives of all shapes and sizes. They practiced the tossing game, Tripp tossing to Hector and Hector tossing to Tripp. Sometimes, they'd try for the occasional crow or pheasant when they could find one. Tripp had the advantage there and could hit them in midflight.

"How do you hit a bird in flight with a fucking knife?" asked Hector.

"It's not that hard," replied Tripp. "When I see them, it's like they are in slow-mo, and I just see where they will be and throw my knife there."

"Very cool, my brother...I wish I could do that."

"We are definitely getting better at this, I think," said Tripp. "I can't wait until they give us decent weapons at the academy. Can you imagine hunting with an actual laser rifle?"

"Too easy," said Hector. "I think I like the knife better. More fun and it's quieter."

The boys played, hunted, and refined their abilities to the point where they always had meat on the table. They became inseparable and often worked together as a team at the academy.

For Chase, it was as if he had inherited all the 523 traits but to a lesser extent. He healed quickly and could see, smell, and even hear better than many of the 523s. But his best asset was speed. He was a gazelle when he ran. Nobody could catch him or even come close, in short or long-distance sprints, and he never seemed to tire. He could run the entire length of the woods without stopping to rest. He quickly excelled at the academy, and his instructors found him to be an excellent team leader, who was able to anticipate problems and solve them by using his fire team's unusual talents.

Regular Piecer competitions were held for platoon leader, and in almost every event, Chase was unbeaten. He could run faster and shoot faster—more accurately than almost any other recruit—including his brother, Loose. Only those unrecovered 523 few, who had shared the same tainted DNA batch, could keep up with him.

Their abilities didn't go unnoticed by their superiors. No one could account for the peculiarities of this batch, though they desperately searched their creation records in the hopes to duplicate the results. They questioned the lab technicians on duty during that time, but no one would acknowledge that anything different had happened from batch 522 to batch 524. They were stymied.

Chester Blanc, one of the two technicians on duty during the creation of batch 523 was repeatedly questioned. Under questioning, he was evasive, at first denying he was on duty when the 523 batch was created. When work logs and security access data were presented showing his signature, time, and date stamps, he admitted to being there, blaming a faulty memory for his prior testimony. The questioning repeated for months, but he never wavered from his story, stating that nothing happened to batch 523. Finally, it was dropped, and Chester disappeared, leaving the Corp to rebuild his family's farm—a farm they later found didn't exist.

Further investigation into his background uncovered that Mr. Blanc had two personnel files, one of which had been intentionally deleted but was recovered by the Corp's forensic team. The deleted file indicated that Mr. Blanc's first application included a background in experimental zoology, while the current undeleted file failed to mention this detail.

Their superiors lamented the decision of "recovering" so many of the 523 batch. They wanted more of these fighters and vowed never to recover any new batches again. Fortunately, Chase and a few others were lucky and had been spared.

The fireteam met at the edge of the forest, next to the stadium and looked over the bombed-out remains of the athletic field.

"Any luck finding your mom, Hector?" asked Gage. "Was she okay?"

"No luck," replied Hector. "Nothing there, just rubble.

Klix got there before we did. Those fuckers are gonna pay if they hurt my mom."

"How 'bout you?"

"No, nothing there," replied Gage.

"I'll help you find them," said Tripp. "Every Piecer house I saw was flattened. It's like they knew where we all lived. If they got out, they would've gone underground. We need to find Chase; he'll know what to do next."

"Okay," said Gage. "First, we'll find Chase, then I'm going to kill me some Klix. They fucked up my house, and if they hurt my mom, they're going to wish they were never born."

They peered through a section of the remaining fence and rubble that surrounded the stadium.

"I don't see it," said Hector. "It's gone, Gage...the *Promise* is gone."

"We took too long to get back," he replied. "We're on our own."

"That sonofabitch left without us," said Tripp. "Great, just great."

"He said he'd wait as long as he could—not forever," replied Gage. "Besides, this place is crawlin' with Klix."

Gage surveyed the area before turning back to them.

"Okay," he said calmly. "We have our orders: get ships and rendezvous. He's got his ship; now we gotta get ours."

"Wait," said Tripp, looking out over the sparkling field. "Our Stars are out there."

"So, who cares about that now? They probably don't work from the EMP anyway."

"I didn't before," said Tripp. "But now that they took it away from us, I want mine...and so will Chase."

"We don't have time for that," said Gage.

"Won't take long; I'm not going to collect them all—just ours."

"If you think you can get them and get back here without being seen or getting killed, then you got two minutes."

Tripp ran out on the field, grabbing stars embedded in the ground wherever he found them, and then came running back. He held out his hand, his fist filled with glimmering Star badges.

"Got 'em," he said, shoving them into his pocket, "let's go."

"You try 'em?" asked Hector.

"Yeah, they're fried...no com."

"Worth a shot."

"I could get more," said Tripp. "Maybe some of them work."

"Forget it," replied Gage. "If these are fried, they're all fried. That's enough."

While the trio was of equal rank, Gage usually took the lead when Chase was gone. It was never voted on; everyone just fell into their respective roles. Gage had no problem giving orders and saw it as a natural process to accomplish the mission. When Chase wasn't around, he assumed the role, and everyone listened.

Tripp never cared for command. He'd stand in front of a speeding troop transport and stop it with his face if ordered to do so. He preferred taking orders to giving them, fearing that someone might get hurt following one of his orders.

Hector was the collector and collaborator of the team. He listened to everyone, collected information, and then said his piece. The four made a great fire team when Chase was with them and a formidable adversary even without him.

"We're gonna need a ship with a worm drive," said Hector. "Not many left...and only in museums. There are two space museums within five hundred miles: New Palm Springs and New Vegas."

"I vote Vegas," said Tripp. "At least then we can grab a drink and do a little gambling."

"New Palm Springs is closer," said Gage. "And closer ain't that close, not without vehicles. And what makes you think Vegas isn't overrun with Klix?"

"Yeah, we can't risk the roads either," said Hector. "Too many fucking Klix."

Hector stopped, sniffing the air. "What's that smell?"

"I don't smell nothin'," said Tripp.

"Shhh!" said Gage, holding up his hand. "Get down."

The three ducked behind trees lining the forest at the stadium. The bushes nearby rustled.

"You hear that?" asked Gage.

"Yeah, I heard it," replied Tripp. "Over there, I think I heard a moan."

"What you smellin', Hector?" asked Gage.

"Smells like flowers or somethin'. I think it's perfume."

"Perfume? You need to get your nose checked out."

Hector sniffed the air again. Gage motioned to Tripp to take position behind the bushes on the far side, while he and Hector approached directly from the front, left and right. Nobody spoke as they moved toward the center bush, which suddenly moved. They each grabbed their combat knives and readied themselves to kill whatever it was. Hector motioned for Gage to move to his right while he pulled back the front bush blocking their view, in one sudden yank.

"Stay back, motherfuckers!" said a seated young woman, holding a large branch as a club.

The woman was obviously scared, possibly in shock, and she appeared to have lost a fair amount of blood from a gash in her forehead. Blood had run down her face, matted in her long blond hair, and stained her sheer yellow dress.

"Perfume," said Hector, smiling to show her he meant no harm. "It's okay...we're Piecers. We won't hurt you."

"I mean it—stay back," she repeated, swinging her club in a circle.

Still smiling, Hector reached forward to help her up, and she swatted at his arm with her club. In an instant, he caught the club in full swing, stopping it, and said, "You won't need this, we're the good guys."

He tossed the club on the ground like a twig and squatted down to face-level. The woman, still frightened, began to weep. Tripp came up from behind, startling her, and she shielded her face and head with both arms.

"It's okay, darlin'," said Tripp. "We're not going to hurt

you. No one is going to hurt you now. What you doin' out here all by yourself?"

The woman sniffled and sobbed a little more before she was finally able to speak.

"My name is Evelyn. Evelyn Tupi, General Tupi's grand-daughter."

"Holy shit," said Tripp. "I hearda you. Tupi would never let any of us near you."

"He was very protective," she said, sniffling. "He took me in when my parents were killed. Have you seen him? Is he okay?"

Hector looked at Gage and Tripp. They looked down and away from Evelyn. Immediately, Evelyn knew her grandfather was gone, and she started sobbing again, almost wailing.

"Umm, sweetheart," said Tripp. "I know you're sad and all, but if you keep that up, you're gonna get us all killed."

Evelyn took a deep breath and silenced herself. "I'm sorry," she whispered. "It's just...I, and then..." Her voice trailed off.

"Here," said Tripp, handing her a canteen. "Looks like you could use a drink."

Hector blocked his arm.

"Not that, you idiot; she needs water—not booze."

"Sorry; she just looked like she could use a drink..."

Evelyn grabbed his canteen, took a big gulp and then coughed, the liquor stronger than she expected.

"What *is* that?" she asked, her voice hoarse from the drink.

"Piecer juice," said Tripp, standing taller and puffing out his chest proudly. "My own recipe."

"Tastes like pure alcohol."

"Yeah, it's a good recipe," said Tripp, smiling.

Evelyn took another swig.

"There ya go, darlin'," said Tripp. "See, Hector, she knows what she wants."

Tripp reached out with his knife and tore into her dress. Evelyn gasped and scooted backwards, still seated. Pulling hard and fast, he ripped a long thin section of her dress, exposing her legs.

"What the fuck you doin'?" asked Gage.

"Nothin', she's hurt. She needs a bandage around that gash in her head to stop the bleeding.

"Oh, sorry," he replied. "I just thought..."

"Yeah, I know what you thought. I'm not an animal...not most days anyways."

"Did you have to rip her dress so far up?"

Tripp smiled. "Nope."

"Hmmph. Dirtbag," Gage snorted.

"Hey, I coulda gone higher. I thought I used amazing restraint."

"Dirtbag," Gage repeated. "I don't know how you can be a 523."

"What? Why?"

"Well, for starters, you got no character. And look at us; I'm gorgeous and black, Hector is fabulously Hispanic, and you, you're about as white as a ghost."

Tripp laughed.

"I came out just fine," he said. "I'm the beauty and you're the beasts."

"523 DNA, my ass...that shit is fucked up," said Gage, spitting.

"They had to have a few ugly guys to balance me and Chase," Tripp continued, watching Gage's reaction carefully. "You know, equal proportions handsome to ugly. You're my ugly brother from another mother."

Gage laughed. "Mmm-hmm, you're equal proportions all right—dumb and stupid."

"Ignore Tripp, Evelyn," said Hector. "We're not all idiots. He has the brain of a rabbit. Can you walk?"

Tripp wrapped the bandage gently around her head to cover her wound and stop the bleeding.

"Gimme your canteen, Gage," Tripp demanded.

Tripp ripped another piece out of Evelyn's dress and poured water from Gage's canteen on to the cloth.

"Hmmph," Gage huffed. "You keep making bandages, and she won't have any dress left."

"Oh, don't listen to the grumpy old man, darlin'. He's just cranky."

"I'm the same age as you, deviant. Watch out for this one, Evelyn."

"There you go," said Tripp, wiping the blood off Evelyn's face. "That's better."

"I can walk," Evelyn replied, blocking his hand from wiping her face any further. "I got hit in the head...by a bleacher, I think, but I can walk."

"You can't walk in those, honey," said Tripp, indicating her shoes.

"Wait, what are you doing?"

Tripp was busy pulling the shoes off of her feet and breaking the heels off of them.

"Not much use for heels in the forest," he said.

"Those were my nicest shoes," said Evelyn, shocked.

"They're better now," said Tripp, handing them back to her. "Trust me."

"I got hit by a bleacher too," said Gage, pointing to his shoulder. "Went in right there...poked out the backside under my shoulder."

Evelyn winced in sympathy, and then looked closely. She saw nothing wrong with his shoulder, only the hole in his fatigues. A look of disbelief came over her.

"Oh, it's healed already," said Gage, smiling. "I'm Gage 523, Piecer Corp, at your service."

Gage took a small bow, finishing up with a flourish of his arm sweeping from his head and down and up again.

Tripp rolled his eyes.

"You are *such* a drama queen." Tripp laughed.

"Ignore my demented brother," Gage said. "He was dropped on his head as a baby— many, many, many times."

Tripp laughed again, crossing his eyes and distorting his face, playing along and trying to make her smile. Gage turned back to Evelyn with an earnest, sad face.

"I'm sorry about your grandfather," he said. "He was a great man. We were all sorry to lose him."

"Thank you," said Evelyn. "You're 523s...the bad batch?"

"Yep, that's us," said Tripp.

"Don't believe everything you've heard about us," Hector said to Evelyn. "We're not so bad...unless we need to be."

Evelyn smiled.

"My grandfather told me about your, umm...batch. Told me you had special abilities none of the other Piecers had."

"Let's just say when they made us, they threw away the mold," Hector replied. "Or they threw the mold in, nobody knows."

Tripp laughed. "Yep, we're special," he said. "But don't worry; we're practically normal, except for these two. I'm Tripp, that's Hector, and you already know Gage."

"I think it was your grandfather that nicknamed us 'the bad batch,'" said Gage.

"Oh, I'm sorry," said Evelyn. "I'm sure he didn't mean anything by it."

"No worries; it's a badge of honor to us. Same batch makes us brothers, same DNA. And bein' bad can be good sometimes."

Gage popped up out of the bushes to reconnoiter.

"Okay; we need to get out of here before the Klix find us," he said. "Let's get back into the woods and head to New Palm Springs."

"We can't fuckin' walk all the way to New Palm Springs," said Tripp.

"Hey! Watch it," said Gage. "There's a lady present."

"Sorry, Evelyn," said Tripp with a pained look on his face.

"It's okay. I've been around the military all my life," said Evelyn. "I've heard lots worse."

"We can't walk all the frickin' way to New Palm Springs," Tripp continued. "Not with a woman. No offense."

"Oh, very smooth," said Gage. "Yeah, much better."

Tripp grinned.

"Offense taken," Evelyn interrupted. "Don't worry about

me. I can take care of myself."

They looked at each other and grimaced, knowing she wouldn't be able to keep up with them. She was a "normie," injured, and a woman.

"These woods don't go all the way to New Palm Springs," Hector whispered to Gage. "Most of the way is desert. And even if they did, Evelyn's not gonna be able to keep up with us."

"I know, I know...I'm workin' on it," said Gage. "I have an idea how we might be able to travel without being seen, but you're not going to like it."

"How's that?" asked Hector.

"We're gonna need a canoe."

"A *canoe*? There's no fuckin river to New Palm Spri—ohh, shit no, don't say the sewers—anything but the fucking sewers."

"There's a small shallow pond nearby, through the woods; usually a canoe or rowboat on shore. Used to go swimmin' there in the summer."

"Can't we find another way?"

Gage laughed. "Sorry, it's the only way."

"Oh, you fucker...you know I hate sewers!"

"Got a better idea?"

Hector crossed his arms and looked away. "No."

Gage laughed again, trying to hold it in.

"Fine," said Hector. "Let's find a fucking canoe."

"Okay. That's the plan then. Tripp, carry Evelyn."

"My pleasure," said Tripp.

Evelyn looked shocked, then angry.

"Carry me? I can walk."

"Evelyn, this isn't personal," said Gage. "But we can walk faster than you can run, without a head injury."

"Well, I'm not going to be carried. I'm not a sack of potatoes."

"Tripp..." said Gage, nodding toward Evelyn.

Tripp leaned into Evelyn after helping her up and pulled her over his shoulder, fireman style.

"Put me down, you jerk," ordered Evelyn, kicking. "Put me down!"

"Sorry, ma'am...no time for pleasantries. That was an order."

Gage pointed toward the woods, and the three took off running with Evelyn over Tripp's shoulder—bouncing with every jump and hop. They ran for fifteen minutes without stopping.

"*Please* let me down," begged Evelyn. "My stomach hurts and my head is throbbing."

"It's okay, Evelyn; we're here," said Tripp, stopping and putting Evelyn on the ground gently.

Gage and Hector stopped, ducking behind trees near the pond.

"Ohh," Evelyn moaned. "My head, it's killing me," she said, holding her hand to her bandage. "I can't take any more bouncing."

Tripp placed his hand over her mouth. Her eyes went wide with surprise.

"Shhh," he said. "Klix."

Evelyn quieted down, her eyes shifting left and right, fear replacing surprise. She started to cry, holding her head with both hands. Three Klix troopers patrolling the woods near the pond were clicking back and forth.

"It hurts so much," she whispered to Tripp, almost crying. "I need some aspirin... anything."

Tripp reached into his pocket and pulled out a small white tablet.

"Here," he said while breaking the tablet in half. "Take this, but just half."

Evelyn popped the half pill in her mouth and swallowed it eagerly.

"Thank you," she whispered to Tripp, who held his finger to his mouth, gesturing to her to be silent.

Evelyn nodded that she understood while Gage signaled to Hector, pointing to the far Klix. Hector pulled his knife and disappeared into the woods. Gage then pointed to the second Klix and made a cutting gesture to his throat. Tripp took off like a stealthy cat, disappearing behind a tree without a sound. Gage turned to Evelyn and put his finger up to his lips.

"Evelyn, stay here and be quiet," he whispered. "Don't come out for anything. Do you understand?"

Evelyn looked at him glassy-eyed and confused before nodding. Gage took off into the brush, heading for the third Klix. Moments later, she heard a few loud clicks and then silence—except for the tweeting of birds and the occasional croaking of a frog.

Hector came out of the woods first, then Tripp, and then Gage. They were heading back to where Evelyn lay hidden, when a fourth Klix appeared with his weapon drawn. He was too far away to rush, and they were too closely grouped together to jump out of the way. The Klix fired a shot at their feet, the laser blast hitting in front of them throwing dirt into the air.

"Do not move," the Klix clicked into his electronic translator.

Most Klix, including the lowliest recruits, carried an electronic translator on their uniform. It enabled them to communicate with other species by turning clicks into other languages and other languages into clicks. Mankind had not yet developed this technology and working Klix translators were highly prized among Piecer soldiers.

"You didn't smell him, Hector?" asked Gage.

"Musta been downwind; Tripp shoulda seen him."

Tripp looked at him and cocked his head in surprise. "Don't blame me...I have great vision—not x-ray vision!"

"Spread out," Gage whispered.

Tripp and Hector started to move sideways when the Klix fired two more shots at their feet.

"Move again and you die, human filth," said the Klix.

"He called you filth," Tripp said to Hector.

"Shut up, you idiot," whispered Hector. "No time to fuck around. Besides, he was looking at you."

"Okay, well...now what?" Gage asked loudly to the Klix.

The Klix spoke into his communicator. There was no reply. The Klix looked left and right for the other three Klix in his squad. He clicked loudly. Still, there was no reply.

"You are my prisoners," he said electronically. "You will come with me. If you resist or try to escape, you will be killed."

Tripp started to walk to the right of Gage—toward the Klix—waving his arms as if the Klix terms were unacceptable.

"I'm not sure how I feel about that," said Tripp, gesturing matter-of-factly. "You see, I'm kinda tired from running through the woods, and I'm not in the mood for another long walk."

The Klix turned his weapon on Tripp and fired, striking him in the chest. Tripp fell back—screaming in pain—and then went silent. Hector dove left and Gage dropped to the ground. The Klix focused his weapon on Gage.

"You move, you die," he clicked loudly into his translator.

"Let me just see about my man," said Gage. "He's wounded."

"Fuck your man," he clicked, pointing his weapon back at Tripp. "He won't need any help soon."

He aimed down the sights of his laser weapon, aiming directly at Tripp's head, and moved his finger to the trigger.

"Don't," said Gage. "He's down...he can't hurt you."

Hector was now moving through the bushes toward the Klix but was still too far away to stop him.

"It's over for him," clicked the alien, starting to pull the trigger. "He will die with honor in battle."

Suddenly, there was a loud crack as the alien's head spun partially left.

"Take that, motherfucker!" Evelyn shouted, swinging a large tree branch club and almost falling over from the blow.

The alien fell like a stone. Evelyn regained her footing and jumped on top of him, clubbing his head to a blackened pulp.

"This is for my grandfather, this is for my parents, and

this is for Tripp, you alien piece of shit!"

Hector hurried over to her and grabbed Evelyn's arm in mid-swing.

"He's gone," he said. "He's gone. You're safe. It's okay."

"Fuck you, alien bitch," she screamed at the dead alien. "Never fuck with a Tupi!"

Evelyn paused, took a deep breath, and looked down at the mass of goo that was the Klix head.

"Oh my God!" she cried, "I *killed* it."

"Yeah...you did," said Hector, "and you saved us all."

"I've never killed anything before."

"Sometimes you have to," said Hector.

Evelyn looked back down at the Klix on the ground, started heaving, and threw up.

"It's okay, Evelyn; you'll be okay," said Hector, putting his hand on her shoulder.

Gage had already moved to Tripp, helping him sit up.

"You all right?"

"No, I'm not all right; that fucker put a laser hole in me. Shit burns. Goddammit, can you see through me?" Tripp asked, looking over his shoulder.

"No, and don't move. You'll be okay. Lucky it sears the blood vessels closed. Let me just cover that shit up. You'll heal."

Evelyn stared at the dead Klix and started laughing.

"Come out, ya fucking Klix," she said, waving her club. "Come out and face me, you pussies."

"Oh God, here she goes," said Hector. "She's losin' it."

Evelyn looked over at the pond, dropped her club, and started walking toward it.

"Oh, I want to go swimming," she said, tossing her dress on the shore, and running straight into the water laughing and splashing.

"Hey, you guys...come on in. It's so warrrrm."

The three soldiers turned to look at her, then back at each other.

Evelyn shouted to them on shore. "Marco!"

"What did you give her, Tripp?" asked Gage sternly.

"You're supposed to say, Polo, you idiots," Evelyn screamed from the water. "Didn't they teach you *anything* at the Piecer Academy?" Evelyn shouted again. "Marco...you guys suck at this."

"I just gave her half a soap—for her headache."

Gage shook his head. "Why you even carry that shit? She's a normie, she can't handle that. Hector, go get her, will you? Tripp's got a hole in him, and I don't want him in that water."

"I only gave her half," said Tripp. "Besides, you never know when you might need 'em. Like when someone puts a fucking hole in your chest with a laser weapon."

Hector waded into the water and Evelyn swam away from him, giggling.

"Aww, c'mon, Evelyn," said Hector. "We have to go."

Evelyn laughed and dove underwater, coming up on the other side of the pond.

"Can't catch me," she yelled, splashing him. "I'm a fish."

Gage yelled to Hector, "Get her now, before she gets us killed."

Hector dove under the water.

"Where are you, Hectorrrrr?" Evelyn called, not seeing him. "Marcoooo."

Hector burst out of the water behind her and grabbed her, throwing her over his shoulder.

"Polo," he said. "Let's go."

Evelyn laughed and kicked her legs. "Wooo!" she screamed. "Spin me!"

"I'm not spinning you."

"C'mon, Hec-tor, Hec...tor—what kind of name is Hec-tor?"

"She's high as a kite," said Hector, placing her on the ground next to Tripp. "Here's your dress, Evelyn. Put it on."

"Oh...hi, Trippy!" she said happily. "Tripper McTrippy, hey, you're the one who tore my dress, you naughty, naughty boy...and you broke my shoes. Those were my best shoes too, you meanie."

Tripp laughed, then cringed from the pain in his chest.

"Ow, shit," he groaned, trying not to laugh. "Yeah, she's wasted."

"I was gonna wear those to my grandpa's graduation ceremony."

Evelyn looked up as if searching her memory and then started to cry. "Oh my God, Grandpa, he's gone. I'm alone, all alone."

"You're not alone," said Tripp. "We're here. We're your friends."

Evelyn grabbed Tripp's head, pulled him closer and kissed him hard on the lips. Then she stood up and looked Hector and Gage in the eyes, reached out and hugged them. Smiling, Tripp stood up, surprised.

"My friends," sobbed Evelyn, "I have friends!"

"Yes, Evelyn," said Gage, "we're your friends."

Evelyn burst out crying, wailing.

"I love you guys," she cried.

"Well, we love you too, Evelyn," said Tripp.

Gage leaned over and put his finger up against her mouth.

"Shhh," he said firmly. "Put your dress back on. It's time to go."

Evelyn nodded, winked back at him, and slipped her dress back on.

"*Shhhh*, gotcha. *Klix*," she said. "Could be anywhere. Don't worry, I got your back."

Gage rolled his eyes. "Okay, Tripp...you got her high, you take care of her.

"I don't mind," said Tripp. "She's kinda funny, and damn, that girl can kiss!"

Evelyn giggled, and kept repeating Tripp's name.

"Tripp, Tripper, Trippy, Trippsky, Tripp Tripp Tripp. You're cute!"

Tripp laughed. "Hey, she thinks I'm cute..."

"She's obviously out of her mind," said Gage. "Shut her

up and let's move out. We're walking until Tripp heals."

Tripp put his hand over Evelyn's mouth. Evelyn stuck out her tongue to lick it and then laughed. "Haha...I wet-willied your hand."

"She's literally a handful," Tripp said quietly, wiping his hand on his pants leg. "Now you hush, darlin', or I'm going to have to hush you."

Evelyn giggled again and put her finger up to her mouth. "Shhhh," she said.

"Hector," said Gage. "Over there, against that tree...the red canoe I told you about. It's still here, and it looks like it's okay. Grab the end and let's go."

"Where to?" asked Hector.

Gage looked around and motioned to his left. Haven't been here in a while, but should be this way...about two klicks east of us should be the entrance to the sewer system."

"Klix?" asked Evelyn. "Where are they? I will fuck them up."

Tripp laughed. "No, he means two kilometers from here, Killer, not *Klix* Klix."

"Let's go," said Gage. "It's a long way and Chase will be waiting."

"Chase who?" asked Evelyn. "Is he gonna chase us? Can I chase him? Chase, ChaChaChase. I knew a Chase once. It was sad."

Tripp ripped off another piece of Evelyn's dress and shoved it into her mouth.

"Mmmphh!" said Evelyn, wide-eyed and turning angry.

Tripp put his finger close to her face, pointing at her. "I warned you; now hush!"

Evelyn whimpered, but she could see by the look on his face that he was not kidding.

"Oh boy," said Hector. "Chase is gonna love this one."

They moved quickly through the woods to the entrance of the sewer system.

"Hector, take care of it," said Gage, pointing to the large padlocked metal door. Hector pulled his combat knife from his boot sheath and slid it into the hasp. "Stand back," he said. "Might fly off at you."

Tripp pulled the cloth from Evelyn's mouth and put his finger to her lips. Evelyn nodded that she understood, and Tripp stepped in front of her to protect her from any shards of lock that might break off. The padlock split in two, and Hector opened the door and stood back, almost gagging.

"My God!" he said. "It smells like shit."

Gage laughed. "What did you expect? It's a sewer. Let's go."

On the wall near the entrance was a bolted placard map of the sewer system.

"Is this really going to take us all the way to New Palm Springs?" asked Tripp.

"According to this map, it does...and no Klix down here."

Gage reached up and ripped the painted metal map off the wall, stashing it in the canoe.

"Fuck me; nothing would come down here," said Hector. "Let's get this over with."

"C'mon, Evelyn," said Tripp.

"Ooh, stinky poo," said Evelyn. "I think I might be sick again."

"Hold your nose," said Tripp.

Evelyn pinched her nose shut and gasped for air. "Thinth is awnful," she said, holding her nose closed. "I think I taste poo."

Tripp laughed.

They carried the canoe into the sewer and set it down on the fast-flowing sludge.

"Whatever you knuckleheads do," Gage said in a loud voice, pausing and then facing Evelyn. "Not you, Evelyn... these two knuckleheads," he said softly. "Don't tip the canoe," he continued in a loud voice.

"Gotcha, Chief," said Tripp. "Tip the canoe."

"Don't fuck around, Tripp," said Gage. "I'm serious."

"Check. Fuck around, tip the canoe, gotcha."

"No problemo here," said Hector. "It would kill me."

"Tripp, hold the canoe while Evelyn gets in. That's an order. I don't want to have to fish her out of the sewage and then ride to New Palm Springs with her covered in shit."

"I'm not an idiot," said Tripp. "Why does everyone think I'm an idiot?"

"Cause you act like an idiot," replied Gage.

"Oh yeah, *that*," said Tripp, laughing. "I got you, Evelyn... climb aboard the Shit Stream Express; next stop, Toity Town."

Gage rolled his eyes and stifled a laugh.

The sewer was an enormous tunnel with concrete ledges on both sides. A trough of watery brown sludge flowed through the center—with rounded concrete walls on the sides and ceilings. Once inside, the tunnel was dark, lit only by blue green lamps extending from the ceiling, casting a garish glow in front and behind them.

Evelyn got into the canoe carefully, then Hector, Gage, and finally Tripp, hopping in at the last moment, pushing them off the side.

"At least it's flowing our way," said Gage.

"Fuck this," said Hector, irritated. "How the fuck does water flow uphill?"

"All this water is pumped," replied Gage. "Part of the New Earth rebuilding project—goes right through the mountains, too."

"This is bullshit," said Hector, spitting.

"Hey, Hector," said Tripp, laughing. "Shit happens."

"Fuck you," Hector replied, tying a bandana over his nose and mouth. "I don't want to die in a fucking sewer."

The muck carried them quickly through the graffiti-covered sewer tunnels.

"Oh my God," said Evelyn. "I think I'm going to be sick again."

Evelyn leaned over the canoe, her face close to the sludge, and then drew her head back quickly from the stench.

"God, it's even worse up close," she gasped.

"You want to hurl in the canoe, you go right ahead," said

Tripp. "Don't you worry, darlin'."

Evelyn took as deep a breath as she dared, still holding her nose, trying to hold back her stomach. They drifted past sprayed graffiti lettering on the wall stating Sixers Rule, Klix Suck Dicks, and worse. Tripp tried to divert Evelyn's attention from the wall, shielding her from the words.

"Hey, Evelyn, you need a drink?"

"No," she replied. "And I've seen worse, Tripp, but thanks."

Tripp looked away, smiled briefly—caught in his diversion.

"Did you guys fight along with them, the Sixers?" Evelyn asked.

"Nah," said Gage. "We were only two by the time the Klix turned tail and ran back to their mommies...if they have mommies...at least most of 'em. Eventually, we returned to the surface, taking back what was left of our cities."

"They should have killed 'em all," said Tripp.

"You got that right," said Gage. "A lot of people died trusting that worthless truce."

"Cha-Cha was right," said Tripp. "He never trusted it."

"And we wouldn't be in this fucking sewer," said Hector, spitting again.

Gage looked around the sewer tunnel and checked his placard map. Every two hours along the way, he repeated the process. They paddled in shifts with paddlers fore and aft. Though the sewer flowed rapidly they paddled with the stream to speed their journey.

"Eight hours in a fucking sewer," said Hector. "Now when people tell me they feel like shit, I'll know exactly what they mean."

Tripp laughed. "Hang in there, brother. Soon this will all be just a stinking memory."

"Stop here," Gage yelled out.

They paddled to the side of a concrete ledge and a new tunnel that led in two directions.

"Thank God," said Hector. "Are we here?"

"I think so," said Gage. "Tripp, how you feeling?"

"Good to go, sir."

"How's Evelyn?"

"She's been better, but the bleeding stopped, and I sutured her wound closed while she was high. She didn't feel a thing."

"Good thinking. Don't need her infected."

"Hector, you want out of here?"

"You don't have to ask me twice," he said, jumping out of the canoe.

"Take that ladder up to the surface and check it out. We should be near New La Quinta; the museum is there."

Hector climbed the ladder and pried the sewer cover open just enough to see out.

"This thing comes out in the street," Hector called down to them, "or what's left of it. Museum is north of our position. Klix are everywhere."

"Okay; c'mon back down."

"No, I'm done with sewers."

"That's an order," said Gage. "We'll be out of here in no time, I promise, but we're not going out in the middle of the street. That's suicide."

"Fine, my nose will never work again," said Hector. "I can't even smell Evelyn's perfume anymore."

Everyone climbed out of the canoe while Hector lowered himself down the ladder and walked over to Gage, who was staring at the map.

"There's a sewer hole cover that comes up just behind the museum," said Gage. "Follow me."

Walking along the ledge, they took the side tunnel north to the sewer exit and climbed up behind the museum.

"Okay," said Gage. "There's a ladder over there. Looks like it leads to the roof. Tripp, you ready?"

"Ready."

"Evelyn, do you think you can make it up the ladder to the roof?"

"I can make it."

"Hector, check for Klix. We'll follow your lead."

"Anything to get out of this shithole."

"You go first, Evelyn," said Tripp.

"What? Why? I'm not climbing a ladder above you in what's left of my dress."

Tripp laughed. "Darlin', I thought we were past such formalities."

"No we are not," Evelyn said indignantly. "I'm not going to have you starin' at my ass all the way up the ladder."

"Why...whatever must you think of me," said Tripp, magnifying his expressions. "I'm shocked, and a little hurt."

Evelyn glared at him in disbelief. "You've been staring at my ass all day," she replied.

"Only because you're in front of me," Tripp said, feigning innocence.

"You go first," she said.

"I think you just want to stare at *my* ass," said Tripp.

Evelyn rolled her eyes. "Nobody wants to look at your scrawny little ass; now get up the ladder."

"Oh, so you *were* looking," said Tripp, laughing. "You little minx you."

"Shut up and get up the ladder."

Tripp overemphasized every step up the ladder, swaying his butt left and right in front of Evelyn's face.

"You're an idiot, you know that?" Evelyn yelled to him.

Tripp laughed and continued his exaggerated climbing. Evelyn turned her head so he couldn't see her smiling.

Hector led them up and over the top to the roof. From there, they could see in every direction, and everywhere they looked there were Klix.

"What now, Chief?" Hector asked Gage.

Gage crept over to the skylight on the roof and peered inside. He could see the starship *Lone Star* on display in the main room below them. The museum was enormous—the size of several airplane hangars. Rockets and airplanes from the bygone days of Earth were on display everywhere, some hanging from the ceiling, others reaching up from the ground to the ceiling. On the wall directly behind the *Lone Star*, a large bright-blue banner hung on the wall welcoming visitors: New La Quinta Space Museum, The Future is Here!

There she is, Gage thought to himself. *All dressed up like a turkey on Thanksgiving waiting for us to climb aboard.*

Gage scurried back to the others.

"I've got some good news and some bad news," said Gage. "Good news is it's the *Lone Star*—that sucker was loaded with weapons. Commissioned in New Texas; they threw every weapon they could think of at her."

"What's the bad news?" asked Hector. "And it better not be sewer-related or you're on your own."

"No," replied Gage. "The bad news is there's a laser security perimeter around the entire ship. Break that beam and every Klix on the outside will be inside in seconds. Ship's below us and no guards that I could see."

"So how are we gonna sneak a fifteen million metric ton spaceship out of a museum in daylight?" asked Hector.

"Who said anything about sneak?"

Chapter Seven

The Blue Angel

A blinding flash of light enveloped the *Promise* for what seemed like several seconds. The ship vibrated like a struck-tuning fork that Chase could feel reverberating in his chest.

"Shit, that's bright!" he said, closing his eyes and turning his head away from the warp bubble light. "Never get used to that."

The light finally dimmed, and Chase opened his eyes. The *Promise's* bridge was back to normal. He scanned the stars ahead of him and his proximity radar.

No Klix. At least he could relax for a minute. *Now where the fuck am I?* he wondered.

Chase spun the ship in a circle to get an idea of the stars around him. There, about 120 degrees to starboard, the familiar rings of Saturn appeared.

"Hello, beautiful," Chase said, patting the *Promise* console. "Thank God I'm still in the solar system."

He quickly flipped off the maneuvering jets after facing the *Promise* directly at Saturn, then toggled the computer speakers back on.

"*Nuclear reactor core, offline,*" said the now-familiar computer voice. "*Nuclear fuel depleted.*"

"Thanks, honey, I'll take it from here," he replied out loud, as if the ship were listening.

He would need fuel, he thought as he checked his control

console. His worm drive was offline, and he didn't have much rocket fuel left either. He knew there was an outpost near here, on Titan, one of Saturn's moons; kind of a dive, but any port in a storm.

Chase reoriented the craft toward Titan and began his descent. He could relax now; the ship's computer would take him the rest of the way. He took a deep breath and exhaled.

The *Promise* touched down near the Blue Angel with a slight bump. The Blue Angel was a fuel depot and bar known to be a rowdy place. As he switched off the engines, Chase checked his guns, spinning the cylinders to make sure that no chamber was missed. He adjusted the holsters over his spacesuit.

No governing authority reached this far out. The only "rule" at the Blue Angel was that weapons were not allowed inside, a rule that everyone still alive had fully ignored. Chase looked at the twin revolvers strapped to his hips. *I'm not going in there naked. Need something to hide these. Where's that coat?*

He pulled on his father's long coat, concealing both pistols and placed his Stetson hat, folded slightly to fit, into one of the deep inside pockets of the coat.

"That'll work," he said, looking down to make sure his guns were hidden. "Shouldn't need these if I get in and out fast. Just need fuel."

The Blue Angel stood out on Titan like a sore thumb—a neon anachronism, a throwback to twentieth century Earth bars. It was the kind of place where you could purchase anything, for the right price: food, fuel, weapons, and if you were lucky, sex.

Chase checked the ship's external sensors. At least this moon had a little gravity. There was a lot of sulfur and methane in the air, though; he couldn't stay out there too long.

He donned his breather helmet and exited the ship, inhaling cautiously. His Piecer spacesuit and boots were built to withstand even the frigid temperatures of Titan, but he didn't want to push his luck. He stepped down the fore ladder and looked around. The front of the bar was well-lit, with a blue neon sign indicating he was at the right place: Shoom's Blue Angel.

Chase chuckled at the curvy neon outline of a female human wearing an old-fashioned Earth bikini. The sign sat atop the building, flickering on and off in the inky darkness.

They sure do like Earth women, he thought. *Where do they get this stuff?*

Another yellow neon arrow with the word "fuel" lit up in English pointed to two large cylindrical tanks behind the building. Chase wondered how English had become so widespread in the galaxy. He remembered his father talking about how Earth scientists had long ago beamed television programs out into space. Apparently, they had a huge following on other worlds. Long dead actors and actresses became intergalactic celebrities. Chase shook his head laughing, took a breath, and instinctively went to hold his nose, his hand blocked by his breather helmet.

Shit! This place reeks of rotten eggs, he thought, *even through the damn breather.*

He made his way toward the entrance of the outpost. It was a desolate location, and nothing moved outside. No wind. No sound. Saturn loomed large above and behind the bar, with its lustrous rings so close you could almost touch them.

Another ship was parked nearby—a black raider, one of the Quargg's flagships. You could hardly see a Quargg ship when it was flying with its navigation lights off. The Quargg realized long ago that the dull matte black ship color acted like a cloaking device, making a ship practically indistinguishable from the blackness of space. Parked next to the Blue Angel, its eerie blue and red lights were on, indicating its security systems were armed, and its environmental systems were operational for any additional crew remaining onboard.

Chase looked over at the ship, but dismissed it.

Quargg scum, he thought. He hated the Quargg—the sticky-fingered bastards were always stealing from their outposts. There was a separate course on the Quargg at the academy and Chase both hated and admired them. They were thieves, but they had defended themselves from the Klix successfully and that alone made them admirable.

Two years before worm-drive tech was invented on Earth, the Klix attacked the nearby world of Quool, pronounced "cwool," the Quargg home planet. The war only lasted two days, with the Klix turning tail and running home. The Quargg were saved because of their penchant for larceny as Chase remembered the story.

On the Quargg planet Quool, there was a meeting at the Ministry of Intelligence and Information Services or the IIS. A Quargg data acquisitions officer, Elam Timit, burst into his supervisor's office, Captain Malton, shouting, "We've done it, we've done it!" Captain Malton had a blue sash over one shoulder and around his chest that stood out against the charcoal black uniform and the alien's dark gray skin. A hefty silver-plated stinger pistol was strapped to the sash, and a large medallion adorned the front of the sash, indicating his rank of captain.

Captain Malton shot up from his chair, clumsily setting down his Bloddo, spilling half of it. Bloddo was a whiskey-like drink said to have originated on the Manakee planet. It was prized for its turpentine-like flavor and hallucinogenic qualities, both visual and auditory. A being intoxicated on Bloddo could often be seen dancing with an imaginary partner to imagined music.

"Shit!" he shouted. "You made me spill my drink."

"I'm sorry, sir, but I had to tell you. We have it, sir," Elam said excitedly.

"Are you sure, Timit? You *better* be right. I need this. I'm not going to stay in this fucking desk job forever."

"No, sir...we have it, their complete plans. Our data scoop obtained the designs to the new Klix trans-warp drive—all their weapons, shields, everything."

"Excellent work, excellent. Are they aware of your intrusion?"

"No, sir."

"Turn the plans over to our fabricators; they will begin work immediately. Continue monitoring for their ship designs. Whatever you can get, send it."

"Yes, sir."

I'll make admiral for this, for sure, thought Malton, licking out his last drop of Bloddo from his spilled cup. There had already been rumors circling about a promotion for him, which he humbly ignored.

He looked up from his drink, noticing Timit was still there watching him.

"Well, don't just stand there, Timit...get the rest of their plans."

"Yes, sir, thank you, sir."

"And I won't forget your loyalty, Elam. You are a master thief if there ever was one. I shall see you are rewarded for your efforts, personally."

"Thank you, sir. I am but your humble servant," said Elam, bowing.

"Now go; get these plans to our factories."

"But sir, wouldn't it be easier to just steal their weapons?"

Captain Malton laughed. "Timit, you are truly Quargg, but we can't get there yet. We will need to build our own ships. Then we can." He paused, smiling before continuing, "*appropriate* their resources to ours."

"Yes, sir. You are most wise, Captain Malton."

The Quargg were infamous in their system as thieves. The very fabric of their society was based on "acquiring" goods from one another, or from the nearby planet of Manakee. To them, theft was the noblest form of work. It required skill, cunning, and what they thought was little effort.

Their current rocket technology only allowed them to pilfer goods from nearby Manakee or Klix-mining stations that were poorly guarded or abandoned. It was time-consuming, travel-wise, but it was all they knew, until the data scoop was developed.

When the Quargg stole plans to an energy repeater from the Manakee planet and were able to boost the signal of their data scoop to reach other star systems, everything changed. They could now steal information from the nearby Tork system where they found the plans for the trans-warp drive, along with every byte of information stored or transmitted on Kattar, the Klix home world.

Elam Timit returned a few hours later.

"Captain Malton," said Elam. "Our fabricators say we can duplicate everything they have."

"Very good, Timit; you have done well."

"But sir, there is one other troubling thing I have discovered in the data scoop."

"And what is that, Timit?"

"The Klix are preparing for an attack."

"Attack? Attack by whom?"

"No, sir...they are preparing to attack *us*, Captain. To attack Quool."

"Quool? But how?"

"They will wait until our planet and their planet are within striking distance, in ten moons."

"Are they? Well, they'll be in for a surprise, won't they, Timit?"

"They will?"

"Of course; how well do you think their weapons will work against their own defensive designs? We'll know everything about their technology. And we'll have the same weapons they do, only we can boost the effectiveness using our energy repeater."

"Ahh, yes, Captain," said Timit, grinning, "and we will know when and where they are coming."

"Exactly, Elam, so we must prepare. Inform the Ministry of Defense. This is a planetary emergency. All resources must be brought to bear. We must prepare to welcome our Klix guests."

Elam laughed.

The Quargg planet built extensive defensive capabilities using the Klix's own plans. They knew exactly how their weapons worked and how to defeat them. They copied their stinger pistols and rifles, adding extra capacity to each type of weapon and doubling their lethality. They copied their shields and boosted the power using the stolen energy repeater to protect their cities from any aerial assault. Then they waited for the Klix to attack, and when they did, the Quargg were ready.

The first attack was a bombing run. The Klix ships unloaded bomb after bomb with little effect—stopped by the Klix's own shield design protecting the Quargg cities.

When the Klix ships landed at secret rendezvous coordinates, they were immediately swarmed with Quargg troops. No matter where they went, the Quargg were waiting for them. The Klix suffered tremendous losses of both ships and soldiers. They tried another assault the next day with the same result and realized it was hopeless; they could not penetrate the Quargg defenses. They retreated back to their home world to assess the damage. The Quargg had won.

Chase took one last look at the Quargg ship before entering the airlock. *I sure would have liked to have seen Klume's face when the Quargg stopped their attack with the Klix's own weapons,* he thought.

The Blue Angel's airlock was a gigantic metallic tunnel that dwarfed him. He stepped inside, looking all around and felt for his guns through his coat.

I hope they pump clean air in this dump.

The door behind him automatically slammed closed, and the airlock pressurized. Chase swallowed and checked his wrist panel for an atmosphere reading. The panel showed green; the air was breathable. He removed his helmet slowly and then took a breath.

"Oh shit," he said, clenching his stomach to keep from vomiting. "It's even worse without the breather."

The tunnel detected his presence, and the too-bright overhead lights came on, making him squint to see. He put on his mirrored Scout Specs to shield his eyes, and the glasses automatically adjusted to block out the harsh overhead lighting.

"Must be some pretty big-ass aliens coming to the bar," he murmured. "This tunnel is gigantic."

The huge metal door ahead of him opened automatically with a burst of pressurized air and a loud *kushhh*. Chase looked in, scanning the bar for a tactical advantage. He pulled his father's folded Stetson-style hat from his inner coat pocket, placed it on his head, and adjusted it so it sat just above his scout specs, obscuring most of his face. Chase looked around the room for any other exits and set his breather helmet on a table near the door.

Always have a way out, he thought, remembering Sergeant Grant's words. *One way in, one way out...not good,* he thought, *gotta keep this low-key.*

The bar was almost empty: just a bartender, a topless dancer dancing to some too loud Grindcore Techno Stripper music, and one portly Quargg. The Quargg was dressed in a flight suit and bright gold-colored sash and was swaying to the music. A hefty silver-plated stinger pistol was strapped to the side of the sash with a large medallion pinned to the front of it.

"Well, *he* sure isn't hiding his weapons and he's some kind of officer," Chase mumbled to himself. "Looks okay though. Drunk, and nobody else here."

The room was decorated to look like a dirty urban Earth bar or strip club from long ago. Tables with soft, comfy chairs of various sizes were scattered around the room. There was a bar on one side of the room and a dance pole in the center of the mini stage. Nearby was a large circular machine, with multiple energy arms attached. It appeared to be a robot charging station.

Two dancing platforms on either side of the stage mimicked go-go dancing cages of old Earth bars. On the walls, neon lights of shapely human female forms buzzed and flickered in gaudy fluorescent colors. Human females were coveted for their beauty and were considered the loveliest of the known alien species. A human woman dancing at the Angel could earn a lot of silver in a brief period of time, but few women would risk their lives this far out.

Earth strip clubs, go-go bars, and dance clubs were emulated throughout the galaxy, and dancers were hard to find. The garish décor was duplicated as closely as possible including the fluorescent and neon lighting. Earth bars were considered Earth's greatest cultural achievement and were very profitable.

Chase figured every planet or moon had at least one of these dives.

The bartender, a short, spindly alien in a top hat with round spectacles, a lime green jacket, matching lime green pants, and multiple face and ear piercings, stood behind his faux wood-covered bar. He watched Chase's every move as he made his way toward him.

Out of the corner of his eye, Chase caught a glimpse of the Quargg officer tugging on the topless red-haired dancer across the room. She was beautiful, and from what he could tell in a quick glance, had a perfect body.

He wondered how such an attractive woman could end up in a dump like this. It couldn't pay *that* much to dance here.

He shifted his attention to the bartender. The short skinny man moved toward him with a scowl, cross-waving his arms at him.

"No. No. No. You are not welcome here," he said in whiny, nasal English. "No. Just keep moving. We don't want your kind here."

"You don't want customers?" asked Chase, looking around at the empty room. "Looks like you could use a few."

"You're some kind of police; I can tell by looking at you."

"Not police. A soldier—a Piecer."

"Piecer, huh...didn't you hear? You were disbanded."

"Bad news travels fast, doesn't it? Look, I don't want any trouble, friend—just looking for fuel."

The bartender looked at him through his round spectacles with tiny red alien eyes, sizing him up from his hat to his space boots.

"Fuel is hard to come by this far out," he said. "It is not inexpensive."

"I'm willing to pay."

The bartender smiled and leaned forward on the bar. "I'm listening."

"I have 1000 chits. That should pay for any fuel you have."

The bartender grabbed the paper chits and examined them closely.

"These Piecer chits are worthless now," he said, throwing them in the air. "Are you trying to fool Shoom?"

Reaching into his coat pocket, Chase said, "How about this?" Chase poured out a pile of silver coins on the bar.

"You—you have *silver*?" asked the bartender, his mouth hanging open.

"It's pure, 99.9%," replied Chase, stacking it into little piles on the bar while watching the bartender's eyes grow wider.

"It will cost you all you have," he said excitedly.

"You don't know how much I have."

"Everything you showed me...all of it, and the sack, everything."

Chase collected the silver, placing it back into the small pouch. The bartender stared at the silver sack, wondering if he had any more. Finally, he turned back to Chase.

"What'll you have?" he asked with a big forced smile. "On the house for anyone who pays in silver."

"Earth whiskey, if you have it."

The bartender nodded and poured a shot glass full. "You're a long way from home, Piecer soldier...where are you headed?"

"Yep, I am, and none of your business," said Chase, throwing the shot back in one gulp. "Where's the fueling station?"

"Behind the building; the pumps are on. You can fuel when you leave. You are leaving, yes?"

"I'll need some trillium too, for my reactor."

The bartender laughed. "We don't have trillium out here, Piecer. You're lucky we have any fuel at all."

In the corner, the shouting escalated between the alien and the dancer.

"I can't go with you now," she said, trying to pull away from the alien. "I must regenerate."

The Quargg laughed as he continued to pull on her arm, spilling a large green jug of Bloddo on the floor.

"Ah, you are playing hard to get with Admiral Malton. You are a coy female. I have heard of this. I like it. You come now," he shouted, "or I will rip your pretty little arm from your body!"

Chase turned toward the Quargg and mumbled under his breath, "No matter where you go in the universe, there's always one more asshole."

The bartender noticed Chase watching the scuffle.

"You like my dancer, Piecer? She is exquisite, yes? You can purchase her services, if you have more silver. She is Courtesan—very special. It is said that an android never tires," he said raising one of his pierced eyebrows up and down.

"Oh? She's a robot? So that's how you got her to work here. I don't have sex with robots," Chase said.

"A Courtesan is more than a robot; she is an android, part robot, yes, but part Soren. The Soren were known for their enchanting beauty and—" He paused for effect, "their *erotic* abilities—"

"Yeah...until the Klix killed 'em all," Chase interrupted. "Their erotic abilities didn't help much then."

"Well, yes, unfortunate that, but that is why this one is very prized now—very special, and hard to come by. You wish to buy her time? I'll give you a good price."

"No," replied Chase, "but I'll take another whiskey."

As the bartender poured the shot, he shifted his gaze to

the dancer then back to Chase. "They were said to drive men mad with their beauty and their sexual expertise. No man could resist them. Some were driven insane after only one night."

The bartender watched Chase's blank expression for any change.

"Many have fought and died over this one already," he added. "You won't find this entertainment at any other station."

"Like I said, I don't have sex with robots," said Chase, looking back toward the dancer. "And I'm crazy enough already."

"Not robot...an *android*, and I will give you a bargain: one night with her for one more bag of silver. You won't get that deal anywhere in the galaxy. I must be crazy to offer it to you, but I like you, and you look like a man who could use a night of passion."

"No thanks."

"Half a bag of silver then; my final offer," said the bartender, growing irritated.

"Look, what's your name again?"

"Shoom. My name is Shoom," he said tipping his tiny hat, exposing his dark beige bald head. I am the proprietor of this establishment."

"Look, Shoom, I don't know how to explain it any clearer...I don't have sex with machines, robots, aliens, or androids. That okay with you?"

The bartender's eyes narrowed, and he clenched his fists on the bar. His face turned bright red with anger, his eyes almost closing.

"Stupid Piecer, I am giving you the deal of a lifetime," he screamed, spitting slightly. "A night with a Courtesan is like no other. Only a fool would refuse me!"

Chase pulled his hands off the bar and wiped the bartender's spittle off his sleeve. Then he pulled back his coat, exposing his holstered pistols. The bartender saw the gleaming handguns and relaxed his face into a smile, forcing himself to calm down.

"Very well, my friend…your loss," said Shoom, sliding the silver sack closer to his side of the bar. "And we don't allow weapons in here."

"I can see that," said Chase, looking at the Quargg's stinger.

The bartender grimaced but did nothing. Chase could hear the dancer pleading louder from the other side of the room.

"I will do whatever you like, but my power is low," she said. "If I do not regenerate, I will cease to function. My programming will not allow that."

"I do not care if you cease to function," said the Quargg, spilling more of his drink as he pulled. "I want your service *now*."

Chase could see she was being pulled farther away from her charging station and was hanging on by one of the station's extended energy arms.

"Hey! Chubs McTubs," Chase shouted to the alien, "let her recharge, you horny bitch."

The alien turned his head to Chase at the bar. "This is not your concern, human. Go fuck yourself."

"Oh good, you understand English."

"Quargg understand all primitive languages."

"Then understand this: let…her…go."

Chase pulled his gun in a blur and pointed it at him. The Quargg ignored him.

"I said let her go," he repeated, pulling the hammer back with a loud click. "The next thing you hear will be a funeral hymn. You can wait."

The alien heard the click and released her wrist. The Courtesan immediately climbed back into the regenerator. The machine hummed, and the dials indicated the Courtesan was recharging.

"Do not interfere with my business," screamed Shoom, pounding on the bar. "Sheen is my Courtesan, and she will do what I say—not what *you* say."

The bartender turned toward the dancer and barked out an order. "Sheen, service the customer."

The Courtesan dutifully climbed out of the regenerator, now showing twenty percent charged.

"Yes, Commander," she replied, moving toward the Quargg.

"Let's see if we can't use up the rest of your energy," said the alien, grasping the Courtesan by her ear, and pulling her head closer to him. "Service me," he hissed, "or I will take you apart."

"My function is to service you," she replied, looking at him, confused.

Sheen began to kiss him on the lips and neck. The alien appeared pleased and then backhanded her across the face. She stumbled backward, caught off guard.

"I do not understand," she said. "I am servicing you."

Sheen looked past Chase at Shoom.

"Do what he says," the bartender yelled. "Service him."

"Yes, Commander."

Sheen moved closer to the alien, her arms ready to block another hit.

"Put your arms down," said the Quargg. "I will not harm you."

Sheen lowered her arms and moved closer to the alien. The Quargg spread his arms wide, welcoming her with a big, pointed, toothy smile. As she got close, he hit her again—hard—and she reeled back falling to the ground.

"Oh, this is wonderful," he yelled to the bartender. "She is worth what I paid you, Shoom."

He turned back to the dancer. "Have you never been with a Quargg, Courtesan?"

"I have not," she replied.

"This is foreplay to Quargg. Come now; service me. This is pleasurable."

Sheen stood again and looked to the bartender for instruction.

"Sheen, service the customer," he shouted once more.

"No more games."

Sheen moved forward, and the alien backhanded her to the ground yet again. Shaken, Sheen got up slowly, appearing pained and confused.

"Sheen," the bartender shouted. "Service him...now!"

"Okay, that's enough," Chase yelled across the room. "Get your jollies somewhere else, you twisted piece of shit."

"Stay out of this, human," the Quargg alien shouted. "This is *my* Courtesan. I paid for her time."

Chase raised his gun. "Your time's up, fuckhead."

The bartender ducked below the bar. A moment later, he popped up with a laser pistol pointed at Chase and fired. Piecer training kicked in, and Chase instinctively ducked, the shot flying just above his head. He reeled around and fired at the bartender, hitting him in the chest. The Quargg heard the shots, drew his weapon, fired at Chase, and missed. Chase pulled his other pistol and fired, hitting the Quargg in the side of the chest. Admiral Malton fell to the ground.

"Why?" Malton asked, his breath shallow. "It is a machine. It has no feelings."

The admiral pressed a lit button on his wristplate, and the button flashed red.

"You are dead now, human. My crew will kill you for this...and for what...a robot whore?"

The Quargg's head fell to the side; his large black almond eyes stared vacantly across the floor stained green with his blood. The Courtesan ran to the bartender lying face up behind the bar.

"Commander," she said, shaking him, trying to wake him. "Commander, what are your orders? I will service the Quargg. What are your orders?"

The bartender, shot dead center in the chest, lay in a pool of his own blood. Sheen passed her hand over him, her eyes looking up as if reading, scanning his body. Sheen immediately turned to Chase.

"My Commander is dead. I have no command."

"I'm sorry," Chase said, "he tried to kill me."

"I am Sheen. I am Courtesan. You killed my Commander. You are my Commander now."

"Oh no," he said, shaking his head. "I'm just Chase. Chase 523, a soldier. I was just defending myself. You'll have to find yourself another Commander."

"I do not understand," said Sheen. "You killed Shoom. You are my Commander."

Sheen turned her head and looked toward the door of the airlock. Staring, she raised her arm. "My heat sensors indicate six armed figures coming this way."

"Run and hide," said Chase. "Get behind something."

"Are you my Commander?"

"No; I'm not."

"Are they my Commander?"

"Not unless you want to die. Hide, goddammit."

"I am Courtesan; I need a Commander."

"Look, I'm not your Commander. Do you have any way to defend yourself?"

Sheen looked straight ahead, scanning her memory. "I have subroutines for complete offensive and defensive capabilities upon command."

"Okay, then, choose one, and defend yourself."

"Yes, Commander," she replied, turning toward the door. "They are here."

A loud burst of pressurized air announced the entry of six armed Quargg as the huge metal door swung open. Sheen grabbed the dead bartender's laser pistol lying on the floor.

"Acquiring targets," she said calmly. "Six active targets—locked on—awaiting your command."

Chase jumped behind the bar, landing next to the dead bartender and Sheen. Seeing him jump, the Quargg opened fire, stinger charges hitting the bar and the bottles behind the bar raining broken glass everywhere.

"Get down!" Chase screamed, pulling Sheen down by her arm.

Sheen squatted down, gun raised, seemingly unfazed.

"Well shoot them, for God's sake," Chase screamed. "*De-*

fend yourself."

"Yes, Commander."

Sheen popped up from behind the bar, pulling the trigger on the laser pistol as fast as she could. Five of the Quargg fell backwards, shot in their heads with a single laser blast each. Sheen pulled the trigger repeatedly, aiming at the sixth Quargg, but nothing happened. The Quargg turned to aim his pistol at her while she continued to pull the trigger on the non-firing weapon.

Chase pulled her down behind the bar as the laser shots passed over her head. Two perfectly round laser holes drilled through the bar, one behind and one in front of Sheen. Light passed through the holes, lighting up the back of the bar and illuminating the sparkling glass dust floating in the air. Sheen turned to Chase, holding up the gun to show him.

"Commander, it appears this weapon is malfunctioning."

"Stay down!" Chase screamed.

"Yes, Commander."

Chase jumped up from behind the bar firing both pistols, and the last remaining Quargg fell backward onto a bar table, dead.

"Thank you, Commander."

"You're welcome, and thank you."

Sheen was caught by surprise.

This was a most unusual Commander. No one had ever thanked Sheen for anything. She wondered if he was defective.

"The threat has been eliminated, Commander," Sheen said.

"Yes...I think we're okay for a while."

Sheen stood up once more and placed the laser pistol gently down on the bar as if she was putting down a drink.

"I do not like this weapon," she said. "It is flawed."

She looked back at him, and the corners of her perfect pink-red lips rose slightly.

"Did you just smile?" asked Chase.

"My programming allows for all natural human expression."

"You just killed five Quargg, and you chose to smile?"

"Yes, Commander, the threat was eliminated. I noticed you smile when the last Quargg fell dead. Is that not the appropriate response?"

"Yeah, well, I'm not complaining." said Chase. "Remind me to never get on your bad side."

"I have no bad sides," she replied. "I am perfectly symmetrical. But I will remind you per your command."

Chase smiled at her remark. "You need to go somewhere, Sheen. That's your name, right?"

Chase stared at her eyes and looked past her, trying not to look at her exposed breasts. He couldn't help notice how beautiful she was with her red hair, red lips, tiny waist, and long legs. Her skin-tight pants looked as if they were painted on and left none of her perfect curves to his imagination.

"Yes, Commander. I am Sheen, I am Courtesan."

"More Quargg will come," he said. "This place isn't safe for you. Don't you have a home or somewhere to live or something?"

"I live with my Commander. It is my function."

"I thought your function was Courtesan?"

"I am a Courtesan. I must be commanded. I have one Commander. You are my Commander. Do you wish me to service you, Commander?"

"What? No."

"As you command."

"And how does one become a Courtesan, anyway?" Chase asked.

Sheen looked straight ahead, scanning her memory. "I do not know," she replied, cocking her head slightly. "How does one become a Piecer soldier?"

Chase started to explain and then sighed. "Fine; maybe we can find you a new commander. Let's get your regen station and refuel. We need to get out of here."

Chapter Eight

Gassing Up

Sheen walked over to her charging station, broke it down, then packed and folded it into one enormous metal trunk.

"I must regenerate soon," she said. "I am at fifteen percent."

"Once we get into space, you can do whatever you like."

"Yes, Commander," she replied.

Chase rolled his eyes, gathered his silver off the bar, and poured himself a last drink.

"Sorry it had to be this way," he said to the dead bartender, holding up a shot glass to salute him. "Never underestimate your opponent."

Chase swallowed the whiskey and cinched the sack of coins shut, putting it back in his coat pocket.

"You're gonna need a helmet out there," said Chase, "some clothes and a space suit, Sheen. It's frigging cold outside. You're going to freeze out there."

Sheen grabbed her top and slipped it over her head, pulling it down around her waist. She flipped the heavy regen trunk up onto her shoulder like it was a feather.

"Yes, Commander, but Sheen does not need a breather as Sheen does not breathe. And my parameters allow my body to function in -360 degrees Celsius. The cold will not affect me."

"You don't breathe, and you don't get cold?"

"No, Commander."

"But your chest moves in and out, and you wear clothing."

"That is merely for presentation, and for my dance performance."

"Oh. Presentation, huh, and you don't get cold. Anything else I should know about?"

Sheen cocked her head and replied, "I must regenerate to live, and I am expert at all forms of sexual and erotic expression."

"No breathing, regeneration, and all forms...gotcha."

"Yes, Commander."

Chase exhaled slowly. "Well, I gotta breathe, and I kinda want to keep doing it, so let's get goin'."

"Yes, Commander."

"You ready?"

"Wait...please, Commander," said Sheen. "I must retrieve my flower."

"Your what?"

"My flower."

"Leave it."

"I cannot. I must have it with me."

Sheen grabbed the small plant in the corner near the stage and placed it into a clear egg-shaped protective enclosure.

"It is a Luminfleur. It is luminescent; it glows purple."

"I can see that...and you need this why?"

Sheen looked forward, scanning her memory. "I do not know; that part of my memory is unclear."

"Where'd you get it?"

"I have always had it—as far back as my memory goes. I am programmed to keep it with me."

"Programmed to keep it for what?"

Sheen paused, scanning her memory for what seemed like a long time.

"Whatever; never mind," Chase shouted, grabbing his breather on the way out of the bar. "C'mon, let's go. We have to refuel and get out of here."

"By your command," she replied.

Chase donned his breather as the pressurized door closed behind them. They walked down the long, bright corridor, exiting the airlock near where the *Promise* had landed.

"You have your own ship, Commander? It is impressive."

"Umm...yes. Thank you. It's a Piecer ship, the starship *Promise*."

"You are a Captain, then?"

"Well, no, just a grunt."

"You are a guh-runt? I am not familiar with this term."

"No, it's just 'grunt,' just a soldier, but a Piecer soldier."

"I have not met a soldier with his own ship. You are a most unusual soldier."

"Nothin' special," he replied. "We need to hurry."

"Yes, Commander."

Chase lowered the cargo ramp, and Sheen ran up to the *Promise* with her regeneration station on one shoulder and her Luminfleur tucked close to her chest. Chase caught up with her and led her through the ship to the crew's quarters, finally stopping in front of a steel cabin door.

"This will be your quarters, Sheen—cabin two. I'm right next to you in cabin one, if you need anything."

"I will have my own cabin?" Sheen asked, surprised.

"Yes; don't you always?"

"No," she replied, "I have not had a room, only my regeneration station."

Chase couldn't help but wonder how she had lived under previous commanders.

"Well, for as long as we are together, you will be part of the crew...with a cabin of your own."

"Thank you, Commander."

"Um, you're welcome; go ahead and regenerate while I fuel up."

"Yes, Commander."

Sheen removed her Luminfluer from its protective capsule and placed it carefully on the small table in her quarters. The plant began to glow and put out a soft lavender light surrounding it and its base. She then went back to the cabin doorway and watched Chase walk down the corridor, until he disappeared.

This is a most unusual Commander, she thought.

She unpacked her regeneration station and climbed in. The machine came to life with a low hum and a soft purple glow in its circular arch. Regeneration had begun.

Chase made his way to the helm and plopped down in the pilot's seat. He pulled the worn photographs of his family from his pocket. Staring at them for a long time, he took a deep breath to focus his thoughts.

I must complete my mission, he thought, *and then find my family.*

Chase punched the thrust buttons and maneuvered the ship to the rear of the Blue Angel while Sheen regenerated. He set down gently behind the bar, near the pumping station.

He donned his breather and exited the *Promise*, hoping there would be enough fuel in the tanks to fill up. There weren't many other stations this far out.

I'd better hurry, he thought, pressing the fuel button on the station's tanks.

A sign posted on the pump station depicted an oxygen tank with fumes escaping, a laser pistol with a slash and a small explosion with flames.

A long arm with a camera scanned the ship, searching for the fuel port. It then retracted with a jerk, and another pipe-like arm extended itself into the fuel port. The pump vibrated as liters of the liquid fuel were transferred to the ship.

"C'mon, c'mon...we haven't got all day," Chase said inside his breather.

Suddenly, someone was coming up behind him. He whirled around, pulling his pistol in one motion.

"Oh, sorry—it's you," he said, replacing his gun in his holster.

Sheen stood in front of him wearing a breather unit.

"I thought you didn't need a breather."

"I do not. I am using the breather's built-in com to communicate with you."

"Oh...right. Sorry."

"My sensors indicate more Quargg are approaching the front entrance. What is your command?"

"My orders are to get outta here before we're toast."

Sheen cocked her head, not entirely understanding Chase's reference to baked Earth bread.

"Okay, that's it...we gotta fly."

"Commander, you have yet to disengage the fuel nozzle."

"Get on board, now!"

"Yes, Commander."

Sheen leapt from the ground onto the top of the boarding ladder in the center of the ship. Chase looked up in disbelief.

"That was quick," he shouted up to her from the ground.

Sheen looked at him, confused.

"You said 'now,'" she replied.

"Never mind; let's go."

Chase climbed the fore ladder, then took his position at the helm and raised all the ladders and ramps. The ship rumbled as he pushed the ignition sequence buttons, and then stopped. He pushed the throttle forward, giving the engines more fuel before trying again. Sheen removed her breather helmet and arrived just in time to hear him.

"C'mon, baby! Start, damn you."

The ship rumbled again, but the engines did not fire.

"Shit, what's wrong now?" he shouted.

Sheen stared straight ahead, her arm extended, scanning the ship.

"Commander Chase, I believe excessive amounts of fuel have collected in the intake combustion chambers of the ship's engines."

"You sayin' I flooded it?"

Sheen paused reexamining her data. "Yes, Commander

Chase," she replied, interpreting Earth slang. "You have flooded it. Please wait a moment to try again. The fuel must evaporate before—"

"We don't have a moment!" he barked, cutting her off. He nodded his head toward a squad of armed Quargg exiting the building and pointing at the ship.

"They're coming. It's now or never, Sheen."

"What is your command?"

"Cross your fingers, honey," said Chase.

"As you command," she replied, crossing her fingers. "Do you wish me to service you now?"

"What?"

"You referred to me as 'honey.' Usually my services are required after that term of endearment."

"No...your services are not required," Chase said in an irritated tone.

"I do not see the purpose of this." She held up both hands with fingers crossed.

"Sheen, I don't have time for this. If we don't get out of here, we're going to be blown apart."

The Quargg opened fire, their laser bolts hitting the *Promise*'s tritanium plating and bouncing off.

"They haven't hit anything important yet," he said, gently stroking the console.

"C'mon, baby," Chase whispered, "just this one time and I'll make sure your tanks are always full."

"You should not make promises that you cannot keep, Commander Chase. Machines do not forget."

"I'll keep that in mind, Sheen."

Chase punched the start button again. The engines fired, and he pushed the throttle forward slowly.

"Sheen, do you know how to operate a gun on a ship?"

Sheen held up her arm and scanned the ship's controls once more.

"It appears to be rudimentary, Commander Chase. I have examined all the ship's controls, systems, and design parameters."

"You got all that with one scan?"

"Two scans, Commander Chase."

As the *Promise* pulled away, the fuel pipe broke, spraying fuel and frosting the ground around the rear of the bar.

"Commander, we have not disengaged with the fuel insertion mechanism, and it continues to spray fuel."

"Good; can you target the spill with the secondary guns using incendiaries?"

The *Promise* rose above the back of the bar area, ascending into the sky.

"Yes, Commander Chase...switching to incendiary projectiles. Do you wish me to continue crossing my fingers?"

"No, just target that spill while I take us out."

"Yes, Commander Chase."

"And stop calling me Commander Chase."

"Yes, Commander."

Sheen entered the coordinates and fired. The fuel exploded in an inferno, sending the Quargg flying and destroying the bar and the surrounding area.

"Nice shot!"

"Thank you, Commander. Awaiting further command."

The ship spun around and leapt to the sky, reaching space in seconds.

"Good girl," Chase said, patting the console. "I won't forget this."

"Is this ship Courtesan?" asked Sheen.

"No, just a ship...but a ship that saved our lives."

"Does this ship service you, Commander?"

"No!" he shouted with obvious irritation in his voice.

He took a breath and then exhaled slowly.

"Please, go finish your regeneration, Sheen."

"Yes, Commander."

"And Sheen, thank you...for back there."

"You are welcome, Commander. I will complete regeneration as you command."

Sheen made her way back to her cabin, evaluating what had taken place in the short time she had met her new Commander. She climbed into her regeneration station and closed down her systems to charge. As she closed her eyes, she wondered what type of Commander this was and if his bizarre behavior would continue. The charging station lit up her cabin, and a whirring sound drifted throughout the corridors of the ship.

In the cockpit, Chase tapped the fuel panel gauge, hoping it was stuck.

"Damn it, we needed more time. A half tank isn't going to get us very far, not with the worm drive offline. We've got to find another depot."

In Sheen's cabin, the intermittent lights flashed faster and faster until finally, at one hundred percent, the lights were continuous. A tiny bleep from the charging computer, and the process was completed. Sheen was fully charged. As her systems came online, her thermo-sensors detected an anomaly in the cargo bay. Someone or something was on board their ship. Sheen clicked the ship's intercom button.

"Commander, I have detected a heat signature in the cargo bay. It may be a malfunction of my sensors, but I have just regenerated and my systems check was normal."

"Check it out and let me know what you find," replied Chase. "And Sheen..."

"Yes, Commander?"

"Be careful."

Sheen smiled.

Chapter Nine

The Anomaly

Sheen headed down the metal ladder leading to the galley, adjacent to the cargo bay. As she entered, she stared at the cargo bay hatch, rescanning the bay with her thermal sensors. Through the door, she could see a blurred humanoid outline floating above the cargo bay floor approximately fifteen feet off the ground. It appeared to be seated with its arms extended.

Unusual, she thought, *I know of no humanoid that hovers.*

Suddenly, the cargo bay hatch slid open. Sheen shaded her eyes from five bright light beams, two on each side and one in the center, coming from an enormous robot-like machine—a mechanized terrain walker that dwarfed the doorway hatch. The main body was an egg-shaped, glasslike cabin. Two enormous metal legs with large four-pronged feet supported the pilot enclosure. The machine filled the cargo bay from top to bottom in the back and stood close to the back exit door. It was suddenly activated with a human at the controls.

For a moment, nothing happened, but as Sheen moved, she realized she was being tracked by twin guns mounted on the sides of the walker. She reached over to the intercom button and clicked it once more.

"Commander, I think you should come down here to see this...come armed."

Chase slapped on his gun belt and ran down the corridor. He slid down the ladder to the galley—using his feet against the rails to slow his descent—and taking the ladder in one step. He stared at the open hatch, eyeing the walker inside.

"What the hell is that and how did it get on my ship?"

"It appears to be a terrain walker, Commander. It is armed with twin laser cannons and a T3 missile launcher. The weapons are trained on us and operational. The pilot operator appears to be humanoid. I do not know how it got on the ship or when. I recommend retreat, Commander."

"Retreat?" said Chase. "I'm not retreating from some stupid-ass walker. Besides, this is my ship...well, I borrowed it, so technically it's mine now."

"You are no match for its weaponry, Commander. It can destroy you easily, even through your body armor."

"Maybe it won't come to that. Let's see what he wants... before we start killing each other."

"Yes, Commander."

"Hey up there, in the walker," screamed Chase, moving forward toward the cargo bay hatch door. He leaned up against the open door, trying to look casual, trying not to alarm the intruder. "I'm Chase. I'm a Piecer soldier. You may have heard of us."

There was a long awkward silence.

"We don't *have* to kill each other, ya know!" Chase shouted.

Chase leaned over and whispered into Sheen's ear. "If this gets ugly, open the cargo bay door and flush that thing into space. Stand away from me, so we're not one big target, and hold on to something."

Sheen nodded and moved back and away. The walker's guns followed her, then switched to Chase who was closer, then back to Sheen, and then back to Chase.

"Look, stranger, you're aboard my ship and you're pointing weapons at me. Any reason I shouldn't kill you where you sit?"

The walker's guns stayed fixed on Chase; a slight tremble

transferred from the controls to the gun barrels. There was no response from the pilot inside. The pilot had long hair and a long beard, a moustache, and thick sideburns. He appeared nervous, wiping sweat with his sleeve from the small strip of hairless brow.

"Do you know what happens when you shoot a missile or laser cannon inside a ship in outer space?" Chase shouted. "It goes boom," he replied to his own question, exploding his hands apart, gesturing with fluttering fingers. "You'll be space glitter in about two seconds. We'll all be space glitter."

The human wiped his sweaty face again—onto his gray flight suit. He shifted his guns back to Sheen, then back to Chase, then he let go of the controls, the guns returning to their default setting pointing straight ahead. He raised his hands, showing he had no weapons.

"How about you come down from there and we talk for a minute," said Chase. "We won't hurt—"

His sentence was interrupted by a violent explosion rocking the ship, almost tipping the walker over and knocking the human inside against the walker's capsuled enclosure. Chase was thrown out of the hatch doorway and against the bulkhead. Sheen was knocked backwards, landing on the floor.

"We are under attack, Commander."

"I noticed. Are you hurt?"

"I am fully functional, Commander."

"*Alert! Quargg Raider Class ship approaching,*" came the voice from the *Promise* computer.

"*Now* she tells us," grumbled Chase.

Sheen scanned through the ship with her heat sensors.

"There is a ship off our port side with a complement of five crew members, two figures on the bridge. I assume that one is the captain."

She staggered to a port window as the ship was hit again by another blast.

"We're not going to be able to take a beating like this much longer," said Chase. "Who the hell is that?"

"It appears to be the Quargg flagship from Titan—where

you found me."

"Get 'em on the com. See if they'll talk."

"Yes, Commander," said Sheen, hailing the other vessel. "Commander, they have responded."

"This is Elam Timit, First Officer of the Quargg vessel *Malton*."

Quargg ships were usually named after their captains, but as this was Admiral Malton's flagship, it had been named in his honor.

"Surrender now or we will destroy you and your ship," said Timit.

"Ask them why they fired on us," whispered Chase.

Sheen pressed the talk button on the open com channel to the Quargg vessel.

"Elam Timit, why are you firing on us?" asked Sheen.

"You killed Admiral Malton and a dozen of our crewmates. You will be taken to Quool to be tried and executed for your crimes."

Sheen released the talk button so they would not be overheard.

Chase signaled to Sheen, pointing in the direction of the helm and the weapons array. "I'll keep them talking. Do you remember your defensive mode on the planet?"

"Yes, Commander; I am incapable of forgetting anything."

"Do you think you can hit them?"

"Yes, Commander…if I can target it, I can hit it," replied Sheen.

"There is no need for discussion, *Piecer* vessel," said Timit, interrupting. "Surrender now or we will destroy you."

Chase hit the talk button on the com. "Well, before you do…there's something you should know."

"And what is that?" asked Timit.

"I was the one who shot your comrades and your admiral, but only after they shot at me first. It was self-defense. Nobody else on this ship had anything to do with it."

Sheen cocked her head, remembering she had shot five of

the six Quargg crew, not understanding Chase's lie.

Chase released the talk button.

"Sheen," Chase whispered. "Prepare to execute your defensive capabilities."

Chase flipped the fire controls from his pilot's station back to the battle station.

"Yes, Commander," she replied, scaling the ladder to take her position.

"You can put forth your defense at your trial," Timit said, laughing. "Right before they execute you and your crew."

There was a brief silence before Chase pressed the talk button once more. "There is one more thing you should know. This ship has a trillium-based fusion powered worm drive. Best-case scenario, you explode this ship, and everything within eighty kilometers will be turned to dust, including you. Worst-case scenario? You create a black hole and get sucked into oblivion!"

There was a slight pause, and then the Quargg ship responded. "Our sensors do not indicate any active nuclear power on your ship," replied Timit.

"Then you need new sensors," replied Chase. "What do you think the WD stands for on the ship?"

There was a long silence and Chase released the ship-to-ship talk button.

"I am ready, Commander," said Sheen over the ship's intercom.

Another blast hit the ship, knocking Chase off his feet.

"Sheen," he screamed to the intercom. "Defend yourself."

Sheen activated the ship's pulse lasers, targeting the Quargg vessel's guns. The lasers were on target but blocked by an invisible barrier in front of each of the Quargg's weapons. The Quargg's defensive shields held, and there was no damage.

"Sheen, target their shields. Look for small, blue-blinking lights below their turrets and target them. Those are their shield generators."

"By your command," said Sheen.

The *Promise* was hit again by another blast.

"Commander, the pulse lasers are damaged and offline."

"Then we're sitting ducks," said Chase. "The secondary guns won't even scratch them. When they board, defend yourself. Quargg always torture their victims to get a confession before they kill them, guilty or not. Don't let them take you alive."

"Yes, Commander. Commander, if you have a chance to get away, you must take it. Do not wait for me."

"We don't leave people behind, Sheen."

"You must. You are my Commander," she said, her voice growing more insistent.

"I'll be fine. Don't worry. And Sheen, if anything happens to me...if the shit hits the fan, take my guns and defend yourself."

"No, you must promise me. Do not wait for me," she repeated louder and more frantically. "Save yourself."

"Don't have time for this now, Sheen."

"Promise me," she insisted.

"Okay, okay; I promise...whatever. We have bigger problems right now."

Suddenly, another voice was heard over the ship's internal intercom.

"Captain, this is Max, the guy in the walker. I have an idea, but you're going to have to trust me."

The ship was rocked again, and a loud creaking could be heard rumbling through the passageways. It was as if the ship was crying out in pain. The *Promise* began to spin slowly—horizontally in circles—its stabilizing gyroscope damaged by the concussion.

"Looks like I have no choice," said Chase. "Anything is better than this. What do you want me to do?"

"Close the hatch to the cargo bay. When it latches closed, wait for my signal and then open the outside cargo door."

"You'll fly out into space."

"That's what I'm hopin' for," he replied, faking laughter to gather his nerve. "I don't want to be space glitter."

Chase grinned, hearing his own words echoed back to him.

He's got balls anyway, I'll give him that, Chase thought. He didn't know what Max was up to, but he wouldn't last long in that walker in space.

"Good luck," Chase said, closing the hatch.

"Thanks," he replied. "Be seein' ya."

Inside the cargo bay, Max grabbed the walker's leg controls, pushing forward with the right leg and back with the left leg, turning the walker in a perfect semi-circle now facing the outside cargo bay door. Then he powered down the walker completely and watched out a cargo bay port window as the Quargg vessel appeared in view.

As the *Promise* spun toward it, Max shouted, "Now!"

Chase slammed the external door release on the cargo bay hatch. The sudden loss of pressure sucked all the contents and the walker into space. Everything inside the cargo bay went tumbling into space—empty fuel barrels, cargo nets, fire extinguishers, and the walker—anything that wasn't tied down was now floating outside the cargo bay. He slammed the door release to close it again, and the now-empty bay pressurized once more.

Inside the walker, Max waited for the optimal moment, drifting, slowly rotating, pretending to be cargo bay debris. He waited, afraid to power up, afraid to tip off the Quargg that he was more than just space junk.

"Your ship is breaking up, Piecer," said Timit over the com. "Too bad. You had your chance."

Max drifted directly behind the Quargg ship's exhaust stream, powered up, and fired a T3 heat-seeking missile into the tail of the Quargg ship. The missile followed the exhaust gases directly through the shields and into the Quargg engine. The Quargg vessel shuddered and then exploded, sending shards of metal everywhere. The *Promise* shook from the blast, and they could hear tiny metal fragments hitting the hull like metallic rain.

Sheen slid back down the ladder to the galley. "What are

your orders, Commander?"

"We need to get the hell out of here before they send more ships. But first, we need to find that walker. That guy saved our ass."

Chase looked out the galley window, hoping to spot the walker among the debris. To his surprise, the walker was clinging to the *Promise* with its foot. Max stared back through the window, smiling and waving. His voice clicked in over the com. "Space glitter, over."

"Get back in here," Chase said over the com.

If I hadn't seen it, I'd never believe it, thought Chase.

"Sheen, open the cargo bay door."

"Yes, Commander."

The door opened, and the walker edged its way along the ship and into the now-empty cargo bay. Chase hit the door release once more, closing the door and pressurizing the bay. Shutting down the walker, Max stepped outside. Chase opened the hatch, stepped in, and quickly pulled his gun. Max brushed the hair out of his face and put his hands in the air, showing he had no weapons. Standing there with his hands up, his face covered in hair, and a dirty, generic space-suit, he looked like the homeless humans of Earth who lived in the remaining rubble of bombed-out cities.

"That's far enough," Chase said. "I don't know whether to shoot you or hug you."

"I can explain," said Max. "Just don't shoot me...or hug me."

"Look," said Chase. "I appreciate what you did to that Quargg vessel, but that doesn't explain what you're doing on my ship."

Seeing he was unarmed, Chase put his gun back in his holster.

"I'm a Mech-Tech specialist IV, a Fixer. Like you, I was genetically engineered—Max 325. Unlike you, I was made for fixing things...not shooting things."

"I've heard of you guys," said Chase. "Weren't you originally Sixer support and then later Piecer support engineers?"

"Yep, an unstoppable force; the Sixers and the Fixers, we kept you guys going. Never worked with the Sixers though... was before my time."

"It doesn't explain why you're hiding on my ship."

"You were my only chance," said Max. "I was a prisoner on Titan, forced to work for that scumbag Shoom. Fixers were disbanded before they disbanded the Piecers. The government didn't want to fund us anymore. We got our walking papers, no ceremony, just hey, there's the door! I left Earth looking for a new home where I wouldn't be seen as a DNA freak or a number."

"Why not go home?"

"What home? Fixers didn't have foster parents. We were brought up in a dormitory with school every day until they sent us out to wherever we were needed. We weren't heroes like you guys. Nobody cares about support people unless they need something."

"Sounds like the government to me," said Chase. "Sorry, I didn't know."

"When I landed to fuel, they forced me to fix their station's environmental systems. They saw what I could do, and they destroyed my ship, stranding me and forcing me to work for them. I needed a ride outta there."

"Where'd you get the walker?"

"It was Shoom's. He collected them—called them his personal mech army. Made me fix whatever was wrong with them. When I saw your ship land, I stole this one and hid in the cargo bay. I figured it would give me a fighting chance if they came after me. I didn't know you were a Piecer, until you hit the com button...or if you'd just shoot me anyway."

"Okay, you earned passage on my ship. That's for sure. I'll drop you off anywhere along our way, but no side trips. Mission comes first."

"Fair enough," replied Max, blowing his hair out of his face.

"Oh, and Max, if you ever point a gun at me again, tell me how where you want me to send your remains."

"Yeah, sorry, won't happen again, and I can help you. I can fix anything you need on this ship to earn my keep."

"Know anything about worm drives?"

"I was weaned on the worm drive," said Max. "I recognized the *Promise* when I saw her. The first worm drive starship ever built. I heard of her. She's beautiful."

"That she is. Welcome aboard, Max," Chase said, extending his hand to shake.

"Thanks, Captain Chase."

"Just Chase is fine...and this is Sheen."

Sheen moved closer, examining Max.

"Sheen, this is Max 325. Max, Sheen."

"He appears to be harmless," she said. "But my sensors indicate he is in need of a cleaning."

Max turned red, brushed his hair out of his face, crossed his arms, and looked away.

"I...there weren't any showers...they kept me in a cage most of the time."

"You can have cabin three, next to Sheen. You'll find everything you need there, scissors, if you need them, and a shaving kit too, if you like."

"Thanks; no barbers on Titan, this hair is getting ridiculous. I can hardly see," he said, blowing his hair out of his face again and grabbing his long beard. "I suppose I could use a shave."

Chase smiled. "If you need anything else, let me know."

Max gazed at Sheen from top to bottom and back again. "Her sensors?" he asked. "Is she the Courtesan they had working in the bar?"

"I am Sheen," she replied. "I am Courtesan."

"You...you have the Courtesan?" Max asked, slack-jawed.

"I don't *really* have her," said Chase. "It's a long story."

Sheen looked at Chase confused. "He is my Commander," she said. "I am Courtesan."

"I never saw her up close," said Max. "They wouldn't let me. She's beautiful, perfect. I envy you."

"Yeah, well, don't. I'm just helping her until she decides

where she wants to go."

Sheen smiled.

"She smiles?" asked Max.

"She's standing right here," said Chase. "Ask her."

"I am fully capable of expressing all human emotive responses," Sheen said.

She then contorted her face, systematically moving from happy, to sad, to frightened, to shy, to pensive, to angry.

"She's gorgeous," said Max. "I mean, *you're* gorgeous."

"Yes, she is," replied Chase. "And very capable—took out five Quargg with five head shots. I wouldn't get on her bad side."

Sheen switched her last angry face to smiling again. "I have no bad sides; I am perfectly symmetrical."

"Perfectly symmetrical," Chase repeated.

Max took a step back, still staring at Sheen. "Have you... you know, with her?" Max whispered to Chase.

"No. I don't have sex with machines," Chase replied curtly.

"Sorry; just wondered," Max said.

Sheen winced, and Chase saw it.

"We don't have that kind of relationship, right, Sheen?"

Sheen looked straight ahead. "I am Courtesan, you are my Commander."

"I'm only her Commander because I killed her Commander."

"You killed Shoom?"

"Yeah, it was self-defense...like I said, it's a long story. Sheen has already proven herself."

Smiling again, Sheen turned back to Chase.

"She's not required to service me or anyone else for that matter," Chase said.

"I owe you one," said Max. "Shoom was the biggest a-hole in the galaxy."

Max paused, looking at Sheen from head to toe.

"Um...so not even *once*, huh?" asked Max. "I heard she's amazing. A lot of guys died trying to steal this one—I mean her—but Shoom had cameras everywhere. It didn't end well for them."

"Yeah, well, men will kill for almost anything."

"Commander Chase," Sheen interrupted. "I am also in need of maintenance. If I may be excused, I would like to return to my cabin to perform my cleansing routine."

"Go ahead. We're okay here."

Sheen shimmied up the ladder with Max and Chase staring upward as she climbed. Max swallowed hard, staring.

"Never?" Max asked. "You've got to be kidding me."

"We only just met and no, never."

Chase exhaled heavily.

"I'll show you your cabin," he said. "You can get cleaned up and get this ship running again. The gyro stabilizer was hit, and the pulse lasers are offline. We need to get out of here."

"Give me five minutes. Stabilizers are easy to fix; probably just knocked out of alignment. Pulse lasers are another story. Depends how badly they were damaged."

Chase walked Max to his cabin, passing by Sheen's open cabin door. Sheen's Luminfleur cast a purple glow in the cabin while Sheen was performing her cleansing routine, washing her legs in her shower cube. Her skin glistened through the clear shower cubicle walls as the water rained on her from above. Chase and Max stopped dead in the doorway staring, unable to speak. Sheen continued cleaning herself, unconcerned that they were watching. Finally, Chase realized they had been staring too long, turned away, and coughed. Sheen stopped, stood up, and turned toward them.

"Yes, Commander? Am I needed?" Sheen asked.

Chase cleared his throat again. "Umm, no, just showing Max to his quarters."

"Yes, you're needed," Max mumbled, too low to be heard.

Max looked at Chase and pointed to the purple glowing plant inside her cabin.

"What the hell is that?"

"She called it a Luminfleur."

"It glows?"

"Yeah...she brought it from the bar."

"Weird," said Max, "but some sea creatures glow, so why not a plant?"

"Commander," said Sheen. "Are you sure my services are not needed? My thermal sensors indicate arousal."

Chase and Max looked at each other accusingly.

"Both of you," she said casually.

Chase and Max looked away.

"Sheen," said Chase.

"Yes, Commander?"

"From now on, please make sure your cabin door is closed during your cleansing cycle."

"Yes, Commander."

"You don't have to on my account," said Max, still under his breath too low to hear.

"You just used up your five minutes drooling," said Chase. "Fix my ship, then shower...if you think you can concentrate."

"Okay, I'll try. I'll have the stabilizers up in no time."

"Just get us running so we can get out of here."

"Will do, Cap...I mean Chase."

"Then for God's sake, take a shower. It's like we're carrying a cargo of onions in here."

Sheen walked to the cabin door naked, her perfect skin dripping, shiny, and wet. She stopped momentarily, looking each of them in the eye, smiling, and then pressed the door lever to close it. The door closed slowly, and Chase and Max stood stunned for a moment.

"Get busy," said Chase. "You have five minutes to get this ship stable."

"Yes, sir, I will."

Max walked away awkwardly down the corridor.

"Stabilizers are on the upper deck," said Chase.

"I'm getting there...just need a second."

This is going to be a problem, thought Chase.

The ship's proximity alarm blared.

A computerized voice announced over the ship's com, *"Alert! Three Quargg battle cruisers approaching. Alert!"*

Chase screamed to Max, "You've got two minutes to stabilize us. We've got company."

Max turned around and scurried up the ladder to the upper deck. Sheen opened her door, fully dressed.

"Commander, there are three Quargg vessels approaching. Do you need me at the helm?"

"Yes, Sheen...I need you on the secondary guns. Pulse lasers are still out."

Max's voice came over the com. "Chase, you've got stabilizers. Kick her in gear. Heading to the pulse lasers now."

"I knew there was a reason not to shoot you. We...are... outta here."

Chase ran to the helm and punched the start engine button.

"Not too much fuel, Commander," said Sheen.

Chase cocked his head, looked at her and grinned, saying nothing. The silence, though short, seemed to make Sheen uncomfortable.

"I apologize, Commander, it is not my place to offer suggestions without being asked."

Chase laughed. "That's okay, Sheen. I can use all the help I can get! Suggest away."

The engines fired, and he set the throttle to three quarters, not wanting to push the damaged ship too hard. The *Promise* sped away from the incoming vessels.

"Are they still behind us?" Chase shouted to Sheen.

"Yes, Commander."

"How many?"

"Ship's sensors indicate three heavy Quargg cruisers in pursuit, and they are closing the gap."

"Sonofabitch," said Chase aloud. "We're gonna have to take our chances."

Chase pushed the throttle forward to full.

"I hope she holds together," he said, patting the console. "Come on, baby, get us outta here."

Sheen looked on annoyed as Chase stroked the console. The ship vibrated as it increased the distance between the *Promise* and the pursuing ships.

"We can't run like this for long," said Chase. "We don't have that much fuel, and she may fall apart."

"My sensors indicate at this rate of fuel burn we have 20.4 of your Earth minutes."

Chase hit the com button. "Max, how 'bout those pulse lasers?"

"Still offline," he replied. "They were hit pretty bad. I don't know that I can fix 'em without replacing 'em."

"Commander, even with pulse lasers restored, this ship is no match for three Quargg cruisers."

"I know, I know...but I feel naked without weapons," Chase mumbled. "Sheen, what's the status on the pursuing vessels?"

"Enemy vessels are in pursuit, but we are maintaining our lead."

"Then we have twenty minutes to come up with a plan," Chase said hitting the com button. "Max, get up to tac-con now."

Chapter Ten

Trillium Schmillium

The "tac-con," or tactical conference room, was a domed cabin at the top of the ship with a windowed ceiling surrounding the room and a view of space all around and above. The furniture and non-windowed walls were dark—almost black—so as not to interfere with the tactical display table and the spectacular view of space.

In the center was a large, computerized "tac-table" capable of projecting holographic displays. It stood solidly in the center of the room surrounded by large, comfortable chairs. The chairs were pushed back out of the way unused as the crew stood at the head and sides of the table.

"How much time we got left, Sheen?" Chase asked from the head of the table.

"At the current rate of fuel burn, we have 17 minutes 29 seconds of fuel remaining."

Max ran to the tactical conference room wearing a new Piecer spacesuit, and took position opposite of Sheen, hearing what she said. Chase punched a button on the table displaying the *Promise* and the pursuing Quargg vessels above the table.

"Hey, you changed your clothes," said Chase. "I hardly recognize you!"

"Had to."

"You shower too?"

"Not yet; seemed like more important things to do...

first—like staying alive."

"Well, my eyes aren't watering," said Chase, watching for a reaction.

"Oh, well, fuck you very much," said Max, grinning. "You wouldn't smell too good after six months without a bath, either."

"Sorry, Sheen," said Max looking across the tac-table. "Please excuse my language."

"I am not offended by language, Max 325," she replied.

"Just Max," he said, turning back to Chase.

"Right," said Chase, smiling. "Sorry, Stinky."

Max rolled his eyes and growled his displeasure.

"We have 16 minutes 15 seconds of fuel remaining," said Sheen.

"Okay; we can't outrun 'em. We can't stand and fight 'em. Any chance the pulse cannons can be fixed?"

"Not in 16 minutes and 15 seconds," replied Max.

"15 minutes and 55 seconds," said Sheen.

"Okay, Sheen, I'll ask you the next time we need an update."

"Yes, Commander."

"Any chance you can do anything with the engines?" asked Chase.

"I'm not a magician. We're at maximum speed now; I can't make them go faster. What's wrong with the worm drive?"

"Nothing, but we have no trillium. We can't even bring the reactor online."

"Trillium schmillium...it's not like we need a lot," said Max. "The walker is nuclear powered. There's some trillium in it, but I don't know if it's enough or if it will even fit in the core."

"Can you salvage it?"

"Maybe, but I'm going to need more time."

"How much more?"

"If everything goes right, probably thirty minutes."

"We don't have that."

Chase looked at Sheen for a moment; she glanced back at him, started to speak, and then stared forward silently.

"They don't make it easy to get it out of the walker," said Max. "And they don't make it easy to get it into the *Promise* reactor. It has to fit and may need to be modified."

"Then we'll need a diversion," said Chase, "something that will buy us time."

Chase looked around the room to see if there was anything that sparked an idea.

"Do we have anything on board that would interest the Quargg? Something they would want to buy? Maybe we can broadcast a good rom-com at 'em or a porno."

"A good rom-com?" asked Max. "First, that's an oxymoron...second, are you high?"

"Well something to buy us time—anything."

"I don't think they'll opt for movie night right now," said Max, "maybe after they kill us, they might want to relax, but not right now."

Chase sighed. "Max, you go get that trillium installed; we'll come up with something to stall them. And don't dilly-dally."

Max rolled his eyes as he left the room running.

"Quargg like me," Sheen said softly. "They paid my commander a lot of money to watch me dance...even more money for other things. Maybe they will take me in trade."

Chase leaned over and kissed Sheen on the head. "We don't trade our friends, Sheen," replied Chase, "but that's not a bad idea. That horny bastard at the bar loved you. If they all like you that much, maybe they'll be up for a little on-board entertainment. How do you feel about dancing for the Quargg again?"

Sheen smiled. "I am yours to command, Commander."

"I told you I would never make you service anyone."

"It is just dancing, and I do not think the Quargg are interested in ancient Earth videos."

"Get the Quargg on the com," said Chase. "Then take your position in front of the helm's console. I'll toggle the ship's cameras at you."

Chase hit the internal com switch. "Max, how's it going down there?"

"So far so good; I have the trillium extracted from the walker. I need another fifteen minutes.

"Make it fast, Stinky, or you know...space glitter."

From the engine room, Max cocked his head at the com and raised the middle fingers of each hand one after the other in disgust.

"Sheen, how much time do we have before we run out of fuel?" asked Chase.

"We have 5 minutes 14 seconds of fuel remaining, Commander."

"Shit! Okay, Sheen...get ready."

"The Quargg have responded, Commander."

"Put it on ship-wide audio broadcast, Sheen," said Chase. "So Max knows what we're doing".

"Quargg vessels, this is Chase 523 of the Piecer Corp—"

"You can't escape us, Captain," the Quargg interrupted. "Please end this futile attempt to flee."

"Flee?" asked Chase. "We're in a hurry to meet up with my Piecer brothers—a whole squadron."

"There is no need to speak falsely, Piecer 523. We know the Piecer Corp was disbanded."

"Speak falsely?" asked Chase, feigning surprise. "We're not fleeing; we're partying with our Courtesan."

There was a brief moment of silence before the Quargg responded. "You have the Courtesan on board your vessel... from the station?"

Chase smiled. "Well, yes. She needed a ride."

Some arguing could be heard before the Quargg cut their com link. A moment later, it was restored.

"You lie," said the Quargg. "You don't have the Courtesan. She is Shoom's. He would never release her."

"Let's just say Shoom doesn't need her anymore," said Chase. "I assure you she is here and quite amazing. Like nothing you have ever seen in your life. If you don't believe me, turn on your ship-to-ship monitors."

Chase pointed at Sheen and cut the mic. "You're on, Sheen. Dance like your life depends on it."

Chase pressed the com link to the ship's entertainment center, patching in some stripper bar music similar to what he'd heard at the Blue Angel.

***

The music drifted through the halls of the ship to Max, working on the trillium.

"Great!" he huffed, nodding his head to the beat of the music, "We're gonna die, and he's listenin' to f-ing music. *Fix the engines, Max. Save us, Max,* while I kick back to some tunes and watch the stripper. New boss, same shit."

Max grabbed the trillium block he had removed from the walker and tried shoving it into the worm-drive reactor. The reactor had a perfectly square receptacle to accommodate the correct-sized trillium block. The walker trillium block was smaller and rectangular. It didn't fit.

He tried putting it in diagonally, hoping it would touch at least two sides of the receptacle. The trillium block had to touch two sides of the reactor receptacle completely to be recognized by the reactor as having a block inserted. It wasn't quite wide enough to reach the corners, and it fell over into the slot and lay on the bottom.

"Stupid piece of shit!" he screamed, carefully removing it so it didn't fall into the bowels of the reactor.

He tried pushing the block in again—horizontally—pushing as hard as he could. It wouldn't budge. It was just a half millimeter too large.

***

Sheen began to gyrate slowly to the music. Chase flipped the switch to the helm cameras and beamed the signal to the three pursuing Quargg vessels. Max flipped on the monitor in the engine room, and seeing Sheen dancing, his mouth fell open. A small light indicating that the monitor had been acti- vated in the engine room turned green. Chase noticed it and clicked the override switch.

The monitor in the engine room went blank.

"What the fuck?" said Max, slapping the monitor, hoping just the right smack would make it work. "The fucking Quargg can watch but I can't?"

Chase opened the com to the engine room. "Get back to work!" he shouted.

Max snorted. "Everyone else gets to watch but I have to work? Aye, aye, Captain Ass Monkey," he said, his voice trailing off.

Chase toggled the com switch again. "I heard that, Stinky. Get my worm drive online first. And you don't have to call me Captain."

Caught off guard, Max nearly dropped the rectangular block of trillium. "Holy shit; just kidding," he replied. "Kidding."

Almost whispering, Max continued, "Don't shoot me you gun-crazy mother-f-er..."

The com clicked in again.

"Heard that too, dipshit. You have less than five minutes before these guys decide they want to blow the crap out of us, or board us and take Sheen."

Max's eyes went wide. "Oh no, they don't," he said to himself. "They're not getting my Courtesan. I plan on having sex with her someday."

Max licked the sides of the trillium rectangle and pushed it against the core receptacle. He pushed hard, and it stuck temporarily, but ninety-nine percent of the block still extended out the side of the fuel core frame. It was making contact, and the core lights were flickering, but it would never work correctly and could fall out. The reactor could explode, if it worked at all.

"You're goin' in, motherfucker!" Max yelled.

He backed up and threw his entire weight into his shoulder against the trillium rectangle, slamming the block into the core. The reactor core lights blinked on, then off, and then on again and remained steady.

"*Trillium core enabled,*" said the computer voice, "*Core initiation sequence begun.*"

"Good old spit...the duct tape of bodily fluids," he mumbled to himself.

Max held his now-aching shoulder and fumbled with the receptacle cover plate, replacing it in seconds. He flipped the com button, shouting, "Chase, the reactor is coming back online."

"Good job, Stinky," replied Chase. "How much time before the worm drive's ready?"

Max sighed. "She's sparking up now, but we're still going to need a few more minutes."

"Do what you can to speed it up. We'll try to buy more time. We'll have to shut the engines off. We have less than a minute of fuel to enter the wormhole, if we ever get one."

Chase cut the engines while Sheen danced provocatively on the bridge. The com link lit up. It was the Quargg lead vessel.

"We see that you have stopped your engines, Captain," the Quargg captain said over the com. "Do you wish to surrender?"

"*Nuclear reactor at sixty percent,*" the ship's computer reported.

"Sheen, we need three more minutes," Chase whispered.

Sheen continued to dance, and Chase could hardly look away. Chase clicked the ship-to-ship com link.

"Quargg vessels, we have had some trouble with video transmission at these speeds. We decided to stop for a moment so you could watch without interruption."

"We do not need to watch any longer. We have decided to let you live, if you send over the Courtesan."

Chase smiled.

"*Nuclear reactor at ninety percent,*" said the ship's computer.

Sheen looked at Chase to see his reaction.

Two minutes, Chase mouthed to Sheen as he clicked open the com link once more.

"Quargg vessels, we have no intention on sending over our Courtesan. We merely stopped as a courtesy to you. But I can see you did not appreciate our friendly gesture."

Chase toggled the com switch off.

"*Nuclear reactor at one hundred percent,*" said the ship's computer.

Chase flipped the internal com switch to patch Max in.

"Max, is there any way to create the wormhole instantly? I don't want to die waiting for it to open—"

"Prepare to be boarded," the Quargg cut in. "If you resist, you will die."

"You can do it," replied Max. "But it's dangerous as hell. You have to initiate the wormhole sequence and bypass the path builder. It will open for a second in one giant burst, and if you're not flying into it at that very moment, it will close and—"

"Blah, blah, blah; just make it happen, Stinky," said Chase. "Set the coordinates for Europa. I'll try to stall."

"Just make it happen, like I'm a fucking wizard. Such an ass!"

Chase's voice trailed off as he turned to the helm where Sheen was dancing. Sheen began removing her skin-tight top, tossing it at the control console. Topless, she continued to play to the cameras, hoping to buy more time for the wormhole to form.

"I'm patchin' the ship's computer and engine control into the wormhole generator," Max said over the intercom. "The engines will fire one second before the wormhole opens fully formed. If we time it just right, we'll be in and gone before the Quargg even know what happened."

"What happens if we time it wrong?" asked Chase.

"We either fly thirty seconds farther away and the Quargg blow the shit out of us, or we make it."

Sheen peeled off her skin-tight pants slowly, gyrating to the music without missing a beat. She was now dancing— only in shiny, simulated leather knee high boots and panties—as she had done many times at the Blue Angel. The

Quargg leered at the monitors on their ships and did nothing more.

Well, if I'm gonna die, this isn't the worst last thing to see, thought Chase, reaching for the engine room video override switch.

The monitor in the reactor room lit up, and Max could once again see Sheen dancing.

"Holy shit!" he said, staring at the monitor.

He forced himself to look away for one moment and initiated the new wormhole sequence. Crossing his fingers on both hands, he mouthed the words, *Please don't blow up, please don't blow up.*

Then he flipped the com button broadcasting over the ship. "Hang on," he said. "Here we go."

Chapter Eleven

Dark Side of Europa

The *Promise* lights flashed off, and the entire ship went dark for several seconds. Chase and Max held their breath, expecting any moment to hit the wormhole, blow up, or be boarded by Quargg. A brilliant flash lit the helm through the windows, and Chase glimpsed Sheen dutifully dancing, a bright shine reflecting from her black boots. He covered his eyes, shielding them from the intense light until finally the light dimmed.

"That's enough, Sheen," he said. "We made it."

Sheen stopped dancing and got dressed, while Chase toggled the intercom.

"You okay in there, Max?"

"All good," replied Max. "We dead?"

"Don't think so; take a look."

Chase toggled the cameras from inside the helm to outside the ship. Jupiter loomed large ahead, and Europa was just starboard of the *Promise*.

"Never thought I'd be so glad to see Jupiter," said Max.

"Get me the status of the worm drive and our fuel, and meet me in the galley. We could all use a drink and maybe some food."

"Roger that," said Max. "Sheen okay? Tell her I asked, okay?"

Chase rolled his eyes in disbelief. "Sheen," said Chase in an exaggerated voice, "Max asked me to pass you a note in gym class. He wants to know if you're okay."

Sheen cocked her head confused. "Yes, Commander...you can tell Max I am perfectly functional. I am unaware of any gym class. What is your command?"

"Max, Sheen says she's fine. Can we all get back to work now?"

"Rogoe," replied Max, grinning from ear to ear.

"Sheen, please scan for any Quargg vessels."

Sheen scanned beyond the perimeter of the ship using onboard sensors and her own thermal scanners. "There are no Quargg vessels in this sector of the galaxy that I can confirm within scanner range."

"Sheen?"

"Yes, Commander?"

"Thank you. You did well."

"I am glad you are pleased, Commander. I danced as if my life depended on it, as ordered."

"They were mesmerized. Hell, I was mesmerized, and Max almost forgot what he was doing."

"Thank you, Commander," she said, blushing slightly.

"Did I embarrass you?" Chase asked.

"No, Commander, but I thought blushing would be an appropriate response."

"Oh right...all human emotive responses—gotcha."

"Yes, Commander."

"Without your dance, we'd be dead and you would be with the Quargg."

"I will never be with another Quargg again," said Sheen, her lips pursed, eyes narrowing. "They are brutish beings."

"Amen to that," said Chase, "now let's go meet Max in the galley for a drink and plan our next move."

"Yes, Commander."

They slid down the galley ladder in two hops. Max was already there with a bottle of Earth whiskey and three shot glasses set out on the table.

"I stole this from Shoom; it's Pappy Van Winkle's Family Reserve, New Kentucky Whiskey; the best in the world. You can't find it anywhere anymore; perfect occasion to break it out. Label says it will put a twinkle in your eye."

Max pulled out the cork gently, not wanting to spill a drop, and poured three shots.

"Here's to the crew of the *Promise*," he said, "who took on three Quargg cruisers and outsmarted 'em all."

"I'll drink to that," said Chase. "Good job with the warp drive. You saved our asses."

"Thanks!" replied Max. "Your dance was amazing, Sheen," he gushed. "I really liked it."

Sheen blushed again.

"She blushes?" Max asked, turning to Chase. "Oh my God, she blushes!"

"I am capable..." Sheen started to say.

"...of expressing all human emotive responses," Max and Chase said, finishing her sentence.

"I'll drink to that," Max added.

Sheen smiled, unsure what to make of their interruption. Chase and Max downed their shots in a quick gulp. Sheen copied their movements, slamming the shot glass on the galley table as they had done. She appeared unfazed by the strong whiskey.

"Wow, you sure can handle your liquor," said Max. "Would you like another?"

"Liquor has no effect on me. My system will filter out the alcohol and other impurities. I have no need of food either."

"Oh," said Max, obviously disappointed, "um, that's great."

"I was merely attempting to participate as a crew member. Is it not required?"

"It is not required," said Chase.

"Then I think I shall not have another," she said. "The taste is unpleasant."

"You can taste things?" asked Chase.

"Yes. I have taste sensors, much like your own."

"Why would you have taste sensors if you don't need to eat?" asked Chase.

Sheen scanned her memory for a few moments. "I have no answer for you. Perhaps taste is helpful in other ways. I have no information as to why I can taste, but I can taste."

"Is there anything you like to taste?" asked Max.

"Chocolate is pleasant," Sheen replied. "It tastes sweet, and the texture is smooth."

"I'll see if we have any chocolate in the ship's stores," said Max.

"Thank you, Max. It is not necessary as I do not need to eat."

"No problem," said Max. "Sometimes it's just nice to taste things because they are pleasant."

Chase rolled his eyes, and Max saw him. "What?"

"Puhleeze," said Chase.

"What, I'm just trying to be nice."

"Fine; be nice on your own time. What's our status?"

"The reactor is still online. Don't know for how long, but it's working."

"And rocket fuel?"

"Not much...maybe 15 seconds at full burn."

"Sheen, can you scan for any ships on the surface?"

"There do not appear to be any ships on this side of Europa. My sensors and the ship's sensors cannot see to the other side until we move into position."

"We may be the first ones here," said Chase. "There is a Piecer station on the far side of Europa. It's colder than shit down there—nobody in their right mind would go there. That's why we picked it for the station and our rendezvous, if the shit went sideways."

"Not much fuel to land this thing," said Max, "and if we did, we'd never get off the ground again without more."

"There's plenty of fuel down there, and weapons, if we can make it to the station. I saw two landing craft in the hold; I think they're Dragonflies. I'll take one to make sure, and be back in no time."

"I'll come with you," said Max. "I love those little ships."

"No...you stay here with Sheen. You handle the engines,

Sheen can take the helm. If anything goes wrong, use the worm drive to get the hell out of here. Find any other Piecers who made it out and regroup with them."

"I will come with you, Commander," said Sheen, stepping forward. "It is my function to stay with my Commander."

"No, Sheen...it's too dangerous."

"You will need me."

"Sheen, I need you here. That's an order...sorry, I mean request. Please stay."

"Yes, Commander."

"Keep the com open. I'll contact you when I reach the station."

"Commander?"

"Yes, Sheen?"

"Be careful."

Chase smiled. "I'll be right back. Don't worry."

"Here, take this," said Max, handing him a tiny pistol that looked like a single shot derringer from Earth's past.

Chase laughed, holding the entire gun in the palm of one hand.

"What the hell is this? I don't need a keychain."

"That's little boom-boom," replied Max, pushing the barrel in Chase's hand away from him so that it wasn't pointed in his direction. "Little boom-boom is your friend. Tuck it behind your back in your belt; too small to be seen."

"Does a tiny flag pop out that says 'boom'?"

"Just make sure you're far away when you use it."

"How far—a mouse's football field?"

"Seriously, fifteen meters at a minimum," said Max sternly. "And take cover if you can."

Chase looked at the tiny pistol closely. "From *this*?"

"There's an old Earth expression 'never judge a book by its cover,'" said Max. "True for guns, too."

Chase grinned and tucked the tiny gun behind his back under his belt. He climbed down to the forward launch bay and into the cockpit of the Dragonfly.

"Chase to *Promise*, can you read me? Over."

"We read you, Commander," said Sheen. "Over."

"Loud and clear, Captain," said Max.

"Roger that...Chase out."

The depressurized launch bay opened, and the tiny Dragonfly was sucked into space below the *Promise*. The small craft looked like its namesake, a dragonfly, or a mini helicopter without a rotor or wings.

I remember training in one of these, thought Chase. *It shouldn't be much different than before. Just need to punch in the coordinates, and the autopilot should do the rest.*

"Chase to the *Promise*, you guys still listening?"

"Yes, Commander."

"Getting the engines ready for that fuel you promised, Chase," Max responded.

"Workin' on it. Don't see much down there; it's pitch black. Wait...the station's lights are on. I'm going to take her in slow. I don't think I'm the first one here."

"Please be careful, Commander," said Sheen, sounding humanly nervous.

"Setting down outside the station," said Chase. "What the hell?"

A crackle followed by a high-pitched whine bled from the *Promise*'s com, then silence.

Chapter Twelve

The Heist of the Lone Star

Gage, Tripp, Evelyn and Hector peered out from behind the ledge wall at the top of the museum.

"Tripp, how's your wound?" asked Gage.

"Almost good as new."

"Almost ain't gonna cut it for this job," he replied.

"I'm fine...really, whaddya need?"

"Not this time. Not with a hole in you."

"You worry too much, Mom," said Tripp. "I can do it."

"Hector, you up for a little B and E?" Gage asked.

"I'm up for anything as long as it ain't in a sewer."

"There's a maintenance winch up here. They must use it to adjust the hanging displays...a sling, too. I'm going to lower you down to the *Lone Star*. You check it out and take care of any guards you run into. Enter through the top hatch, and you won't have to worry about the laser perimeter alarm going off."

"They strip those things pretty good when they put 'em on display, Chief," Hector replied. "I doubt there is any fuel on board or weapons that work."

"I saw some trillium on display," said Gage. "We'll grab that. It may be the real deal. If it's not, we'll have to improvise."

"The Piecer armory is near here," said Tripp. "We can get weapons and fuel there, if we can make it out of here."

"How do you plan on getting the ship out?" asked Hector.

"I plan to fly us right out the window," said Gage.

"For real?" asked Tripp. "You're just going to crash through the wall?"

"Hull is tritanium; won't even scratch it."

"We're still gonna need fuel," Tripp replied.

"There has to be some fuel around here somewhere... something we can use."

"I doubt they keep jet fuel in a museum; too dangerous."

"Something—anything—just some fuel of some kind. The museum has to have backup generators," said Gage. "They probably run on diesel."

"You can burn diesel in the *Lone Star* engines?" asked Tripp.

"We'll need some liquid oxygen to add to the diesel...a lot of it, but they should have that on board the *Lone Star* as backup O2."

"How you gonna get the O2 into the fuel tank?"

"They have injector valves inside the ship that should work."

"Lots of *shoulds* in this plan."

"I know, I know, but I seen it done in a training video at the academy," said Gage. "For some reason, it always stuck with me."

"Okay...but where's the generator?"

"Usually in the basement," said Gage.

"If we pull this off, it'll be a goddamn miracle," said Tripp.

"Tripp," said Gage, "climb back down and gain entry into the basement from behind the building. Check for fuel and report back. Let's make a miracle."

"Roger that, Chief."

"What do you want me to do?" asked Evelyn.

"You keep an eye on Hector while I lower him down to the *Lone Star*. Make sure he's okay."

Tripp slipped over the edge of the building and disappeared, while Hector climbed into the sling.

"What are you doing?" Gage asked while Hector slid face downward, his legs wrapped around both cables at the sling.

"I'm not goin' down there ass first," he replied. "I wanna see what I'm getting into."

"Roger that. Oh, and check for O2 when you get in there. We're gonna need it."

"Will do, Chief."

"Here we go; you ready?"

"Ready."

"Evelyn, you let me know if he gets in trouble, and I'll stop."

Gage started lowering Hector slowly. Hector clenched his combat knife in his teeth, while his arms dangled forward. Blood rushed to his head, and he could hear his heartbeat pounding in his ears.

The museum was enormous. The ceiling height alone was easily one hundred meters high, to accommodate the airplanes hanging from the ceiling and to house the *Lone Star*.

"Wait," Evelyn whispered frantically, "Klix!"

A Klix guard had entered the building and was looking around. He too was limited by the ship's laser perimeter and the small safe non-laser zone at the door.

Hector froze.

Don't look up, he thought, *please don't look up*.

The guard turned around and was about to leave, when he abruptly turned back again. Evelyn and Gage ducked slightly below the skylight rim and remained perfectly still. Hector hung without moving a muscle. Suddenly, they heard a clicking noise from outside, and the guard turned around and walked out.

"That was close," said Evelyn.

"Hector okay?" asked Gage.

"Yeah, he just gave me a thumbs up."

Gage started lowering him again, and soon Hector's hands touched the *Lone Star*. He quickly slid out of the harness and gave it a tug, indicating he made it and was free of the rigging. Gage cranked the harness back up while Hector opened the top hatch on the ship and climbed silently down the ladder.

"Watch for his signal, Evelyn; Tripp's back."

Evelyn watched for Hector through the skylight while Gage talked to Tripp returning from his recon mission.

"Anything we can use?" he asked Tripp.

"They have a big tank of diesel...mostly full—must weigh a ton. No way to get that up here, and it's bolted to the floor anyway. But they *do* have two 55-gallon drums of diesel as back up."

"Two drums won't get us off the ground, even if we burn mostly O2."

"That big tank ain't goin' nowhere," said Tripp.

"You see any fire hoses around?"

"Yeah, a few on the walls by the tank. Why?"

"They got couplers, and there's usually a manual pump to get the barrels into the main tank."

"You gonna pump that shit all the way up to the *Lone Star*?"

"Nope...you are," said Gage. "We can start with the 55-gallon drums, but we're gonna need it all. Lower me down on the sling; I'm going to grab some of the fire hoses on the wall. We're gonna need a lot of hose."

"You really think this will work?" asked Tripp.

"Has to. Besides, it's not easy making a miracle."

Tripp lowered Gage in the sling and he started to swing closer and closer to the wall. He grabbed onto the fire hose cabinet handle and opened it. He tied the fire hose end to his sling and then unscrewed the coupling from the water pipe on the wall. Giving a thumbs up, Tripp cranked him back to the roof with the hose trailing behind.

"That's one," Gage said. "Let's get another one."

They repeated the process until they had three long hoses on the roof.

"Couple these together. They're pretty heavy, Tripp...you think you can handle them all the way back to the basement generator room?"

"Tripp strong, me carry hose," Tripp said in his best cave-man voice.

"Stop foolin' around; you're still healing."

"I can carry a hose, Chief. I'm fine."

"Okay...these are long enough to go down to the *Lone Star* and back down the building. You'll need the others from the generator room to hook up to these. Grab them, hook them up to the pump and then the big tank. You're gonna have to crank pretty fast to get that shit all the way up here, but once its flowing down to the *Lone Star*, the siphon effect should empty the tank. I'll let you know when to start pumpin'."

"Roger that, Chief, but first I'll bring you the barrels—then we can pump the rest."

Gage and Tripp played out the winch line down the side of the building. Tripp watched for Klix, but most had been called to the street in front. They quickly raised the two 55-gallon drums of diesel to the roof, and Gage pulled in their sling.

Tripp ran back to the generator room and grabbed the two hoses on the wall, connecting them to the hose trailing down from the roof. Then he went back to the generator room door, and waited for Gage's signal.

"Hector come out yet, Evelyn?" Gage asked.

"He's coming out now. He's waving for us to come down."

"Okay; let's get the fuel down to him, then we'll follow up with the hose."

They lowered the fuel to a waiting Hector, who immediately poured the barrel into the top port fuel tank inlet. Some of the diesel spilled onto the wing as it chugged from the drum. When the barrel was empty, Hector signaled for the second one, and soon both barrels were empty.

Gage lowered the one end of the hose to Hector and he inserted the end into the fuel inlet of the Lone Star. Then he signaled to Tripp at the generator room. Tripp opened the valve on the big tank and could see the fuel filling the fire hose from gravity alone, and then it stopped.

Time to start pumping, he thought.

Tripp spun the handle on the manual pump as fast as he could and watched as the fuel started flowing once again.

Hector waited for the flat fire hose to fill. At first nothing happened, while Tripp frantically spun the manual pump crank. Suddenly, a few drips came through Hector's end until finally the fuel began to flow. Hector signaled to Gage up on the roof that it was working. Tripp continued spinning the pump crank a few more turns, then ran back to the ladder and climbed up to the roof.

"You did good," Gage said. "Won't take too long with the size of that hose."

"My arm hurts," replied Tripp. "That's not that easy to crank that shit all the way up here."

"You want me to kiss it and make it all better?" asked Gage, rolling his eyes.

"Yes," replied Tripp, holding his arm closer to Gage.

"You're an idiot."

Tripp laughed and pulled his arm back.

Gage turned back to Evelyn, whispering, "Evelyn, you go first, then Tripp. I'll follow you both. Tell Hector to keep that hose flowing until we empty that tank."

They lowered Evelyn quickly into the waiting arms of Hector. She signaled okay, and Tripp went next.

"Gage wants us below...said to meet him in the helm," Tripp said.

"Is he coming?" asked Hector. "Fuel is flowing, and I got those O2 tanks he wanted and attached them all to the fuel valves. We better not need backup O2. I used them all."

"He's coming, but he said he wanted to do some shopping first."

"Shopping?"

"I didn't ask."

"What is that crazy mother up to now?" asked Hector.

"You probably don't want to know," said Tripp. "Let's get below. He said to get everything ready. We may have to leave in a hurry."

The three descended the ladder, leaving the hatch open for Gage and the fuel hose connected and flowing into the *Lone Star*. Gage stuffed a rag into the winch mechanism hoping to slow his descent. He was the last one on the roof and had no one to lower him gently to the *Lone Star*. He unwound the cable, threading the rag into the gears until it caught.

Here goes nothing, he thought. *I think I'll go ass first...no need to land on this beautiful face.*

Gage slipped off the edge of the winch housing, and the sling descended slowly.

Shit, that worked.

His weight kept the winch going, and he surveyed the area below. He turned to look at the trillium display when he suddenly fell ten feet, slowed and then stopped.

What the fuck? he thought. *Damn rag is slippin'.*

He jiggled up and down, trying to get the winch to restart. He wiggled harder, jumping up and down in the sling. Suddenly, the winch responded, and he dropped—free falling still in the sling.

The sling stopped with a sudden jerk at the end of the cable just above the ship. He hung motionless for a moment to get his bearings and then slid face-first like Hector had done, with his arms hanging below him and his ankles holding him on the sling. Then he started swinging his arms. Each movement made him swing farther and farther from the ship—back and forth—above the laser perimeter alarm beams.

"There it is," he said as he swung by one of the museum's displays, "trillium."

His next swing took him directly over the trillium display, and he reached out to grab the case. His momentum took him past the glass case, and it slipped through his fingers. He swung back past the *Lone Star*, dangerously close to the wall.

"Now or never," he mumbled to himself as his arc brought him over the display yet again. He reached out and grabbed the corners of the glass enclosure, grunting as he grabbed on. Now suspended above the case, he tried to pull the case up. It wouldn't budge. It was locked down, attached to the floor.

"Okay, well so much for subtlety," he said, reaching with one hand for his combat knife while clinging to the case with his other hand. "Time to get this party started."

He grabbed the blade end of his knife and smashed the top of the display case with the thick metal hilt. The glass crashed to the ground and broke the laser beam security web across the floor. Alarms blared and red lights flashed. When the glass broke, his grip was gone, and he grabbed onto the corner of the display case frame.

"Welcome, New Mart shoppers," he said to himself. "There is a special on trillium in aisle one. First come...first served. Three, please."

In the case were three glowing blocks of trillium, showing the evolution of the fuel cells. One of the earlier versions was pyramid-shaped, one was rectangular, and the one on the end was a state-of-the-art trillium cube. Trillium was one of the safest fuels ever created. It was non-volatile and could be handled safely in its specially designed container, without any fear of radiation or explosion. Gage grabbed each of the trillium objects and stuffed them into the top of his fatigues.

They look real, he thought. They were heavy enough to be real, and they were glowing. It was time to go.

He let go of the display case and swung back toward the *Lone Star,* pulling himself up onto the sling in a seated position. Klix guards burst into the museum from every door, spotted him, clicked orders to each other, and then started shooting.

Gage jumped onto the *Lone Star* running, with Klix firing at him as he ran. He jumped into the open hatch—not touching the ladder—and landed with a loud thud on the deck below.

"Somebody get the hatch," he screamed.

Evelyn crawled up the ladder and pulled the hatch door closed. It was stuck.

"Someone help Evelyn!" Gage yelled while heading for the helm.

Tripp ran back to the ladder and climbed up beside her. One of the Klix soldiers was holding onto the bottom of the hatch to keep it from closing.

"Hang on Evelyn...I gotcha."

Tripp pulled his combat knife and sliced the Klix's hand off with one chop. Muffled click-screaming could be heard from the other side of the hatch as the hand plopped to the floor inside the *Lone Star*. The latch slammed shut, and Tripp spun the hatch door wheel, locking it tight.

"We're good to go, Gage," he shouted. "Get us the fuck out of here."

Evelyn looked at him and then hugged him. "Thank you," she said.

"Well, thank you," Tripp said, enjoying his hug and squeezing her back hard. There was an awkward moment as the hug lasted a bit too long. Tripp let go and picked up the Klix hand, offering it to Evelyn.

"I'm here for you, Evelyn—if you ever need a hand," he said, grinning.

Evelyn pushed him away. "God, you're such an idiot. Get that disgusting thing out of my face."

Evelyn stormed off and headed to the helm.

"What? I was just kiddin'," he called after her, using the hand to scratch his head.

"I'll never figure women out," he said, now talking to the hand. "I wonder if Klix women have a sense of humor."

Then he shook the hand back and forth as if the hand was answering him, "no."

"I didn't think so. No wonder you're such a bunch of bloodthirsty savages."

He threw the hand into the ship's bio-disposal unit, where it instantly vaporized. Tripp headed forward to the helm, apologizing along the way.

"C'mon, Evelyn...don't be mad. I was just messin' around."

Hector came forward to the helm and sat next to Gage, who had just flipped on the ship's forward cameras. The ship's controls lit up, and Gage scanned the instrument panel for fuel. The fuel indicator showed fuel in the tanks, but not much.

"How's that fuel coming, Hector?"

"Still flowing."

"You attach the O2 to the fuel intake valves?" Gage shouted.

"Roger that; opened 'em up after I poured in the first two barrels."

"Good job. Here goes nothin'. Fire up those engines."

"Hose is still drainin', Chief—slower, but still going."

"Goddammit. Tripp, disconnect it...we're leaving."

"You got it, Boss. Be right back. Don't leave without me."

He made his way to the fuel inlet port and uncoupled the hose, tossing it to the ground.

A stinger bolt flew past him from the right, and he knew he was not alone. He spun around and in one motion, let his knife fly, catching the Klix guard in the chest and knocking him back onto the top of the ship.

He ran back to the hatch, grabbing his knife from the dead Klix chest along the way.

"You shouldn't sneak up on people," he muttered. "It's rude."

He jumped into the still-open hatch, hitting the deck below with a roll to his feet to break his fall. Without stopping, he clambered back up to the top of the ladder, and closed the hatch.

"Hit it, Hector. Go, go, go!"

Hector hit the ignition button. The *Lone Star* vibrated and shuddered, but nothing happened.

"Give it a shitload more fuel," said Gage. "Tank's been dry a long time."

"Roger that, Chief."

A loud bang echoed inside the museum, coming from the engines.

"Don't worry; probably just excess O2 exploding."

The Klix were now firing at the windows of the *Lone Star*, hoping to find an area of the ship their laser bolts could penetrate.

"The fuckin' Klix are shooting the crap out of us," said Gage. "They can't hurt us for now, but it won't be long before they pull out the big stuff. Turn on the aft camera."

The screen lit up, and they could see two Klix soldiers carrying what looked like a large crate, and placing it under the ship's tail.

"Explosives!" Gage cried. "They're gonna blow us up."

Hector pushed the throttle forward and hit the ignition again. The engines stuttered to life. Loud bangs exploded from the engine intermittently—with puffs of black smoke belching from the engines.

"It's working," shouted Hector, "we got engines."

"Get those flaps up," Gage ordered. "Keep giving her as much fuel as she needs. Take us outta here."

Hector hit the throttle hard, and the ship shuddered and rose, black smoke billowing from the stuttering engines.

"I don't think she likes the diesel, but she loves the O2," said Hector. "Which way?"

"It's all she gets for now," said Gage, "and straight through the fucking wall."

Hector pushed the yoke forward, and the *Lone Star* pushed through the wall like it was made of Legos. Bricks and cinder blocks hit the outer hull and bounced off onto the Klix below. There was a sudden explosion from below and behind—which shook the entire building. The blast blew them farther into the air.

"Hector, get us outta here!" said Gage.

"Aye, aye, Chief," said Hector, plunging the throttle as far as it would go. The *Lone Star* shot up into the sky.

"Get ready for company; we won't be alone for long."

"Tripp, check out the weapons. Does anything work on this ship?"

"Negative...display only. Guns are real, but no ammo. The

rockets are fake. Pulse lasers are charging, and they look like they work, but it will take a while."

Gage walked back to the engine room to the nuclear core and pulled out the square trillium cube from his fatigues.

"I hope this shit is real," he said, pushing the cube into the reactor receptacle.

Nothing happened. He tapped the cube with his fist, and the cube blinked on, then off.

"What the fuck!"

He removed the cube, shook it, and could hear rattling inside. As he shook it, it blinked on then off. He examined the cube more closely and saw the slightest notch in the corner of the cube. He picked at it with his fingernail, and a semi-transparent decal picture of wires peeled off the cube. He squeezed the cube hard and it cracked, splintering in his hand. He grabbed the other two blocks and threw them against the wall, shattering them into pieces.

"Goddamn plastic shit; it's fake. Everything is fake."

Gage came back to the helm swearing.

"We need weapons, Hector. And fuel...and we got no trillium either. Plot a course for the armory. We have to get in and get out fast."

"No sweat, Chief. I know the armory like the back of my hand."

"Do ship sensors work?"

"Sensors are online and operational."

"Take us above the armory, but keep our distance."

"Roger that," said Hector.

Minutes later they were over the armory.

"Hector, scan for Klix."

Hector scanned the armory for any sign of life.

"Bad news, Chief; armory looks destroyed. Nothing left."

"Those fuckers," said Gage. "They hit the armory too. We're fucked."

"Maybe they missed the tombs," said Hector. "They're pretty well-hidden."

"What's in the tombs," asked Gage. "Anything useful?"

"Everything," Hector said, smiling. "That's where they keep the good shit."

"Better be a shitload of fuel in there," said Gage. "And some trillium. We burned up most of that diesel and O2 already. We land and we're not going to be able to get airborne again and without trillium, we'll never get to Alpha-Seven."

"Should be," replied Hector. "Always was."

"Tripp, I'm gonna need you," said Gage." Stop making puppy eyes at Evelyn and pay attention."

"Puppy eyes? I was not."

"Whatever. We're setting down at the tombs. I want you and Hector to get in and out with anything and everything you can carry. And keep your eyes open for trillium. Got it?"

"Yes, sir," said Tripp in a dead serious tone.

"Oh, and if you see any food and water in there, grab it. We're gonna need that too."

Hector dropped the ship from space like a silent stone. He slipped in, landing behind what was left of the burned-out armory.

"Tombs are nearby," Hector said to Tripp. "Let's go."

"You guys ain't back in twenty minutes, we're leaving without you.

"Understood," Tripp and Hector said in unison.

"If we're not back in twenty minutes," said Hector. "We're not coming back."

"Keep your eyes and ears open out there," said Gage. "No heroics. Just get the shit and get out."

Tripp opened the hatch on the top of the ship, and he and Hector peered out. The area was cratered with bomb blasts, debris, a crashed Klix ship, and dead bodies—human and Klix.

"Looks like they tried to fight back," said Tripp.

"There were just too many and they had working weapons," replied Hector.

"You scared?" asked Tripp.

"Fuck no," said Hector. "You?"

"Fuck no."

They hesitated—neither moving forward—each taking a long look around the entire armory, taking in the devastation.

"You lyin'?" asked Hector.

"Fuck yes. You?"

"Hell yes," said Hector. "Poor souls didn't have a chance. I don't want to be one of 'em."

"Let's hurry," said Tripp. "I don't want to be one of 'em either."

They climbed down the ship's ladder and headed for the tombs double time. The tombs were underground with the entrance embedded in a small hill, hidden from view with a false front of bushes and shrubbery. Hector slashed at the bushes with his knife, revealing the enormous tritanium door.

"Looks like they didn't know about the tombs," said Hector. "Lucky for us.

"What's in there?" asked Tripp.

Hector smiled. "Anything and everything you could want for a kick ass Fourth of July party."

Tripp laughed. "I love pyrotechnics," he said. "Doors locked...of course. How we gonna get through that?"

"No problemo," said Hector, placing his combat knife in between the lock and the doorjamb.

"Stand back," he said, moving a few feet back.

Hector ran toward the door and jumped up and at the tritanium combat knife hilt from an angle, popping the door open in one thrust.

"Nicely done," said Tripp. "How'd you know that would work?"

"I used to sneak in here with one of the base nurses for a little R and R; super strong lock, super strong door, super stupid design; you know, government work."

"You dog!" said Tripp, laughing. "I didn't know you had it in you."

"I am a man of many talents," Hector said, smiling back. "As she would happily attest."

They climbed down the stairs into the pitch-black tombs. Hector took a lantern from a shelf in the corner and lit it, bathing the corridor in lamplight.

"It's not much, but I left it here in case I ever came back. Runs on rocket fuel. Kind of an antique, but it works."

"This is a whole side of you I never knew," said Tripp.

"There's a *lot* about me you don't know," said Hector. "I'm not just an extraordinary lover."

"And here comes the bullshit," said Tripp.

They walked into the main chamber of the tombs and saw munitions stacked up everywhere.

"Holy shit, it's Christmas," said Tripp. "MREs, water, guns, fuel, rockets...you name it, it's here."

"Grab all the food and water you can first. Take a laser pistol sidearm. These were underground and probably unaffected by the EMP. These tombs are basically a big tritanium box buried under this hill."

"Who are you?" asked Tripp. "What happened to Hector the lackadaisical fuckup brother of mine?"

"Eat me. Grab a gun and all the food and water you can carry. And check all the cabinets. They used to have some trillium stored down here. Shit lasts forever, so unless somebody stole it, should be some."

Tripp opened each tall steel cabinet, finding rifles, sidearms, grenades, and MREs. As he made his way deeper into the tombs, he found more cabinets. Tripp's bird vision kicked in, and he could see all the way to the end of the tombs even without Hector's lamp.

"Hector, you see that?"

"I can't see shit that ain't lit by this lantern," he replied.

"At the end of the hall—way in the back—is that cabinet glowing?"

"I see nothing but black. Go check it out," Hector said, offering him the lantern. "You need this?"

"Nah, I'm good. Be right back."

Tripp disappeared into the inky black tunnel.

"You okay?" asked Hector.

"Yeah, it's getting brighter back here."

Tripp moved closer to the glowing cabinet and threw open the steel door. Suddenly the back of the tunnel lit up as if Hector was standing there with the lantern.

"Holy shit, Hector...trillium! I think I found our Christmas tree and it's all lit up."

"Grab some and let's get the fuck out of here. Gage ain't gonna wait forever."

"Roger that; what size?"

"What size?"

"Yeah, there's three kinds in here: square, rectangular and pyramid-shaped. Which one?"

"Fuck if I know. Take one of each. One of them should work."

Tripp slipped three trillium blocks into his pockets, making sure they didn't rotate to the front of his pants—too close to his manhood.

I hope this shit don't make me sterile, he thought, pushing the figures into his pockets to the sides of his legs.

"Hurry up," said Hector. "We don't have all day."

Tripp began to sprint through the darkness, his pants lighting his way.

Hector laughed. "Are your pants glowing or are you just happy to see me?"

"Oh, you're a riot," said Tripp, fake laughing. "I will light your fire with what's in these pants, baby."

Hector laughed, and Tripp looked beyond him, with the extra light from his pants.

"Did you see this?" he asked, pulling a huge tarp away. "A four-wheeled ATV!"

"No shit. See if it has fuel."

"Fuel gauge says full."

"Let's load this sucker up. We're taking it back to the ship. It will handle the stairs easily."

"Roger that. That's how they got it in here."

They loaded up the ATV with food, water, and munitions before starting it up.

"Yep," said Hector, "if this thing starts, the guns will work too."

"Grab those ship-to-ship rockets and let's go. Ammo for the ship's guns is in those crates. Grab those and grab those jet fuel canisters—as many as we can fit."

"See this?" asked Tripp. "This thing has a trailer too!"

"Hook it up and load it up. We're not comin' back."

They hooked up the two-wheeled trailer loaded with munitions and fuel and took off up the stairs—bumping toward the door—with Tripp's pants and their lantern lighting the way.

"Back to the ship," said Tripp.

"One more thing" said Hector, tossing his jet fuel lantern back over his shoulder and down the steps into the tombs.

"Why you do that?" asked Tripp.

"Don't need it with your pants on board, and I don't want the Klix to get any shit from us."

"Who are you?" exclaimed Tripp. "I don't even know you anymore."

Hector smiled, and in a semi-serious narrator's voice, he said, "Lo and behold, his pants shall light the way."

"Hilarious," said Tripp.

"You might want to hurry up," said Hector, looking back to the now flaming stairs. "Ya know?"

They burst out of the door and onto the field, with Tripp gunning the engine back to the ship. Hector climbed up the ship's ladder as a huge fireball explosion nearly knocked him off his perch. He pushed the button to the cargo bay door, lowering the cargo ramp to the ground. Tripp drove the four-wheeler and trailer up the ramp and into the cargo bay.

"Santa's here kiddies!" Tripp shouted, jumping out of the driver's seat. "I have presents for all the good boys and girls... even you too, Gagey-poo."

"Will you quit clowning!" screamed Gage. "We gotta get out of here."

"You don't want to know what Santa brought you, grouchy ol' Gage?"

Gage looked at him sternly. Tripp smiled back and pointed to the trailer. "I brought you working laser rifles, pistols, and ship-to-ship missiles," he said, talking like he was an adult cheering up a child. "Wouldn't you like some *working* weapons for Christmas? You want some? Hmm? Dontcha?"

Gage held back a smile and then busted out laughing. "You're nuts, ya know. I don't know what fell into your DNA, but I think it was two cups crazy, and one cup loon."

"Ooh," Tripp continued, "somebody needs a naaaap."

Gage laughed more.

"I have treats and water for everyone," said Tripp, throwing MREs in their foiled pouches. "Fuel for our ship and one more thing..."

Tripp reached into his pockets and pulled out the glowing trillium pieces. "I hope you know I risked my future generations for you."

Gage smiled seeing the luminous blocks in his hand. "Good job, you two. If there still *was* a Corp, I'd promote you."

"Aw, crap," said Tripp. "I always wanted to be an officer... just not bossy like some people," he said, looking over at Gage. "But this was all Hector. I just went with him. If anyone should be promoted, it would be him."

"He's just sayin' that to get in my pants," said Hector, grinning. "And Tripp found the trillium with his bird eyes."

Tripp laughed and blew Hector a kiss, mouthing *oh yeah* to him.

"Everybody eat and drink something," said Gage. "I don't want anyone passing out. Hector, Tripp, get that fuel and the working munitions loaded before we get off the ground. That explosion will bring looky-loos for sure."

Evelyn stood at the back of the cargo bay with her arms crossed watching.

"Hey, Evelyn, I brought you something too," said Tripp.
"You did?"
"I found a whole shitload of chocolate."

"A whole shitload? You make it sound so appealing, especially after riding around in the sewers."

"No; I mean, yeah...a whole case. You want some?"

Tripp handed her a block of chocolate.

"Thank you," she said, biting off a big piece and then swallowing. "Oh my God, I almost forgot what chocolate tastes like."

"You're welcome, darlin'. There's plenty more."

"Yeah," she replied while chewing. "A shitload. I heard."

Glad you like it," he said. "Hey, Gage, want some? This is the good stuff."

"Thanks," said Gage, breaking off a piece. "You guys did well."

Everyone ate and drank quickly. Tripp and Hector dumped the display rocket models and attached the real rockets to the bow of the ship. Strip after strip of ammunition was fed into the *Lone Star*'s forward guns until the crates were empty. The fuel canisters were poured into the *Lone Star*'s thirsty engines, tossing the empties on the ground. By the time they were done, the laser cannons were charged and ready to go.

"We are ready to rock and roll," said Gage, stopping in mid-thought. "Wait...one more thing. Be right back."

Gage walked back to the engine room to the nuclear core with the new trillium blocks Tripp had given him. "This shit better be the real deal," he said, pushing the cube into the reactor receptacle.

The reactor core lights blinked on and remained steady.

"*Trillium core enabled,*" said the computer voice. "*Core initiation sequence begun.*"

Gage took a step back quickly.

"*Nuclear reactor at sixty percent,*" said the ship's computer.

"Hot damn, it's real!" Gage screamed. "We got our worm drive."

"*Nuclear reactor at eighty percent,*" said the ship's computer.

Gage ran back to the helm. "Nuclear reactor is online and charging. Everyone get ready. Hector, set a course for Europa. And get us the fuck back in space."

"Roger that," said Hector. "Europa, it is."

The ship took off vertically and reached space in less than twenty seconds. The engines belched out the last drops of diesel in black smoky puffs, then burned clear.

"*Alert: three Klix enemy vessels, scout class, approaching on an intercept vector, alert,*" blared the ship's computer.

"We've got company," Hector screamed.

"*Nuclear reactor at one hundred percent,*" said the ship's computer.

"Initiate wormhole. Everyone hold on and get ready to shield your eyes," said Gage. "This shit gets bright. Hit it, Hector."

Hector engaged the worm drive, and a milky-white mist bubble appeared in front of them. A Klix ship flew in behind them, firing a shot across the bow.

"I think they want us to stop," said Tripp.

"Fuck them," said Gage. "Now, Hector! Take us in. They won't follow; they don't know where we're going. They follow us in and they can end up anywhere in the universe."

Hector pushed the yoke forward, pushing the throttle to the max. The *Lone Star* lurched forward into the misty ball of spinning stars.

Chapter Thirteen

Europa, the Pwyll Crater

As Chase steered the Dragonfly closer to the dark side of Europa, he could see lights inside the Pwyll crater.

I'm not the first one here that's for sure, Chase thought. As he looked closer, he saw two ships parked just outside the station on opposite sides, a Quargg cargo ship and a Klix scout ship. *What's a Klix ship and a Quargg ship doin' here? They're sworn enemies.*

The Pwyll crater was enormous—almost twenty-five kilometers across—with many smaller but sizeable impact craters inside the main crater itself. The artificial atmosphere shield generated from the station was on, covering the entire crater and keeping it warm enough to melt the icy crust on the surface below it.

Chase turned off the Dragonfly's lights and slipped in behind a small mound of orange-brown silica sand inside one of the smaller craters. He opened the Dragonfly's canopy and took a breath.

At least I won't need this stupid breather, he thought, tossing it into the Dragonfly. *But I'll wear my hat; I like the hat.*

Chase placed his father's Stetson on his head and checked his guns. He crept up over the sand mound toward the station. As he passed one of the many smaller craters to his left, he heard a muffled scream. He peered over the top rim of the crater to get a better look. In the center, six Klix were holding a small, thin, female Quargg prisoner on her knees with her hands tied behind a square metal beam buried in the crater floor. A thick cord was tied around her waist, holding her upright against the pole. She was wearing a tight, flexible gray and black spacesuit that looked like a diver's wet suit. She had a large, hairless oval-round head with black almond eyes, yet Chase could tell she was sobbing. Some things are universal.

Dark green blood stained the sand around the pole, and she appeared to have been beaten. One of the Klix was on his knees and was taunting her and licking her face. The Quargg squirmed to free herself, screamed again, and then slumped forward. At first, the Klix were unaware of Chase as he walked up to them—pulling both guns.

"Let her go," he shouted, pointing each pistol, one left one right.

The Klix were surprised, shouting to each other in a frenzy of clicks. A Klix rifleman pulled his laser rifle and was about to shoot when Chase fired his left-hand .357, sending a bullet to the Klix chest. The rifleman flew backwards—firing into the air—with his black blood spurting from his chest wound.

"Anyone moves and they're next," Chase shouted. "Cut her loose."

The largest Klix, wearing captain insignia on his vest, spoke into his translator.

"Do not interfere with Klix affairs," he said. "You have no jurisdiction here."

"I'm going to count to three," said Chase. "If she is not freed by three, your captain here dies next."

Their captain scowled and called out an order to his men.

"Release the Quargg bitch," he clicked, using his translator for Chase's benefit.

The kneeling Klix untied her, and she staggered to her feet toward Chase. Chase offered her his arm, still holding his guns on the Klix.

"Can you walk?" Chase asked while she grabbed his arm.

"Yes," she replied weakly.

"Are you hurt?"

178

"They beat me, but I will live."

"Can you make it back to your ship?"

"I think so."

"Then get out of here. There may be more nearby."

"Who are you?" she asked as she started to walk away.

"Name's Chase, Chase 523 of Earth's Piecer Corp."

"Thank you, Piecer Chase 523. I will not forget this."

"Go...hurry!"

The Quargg female started walking fast, looked back, and then ran toward her ship. Chase held his guns pointed at the remaining Klix waiting until her ship took off before speaking to the Klix again.

"You scumbags always pick on girls?"

"Fuck you, Piecer," shouted the captain. "The Quargg bitch stole from us."

"*Stole* from you?" he asked. "One woman took something from a squad of Klix. Yeah, that's likely."

"She was stealing weapons from the station."

"Last time I checked, that's not your station. If anything, she was stealing from the Piecer Corp."

"When the Piecers disbanded, we claimed this station for the Klix Supremacy. She was taking from us. You know nothing."

"I know enough to know you're not supposed to hit girls, you fucking scumbags. And you, pervert—with your tongue out—all licking her face and shit, what the fuck is wrong with you? You're not supposed to beat or lick your prisoners."

Chase fired his left-hand .357 into the still-kneeling Klix's knee. The Klix fell over in pain, grabbing his knee squealing loud clicks, while the others clicked back and forth among themselves. The captain moved for his stinger pistol, and Chase pulled back the hammer on his right-hand pistol.

"You don't want to do that," he said. "He'll live. Tend to his wounds or whatever you scumbags do."

The Klix captain clicked an order to the Klix soldier standing closest to the wounded Klix writhing on the ground. He leaned over, pulling a long blade from his side and then sliced open the injured Klix neck. The injured Klix stopped moving, and his attacker wiped his blade in the sand to clean off his blood. The captain then turned back to Chase.

"You didn't have to shoot our engineer," he clicked into his translator.

"You didn't have to slit his throat, either."

"A wounded man is of no use to us. We gave him honor to die on the battlefield."

"Tell you what...you don't torture people and I won't shoot your engineer. How's that?"

"You're a fool. Do you think our ship is not monitoring us? Do you think we will let you leave here alive?"

"I'll take my chances," Chase said, tipping his hat back with the barrel of his .357 for a better view. "Now, I'll be leaving, and remember, anyone moves and your captain here dies first. So simple even you idiots can understand."

Can't fight them all now, he thought. *Not with these weapons. I don't even know how many there are...*

Chase walked backward keeping his guns trained on the captain in front of him, hoping to clear the sand mound before any other Klix showed up. As he reached the crest of the smaller crater backing up, he saw a dozen Klix appear on the opposite side.

The captain click-screamed, pointing at Chase.

The Klix pulled their weapons and began firing. Chase emptied his left pistol, killing four Klix in a flurry of fire. The new squad charged forward, and Chase jumped and rolled behind the sand mound to a kneeling position. Chase fired his right-hand pistol as fast as he could, killing another four Klix.

The eight remaining Klix hid behind rocks on the crater floor, firing their laser weapons as quickly as they could. Chase pulled the trigger of his .357 in his left hand, and it clicked. He tried the right and it clicked. He reached around his gun belt for more cartridges—loading each gun quickly—while taking the occasional shot to keep the aliens at bay. Once fully loaded, Chase jumped up and started firing, taking down three more Klix before his guns were empty again and the hammers were clicking against already spent shells. Chase ducked back down behind the sand mound. There was a long uneasy silence until the Klix Captain spoke.

"Your weapons are empty," the officer shouted. "I think we will torture you to death. Yes...that would amuse me. I will slowly peel your skin from your body, Piecer. We destroyed your kind on Earth and now? Now you are alone. Your planet will be ours soon, and you can do nothing. Your last thoughts will be how you failed."

"There must be some universal rule," Chase mumbled to himself, "that says assholes must blather on. Blah, blah, blah, I'm going to kill you, blah, blah, blah, you will suffer. It's like they all have the same shitty speech writer."

"Time to die, Piecer; you have no weapons. There is nothing you can do."

Chase reached around his back, pulling the tiny derringer tucked in his belt. Standing up, he pointed it at the Klix.

"I have this," he said, pulling out the tiny gun Max had given him.

"What's that?" asked the Klix, pointing and laughing. "An Earth toy?"

"This?" said Chase showing the weapon to them. "This is little boom-boom."

All the Klix started click-laughing.

"There are five of us. What do you think you are going to do with that?"

"I'm going to kill you all...unless you back the hell out of here."

They all laughed again.

"I'm going to count to three," Chase said out loud, aiming the tiny pistol at them, "and if you don't go back to your ship, you will die right here—right now."

"Then you have three seconds to live, Piecer fool. You cannot kill us all with a toy."

"You're wrong about that. Better make peace with your god if you have one."

I hope this thing works, Chase thought. *Or I'm in deep*

shit.

The captain muted his translator and clicked to his men. His men nodded and smiled nervously, looking at Chase.

"One..." said Chase out loud, pulling the trigger of the tiny gun.

A mini-bullet rocket flew out of the barrel with a popping sound. He moved backward, hoping to put some distance between himself, the Klix, and the mini rocket.

The Klix watched, first with surprise and then amusement. The tiny missile-bullet flew directly at them, and then—just before it reached its target—flew straight up above the Klix and out of sight. The Klix started click-laughing; some doubled over and pointed at the sky.

"Stupid Piecer, your little toy gun missed."

Suddenly, a screaming whine grew louder and louder as it approached them from above until the tiny missile flew down into the ground in the middle of them. Their eyes followed the missile down for a second until a huge explosion sent them, the dirt, and rocks flying in all directions. The Klix lay dead or dying around a small crater made by the blast.

Chase walked up to the bleeding captain who was gasping, taking his last breaths.

"I thought—I thought you were going to count to three," he clicked into his translator. His hand slumped from the translator, and his head fell to his chest as he died.

"I lied," said Chase, staring at the still-smoking pistol.

I owe Max for this one.

Chase put the tiny gun back behind his belt and headed out of the small crater and back toward the station's lights. He passed the Klix ship—its lights still on—and its engines putting out a low hum.

I wonder if there is anyone left on board, he thought, keeping a close eye on the ship. *I guess I'll find out soon enough...but first things first.*

The abandoned station was dug into the side of the Pwyll crater wall. It was fully operational, generating the heated, oxygenated atmosphere bubble all around them, and providing inside and outdoor lighting. Someone had obviously been inside to activate the station's systems. Chase proceeded cautiously, pulling his combat knife—his only remaining weapon.

He crept inside the open giant metal door of the station, looking for fuel and ammo for the *Promise*. Inside, stacks of weapon boxes were smashed open, their contents looted. It appeared that some of the station's weapons had already been taken and the thief had been interrupted before they could clear out. Pallet upon pallet of weapons remained intact, and Chase smiled. He pulled a laser rifle from one of the crates and shot it at the ceiling. A huge chunk of rock crashed to the floor and broke into pieces.

"They work, but we're gonna need fuel too."

The station was large, with tunnels extending underground in all directions. Rooms filled with munitions, fuel, food, and water lined the corridors. Chase found the radio room and contacted the *Promise*.

On board the *Promise,* a transmission came through.

"Sheen, Max, can you hear me...over?" came Chase's voice.

"We can hear you, Commander," Sheen replied.

"Loud and clear, Chase," said Max.

"Commander, you are unhurt?" asked Sheen.

"I'm fine. Everything we need is here. Land the *Promise* at these coordinates and we'll fill her up."

"Yes, Commander," Sheen said, smiling.

A sudden blast from the *Promise*'s computer interrupted them. "*Alert, the Piecer vessel Lone Star approaching, alert!*"

"Commander, the Piecer vessel *Lone Star* has appeared," said Sheen.

"Have they contacted you?"

"No," replied Sheen. "They only just emerged from a wormhole."

"Hail them. Find out who is on board. We need all the help we can get."

The *Lone Star* activated their weapon systems, pointing them at the *Promise*. Sheen hit the com button. "*Lone Star* ship, this is the Piecer ship *Promise*, under the command of Chase 523. You have raised your weapons. Identify yourself or we will destroy you."

Max muted the mic. "Our secondary guns are live, Sheen," he said. "But that's all we got for now. If they fire a shot, try to take 'em out...before they take us out."

"Understood," Sheen replied.

"This is Gage 523, of the Piecer ship *Lone Star*. Good to see you again, Chase."

Sheen hit the com button again. "Captain of the *Lone Star*, this is Sheen—in temporary command of the *Promise*. Commander Chase is on Europa at the Pwyll Station."

A sudden squawk from the radio interrupted them. "Gage, you made it!" said Chase, cutting in from the planet. "Looks like you found a ship of your own. Well done."

"Rendezvousing as ordered, Chief; how can we help?"

"Tripp and Hector okay?"

"They're fine. Tripp took one in the chest, but he's healed. Hector's okay...oh, and Chase, we have a passenger."

"There's fuel, provisions and munitions down here. You can follow the *Promise* down so you can stock up. You won't need breathers either; the atmosphere bubble is operational. You can introduce me to your passenger when you get here."

"Roger that," said Gage. "Down in a minute."

"Oh, and Gage..." said Chase, "you'll see a Klix ship parked nearby. I think it's unmanned, but be careful."

"Roger that," said Gage. "We're headed down now."

The *Lone Star* followed the *Promise*'s trajectory down to the Pwyll crater and landed just north of the area the Quargg prisoner had been held. Tripp, Hector, and Gage grabbed weapons and headed down the cargo bay ramp toward the station.

"Look alive," said Gage. "No tellin' what's out there."

As they walked toward the station, Gage, Tripp, and Hector saw the blood stains and blackened, half-melted iron beam, now standing bent over in the sand. Dead Klix bodies and body parts were strewn everywhere in a blast radius of the melted iron.

"Looks like Chase was here already," said Tripp. "Must be a dozen dead Klix."

"Eighteen that I could see," Hector corrected. "If you count body parts!"

"Grab any translators that are operational," said Gage. "We may need 'em."

Hector and Tripp picked through the remains, gathered up the few translators they could find that worked, and then headed into the station. Gage walked in, looked around and saw no one.

"We sure that was Chase on the com?" Gage asked.

"It was him," said Tripp.

"Him," followed Hector.

Suddenly, from behind them, someone yelled, "Freeze!"

Chapter Fourteen

The Passengers

They turned slowly around to find Chase smiling at them.

"You fucker, I nearly shit myself," said Gage, grabbing him and hugging him.

Tripp and Hector grabbed him too.

"I knew you were too ornery to die!" said Hector.

"Good to see you, Cha-Cha," said Tripp.

"Heard you took one in the chest," Chase replied, looking for a wound.

"Yeah, no big thing, but you get shot with a laser rifle and it sears a hole right through you. I could see right through me. Hurt like a motherfucker, too."

"Glad you're okay. I actually missed you guys."

"Aww...there you go getting all mushy on us," said Hector.

"I told you he loves us," said Tripp. "Mostly me, but you too—a little."

"So who's this Sheen in command of your ship?" asked Gage.

"Some asshole was holding her prisoner on Titan; she's a Courtesan."

"A courte-what?"

"A Courtesan; kinda like a sex robot, but an android...a person, not really a robot. She's my passenger. Long story.

She saved my life. I'll tell you after we empty the station."

Hector and Tripp looked at each other wide-eyed and stared.

Chase snapped his fingers in front of them twice. "Okay, you two," said Chase, "stop thinking about Sheen, and get back to business."

"Right," said Tripp. "Sorry. We hit an armory before we left Earth. Got tons of goodies, but you can't have too much ammo."

"Nice," said Chase. "I was out of ammo and fuel—dead in the water until Max showed up. No weapons, no worm drive, nothin'. I thought it was the end of the line."

"Who's Max?"

"He's my genius stowaway. He's a Fixer."

"A stowaway and you didn't shoot him?"

"Almost did," said Chase, laughing. "Lucky I didn't."

"Eighteen dead Klix...looks like you been busy," said Hector.

"I was lucky Max gave me this." Chase pulled out the tiny pistol and showed it to them. "Saved my life."

Tripp burst out laughing. "What the *hell* is that?"

"Max called it 'little boom-boom.'"

"Does it work?"

"You see that crater full of dead Klix?" They nodded. "Little boom-boom."

"You're shittin' me!"

"I shit you not, Gage..."

"Can I get one? I gotta meet this guy. I want one."

"You can ask him. If you need anything fixed on your ship, Max is your guy."

Gage moved closer to Chase, keeping his voice low. "You check out that Klix ship yet?" he asked. "Should we be worried?"

"Not yet; I wanted to get supplies to the *Promise*. I don't like my crew floating around in space like a sitting duck."

"Tripp, Hector," said Gage, "check out that Klix ship...and don't get fancy out there."

"Roger that," said Tripp, "nothin' fancy; just our usual fabulous job. Check."

"Don't wait up," replied Hector, heading out the door with Tripp.

"I don't like those knuckleheads out there alone," said Gage. "If they're not back soon, I'm going after them."

"We'll both go after them," said Chase. "But I haven't seen any more Klix. It's been quiet since I got inside the station."

Hector and Tripp ran to the Klix ship, approaching the hatch from opposite sides. They could hear the low hum of the engines and could see the ship's lights were on and operational. A ladder was down and the hatch open.

"Let's just knock on the door and see who answers," said Tripp.

Hector moved to the left of the open hatch, while Tripp climbed the ladder. "Direct and crazy," said Hector. "I like it."

Tripp banged his rifle butt on the hull surrounding the hatch door. There was no response.

"Whaddya think?" asked Hector.

"I think Chase already took care of this crew."

Tripp climbed into the alien craft, checking left and right before calling to Hector.

"All clear so far; c'mon up."

Tripp and Hector moved through the ship, deck by deck. The ship's power supply pulsed in the background.

"It's a worm-drive ship, for sure," said Hector. "I have no idea what all this alien shit means, but it looks like it to me."

"I don't read Klix," said Tripp.

"You got one of those translators?" asked Hector.

"Yep...why?"

"Hold it up to the writing and watch the screen. It'll translate that crap."

Tripp held the translator in front of the console buttons. As he passed over the alien labels, English words appeared on the screen: Initiate Trans-Warp Sequence.

"I told you this was a worm-drive ship," said Hector.

"Fucking Klix," said Tripp. "We should blow it up. There have to be some explosives at the station we can use."

"No. Before we blow it up, we need to see what Chase and Gage want us to do with it. Worm-drive ships are hard to come by, even if it is a Klix ship."

"Shit, I want to blow it up," Tripp said, spitting on it.

"Maybe later," said Hector. "Not without orders."

"How 'bout that sex robot?" said Tripp. "You believe that shit? He called her Sheen... said she was a Courtesan."

"So I heard!" replied Hector. "Said she saved his life, too."

Tripp laughed. "She can save me too—over and over again."

"Me too," said Hector. "But I'll go first, I don't want your sloppy seconds."

"Excuse me? My seconds are never sloppy."

"Uh-huh...nothin' here; let's go."

Tripp and Hector double-timed it back to the station, running inside through the station's door. Gage and Chase were busy checking supplies when they heard footsteps rapidly approaching. Gage dropped down to one knee, taking aim with his laser rifle, while Chase instinctively pulled both pistols forgetting they were empty.

"Whoa, whoa, whoa...we come in peace!" said Tripp, raising his hands.

"Find anything?" asked Gage.

"Nada," replied Tripp, shaking his head. "Ship's empty but fully functional."

"It's a Klix version of a worm-drive ship," said Hector. "They call it trans-warp. You musta killed the crew, Boss."

"Can I blow it up?" asked Tripp.

"No," said Chase, "maybe we can use her."

"Use her?" asked Gage. "For *what*?"

"Not sure yet. First, I need to take care of my crew."

Chase pressed the button on the station's radio, contacting the *Promise*.

"Sheen, Max, the station's all clear. Come on in and meet

the guys. We been dodging bullets and bad guys for long enough; time to take a break, eat some dinner, and resupply."

"Yes, Commander," Sheen replied. "I will inform Max."

"We have a jeep and trailer if that helps," Tripp interrupted. "You can haul a lot of this stuff out to the *Promise* in one run."

"That's great," said Chase. "That'll help."

"I can bring Evelyn too," said Tripp.

"Evelyn?" asked Chase. "Who's Evelyn?"

"Our passenger," said Gage. "I told you over the com we had a passenger. She's Tupi's granddaughter, Evelyn."

"Eve," Chase said to himself, too low to hear.

Gage snapped his fingers twice in front of Chase's face. Chase stared straight ahead, lost in thought.

"You okay? Where'd you go?"

"Oh, yeah…I'm fine. Yes, everyone should meet here."

"Hector, can you still cook?" asked Chase.

"Not much to cooking MREs," said Hector, "just heat 'em and eat 'em, but I'll try to make it nice for everyone."

"Could be our last decent meal for a while," said Chase. "We could use a little recharge ourselves."

"On my way," said Tripp. "Back as soon as I get the trailer hooked up to the jeep again."

Tripp exited the station while Hector gathered supplies, placing them on a table in the mess hall. Then he began foraging through the station for supplies.

"Hey! They have a kitchen," Hector yelled. "Won't be hard to cook this up."

Hector disappeared into the kitchen, and the sounds of pots and pans clanging in the background echoed through the halls.

"You have a plan?" Gage asked Chase.

"Nope; just a mission."

"And that is?"

"First, we're going to rid the Earth of the Klix once and for all, and then I promised myself I'd find my parents and my brother, Loose, if they're still alive."

"Any ideas?"

"Still percolating," said Chase.

Just then, Sheen and Max walked inside the station.

"We are here, Commander—per your request," said Sheen.

Gage stopped and stared at Sheen. "Well, who is this *lovely* creature?" he asked, smiling.

"This is Sheen," said Chase. "My passenger and new first officer I told you about."

"Well, it is my deepest pleasure to meet you," said Gage, grinning ear to ear.

Here we go again, thought Chase. "Sheen is a Courtesan," he said, introducing her.

"I am Courtesan," Sheen repeated.

"You can stop drooling," said Chase. "Max already beat you to it."

"Oh...sorry, Max, is this your lady?"

"I wish. We're just crewmates. I'm Max," he said, extending his hand out to shake.

"Name's Gage," he replied, shaking Max's hand. "I heard a lot about you already."

"Anything good?"

"All good. I hear you're a Fixer."

"I am."

"Tell me about that little gun you gave Chase. He said it saved his life."

"Oh, it did, did it? Glad to hear it. A little boom-boom can come in handy when you need it."

Max smiled and laughed as he explained how it worked. He soon realized Gage wasn't listening and was staring at Sheen.

"So what exactly *is* a Courtesan?" Gage asked Max.

Max explained and Gage's eyes widened as he turned and stared at Sheen. "For real?"

Max shook his head left and right.

"Have you?"

Max shook his head left and right again.

"Has he?"

"No; the stupid shit said he wouldn't."

"You gonna?"

"Gonna try."

"Mind if I try?"

"Not at all—if she'll let you."

Gage and Max stared at Sheen and then resumed their conversation. Sheen walked up to Chase and waved her hand over him, scanning him for injury.

"Are you hurt, Commander? Were you damaged?"

She finished her scan and then gently touched and prodded his shoulders, arms and chest—checking for wounds. Chase laughed.

"Whatcha doin? I'm fine," he said. "Really; not a scratch."

Sheen smiled broadly. "My system was malfunctioning while you were gone. It has not happened before."

"Shouldn't I be scanning you, then?" asked Chase, laughing. "Are you okay?"

"I do not know. I was twitchy while you were gone, and I could not focus my thoughts."

"Twitchy? You mean nervous?"

"I do not know what nervous feels like. I was concerned that you needed me, Commander...that I failed you somehow."

"You didn't fail me. I asked you to stay behind and you did. Thank you."

Sheen smiled again. "I feel like I am malfunctioning again, Commander."

"I think we all need a little rest and some food, Sheen. Let me introduce you to Hector—he's cooking up some food for the crew."

They walked into the kitchen off the main corridor. Hector was ripping open foil packets of MREs and dumping their contents into bowls.

"Hector, this is Sheen, my first officer."

"Holy shi—Señorita, I am Hector—at your service. It is

very nice to meet you," he said while taking her hand and kissing it.

"Okay, Casanova, back off. Sheen's not on the menu."

"Do you wish me to service him, Commander?"

"No, Sheen."

"He appears to be aroused."

"He's always like that. Vegetables arouse this guy."

"What does service mean?" said Hector. "Does it mean what I *hope* it means?"

"Never mind," said Chase. "Sheen is adjusting to her independence. She and Max were prisoners on Titan."

Sheen looked at Hector and gestured toward Chase. "My Commander saved me from the Quargg and Shoom."

"Your Commander?" asked Hector.

"Yes. Commander Chase is my Commander."

Hector looked at Sheen and then stared at Chase. "Are you shittin' me?" asked Hector, his brow furrowed.

"It's a long story," said Chase. "I'll tell you over dinner."

"Can I be of service to you, Hector?"

"Yes!" he replied immediately.

"She means do you need any help preparing the dinner, Lover Boy. I'll be over there, Sheen," said Chase, "talking to Gage and Max, if you need me."

"Yes, Commander."

"Oh. Okay," said Hector. "I guess I *could* use some help. I've got a big pot of boiling noodles. Maybe you can help me get that over to the table. There are some oven mitts over here. I'll take one handle and you take..."

Sheen reached over and grabbed the still-boiling pot of noodles, carried it to the table and returned. "Can I be of any further assistance?" she asked.

Hector stood staring. "That wasn't too hot for you, or too heavy?"

"Oh, it was very hot. You have done well, Hector," she replied, patting Hector on the shoulder.

"That was fifty pounds of boiling water and noodles," said Hector.

"Twenty-three point five eight kilograms, approximately—at one hundred degrees Celsius," Sheen replied. "This is cooking, is it not?"

"Yes. Um, you never cooked before?"

"No. I have never been tasked for cooking."

"What have you been tasked for?"

"I am Sheen. I have been tasked as Courtesan. I am expert in all forms of sexual expression. Do you need further assistance?"

Hector stared at her, stunned, searching for any part of her that looked mechanical or robotic.

"Um...uh...you can help me set the table, if you don't mind."

"I will gladly help you, crewman Hector," Sheen said, reaching out to shake hands. "It is nice to meet you."

"Thank you," said Hector, lingering over their handshake feeling her skin. "And thank you for helping me."

Hector and Sheen brought the food to the table with plates and settings for seven people. Sheen sat down and then suddenly jumped up from the table. Pulling a laser rifle, she aimed it at the door. "Commander! Two life forms are approaching; one is armed."

Chapter Fifteen

Meet Me in the Woods

Tripp returned with the jeep and trailer and walked into the Pwyll station with Evelyn Tupi. As he walked through the station door, Tripp saw Sheen holding a laser rifle and jumped in front of Evelyn to shield her.

"Whoa, whoa, whoa...why is it whenever I walk into a room, people are pointing guns at me?" asked Tripp. "We're *friendlies!*" he shouted.

"It's okay, Sheen, they're with us," said Chase.

"Yes, Commander," said Sheen, leaning the laser rifle against the wall and sitting down again.

"Who the fuck is that?" asked Tripp, still standing in front of Evelyn.

"This is Sheen," replied Chase. "She's my first officer."

"Sheen, this is Tripp, and..."

Evelyn stood behind Tripp, trembling. As she recognized Chase's voice, her heart started beating faster, and her palms began to sweat.

What am I going to say? she thought. *What can I say? What if he doesn't remember me? What if he hates me?*

Six years earlier, there was little thought of another war. The years had gone by quickly and only the monuments to the Sixers and vast cemeteries remained to remind people of what happened. The Corp continued to breed and train young men for service, but as time went on, cadets thought

197

more about outside activities and women, especially.

Unless a cadet was placed in a foster family where a "normie" female sister lived, Piecer cadets had little or no experience with girls or women, other than their foster mothers. There was little time devoted to sex education at the Piecer Academy, simply because the cadets were discouraged from any relationships with the opposite sex.

Of course, these extra-normal young men—like all young men—bragged constantly about their conquests, both real and imagined. Loose was an especially loud braggart about the girls he had met and how they worshiped him. He would tell the others that he was dating three girls at a time and that he was having sex with all of them. Chase never believed him. He knew Loose was at home, in his room alone, and that he rarely left. He didn't really have any friends and certainly no girlfriends.

Chase never thought much about sex or women; to Chase, girls were for "normies." He didn't understand all the hoopla, and if it didn't relate to his mission, he didn't care. To him, the Piecer Corp was everything, and the Corp was about the mission. There was no time for anything else until the unexpected happened.

It was fall, and some of the trees were starting to change color. It was getting cooler and the sun was setting earlier; a perfect day for a run, a perfect day for a race. Now that the boys were older, Martin would let them run the woods alone—as long as they were home in time for dinner.

Chase had just turned sixteen, and he and Loose started the day as usual, taunting each other. Loose was feeling especially cocky that day so he bet Chase his dessert that he would beat him across the woods. Chase smiled and teased him.

"I feel bad beating you *and* eating your dessert too, but if you're dumb enough to bet me, I'm man enough to win."

"Not today," said Loose. "I'm gonna crush you like a bug."

The boys were both wearing shorts and a rugged type of boot-sneaker combination developed by the Corp for training that the cadets called 'beakers' or 'beaks' for short. The shoes were comfortable and solid—laced with a rubber wire combination—with sturdy rubber cleats that absorbed impact to the foot and legs while digging into obstacles for sure footing.

"Count of three," said Loose. "You ready?"

"Ready. I can already taste it."

"One, two..."

Chase was ready and in position to take off running. He planted his feet and rubber cleats firmly in the soil, making sure there were no leaves or twigs under him to cause him to slip. Loose did the same next to him, but just before starting off, he reached over and pulled Chase's shorts to his ankles.

"Three!" he yelled, taking off laughing.

Chase took off on three, not realizing what had happened and fell forward.

"Oh, you fucking cheat," he screamed, laughing and stumbling, picking his shorts up. "You will pay for that."

Loose had a good head start on him now, but the woods were Chase's domain. He knew every trail, path, log, stream and tree. He flew left of Loose, running down the stream that meandered through the woods. It was wet and slippery, and he knew he had to be more careful. But he didn't want to lose—not to Loose—especially after he cheated.

Flying down the stream, he knew he would beat Loose easily, but as he turned a bend in the creek, he caught a glimpse of something blue out of the corner of his eye. He looked back briefly to see what it was. When he turned back, he wasn't ready for the low limb which he instantly ducked, or the rock in the stream that he deftly jumped over, or the patch of wet leaves that sent him flying face first into the soggy creek bed. He landed with a loud *whump*, slid for a dozen feet, and then stopped. He struggled for air for a moment or two and turned over on his back, pulling his head out of the water. Looking up—silhouetted by the sun through the trees—stood a beautiful young woman, her blond hair glistening from the sunlight behind her. She looked like an angel.

"You okay?" she asked, holding out her hand to help him up.

Chase pulled himself together quickly, embarrassed and not wanting to look weak in front of a girl.

"I'm fine," he said. "Happens all the time."

"Really?" she said, smiling. "Looks painful."

She moved closer, and Chase took her hand. When their fingers touched, he felt an unfamiliar tingle; a pleasant electricity. He marveled at the softness of her skin and how tiny and slender her hand and fingers were compared to his. He didn't want to let go.

"I'll be fine," he said, pulling himself up and releasing her hand.

"I'm Eve," she said.

"Chase," he replied, holding out a soggy hand to shake.

"Nice to meet you, Chase," she said. "Where you goin' in such a hurry?"

"Oh, nowhere...not going anywhere, really, just runnin', racin' my brother."

Chase looked back up the creek and to the woods where his brother would be headed.

"Probably lost by now, though."

"Oh, too bad. Gentlemen's bet?"

"No, we bet dessert."

"Ouch. Sorry to hear that."

"It's okay. Have to let him win sometimes."

"Oh, you let him win, huh...by falling in the creek?" Eve laughed. "Good strategy," she said, laughing harder. "Though you *might* want to consider just running slower."

Chase stared at her beautiful face, her smile, and the way the light sparkled on her shoulder-length blond hair. She was wearing a short baby blue sun dress and was carrying her shoes so they wouldn't get wet in the creek. Eve caught him staring at her not responding.

"I said you might want to just go slower...in the race... against your brother."

Chase laughed, realizing how ridiculous his explanation was and that he was staring, so he decided to go with his story.

"Oh, he'd never believe that. I always beat him. If I just slowed down, he would know. I had to come up with something to fool him, and that is why I dove into the creek bed face first."

"Really? So it was your plan all along?"

"Absolutely," he said.

"Well, I have to say...that was one of the best executions of a plan that I have seen in a long time. You actually looked like you slipped and fell flat on your face. Fooled me completely."

"All part of my plan—in case he saw me," said Chase, blowing on his knuckles and polishing them on his shirt. "I'm practically a strategic genius."

God, I sound like an idiot, Chase thought.

Eve smiled, turned around, held up part of her dress over one leg—as if keeping it from hanging in the water—and started skimming her foot back and forth over the top of the water in the creek bed.

"Practically," she said with a wry smile.

Chase was still dripping, and wiped his face with his arm.

"Isn't it wonderful?" she asked.

"What?"

"The woods; it's so beautiful here."

Chase stared at her willowy figure, her dress backlit by the sun as she stepped through the stream, splashing and laughing.

"It is," he said. "It's my favorite place."

"Mine too," she said, stopping. "It's magical, don't you think?"

Staring, he swallowed hard, his throat dry. "It is. I sometimes come out here just to think...to clear my head."

"And what do you think about when you come here?"

Chase paused for a moment, thinking about what would sound good. "Mostly about stuff, you know."

Oh my God, he thought. *What is wrong with me? 'Mostly about stuff?' I'm a moron.*

Eve swirled her toe across the top of the water. "Are you hungry?"

"Starving," he said. "I skipped lunch today."

"I have a sandwich I didn't eat. You want it?"

Eve walked over to the log she'd been sitting on when Chase had run by. She opened the lid of her picnic basket, pulled out a sandwich, and handed it to him.

"It's some kind of meat. I stopped asking a long time ago."

"Thanks," he said. "You sure you don't want it?"

"No; I ate before I came out. I just brought it in case I got hungry."

Chase sat down on the opposite side of the log.

"I don't bite," she said.

"What?"

"I don't bite."

Chase paused mid-chew, looking at her over his sandwich. "Never said ya did!"

"Kinda hard to talk when you're on the other side of the log."

"I can hear you. I have really good hearing."

Eve crossed her long legs, and leaned back, eyes closed. "I just love it here," she said. "I come here all the time."

"You do? I never saw ya."

"I try to. I try to come at least once a week—just to soak it all in."

Chase finished his sandwich in two bites and looked around. "Yeah, it's a nice spot," he said, chewing .

He looked over at Eve, the sun streaming on her smiling face. "It *is* beautiful here," he said staring, "peaceful, ya know?"

"You want some cake?" she asked. "You should be rewarded."

"Rewarded? Rewarded for what?"

"You know, for being so nice to your brother...for letting

202

him win by falling on your face."

Chase laughed. "Oh yeah, that. You're right. I should."

Eve pulled out a piece of chocolate cake from her basket. "You mind if we share?"

"'Course not. It's your cake," said Chase.

"Do you mind my germs?" she asked. "I only have one fork. I don't have cooties or anything."

"Oh, I don't mind. I don't really get sick."

Eve laughed and sat down next to him with the cake on a paper plate and one fork. "How come I've never seen you at school?" she asked.

The words that stumbled out of his mouth surprised him. "I'm...I'm home schooled," he said, stuttering.

"Oh, that would be nice. I hate my school. Everyone there is so cliquey."

"Yeah," said Chase nodding, having no clue what she was talking about. "I hate cliquey stuff."

"Me too," said Eve. "People can be so mean for no reason."

"People are mean to you?"

"Sometimes."

"Why?"

"My grandfather says it's because I'm pretty."

"You are pretty, that's for sure."

"Thanks," she said, turning away smiling. "That's nice of you to say."

"You probably hear that a lot."

"Sometimes, but it's more important what's inside."

"Most people probably never get past your outsides, I guess," he replied, trying not to stare.

"They're not looking," she replied. "They see pretty and think, 'dumb.'"

"I can see why," he said, quickly correcting himself, "not the dumb part, the pretty part."

Eve laughed. Chase took one last long look at Eve and stood up.

"Well, it's getting late," he said. "I should get going before

I'm in trouble."

"Maybe I'll see you the next time you race your brother," said Eve.

"Maybe...usually don't come this way, though—you know, too slippery."

"Right, yeah, you wouldn't want to slip and fall, unless that's your plan."

Chase smiled. "Right."

"I'll see you around, then? Nice meeting you, Chase."

"Umm, me too, Eve. Thanks for the sandwich...and the cake, too."

Eve gathered her picnic basket and turned before heading away from the log. "Catch you later, Chase," she said, smiling over her shoulder.

Chase waved; staring for a moment, then took off for home knowing he had lost the race and not caring. All along the way home, he couldn't get his mind off of Eve. When he arrived, Loose taunted him.

"Hey, loser...I beat you by an hour. You suck."

"Yeah; whatever," said Chase, waving him off.

"I get your dessert."

"I know. You won...you can have it, even if you did cheat."

Loose looked at him sideways. "You don't care?"

"Not really. I already had a dessert—in the woods. I met someone."

"Who?"

"Nobody. Just a girl named Eve."

"Eve who?"

"I don't know...just Eve."

"You liar. What she look like?"

"On a scale of one to ten, she was a twenty."

"Bullshit!"

"Okay; bullshit."

Chase walked off in a daze, heading to his room.

"Where?" asked Loose. "How old was she? You're lyin'. Mom, Chase is making shit up."

Chase never told Loose where he met Eve. All day every

day, she was all he could think about. When they would go out for a run and Loose would challenge him to a race, Chase would always agree. As soon as Loose was out of sight, he would veer off to the creek just to see if Eve was there.

A week went by and he didn't see her, then one day, there she was—on the same log with her picnic basket. She was lying on her back, simply staring up at the sky, her long blond hair spilling over the log like molten gold. She was wearing faded blue jean overalls, a tight form-fitting white t-shirt and "beaks." Chase walked up to her from the brush.

"Hi, Chase," she said, squinting. "That you?"

"The one and only!" he said, fumbling for words.

"I brought you a sandwich and a piece of cake...two forks this time," she said, smiling.

"Hey...thanks. How'd you know I'd be here?"

"I didn't, but I hoped so."

She hoped so? he thought, his heart beating faster.

"I hoped you'd be here too," he said. "I liked running into you the other day."

"I think you like my cake," Eve said, teasing.

"No," said Chase quickly, realizing too late that she was just kidding.

Chase walked up to the log and sat down next to her. "I ran by here every day to see if you were here," he confessed.

"You did? I wish I had known, but I sometimes have a hard time getting away."

"You do? Why?"

"My grandfather is very protective of me. He doesn't like me going out alone."

"He's a smart man. You probably shouldn't be out alone."

"Oh, I can take care of myself...and besides," she said smiling, "I'm not alone, am I?"

Chase smiled back, and they talked and talked until just before dusk.

"Are you going to be here again?" he asked.

"Whenever I can. I can usually slip out on Wednesdays. Are you?"

"Whenever I can."

They stared at each other for a moment, looking into each other's eyes.

"Will your boyfriend be mad that you're out here with me?" Chase asked clumsily.

"What makes you think I have a boyfriend?"

"You're too pretty not to have a boyfriend."

"Well, I don't...at least not anymore. Most boys are just too dumb, and some are just nasty."

Chase smiled again. "It's getting dark," he said. "Let me walk you back through the woods. Make sure you get home okay."

"You don't have to. I really can take care of myself."

Chase was feeling playful, bold, and protective. "What if someone comes up behind you like this?"

He grabbed Eve from behind, locking his arm around the front of her shoulders. Eve immediately jabbed him in the stomach with her elbow and flipped him on the ground in front of her. Chase was stunned and embarrassed.

"Sorry!" said Eve. "My training kicked in."

"Training...what training?"

"My grandfather made sure I took martial arts. I'm pretty good at defending myself."

"I'll say. That was a great move."

"Thanks. Did I hurt you?"

"Nah, I can take it."

Chase got up and brushed himself off. "Well, what happens when someone comes at you from the front..." he said, pretending to lunge forward.

As he got closer, Eve grabbed him by his shirt and rolled backward on the ground, pushing him up and over with her leg. Chase landed with a thud on his back behind her.

"Ugh," said Chase. "I give."

Eve jumped on top of him, pinning his arms down. "I win," she said. "See! I can take care of myself."

"Oh really," said Chase, laughing.

He spun his arms around hers and rolled to the right. Eve

rolled with him, and soon, Chase was on top of her. He held her arms to the ground.

"You have to always be ready," he said, "or they'll getcha."

Eve lay back on the ground, panting from her fight. She looked up at him and smiled. "You're very good," she said. "Let me tell you something," she said whispering.

"What?"

"I need my arms," she said.

"Oh; sorry," he said, getting off her arms but still straddling her waist.

"I have a secret," she whispered softly, cupping her mouth in her hand but still too low to hear.

"You have a *what*?"

"I have a *secret*," she whispered again even lower than before. "Come closer and I'll tell you."

Chase moved in close, putting his ear next to her hand and mouth to hear. "What do you have?"

"A secret."

"What's your secret?"

"I have a secret crush on a boy I met in the woods," she whispered.

Eve grabbed his face, pulled him closer, and kissed him on the lips. Chase hesitated and then kissed her back softly, lingering with the most passionate kiss he dared take. Eve smiled. Chase smiled so hard he turned away from Eve, embarrassed. He had never been kissed before by anyone other than his mom. He couldn't stop smiling. He looked at her face, her perfect nose, her perfect lips, her beautiful eyes and held his breath. *How can this be...*he wondered, *that she likes me?* The woods truly were a magical place.

Chase and Eve continued to meet every week, on Wednesdays. Chase grew to love Wednesdays and often had trouble sleeping on Tuesday nights. Eve would always bring him a sandwich and some type of dessert. He would lie in her lap as she broke off pieces of the sandwich and fed it to him. Sometimes they would just sit on their log, staring at the running water going by and hope that the day would never end.

Loose had caught on to Chase's race gambit, but he let Chase continue to think he was being fooled. Loose would start off running, and when Chase was out of sight, he would stop and carefully loop back to follow Chase to see where he was meeting this mysterious girl Eve. Many times Chase was just too fast and would disappear in the woods, but Loose's tracking skills were exceptional, and he quickly found where Chase was going.

Loose watched Chase and Eve from behind bushes, making sure he was not seen. He moved closer when he saw them kissing and watched eagerly.

Chase was right, Loose thought. *She's beautiful; the most beautiful girl I've ever seen.*

Sometimes he would close his eyes and imagine that he was Chase kissing Eve.

Why don't girls like me? he thought. *I'm stronger than Chase, smarter, and better looking, too. She should be with me, not him.*

Loose always made sure he beat Chase home to keep up his ruse, taunting him about losing as before. It was becoming obvious that he won their races every Wednesday— Eve's day—but he played it up like the bad winner he usually was. He didn't want Chase to know he knew where he was meeting Eve.

A few weeks went by and another Wednesday arrived. Chase was anxious to go for a run in the woods to see Eve. He and Loose were leaving the stadium, having gone through several hours of drills and weight training.

"You wanna race?" Chase asked. "Desserts again?"

"Sure," said Loose, "but Sergeant Grant wants to see you at the barracks, and he didn't look too happy."

"What? Why? I didn't do nothin'."

"How should I know? I'm just tellin' you what he said."

"At the barracks? He was *just* here in the stadium. Why didn't he talk to me then?"

"Dunno. He said, 'pronto.'"

"Fuck; now what?"

"Catch up to me and we'll finish that race," said Loose. "I'll wait; I could use an extra dessert today."

"Okay; I'll be right there."

Chase took off to find his drill sergeant while Loose took off for the woods. When Chase got to the barracks, he looked for Sergeant Grant everywhere. He searched all the barracks without any luck. He stopped one of the other cadets.

"You seen Grant anywhere?" he asked.

"Nope, not since drills."

Chase asked another cadet and got the same answer. He took off back to the stadium, retracing his route in case he somehow missed him. When he got to the stadium, he saw his drill sergeant gathering his gear.

"Sergeant Grant, Chase 523 reporting as requested, Sir."

"Chase? Reporting for what? Drills are over, son."

"Cadet Loose said you wanted to see me."

"I think Cadet Loose must be pullin' your leg. I never asked to see you."

A sick feeling grew in Chase's stomach. In a moment, he knew.

"Eve!"

He ran from the stadium—barely able to breathe—hitting the woods flying, taking logs and bushes in stride like he was running hurdles. He blasted through bushes he couldn't hop, breaking limbs and branches of trees in the way, making a bee line for their log, for Eve.

Meanwhile, Loose had made his way through the woods to the log across the stream. When he approached, Eve was lying down on the log, staring up at the sky. She was wearing form-fitting pants that looked painted on, a loose-fitting butterfly-button shirt, and boot shoes similar to beaks. Her picnic basket was at the side of the log, and she was waiting for Chase. She heard footsteps coming her way.

"I've been waiting for you," she said, without looking.

"I've been waiting to meet you for a long time, too," Loose replied.

209

Eve sat up frightened, knowing it was not Chase's voice.

"Who are you?" she said, straightening up.

"Oh, I'm Chase's brother, Loose. He told me to meet you and tell you he was going to be late."

Eve relaxed. "Oh, so you're the brother he races for dessert?"

"Yep," he said, sitting down on the log right next to her. "I'm the one who always wins!"

Eve scooted a little away from him.

"Where you goin'?" Loose asked.

"Goin'? Nowhere. Just needing a little space."

"I'm not going to hurt you," he said.

"I...I didn't think you were," she replied nervously.

"You like Chase, huh?" he asked.

"Yes, very much."

"Well, he likes you too—very much. I can tell. He tried to keep you a secret from me."

Eve smiled. "He did?"

"Yeah. He mentioned you and all, but he didn't tell me he was meeting you every week."

"Oh, well, I'm sure he must have his reasons."

"We share everything you know, me and Chase."

"You do?"

"Yeah, we're brothers. Piecer Corp brothers, ya know?"

"Chase is a Piecer cadet?"

"You didn't know? He didn't tell you?"

"No, he said he was home schooled."

Loose laughed. "Well, he's a fuckin' liar."

Eve looked away, trying to hide her reactions from him.

"He's a Piecer...born and bred, just like me."

"When is he coming?"

"He may be a while. I think he was going to meet my girl."

"What? Is he seeing someone else?"

"He didn't tell you that? What a dog. Yeah, he's with my girlfriend now. We share our women."

"That doesn't sound like him to me. Chase wouldn't do that."

Loose scooted even closer to Eve and put his arm around her. "I know this is probably hard for you to hear, but Chase is kind of a hound dog. He sleeps with a lot of girls. If I know 'em, I share 'em with him. And if he knows 'em, he shares 'em with me! That's what we do."

Loose stared at Eve, slowly looking at her body up and down. "I can see why he kept you a secret; you're prettier than all of 'em."

Eve tried to scoot down the log, but Loose wouldn't let her, his arm now holding her there. "My Piecer brothers and I have a deal; what's mine is theirs and what's theirs is mine."

Eve spun out of his arm and stood up. "I'm not something of Chase's that he can share."

"Oh, I think you are," said Loose. "I seen you from the bushes. You and Chase makin' out—tonguin' each other. All I want is some of that...and *maybe* a little more."

"Well, you can go fuck yourself," said Eve, gathering her things. "I'm leaving."

Loose jumped up and grabbed her from behind. Eve instinctively jabbed him in the gut and flipped him over.

"Oh, you wanna play, huh?" said Loose. "I like a girl with spunk."

"Leave me alone, motherfucker. I'm not playin'."

"Ooh, she talks dirty too."

Loose got to his feet and lunged left. Eve prepared herself to take him down, but then he lunged right.

"Don't know where I'm goin', do ya?"

Loose ran right then jerked left again, hitting Eve in the stomach with his shoulder hard. The blow knocked the wind out of her, and she fell on her back. Loose jumped on top of her, pinning her down with his knees. She struggled for air and struggled to get free, but he was too strong and too heavy.

"Let's see what you got in there," said Loose, grabbing at her shirt and pulling it apart.

Eve screamed as he pulled her shirt apart, the butterfly-buttons popping into the leaves, landing around the old log. Loose pulled his combat knife from his boot and held it in front of her face.

"Let's see 'em," he said, grinning, cutting through the front of her bra.

Eve screamed again, and he covered her mouth with his hand.

Chase was tearing through the forest in a blur. He heard Eve scream and his feet barely touched the ground. He got to the log at full speed and saw Loose on top of her. He leapt at him from ten feet away, like a panther on his prey, the momentum of his run carrying him through the air. He hit Loose hard from the side knocking him off of Eve.

"Get off of her, you motherfucker. I'm going to kill you!" Chase shouted.

They rolled in the woods, leaping to their feet, facing off against each other.

Eve struggled to her feet crying and pulled her shirt closed. She searched the ground for her shirt buttons not thinking, hoping to put them back to close her shirt. She knelt down—dazed and sobbing—trying to pick up those she could find.

Loose still had his knife pulled and held it in front of him. "I was just having a little fun. She came on to me."

"I'm going to beat the livin' shit outta you."

Loose held up the knife again. "I'll use it!" he screamed.

Chase ignored him, jumping on top of him, grabbing his knife hand, holding it at bay. Loose punched him and Chase took the hit without feeling it, barely turning his face from the blow. Chase's eyes narrowed. He had felt anger before but not like this. He was going to kill Loose, and it was all he could think about. He grabbed Loose's hand and beat it against the ground until he dropped the knife. Then he began hitting Loose in the face—hard.

With the first hit, Loose's head snapped back into the dirt with a thud. Chase changed hands and hit him from the left then the right then the left. Loose's face was covered in blood. Chase continued hitting him, the fury inside released but not abated with every blow. Loose's eyes rolled unconscious and Chase kept hitting. He couldn't stop himself. He didn't *want* to stop himself. He hit harder and faster.

"Stop it, Chase!" Eve screamed. "You'll kill him."

Chase hit him again and again, breathing like a raging bull, sweat pouring out of his face.

"Chase, stop it...please," Eve screamed once more.

Chase pulled his fist back to hit Loose again, and then Eve's plea penetrated his anger. "Don't kill him; that's not you."

He stopped mid-swing, stood up, and ran to Eve, who was kneeling nearby weeping.

"Are you okay? Did he hurt you?"

"I'm okay," she said. "I should...I just have to go home."

"I'll take you."

"No. I want to go alone."

He reached out to put his hand on her shoulder to comfort her, and she pulled away sharply. "You should have said something," she sobbed. "You lied to me. You're a Piecer!"

"I didn't mean to lie," he said. "I don't know why I didn't tell you. Please don't go. He will never bother you again. I promise."

"No; I have to go," she said, turning abruptly, heading off running into the woods.

Eve disappeared in the woods, and Chase sat down on the log—their log. He saw Eve's picnic basket, its contents strewn about the forest floor and began to weep. He heard Loose moan from the woods, and then spat in his direction. Chase grabbed Eve's basket, stood up and left.

Carrying Eve's basket, Chase arrived at his house and headed straight for his room.

"Hi, Son; whatcha got there?" his father asked.

Chase hardly heard him.

"You okay?" his father asked, seeing he was upset. "Seen Loose?"

"Fuck Loose," said Chase, running upstairs to his room

and slamming his door.

Loose made it home several hours later and told his father he had gotten jumped in the woods. Martin knew better—having seen the blood on Chase's knuckles and clothes—but he didn't pry.

Things were very tense in the house for a long time with neither boy speaking to the other unless they had to. Loose avoided Chase, often flinching whenever he came near him.

Chase went to the woods every Wednesday, carrying Eve's basket, hoping to see her, hoping to return it to her. But she was never there and he thought he would never see her again until she walked into the Pwyll station.

Chapter Sixteen

Night on Europa

"This is Evelyn," said Tripp, "Evelyn Tupi...General Tupi's granddaughter."

Evelyn shook her hands back and forth, trying to calm herself and dry her sweaty hands. Tripp stepped aside, revealing Evelyn standing behind him. Evelyn waved meekly.

"Hello, Chase," she said softly, afraid to look directly at him.

"Hello, Eve..." Chase replied.

"Eve?" asked Tripp. "You guys know each other?"

Eve and Chase looked at each other and then away, saying simultaneously, "We've met."

"Oh great," said Hector, "only two women around for 300 million miles and Chase knows 'em both."

There was an awkward silence for a moment until Sheen spoke up. "I am Sheen. I am Courtesan. You are human female, yes?" Sheen did not wait for a response and scanned her carefully. "We are similar, yes?"

Eve looked confused. "Similar?" she asked. "I'm not sure what you mean."

"You have breasts, Sheen has breasts. You have a tiny waist, Sheen has a tiny waist. You have long legs, Sheen has long legs. You are pretty, Sheen is pretty. Are you Courtesan?" asked Sheen.

"I don't know what that is," Evelyn replied.

"Do you service men or women or both?"

Eve looked around the room, looking for any help in understanding.

"Sheen is going through a period of adjustment," said Chase. "She was being exploited by a real, umm...*jerk*, until we met. I just helped her get away."

"Commander Chase saved me from Shoom, from Quargg. He is my Commander. He is a good Commander."

"I still don't get it," Eve said. "Sorry."

Sheen cocked her head, trying to understand why she couldn't communicate with Eve. "Commander, am I not speaking correctly?" she asked Chase.

"No, Sheen...you are doing fine. Eve's just not familiar with a Courtesan."

Sheen straightened her head. "Ah, Sheen understands," she said, looking at Eve. "I am Courtesan. I have one Commander. He killed Shoom. Chase 523 is my Commander now. I do what Chase 523 says. I service who Chase 523 says."

Eve's eyes widened. "You mean service like *sex*?"

"Yes," said Sheen. "Service like sex. Do you service men, women, or both?"

"What? No!"

"You are not Courtesan. I am Courtesan. For what task are you purposed? Do you have a Commander? I service who Chase 523 says."

"Well, how nice for Chase 523, then," said Eve, staring at Chase in disbelief.

"It's not like that," said Chase. "I rescued her from servicing anyone—ever. Honest!"

"Chase 523 freed me. He does not make me do service. Have you serviced men?" asked Sheen.

The room grew completely quiet. The sound of the station's generators grew quite loud in the background. All the Piecers and Max stared at Evelyn, waiting for her response. Evelyn's cheeks flushed red until she walked up to Sheen and extended her hand. "I'm Evelyn Tupi," she said. "Nice to meet you."

"I am familiar with the shaking of the hand. I have no weapons either," said Sheen. "It is nice to meet you too, Evelyn Eve Tupi."

"Just Evelyn," she replied still shaking her hand.

"This is Max," said Chase. "He's a Fixer, my engineer on the *Promise*; saved my life a couple of times already."

"Nice to meet you, Max," said Evelyn.

Max stared at Evelyn his mouth agape. She was every bit as beautiful as Sheen, only human and blond. Sheen studied Evelyn closely.

"Tripp, this is Max, the Fixer I mentioned."

"How's it goin?" said Tripp. "Chase told us about you. I like that little boom thing you put together."

"Thanks," said Max. "Just a little something I cooked up on Titan. It's what I call a WLR."

"A WLR?"

"Weapon of Last Resort. When the shit hits the fan, you need a WLR. I had a lot of spare time on my hands."

"Would you mind making me one if you have the time? Could come in handy someday."

"Sure; not hard...catch me later."

"Thanks," Tripp replied. "I'll do that."

"Let's eat, everybody," said Chase. "We have a lot to do and not much time."

Hector passed bowls of combined MREs up and down the table.

"I'm starving," said Evelyn. "All I had to eat was the chocolate Tripp gave me."

"I'm starving," Sheen mimicked, still watching her every move.

"What's the plan, Chase?" asked Tripp.

"It's going to take a while to empty this place. I say we spend the night here. There are enough rooms for everyone with cots for all, food and water."

"Then what?" asked Gage.

"I've been thinking about that. The Klix took us all out

with that EMP blast—killed our weapons and electronics. Only reason theirs worked is because they were out of range of the blast. We now have working weapons...lots of them. Max, can you rig an EMP blast?"

"I'd need some nuclear fuel," he said. "There's weapons here, some explosives, but nothing big."

Gage reached into his suit and set the triangular and rectangular trillium objects down on the table. "Will these work?" he asked with a smile.

"Trillium!" Max shouted. "That's the same kind that goes into my mech and an extra. Just need one. Yeah, these will do. Give me a few hours, and you'll have your EMP device." He looked down at his empty cup. "I'll be right back. I need to get something."

"Glad he's with us." Tripp laughed as Max disappeared down the station's halls.

"Me too," said Chase.

"So, what are we going to do with an EMP?" asked Hector.

"We have three ships—including the Klix ship—plus the two Dragonflies. We can empty this place and take the weapons to the survivors on Earth. But they're going to need a little help, and that's where the EMP blast comes in. We stay just outside of orbit, then send the EMP into the atmosphere in the middle of the Klix ships. Anything inside the Earth's atmosphere will fall like rocks. Their rifles and pistols should fry just like ours did. Then we find human survivors, distribute the working weapons, and kick their ass back to Klixland."

"What about their ships in space?" asked Hector. "They won't be affected by the blast."

"Shouldn't be too many and we'll have to deal with those ourselves," said Chase.

"Just might work," said Gage, "with a little luck."

"It has to work," said Chase. "They're depending on us. Sheen, can you please return my Dragonfly to the *Promise* when you get a chance?"

"Yes, Commander," she said, standing.

"Let her stay," said Tripp. "We just sat down."

"She can stay," said Chase. "You don't have to go now, Sheen...just whenever you get a chance."

"I will stay," she replied, sitting again, "and eat with the crew. Then I will do as you ask, Commander."

"Thank you, Sheen."

Sheen smiled as Max appeared with a bottle of whiskey and set it on the table. "I brought this from the ship. It's the best."

Tripp sniffed his tumbler and smiled. "Wow; thanks... this is the good stuff. You wanna try some of my Piecer Juice?"

"Umm...no thanks," said Max. "We used to use that to loosen rusted bolts. Tastes like acetone."

"It's not *that* bad," said Tripp, laughing. "Well, maybe a little."

Tripp poured Sheen a half tumbler full. "Here you go, Darlin'...some of the good stuff."

Evelyn drilled a look at Tripp.

"You're wasting your time," said Max, "*and* good whiskey."

Tripp looked at him, confused.

"Doesn't affect her," said Max. "She filters out the alcohol."

"Ahem," said Evelyn, holding out her glass.

"Ahem," said Sheen, standing up and holding out her half-full glass.

Tripp poured Evelyn a drink and added a little more to Sheen's glass. "See," he said. "She likes it."

"No," said Max. "She's being polite. She's an android—a Courtesan. She's just being part of the crew."

"You mean like a robot?" asked Tripp, staring at Sheen.

"Part robot; I'm not sure which parts."

"No fuckin way," said Tripp. "She looks so real."

"I am real," said Sheen with a puzzled look on her face.

Tripp leaned over the table, reached out and squeezed

Sheen's right breast and then her left breast.

"They *feel* so real," he said. "Amazing!"

Everyone stopped talking and stared, stunned.

"Sheen," said Chase. "Did you say Tripp 523 could touch your breasts?"

"No, Commander."

"Sheen, defend yourself."

Tripp looked over at Chase, laughing. "Defend herself from what? I just—"

In a flash, Sheen punched Tripp open-handed—flat in the chest. Tripp flew across the room, landing on a pile of empty rifle crates.

"*Sheen*," Evelyn screamed. "Don't!"

"Commander Chase ordered me to defend myself."

"Well, stop listening to Commander Chase."

Evelyn ran over to Tripp to see if he was injured. "Are you all right?" she asked, bending over, helping him to his feet.

"I'm fine. What the *fuck* was that?"

Chase smiled. "Sorry...Sheen is just learning how to defend herself. And we don't touch our friends unless invited."

"Well you could have just said something," said Tripp, rubbing his chest.

"I didn't think I had to tell a crewmember not to touch another crewmember's boobs!"

"Oh, right. Shit. Sorry, Sheen. I thought that you were just a rob—well, I'm sorry."

"I can only be touched if my Commander orders it," Sheen said.

"No, Sheen," said Chase. "You can only be touched if you *want* to be touched."

Sheen cocked her head, clearly confused. "I do not understand, Commander, but I will only be touched if I wish it... per your orders."

She sat down and looked at her glass. "Commander, is it required?" Sheen asked, pointing to the whiskey.

"No, Sheen; it is not."

"Then I think not," said Sheen. "It tastes like fuel."

Evelyn returned to her seat, sitting further from Sheen than before. "You don't have to ask him permission for everything that you do," said Evelyn, irritated.

"He is my Commander," she replied.

"But he freed you. You can do what you want!"

Sheen looked confused. "I want what my Commander wants."

Eve lifted her glass and flipped her head backwards, taking the shot in one gulp and slamming the cup on the table.

Sheen watched closely, picked up her cup and did the same.

"I thought you didn't like it," said Evelyn.

"It is unpleasant," Sheen replied.

"Then why did you drink it?"

"The crew is drinking. Sheen is part of the crew. Sheen will drink."

Chase stared at Eve, watching her interact with Sheen, smiling. Sheen saw him, looked at Eve, then back at Chase.

"Do you wish Evelyn to service you Commander?"

Chase turned white, then red. "What? No!"

"You appear to be looking at Evelyn and you are arous—"

"Sheen!" he screamed, interrupting her. "If I need an update, I'll ask you."

"Yes, Commander."

Evelyn leaned over and whispered into Sheen's ear, "You don't have to do what he says, you know."

Sheen looked perplexed. She followed Evelyn's example and leaned over, whispering back loudly in Evelyn's ear, "He is my Commander. I must."

"You said he freed you."

"Yes...but he is my Commander."

"But you don't have to listen to him."

"But I want to listen to him."

Evelyn leaned back and away. "*Pfft*," she said.

Sheen leaned back, copying her movements. "*Pfft*," Sheen said.

Evelyn tapped her glass on the table.

"More?" asked Tripp.

"Please."

Sheen looked at Evelyn, reached for her own glass, and then looked at Chase, who shook his head left and right. Then she set it down without tapping. Chase coughed to get everyone's attention.

"Tomorrow, we take off for Earth's moon. Evelyn can stay here with Max and Sheen; they aren't soldiers. We'll leave plenty of provisions here."

"What?" asked Max. "Do we have a say in this?"

"Well, sure; I just thought…"

"Earth's my home, too."

"And mine," said Evelyn. "They killed my parents, my grandfather, and my friends."

"Commander, are you ordering me to stay here?" asked Sheen.

"No, Sheen. You can do what you want to do."

"The Klix destroyed Sheen's people. Sheen will avenge Soren. Sheen will help."

"Besides," said Max, "you need all the help you can get."

"They're right," said Gage, "three ships and two Dragonflies—with four guys—is near impossible…even with the computers running the ships."

"Thank you, everyone; I appreciate it, I do. I just didn't want to assume to put you in harm's way."

"We're already in harm's way," said Max. "Anywhere the Klix are on the loose is harm's way. They have to be stopped."

"You're not leaving me here," said Evelyn, picking up Sheen's laser rifle. She flipped a switch, and the weapon charged with a familiar whine. "Besides, I know how to handle myself."

Evelyn aimed the rifle at a small rock on the ground just outside the door and pulled the trigger. The rock jumped, and she fired again, hitting it mid-air before it landed from the first shot.

"Impressive," said Tripp. "I didn't know you can shoot."

"You don't know anything about me," she said angrily.

"What'd I do?" asked Tripp, looking confused.

Evelyn leaned the rifle back against the wall and scooted in closer to Sheen.

"Okay," said Chase, "if you're sure, then everyone goes. Sheen and I will handle the Klix ship. Sheen, you'll need your regen machine. Be sure to transfer it from the Promise. And please bring the ammo in my coat from the Promise too. I need to reload my guns."

"You want a working Stinger, Boss?" asked Hector. "We have plenty."

"No thanks; I've been pretty lucky with these so far."

"Roger that," replied Hector.

"Gage and Evelyn can take the Promise," Chase continued. "Hector and Tripp can handle the Lone Star."

"We oughta rename that piece of shit Klix ship, Chief," said Tripp. "It's ours now...it's a Piecer ship."

"Umm, where the hell do I go?" Max interrupted.

"Oh; sorry. Max, I need you on the Klix ship." Chase smiled. "Any suggestions for a ship name?"

"How about the Vengeance?" asked Max. "Seems fitting."

"Vengeance sounds good to me, Boss," said Gage.

"I like it," said Hector. "Has a nice menacing ring to it."

"Vengeance is one of my favorite things," said Tripp, smiling. "It's right up there with revenge."

"Max, do you think you can figure out how the Klix ship... um, the Vengeance works?"

"Sure—as long as we have a translator."

Tripp tossed him one of the translators they picked up earlier. "I know this one works; tested it."

"Thanks," said Max. "We're good to go, Chase."

"Everyone, please eat as much as you like. Hydrate yourselves and get a good night's rest. We're leaving at 0600. There are plenty of rooms here for everyone. Take whatever you want to make yourself comfortable for the night. I don't know when we'll get off these ships again."

"Yes, Commander."

Chase held up his glass, high in front of him. "A toast…" he said, his eyes lingering on Evelyn. "To all our loved ones, our families, and for Mother Earth."

Everyone stood up and raised their cups, including Sheen.

"For Earth," they all said in unison.

"And for Soren," said Sheen. "My home."

"For Soren," everyone added, lifting their glasses higher.

Tripp took a seat on the opposite side of Evelyn and Sheen. Everyone finished their dinner, exchanging stories of how they acquired their ships and ended up at the station.

"I've got some work to do," said Max, gathering the trillium objects and standing up from the table. "I found some parts for the pulse laser array; should be easy to fix now. See you all in the morning…g'nite." Max left the table and headed to his room, carrying the trillium.

"I'm getting some sack time," Chase said, standing. "I suggest you all do the same."

"I'll check the ships and gear," said Hector, "then get some shut-eye."

"Probably not a bad idea," said Gage. "I'm right behind you."

Sheen stood up immediately. "Yes, Commander."

"You don't have to go," said Evelyn, holding Sheen's arm. "It was just a suggestion."

Sheen stared ahead as if trying to figure out what "suggestion" meant, and then sat back down next to Evelyn. "Sheen will stay with Evelyn Tupi," she said. "It was just a suggestion."

"That's right," Evelyn said glaring at Chase. "Sheen is staying."

"Fine with me; Sheen can do what she wants," said Chase "Good night, everyone… and thank you."

"Oh! Did you see the way he said that?" Evelyn whispered to Sheen.

"Yes," said Sheen. "Commander Chase wished us all a good night and thanked us. He is a good Commander."

"No...it was how he said it," Evelyn said. "Like, Sheen can do what she wants— knowing that I asked you to stay."

"Sheen does not understand. Did you not want me to stay?"

"No, I wanted you to stay, but it's just he can't tell you what to do."

"Commander Chase said Sheen can do what Sheen wants. Did you not hear him?"

"Yes...I heard him," she said, "but it was sooo condescending."

Sheen paused, thinking for a moment. "I do not think Commander Chase was patronizing me." She lifted her arm and scanned Evelyn. "Are you ill, Evelyn Tupi?"

"What? No."

Tripp watched their interaction amused, trying not to laugh.

Sheen continued her scan. "Ah, you are aroused. Do you wish me to call Commander Chase to service you?"

"What? No! I am not aroused...not by him, anyway."

Tripp looked up, smiling.

"Ah, you are aroused by Sheen, then? Do you wish me to service you?"

"What? No! Look, I'm not aroused, okay?"

"Perhaps Sheen is malfunctioning. After returning Commander Chase's dragon fly to the Promise, I will regenerate and perform a systems check. Sheen will return soon," she said, getting up from the table.

"We can bunk together," said Evelyn. "I'll get our room ready."

Sheen paused, scanning her memory banks for the term "bunk. "Very well, Evelyn Tupi...we will 'bunk' together upon my return."

Sheen walked out toward the Promise, leaving Evelyn and Tripp alone at the table.

"Did you want another one, Evelyn?" asked Tripp, pouring himself another whiskey.

"Hell yes; one more to help me sleep."

"Are you still in love with him?" Tripp asked, handing her a shot.

"What? Who? Hell no."

"You can't bullshit a bullshitter. What happened between you two?"

Evelyn looked at him in disbelief and started to cry. Tripp got up and moved next to her. "Oh shit, sorry," said Tripp. "I didn't mean anything by it. Don't cry. You don't have to tell me anything. Here, have another drink. Have the whole bottle."

Eve threw the shot back and swallowed. "It was a long time ago. We met in the woods, and I fell in love with him... until..." She looked down and away.

"Until what?"

"His brother, Loose—he tried to rape me."

"Never liked that guy; something off about him. Surprised Chase didn't kill him."

"He would have. I stopped him."

"Never known anyone who could stop Chase from doing anything. He must have really loved you."

"Oh, Tripp, I don't know what to do. It was so long ago, but seeing him now..." Evelyn threw her arms around Tripp and sobbed.

"There, there, darlin', it's okay. We'll probably all be dead tomorrow anyway, so no worries."

Eve stopped sobbing, looked up at him and then burst out laughing. "You're crazy, you know that?"

"So people tell me," he replied, "repeatedly!" He grinned.

Evelyn wiped her eyes and let out a deep breath. "Thanks; you've been a good friend to me."

Tripp looked Evelyn in the eyes, unblinking. "You're welcome to bunk with me tonight if you like," he said.

"What? Oh. I don't know. I'm supposed to bunk with Sheen. I..."

"I understand," said Tripp. "The heart wants what the heart wants. Offer is open anytime."

Evelyn reached out and hugged Tripp. "Thank you,

though. I should go. I have to get our room ready. Sheen's and mine."

"I know. You're bunkin' with Sheen. Gotcha. Goodnight then, Evelyn," said Tripp. "If you change your mind, I won't be sleeping. I never sleep before a fight."

Evelyn got up, took a long look at Tripp, then turned away to find her room. Tripp sat alone staring and poured one more drink.

"Well, Tripp ol' boy," he said, toasting himself, "it's been a good run. If we die tomorrow, we're gonna take a helluva lotta Klix with us!" He raised his glass. "To battle." Then he gulped down the shot in one swallow.

As he set his glass down, Sheen walked back into the room, having finished her regeneration cycle. "Tripp 523, have you seen Evelyn Tupi?" she asked.

"I have," he said. "She went off to make up your room—hers and yours."

Tripp looked down at the table and poured another whiskey.

"Are you all right, Tripp 523? I hope I did not damage you."

"Nah; you didn't damage me. I had it coming. I'm sorry about grabbing your boobs."

"You did not hurt me," said Sheen. "You were very gentle."

"I've never met an android before," Tripp said, "and it's just that you are so gosh darn beautiful."

Sheen blushed on cue. "Thank you. Are you certain you are undamaged?"

"From your punch? Oh yeah...I heal really fast."

Sheen paused watching him. "I detect melancholy in your demeanor."

"It's nothing. I just got shot down by Evelyn, and I'll probably die tomorrow. Just wanted to have sex one more time before I died...and not with myself. Looks like that's not gonna happen."

Sheen stood silent for a moment. "If you have sex, you

227

would feel better, yes?"

"Hell yes."

"I could service you," she said. "I am Courtesan."

"I thought you could only service whoever your commander tells you to service?"

"No. Commander Chase freed me. Sheen can do service when Sheen wants."

"Well, do you want to?"

"You will feel better, yes?"

"Hell yes!"

"Then Sheen will service you," she replied, smiling.

"Well...then prepare yourself, Darlin'—for a night of passion like no other."

Sheen looked confused. "I do not think this will take all night," she replied. "I think five to ten of your Earth minutes."

"What? No way. You've never been with Tripp 523! I'm going to rock you all night long."

"I do not know what that means," said Sheen, "but we should hurry. Evelyn is waiting for me."

"Well, she's going to wait a longggg time."

"Come; we will find a room to use," said Sheen.

"I'm right behind you," said Tripp, jumping up from the table.

Sheen and Tripp disappeared into one of the many vacant rooms and closed the door. Four minutes later, a loud scream was heard coming from the room.

Chase ran to the hallway. Gage and Hector soon followed, stopping in front of the source of the scream, weapons drawn toward the door. Sheen exited the room and closed the door quietly.

"Is everything all right? Did he try something?" asked Chase.

"He tried several things," said Sheen, "but nothing I am unaccustomed to."

"Did you kill him?"

"No; I did not kill him. I serviced him. Tripp 523 is happy

now. He did not want to die without sex one more time. Is that acceptable, Commander?"

Chase laughed. "As long as you wanted to. It's up to you."

"It was acceptable to me, and it did not take long," Sheen said. "Only four of your Earth minutes. Now I must hurry and meet my friend Evelyn Tupi."

Gage and Hector looked at Chase. They all started laughing, trying not to laugh too loud outside Tripp's door.

"I hope she didn't hurt him," Chase said, "our little four-minute stud."

Hector and Gage looked at Chase again.

"We don't want to die without sex either!" said Hector. "Do we get a turn with your Courtesan?"

"It's not up to me," Chase answered. "And it looks like your chance just walked away."

"Wait for us!" Hector yelled down the hall, but it was too late. Sheen had disappeared into Evelyn's room.

Chapter Seventeen

Bunk Mates

Sheen knocked on the door to Evelyn's room and walked in. "I am here, Evelyn Tupi. We can begin our bunking together."

"Please, just call me, Evelyn. I made up one of these cots for you."

"Thank you, Evelyn...but Sheen does not need sleep. I have regenerated and performed a systems check. My system is fully functional."

Sheen scanned Evelyn again and cocked her head. "You appear to be functioning normally. Your head injury appears to be healing, and your white blood cell count is normal. You have no infection, but I do detect melancholy—much like Tripp 523."

"I'm okay," said Evelyn, sitting down on her cot next to Sheen's. "It's just...I didn't expect..." She put her face in her hands and started crying.

"Are you malfunctioning, Evelyn?"

"What? No, I'm okay."

"Are you sad because you are going to die tomorrow?"

"What? I'm not going to die tomorrow."

"Our chances of survival against the Klix forces are 1,568,472 to 1."

"You don't know that. You can't know that."

"There are seven of us. They are legion. We cannot succeed against overwhelming forces."

Evelyn started crying again, and Sheen sat down next to her. She scanned her memory banks and then hesitantly put her arm around Evelyn, awkwardly patting her back. Evelyn put her head against Sheen's shoulder and sobbed.

"I didn't expect to see him again," said Evelyn. "I didn't think I had feelings for him anymore, but it all came back. I still love him."

"Who do you love?" asked Sheen.

"Chase...your commander, Chase"

Sheen stared straight ahead, thinking. "Commander Chase is a good Commander. Many have saved Sheen from other commanders only to take Sheen home to service them exclusively. Only Commander Chase saved me to free me. Yes; he is deserving of love."

Evelyn looked up at her in surprise. "Do you love him?"

Sheen stared straight ahead, tilting her head occasionally as if considering another possibility. "I do not know how to answer you. I have not known love. With Commander Chase, I feel happy. I feel safe. I feel valued. When he is away, I feel twitchy and malfunction."

"So, you do love him!"

"Do I? Is malfunction love?"

"He makes you happy. You feel safe and protected, and when he's gone...you feel twitchy?"

"Yes. I fear something is wrong with my internal system."

"That's love."

"How can I fix love?"

"You can't fix it."

"Should I cry with you then, Evelyn?"

"Do you want to cry?"

"No. It appears purposeless. Why do you do it?"

"Because I'm sad."

"Does crying fix love?"

"No."

"Does it make you not sad?"

"No."

"Then it is pointless."

"Humans cry when they are sad, that's all. Sometimes they feel better afterward."

"Humans are strange beings. I have often thought on why my maker modeled me after a human female. Human females are sought after by many species, but I do not understand why. They cry for no purpose. They are not strong. And they talk a lot."

"We are strong," said Evelyn, irritated, "and we don't cry for no purpose—we have purposes, reasons—and we don't talk a lot, either."

"I am sorry, Evelyn Tupi. I have only met one human female. Sheen should not assume all human females are the same."

"What? I'm the only human female you ever met?"

"Yes."

"I don't talk a lot," she insisted. "Nobody says I talk a lot. Why do you think I talk a lot?"

"In the brief period of time that I have been in your presence, you have spent sixty-two percent of your time talking."

Evelyn's expression changed from surprise to anger. "I think you're jealous."

Sheen looked straight ahead again, thinking for a moment. "I do not feel resentment or rivalry toward you, Evelyn...nor do I feel suspicious of you. I think I am not jealous. If you wish to be with Commander Chase, then Sheen will be happy."

"You don't want to be with him?"

"Yes. I do. He is my Commander."

"Well, what if he picks me?"

"I do not understand. Does picking you exclude me?" asked Sheen.

"Well, yes, obviously."

"I do not understand. Do you wish him to be alone with you forever?"

"Well, no, not alone. He can still have friends, and his Piecer brothers."

"So, you would exclude only Sheen?"

"Well, no. You could still be friends. You just couldn't, well, you know, service him."

"I do not service him now."

"That's good," said Evelyn, smiling. "Yes, that's very good."

"Then we are still friends, Evelyn?"

"Yes...we are still friends, Sheen."

"I am glad Evelyn is my friend."

Evelyn walked over to the sink and looked into the shiny metal mirror bolted to the wall above it. "Oh God, I'm a mess. No wonder he's ignoring me."

Sheen looked at her, perplexed. "Who is ignoring you?"

"Chase, Commander Chase."

"I do not understand. He spoke with everyone."

"I don't mean ignoring ignoring...I mean, he hasn't looked at me like he used to in the woods."

"I am not familiar with the term, 'ignoring ignoring,' but Commander Chase is concerned about the mission, Evelyn. You are not ignored."

Evelyn grabbed a small bag from her pocket and poured the contents on the sink counter. Sheen looked over the items, puzzled.

"What are these objects?" she asked. "What do they do?"

"Those are my face. I have to fix my face."

"Ah...tools. Sheen understands. Is your face damaged?"

"No not damaged, it's just a mess. Haven't you ever seen cosmetics before?"

"Your face seems arranged properly," said Sheen, scanning her memory for cosmetics. "Oh! Sheen understands. Powder, mascara, lipstick, and blush: things to beautify the face."

"I'm not letting him go this time," Evelyn said, "not until I find out how he feels about me."

Sheen watched with amazement as Evelyn brushed powder over her face, then applied blush, mascara, and a dab of lip gloss to her lips. Standing behind her, Sheen mimicked

Eve's movements exactly.

"That's better," said Evelyn, turning her head left, then right. "That gash is pretty ugly, though. Ugh!"

Evelyn turned to the mirror and pressed her lips together to even out her lip gloss. Sheen examined the powder and gloss, then scanned it with her hand.

"I do not understand why you use these," said Sheen. "Is it necessary?"

"Very! Besides, I've seen your face, and you use them all the time."

"Sheen does not need cosmetics," she replied. "I can change my appearance at will. Observe, Evelyn."

Evelyn stared at Sheen's face while her skin transformed, imitating the makeup Evelyn had applied identically.

"That's amazing. How do you do that?"

Sheen smiled. "I can change more than my skin. Observe, Evelyn." Sheen then transformed the color and length of her hair from red, to brown, to blond. "It is all part of my system parameters."

"Can you change everything about you?"

"No. My parameters are limited. I cannot grow taller or shorter, as my frame is of a preset size. But I can do this," she said, pointing at her chest.

Her breasts grew several sizes larger and then shrank to practically nothing. Evelyn stared at her—stunned—watching Sheen's transformations.

"I bet that comes in handy," said Evelyn.

"I was designed to please many different species with many different tastes."

"Who designed you?"

"I do not know, Evelyn. My memory was erased. I have only fragments of memories and not many of those."

"Oh how sad. That must be awful."

"It is not awful. It is all I have ever known. I'm a Courte-san, an android from Soren, and a twin."

"You have a sister?"

"Not sister, but twin. I have been told there is another

Sheen just like me, but not like me. We have the same body and software, but our Soren brains are different."

"That is so weird to have a twin you never met."

"Not weird to Sheen. It is normal."

"Do you want to find her?"

"I have not thought much on it. I have no reason to seek her out."

"Maybe she knows who made you."

Sheen cocked her head, thinking. "It is possible. I have not considered that my twin would know more than I do."

"Does she look just like you, then?"

"Perhaps, but a Courtesan can change their features as well. Observe."

Sheen seemed to be concentrating as her nose shifted up—then in slightly—her eyes widening to match Evelyn's, and her lips adjusting to match exactly. In less than a minute, they looked identical, including Evelyn's forehead wound. The only difference was their clothes.

"You—you look exactly like me," she said. "That's amazing!"

"I am pretty like Evelyn now," said Sheen with a smile.

"You were pretty before," said Evelyn. "Change back; it's too creepy talking to myself."

Sheen focused straight ahead, and her features returned to her original face. As Evelyn watched, Sheen shook her head. Her blond hair rippled and began to shimmer. Starting from her scalp, the blond color glowed pink, then traveled through to the tips of her hair. The glowing pink color darkened, returning to her original deep ruby red color.

"I am Sheen again," she said.

"We humans have to use makeup—um...cosmetics to change our faces. It's a pain, but you get used to it."

"Does Commander Chase like these cosmetics?"

"He never said anything about it, but probably. A lotta guys do."

"Then Sheen will do cosmetics like Evelyn."

Sheen stared momentarily, and her face returned to appear like the cosmetics Evelyn had applied.

"You look great, Sheen, but remember no servicing Commander Chase."

"Thank you, Evelyn. Yes, no servicing Commander Chase. He does not wish it."

"That's right, Sheen; Commander Chase does not wish it," Evelyn said, smiling.

"Tripp 523 wished it. He had melancholy, so Sheen serviced him."

Evelyn stopped smiling, stunned. "What? You...you had sex with Tripp?"

"Yes. He was sad. He did not want to die sad. He is happy now."

"Why would you have sex with Tripp?"

"He asked me to service him. He did not want to die before having sex one more time. He said he got shot down by Evelyn for service, so I serviced him. It did not take long."

"Whatever, Sheen!"

Sheen raised her arm to scan Evelyn. "Your blood pressure is elevated, and your heart is accelerated. Is Evelyn angry at Sheen?"

"Stop scanning me," Evelyn screamed.

"I only serviced Tripp 523 because he was sad. Was it wrong?"

"Well, you can't go around servicing everyone just because they're sad."

"He will be dead tomorrow. You would not service him. I think it was not wrong."

"No, it's not wrong. You didn't do anything wrong. I just... oh, never mind."

"Does Evelyn love Tripp 523 too?"

"What? No. We only just met. He's just been very kind to me."

"Sheen does not understand. You would not service him because he has been kind to you? You should meet Quargg. They are not kind. You would service them."

"No. People just don't go around servicing everyone they

meet."

"They do not?"

"No...they do not."

"Everyone who I have met wanted Sheen to service them."

"That's just men."

"No, not just men."

"Well, that's because you're a sex robot."

"Sheen is not a robot, Evelyn. Sheen is android."

"Yeah, but all you do is have sex with everyone."

"I was designed as Courtesan. I am expert at servicing all known species of life forms throughout many galaxies."

"That's gross."

"I do not understand. What is gross?"

"I mean it's disgusting."

"Why is it disgusting? I am Courtesan. I am expert at service. I have satisfied many customers."

"That was your old life. You don't have to service...I mean, have sex with anyone unless you love them."

"I do not know love. Do you plan to service Commander Chase?"

"What? No. I don't plan it."

"He will be dead tomorrow. If you love him, you should service him. He should die happy."

"Stop saying that. We're not going to die tomorrow."

"Our chances of survival against the Klix forces are 1,567,949 to 1."

"Stop saying that too," Evelyn said, gathering her cosmetics. "And why has it changed?"

Sheen paused for a moment, redoing her calculation. "You are correct, Evelyn; our odds have improved slightly. Perhaps Tripp is happy now and he will fight better in the upcoming battle. I will need to reexamine my data."

"Ugh! Now you're just trying to make me mad."

"I assure you, Evelyn...I am not trying to make you mad."

"Well, you are. I have to go before Chase goes to sleep."

Evelyn stepped back from the mirror and took a long

look, extending her left leg through the slit Tripp had cut in her dress. She then reached for the smaller square ripped out to clean her wound and pulled it apart—up to her waist—exposing her long right leg.

"Is ripping your dress more makeup?" asked Sheen.

Evelyn turned around, glared, and then smiled at Sheen. "That was an accident. Let's just forget about it."

"Sheen does not forget."

"Okay then, just remember it was an accident...and don't tell anyone, okay?"

"Sheen will remember. It was an accident. Sheen will not disclose this accident. Are we going to bunk together now?"

"Umm, yes sure, when I get back...yeah, but don't wait up for me."

"I detect arousal in your system. Do you wish Sheen to service you?"

"No. We'll talk when I get back, and stop scanning me."

Evelyn opened the door and found Max standing outside. It startled her.

"And what do you want?" she asked in an irritated voice.

"I was looking for Sheen. Is she here?"

"Right behind me; I was just leaving."

"I am here, Max 325," Sheen said.

"Can I come in?" he asked.

Evelyn walked down the corridor toward Chase's room, leaving the door open behind her.

"Yes, Max...come in," said Sheen. "Ah, you have performed your maintenance and have changed your appearance."

"My what?"

"Your cleansing routine."

"Oh that. Yeah, I took a shower, cut my hair and shaved, but I'm feeling really bad. There's a rumor that we're going to die tomorrow."

"I'm not supposed to say that. Evelyn Tupi does not like that."

Max hung his head low, staring at the floor.

Sheen scanned him. "I detect melancholy in your demeanor...and arousal."

Max sighed heavily, looking up with pouty eyes. "It's just that I was held prisoner by that scumbag Shoom for six months, and I haven't had sex in over a year."

"Ah, and Max does not wish to die without having sex one more time, yes?"

"Well, now that you mention it—yes."

"Very well, Max; Sheen will service you before you die. You can be happy again."

"Thank you, Sheen. When do you want to do it?"

"I will service you now, Max," said Sheen, closing the door.

Max grinned enthusiastically while Sheen removed her clothes and helped Max out of his. Max shivered in the cold station. Sheen concentrated momentarily, raising her body temperature.

"You are aroused. That is good. This will not take long."

"I'm in no hurry."

"Hold me, Max, and I will warm you."

Max reached out and hugged Sheen. Several minutes later, a loud scream was heard echoing throughout the station's corridors. Gage and Hector ran to Sheen's door weapons drawn.

"Everything all right in there?" asked Gage.

Fully clothed, Sheen stepped out into the corridor and closed the door behind her.

"Yes; everything is fine. Max was melancholy and I serviced him. Max is happy now. He is resting."

A moment later, the door opened and Max appeared dazed with his flight suit only partially on. He wobbled out into the hallway drunk-like, grinning.

"You okay, Max?" asked Hector, laughing.

Max giggled and weaved down the hall, back to his room.

"He had not been serviced in a long time," said Sheen. "He is happy now."

Gage looked at Hector and Hector at Gage.

"Sheen," said Hector, "we have not been serviced in a really long time, either."

"And you are going to die tomorrow," Sheen added.

"We are?" asked Gage.

"Our chances of survival against the Klix forces are 1,567,732 to 1."

"That can't be right," said Gage.

Sheen stared ahead, thinking. "It is approximate, but it is correct."

"Are you sure?" asked Hector.

"It is highly probable."

"Well, shit," said Gage. "I wasn't planning on dying, maybe Hector, but not me."

Hector looked at him surprised.

"The odds have improved recently," said Sheen., "but you should both prepare for that eventuality."

"I don't want to die," said Hector, "not yet anyway. How about you, Sheen...are you prepared to die?"

"I have already died once; it is not pleasant. I do not wish it, but the Klix must be stopped. If I die trying, then Sheen died trying, and that is all a sentient being can do."

"Aren't you sad?" asked Hector, looking concerned.

Sheen stared straight ahead for a moment. "I am feeling melancholy," she said. "I have not known friends before, and now that I have friends, I do not wish to lose them. I have not had a kind Commander, and now that I have one, I feel the loss of him even though it has not happened yet. I do not like this feeling. It is discomforting."

Hector stepped forward and put his arm around her. "Do you wish me to service you, Sheen?"

Gage gave Hector a look of shock. "Hey, I can service you too, Sheen! I mean, if you feel bad," Gage added.

Sheen cocked her head, thinking. "No one has ever offered to service Sheen. I do not need service, but thank you. I could service you—if you both wish it?"

Gage and Hector nodded vigorously.

"Very well; come in, and I will service you now."

Hector and Gage bumped into each other trying to get through the door first. Sheen looked back over her shoulder and smiled as she removed her clothes and closed the door. Several minutes went by before two loud screams echoed down the corridors. Nobody responded.

***

Earlier, down the hall, Evelyn knocked on Chase's door softly.

"Who is it?" he asked.

"It's me, Evelyn...Eve. Can I come in?"

"Door's open."

Eve stepped in barefoot, wearing what was left of her torn dress, her long legs exposed from her waist to her feet by the slits in the dress. Chase's room was like every other sleeping quarters in the station: lockers, a bench, a small table bolted to the floor, a sink, and room for a cot he had set up in the corner of the room. It was like a more comfortable version of a prison cell, or a cheap motel room without a bed. It was dimly lit overhead by the same unflattering lights used throughout the station.

"Looks like you need some better clothes for tomorrow," Chase said, eyeing her damaged dress and long legs. "There are some flight suits in here you can probably fit, and some boots."

"Thanks; this dress is mostly rags now," she said, reaching down to pull her dress closed, exposing even more leg.

"Sure is ripped up," said Chase, smiling, staring at her legs. "Still, you do make rags look good."

Eve smiled, feigning embarrassment at her torn dress. There was an awkward silence for several moments that seemed eternal. Their eyes met, and they both started to speak.

"I meant to..." they said simultaneously.

"I'm sorry," said Chase, laughing. "You go ahead."

"I just wanted to say I'm sorry, Chase—for what happened."

"You're sorry? You didn't do anything. I've felt terrible ever since."

"It wasn't your fault. You saved me. I never thanked you for that."

"It should never have happened. I should never have trusted Loose."

"I meant to come back," Eve said, "to the log...but I just couldn't. And my grandfather, he kept a close eye on me after that. He never blamed you, though. He knew it was Loose. That's why he was so hard on him all the time."

"It's okay. I understand, and I'm sorry about your grandfather. He was a great man."

"He was. He liked you."

"He did?"

"He said you were different from the others. Said you were better...that you had a gentle streak."

"Well, then, he didn't know me very well."

"I think he did."

Eve looked down at the floor then at Chase, gathering her courage. "I missed you, Chase."

"I missed you too, Eve—every day that I went back to that log, I missed you. I was miserable for a long time. Then I just went numb and concentrated on my duties. I haven't felt anything for anyone since. Until I saw you walk in with Tripp."

"Oh, Chase, I wanted to see you every day too...and be with you, and hold you, but I couldn't; I couldn't go back there."

"It's okay; probably for the best. I'm a Piecer soldier. I should've told you that from the start. Piecers fight and die. There is no place for you in my world. You would only get hurt."

"Sheen says we are all going to die tomorrow—that the odds are against us."

"Maybe, maybe not...nobody can know the future, not

even Sheen."

"But there are so many Klix and so few of us."

"Remember that day in the woods when I was worried about you walking home?"

"Yes."

"And you flipped me twice, even though I was much bigger and stronger than you?"

"Yes, but..."

"Sometimes a smaller force can overcome a bigger force. I have no plans on dying tomorrow."

Chase turned from her and rummaged through his compartment's lockers, opening doors and closing them until he came upon one with a flight suit.

"Here, this should fit you. Might be a little baggy, but it does have body armor built in, so that should help. And here's some boots."

Eve held her arms out, palms up, ready to take the clothes from him. He laid the flight suit on both arms flat, and then the boots on top of the suit. One of the boots tipped and started to fall. They both immediately ducked to catch it, bumping their heads against each other.

"Ow—shit!" cried Eve, dropping everything and holding her head wound. "Sonofabitch..."

"I'm so sorry," said Chase, reaching out to hold her up. "I was just trying..."

Eve grabbed the gash on her head with one hand and steadied herself by holding Chase's arm. Then she started laughing. "I keep getting hit in the head," she said. "I think the universe is trying to tell me something."

Chase laughed. "Here, let me look at it." Eve dropped her hand from her wound, and Chase moved closer to examine it. "Looks okay; not bleeding. I'm really sor—"

Eve pulled him closer and kissed him on the lips. Chase's heart was racing. He kissed her back, starting with her lips, then her face and neck.

"I've missed you so much for so long," he said. "I never thought I would see you again."

244

"Oh, Chase," said Eve, kissing him more. "I thought about you every day. Do you...do you still care about me?"

"I've never thought about anyone else!"

They stopped kissing for a moment and stared into each other's eyes.

"I love you, Chase Chambers...do you know that?"

"I love you too, Eve Tupi—more than you know."

Two loud screams echoed from down the hall, then all was quiet. Chase and Evelyn looked at each other and both started laughing.

"Busy night," said Chase. "I hope she didn't kill them."

Eve smiled. "Do you mind if I change in here? Sheen's in my room and she sounds...busy."

"No of course not; I'll turn around."

"You don't have to," said Eve slipping off her ripped dress, standing in front of him in only her panties and bra.

"You're so beautiful," Chase said, "even more beautiful than I remember."

Eve lifted her arm—joking to break the tension—pretending to scan Chase like Sheen. "I detect arousal," she said in a robotic voice.

She unhooked her bra, letting it fall to the floor. Chase's eyes followed it, embarrassed to be caught staring. Eve then slipped off her panties. Standing naked in front of him, her arms slightly turned out at her sides—palms forward—displaying herself to him. She paused for a moment while Chase stared. He swallowed nervously. Then she moved toward him, unzipped his flight suit, and slipped the suit from his wide shoulders. Her hands brushed his shoulders as she removed the suit, and he remembered that time at the creek when their hands first touched and the tingle when their hands met. He shivered, not from the cold, but from the soft electricity of her touch.

"This is long overdue," she said.

"Yes it is," said Chase. "I love you, Eve. I've loved you from the first day we met."

As Chase reached out and hugged her close to him, his

powerful arms enveloped her, and she buried her face and long blond hair in his chest. Chase stroked her hair and caressed her cheek, wishing the moment would never end.

"I love you too, Chase," she said, embracing him. "I feel so safe when you hold me. Don't ever let me go."

"I will love you until the day I die," he said.

Eve looked down and away, saddened and worried.

"Don't worry, my love. I have no plans on dying anytime soon."

He squeezed her close, feeling her against him, feeling her breathing, her slender smallness against his large frame. She felt like a fragile bird in his arms, and he was careful not to squeeze her too tightly. He held her close and didn't want to let go. Finally, he picked her up and took her to the bedroll he had made up on one of the cots.

"This isn't how I wanted it to be," he said. "I wanted it to be special. I hoped we would have a big soft bed in a lavish room somewhere—not this dank room on a frozen moon. And time...I wanted more time."

"This is fine," she said, as he laid her down on the cot, "more than fine. And this is all the time we have—right now, in this moment."

Chase kissed her gently.

Chapter Eighteen

0600 Hours

The next morning, Chase entered the station's kitchen hearing whistling and the sound of pots and pans softly clanging.

"Morning, Hector," Chase said. "Get any sleep?" "Not much," he replied, grinning and continuing his whistling.

"You're sure cheerful this morning."

"Am I?" he asked, shaking a pan full of dehydrated eggs as if to music. "Hadn't noticed."

"You're whistling. I've never heard you whistle in your life."

"Huh...funny," said Hector, going back to whistling and shaking the pan. "I thought I would make breakfast for everyone before we leave."

"That's very nice of you," Chase said, looking at him suspiciously. "Thanks."

"Could be our last meal. We gonna die today, Boss?"

"No. Nobody dies today; nobody except the Klix."

"Roger that," he said, flipping the eggs in the air and spinning around to catch them in the pan.

"What's gotten into you?"

"Me? Nothin'; I'm just happy."

"Couldn't have anything to do with Sheen and those bloodcurdling screams I heard last night, could it?"

"Could be...she is an angel. I mean dios mio; I thought I died and went to heaven. I think I'm in love."

Chase laughed. "I didn't know you speak Spanish."

"Un poco. I am more worldly than you know."

"What else can you say?"

"Dos cervezas por favor and ¿Dónde está el baño? You need the last one if you know the first one. But that's about it."

Chase laughed. "So she's that good, huh?"

"She knows things even I don't know."

"No way! Things that even you don't know? How is that possible?"

Hector raised his eyebrows and curled his lip, knowing Chase was messing with him. "You look pretty relaxed yourself, Boss," Hector said wryly.

Chase looked away, slightly embarrassed, caught off guard. "I'm good; fine."

"Uh-huh. I saw Evelyn tiptoeing it down the hall around 0500 hours, coming from your direction. Looked like she had just robbed a bank and was making her getaway."

"Don't know anything about that," said Chase, clearing his throat.

"Uh-huh."

"You seen Max?" Chase asked, changing the subject.

"Speak of the devil," said Hector, "and the devil appears."

Max entered the kitchen whistling and placed a small package on the counter.

"Your EMP, Chase...tiny package—big boom. Oh, and the pulse lasers are fixed."

"Thanks, Max. This little thing?"

"Yep; I call it Big Boom-Boom. It will knock out any electronics in orbit and on the surface anywhere."

"You look so different," said Chase. "Are you wearing cologne?"

"Nope...just showered, shaved and cut my hair, but same ol' me," Max said, now whistling in harmony with Hector. "I am hungry though, and those eggs smell heavenly, Hector."

"Lots of whistling and heaven-talk today," said Chase. "You didn't by any chance pay a visit to Sheen last night, did you?"

"A gentleman never kisses and tells," said Max, smiling from ear to ear, "but oh my God, yessss."

"Seems like Sheen was very busy last night."

"I'm gonna marry that girl," said Max. "I swear to God I am."

"Oh no you're not," said Hector. "I got first dibs."

"Dibs schmibs...there are no dibs. May the best man win."

"Done," said Hector. "You can be the best man at our wedding."

"You can be the flower girl at my wedding," said Max.

Hector slammed down the pan of eggs. "I will show you 'flower girl at your wedding' when I cut you in two."

"Whoa, whoa, whoa, knock it off," said Chase. "Save it for the Klix. Where's Tripp and Gage?"

Tripp and Gage entered the kitchen, dancing and singing, "Cha cha cha."

"Good morning, ya'll," said Tripp. "Wow, what a great day to start a war. Cha cha cha."

"You mean to finish a war, doncha?" asked Gage. "Cha cha cha."

Chase rolled his eyes.

"Expertly put, my good man—expertly put."

"Why thank you, my good man, thank you."

Locking their arms at their elbows, they spun each other around, uncoupling to face Chase.

"Ta-da! Reporting for duty," said Tripp. "Let's kick some Klix ass."

"Roger that, my brother," said Gage. "It's ass-whoopin' time."

"I'm glad to see everyone is in such a good mood and ready for a fight. Anyone seen Sheen?"

Evelyn walked into the room wearing a flight suit and boots. Everyone stopped and stared.

"What? I changed my dress. So what?"

Nobody said a word.

"What? Did you tell them?" she asked Chase, her eyes

wide and in shock.

Everyone stared at Evelyn. Chase shook his head left and right, but it was too late.

"You told them we slept together last night?"

"Nope," he replied.

Hector, Gage, and Max smiled and stared. Tripp laughed out loud. Evelyn stopped talking, stunned, and turned bright red.

"Well...well, I don't care who knows it. We're all probably going to die today anyway, so stop grinning at me like a bunch of adolescent baboons."

"Ooh, she's got your number, Tripp," Hector said, laughing.

"Nobody is dying today," said Chase. "Let's everyone mind their own business and grab some chow. Please sit down at the table and eat before we take off."

"I am here, Commander," said Sheen, entering the room. "I am minding my own business per your orders, but Sheen does not need breakfast. I am fully charged."

Max jumped over to the table and pulled out a chair for her. "Here, Sheen...sit here— next to me."

"No," said Hector. "I set the table and put Sheen at the end of the table next to me."

"Well you don't get to save seats," said Max. "Sheen, do you want to sit over here by me?"

Chase squeezed the bridge of his nose, looked down, and sighed.

"Sheen can sit anywhere," Sheen said. "As I am not eating and it does not matter where I sit."

"You can sit by me, Darlin', if you like. I think we had a moment last night... something special."

"Bullshit," said Gage. "We had the moment last night— Sheen and I. You were just a brief chore. Sheen will want to sit by her Gage-baby."

Tripp burst out laughing. "Gage-baby? Oh my God. Isn't that what your mom used to call you? Dude, you have mommy issues." Tripp kept laughing.

"Stuff it, four-minute man."

"Sheen, would you mind taking the seat on the end of the table...in the middle?" requested Chase. "That way, you can sit with everyone."

"Yes, Commander."

Chase stood at the opposite end, the head of the table; Eve sat next to him at his right hand. "I've made a slight revision to our attack plan, if there are no objections."

Everyone looked up at Chase, wondering what changed. While everyone was looking at Chase, Max shifted himself closer to Sheen.

"Max and I will still handle the Vengeance, but Eve...um, Evelyn, will come with us, me and Max. Sheen will be on the Promise with Tripp. Gage and Hector can handle the Lone Star."

"Well, shit," said Gage, "that's convenient."

Chase looked at him, surprised.

"I mean, sure...that's fine, Chase; sorry—whatever you say."

"Hot damn!" said Tripp. "Don't worry, Darlin'...I'll take good care of you."

"Sheen will be in command of the Promise, Tripp. She is already familiar with the ship."

"What?"

"You will be her first officer."

"I'm okay with that. Sheen, Darlin', you can tell me to do anything you want. And I do mean anything."

Max glared at him.

"Commander," interrupted Sheen, "I do not understand. Sheen should be with you. I should be with my Commander; it is my function."

"I will not order you to take command of the Promise, Sheen. I'm asking you to do it as a favor to me."

Sheen stared and cocked her head. "Is this change because Evelyn serviced you?" she asked. "Sheen can service you and you will change your mind, yes?"

Evelyn glared at Sheen.

"No, Sheen; it's not that. It's just that I've known Evelyn for a long time, and I let her down once. I don't...I can't do that again."

Sheen looked at Evelyn and then Chase. "I will command the Promise as you wish, Commander. I will comply with your request."

"Thank you. I appreciate that, Sheen. Please transfer your regen machine back to the Promise."

Max stood up from the table. "I could fly the Promise with Sheen."

"Then who would fly the Vengeance? And I need you to deploy the EMP blast."

Max sat down, huffed, and crossed his arms. "Fine," he said, "let's kill those sons of bitches and get this shit over with."

"Look, I know we have all become...close friends. I know we would all like to be together, but that is not the mission. Our families and the Earth are depending on us to do our best and put all feelings aside. I know I am asking for your indulgence with Eve flying with me, but I do not think I would be at my best worrying about her on another ship. Can you forgive me for that?"

"Nothing to forgive, Chief," said Gage. "Mission comes first."

"No problemo, Boss," replied Hector.

"Hell, I'm fine with it," said Tripp. "Sheen and I will make a great team."

"Me too," said Max.

"Thank you everyone. I—we both appreciate it." Chase reached forward and picked up a glass. "I know it's just powdered orange juice, but I would like to toast to our mission's success."

Everyone raised their cup.

"To a successful mission, a free Earth, and for those who were lost on Soren," said Chase. "We leave in ten minutes. Check your weapons and check your ships; we rendezvous on the dark side of Earth's moon."

Chapter Nineteen

Things Get Sticky

"Okay, everyone...time to go," said Chase. "You have your coordinates. We'll rendezvous at the moon. We go in first, using the Vengeance as cover, deploy Big Boom-Boom, and worm back to the moon until the blast goes off. They won't suspect one of their own ships in orbit."

"Roger that," said Tripp. "Where we go after that?"

"After the blast goes off, they'll be pretty busy trying to figure out what happened. They won't have any working weapons or communications. Any ships not in space should come crashing down. We land at the stadium field; plenty of room and close to where any surviving Piecers could be hiding. We need to get the weapons to our guys first. Gage, you know the underground pretty well; you and Hector hook up the jeep and trailer and get those weapons to any survivors down there."

"Consider it done, Chief," said Gage.

"Jeep and trailer already loaded," said Hector. "We're good to go."

"Sheen, you and Tripp provide cover when you get there. If you see any Klix, take 'em out."

"Yes, Commander."

"You got it, Cha-Cha."

"It's important that we get the weapons delivered to our people," said Chase. "Distribute as many as you can...as quickly as you can, then hightail it back to the ship to get more. Max, Eve, and I will run interference if any ships come in from space. You're gonna need to figure out the weapons systems on the Vengeance pretty quick, Max."

"No problem, Captain—got my translator right here. A ship's a ship, a gun's a gun."

"Eve, stay on the com with these guys. We'll monitor the Klix from up here and relay the details."

"I can do that," said Eve.

"If anything goes wrong, we all head back to the moon and regroup."

"Roger that, Chief," said Gage.

"And Sheen?"

"Yes, Commander?"

"Whatever happens, defend yourself."

"Yes, Commander."

The crew finished their food and gathered their personal belongings. Gage caught Chase's eye and nodded, giving him a thumbs up. Hector patted Chase on the butt, saying, "Good hunting, Boss." Tripp walked by and winked at Chase, whispering, "Kill 'em all, Cha-Cha."

Chase smiled and nodded. "Keep your wits about you and stay the fuck alive."

"You got that right," said Max. "Stay the fuck alive, you guys—and watch out for Sheen." They all walked out to their ships, waving each other off with a half salute.

Chase, Max, and Eve climbed aboard the Vengeance, its engines still running.

"Max, how's our fuel? Thing's been running all night."

Max held up the translator and found the fuel gauge. "Says we're mostly full, if I'm reading this thing right."

"Get us into space, Max."

The Vengeance's engines hummed louder, and the ship took off vertically from the Pwyll crater into space.

"I need to see what's out there, Max; gimme a screen, a window, something."

"Comin' up now, Chase."

The entire front of the ship became transparent, and Chase could see through everything from where he stood.

"Pretty neat trick," said Chase, "wonder how they do that? Max, figure out the weapons systems and get back to me. Eve, see if Max can show you how to work the com."

"Gage gave me another translator," she said. "Gimme a minute, and I should have something."

***

Back at the Pwyll station, Tripp and Sheen climbed into the Promise. Sheen looked overhead at the Klix scout ship disappearing into space before closing the hatch.

"You're worried about him, aren't you?" asked Tripp.

"I am feeling twitchy. I do not like twitchy. A Courtesan should be with her Commander."

"That's normal before a fight—or when someone you love is heading for a fight."

"Do you love Chase 523?" Sheen asked. "Are you twitchy?"

"Love him? Hell yeah. He's my brother; he's family. He's always been there for me and makes sure I don't screw up."

"Do you screw up often?"

"Too often, I'm afraid."

"Do not screw up today, Tripp 523. I am in command of the Promise, and I do not wish to fail my Commander."

"No worries there, Darlin'...too much at stake. Dammit, now I'm feelin' twitchy!"

"Very well, Tripp 523. Sheen will do what is necessary— for Soren and for Earth. It is how you say in your world, 'time to put it back.'"

"Close, Darlin', but I think you mean payback time," Tripp corrected.

Sheen cocked her head. "Yes; it is payback time."

The Promise's engines burst to life and shot into space.

"Set our coordinates for Earth's moon," said Sheen. "Initiate wormhole sequence."

"Roger that, Darlin'."

Sheen smiled as they slid into the wormhole, leaving the

Klix scout ship last to worm out.

***

"You think we got a chance?" Hector asked Gage as they climbed the ramp to the Lone Star. "I don't much feel like dyin' today."

"I ain't dyin' today," Gage replied. "I got a date with Sheen after this thing is all over."

"You got a what?"

"I arranged a debrief...to discuss our mission and our strategy. I'm planning to get debriefed myself."

"You dog! You better hope Sheen doesn't get mad when she figures you out. You saw what happened to Tripp."

"I'm her little Gage-baby, I may show up de-briefed."

"I'm coming with you."

"Oh no; two's company, you're a crowd."

"C'mon...it was fine last night."

"I need some alone time with my lady."

"I'll make my own date, then."

"It's a free galaxy...at least it will be soon."

"Fuckin-A man; fuckin-A. Let's kick some Klix butt."

"Let's do."

The Lone Star's engines wound up, and Gage throttled them like an impatient dragster. He held the throttle open and blasted straight up into space.

"Coordinates for the moon are set," said Hector. "Wormhole is forming."

"Okay, assholes...here we come," said Gage.

***

"The Vengeance is pretty easy to figure out, Chase," said Max. "Nothing special here, but some of the panels feel weird or greasy—sticky—like they've just been serviced or some-thin'."

"I don't know," said Eve. "Something's wrong. I can feel it. Call it a woman's intuition."

"Just battle jitters," said Chase. "We'll be fine. Max, did you enter the coordinates for the moon?"

"Ready when you are, Chase," Max replied.

"The Lone Star and the Promise are entering their wormholes; let's not be last to the dance."

"Roger that; wormhole sequence engaged—here we go."

The Vengeance hummed and shot forward into the spinning whirlpool of stars.

Chapter Twenty

The Moon

The Promise was the first ship to arrive at Earth's moon.

"Tripp 523, make sure we orbit in sync with the moon and remain hidden from Earth," Sheen called out.

"Roger that, Sheen; ship is locked in sync with the moon."

"We will wait for the others to arrive," said Sheen. "Check weapons and be prepared for any Klix ships in the area."

The Lone Star appeared through a swirling bubble mist, off the port side of the Promise.

"Sheen, this is Gage on the Lone Star...we are in position."

"This is Sheen of the Piecer ship Promise. We will await Commander Chase before proceeding."

The two ships waited, expecting a wormhole to open and the Klix ship Vengeance to appear.

"Sheen, this is Gage—it's been ten minutes. Did they say anything to you before they left? Were they having any trouble?"

"Negative, Gage 523...their ship was running all night without incident. They should have been right behind us—though I am not familiar with Klix wormhole technology."

"I don't like it," said Gage. "It's not like Chase to be late."

"We will wait," said Sheen. "I am following orders."

"Roger that, but I still don't like it. Ten more minutes and

I'm going to look for him— orders or not."

"Affirmative," replied Sheen.

The two ships floated side by side—in concert with the moon, waiting— wondering when Chase's ship would appear.

***

The Vengeance slid through the wormhole with a slight spin, forcing it to level out as it exited. After leveling out, the ship stopped dead. The transparent window disappeared.

"What's going on, Max?" Chase screamed. "I can't see shit!"

"I don't know; the engines just cut out. Everything is offline, except communications."

"Eve, see if you can contact the Promise or the Lone Star."

"Lone Star, Promise, this is Evelyn...do you read me— over?"

There was no response.

"Lone Star, Promise, this is Evelyn...do you read me... over?"

"Hello, Eve," came the reply. "It's nice to hear your voice again."

"Who...who is this? Identify yourself."

"You don't remember me? Pity. I remember you."

The Klix engines started back up, and the transparent window opened. Klix ships had surrounded them with one scout ship—bow-to-bow—facing them. The other ship's window soon became transparent, and standing on the bridge of the other ship was Loose, surrounded by Klix soldiers.

"Max, where the fuck are we?" Chase yelled.

"I don't know. I put in the coordinates for Earth's moon."

"You can forget your big plans, Chase!" said Loose, laughing, "or whatever it is you've cooked up. It's over. Do you think we weren't monitoring our own ship?"

There was a long pause and silence over the com.

"Wondering where you are or how you got here, brother?"

"Loose, you're okay. Thank God. I was going to look for you after I found Mom and Dad."

"Oh, how touching, but I already found them. No need to worry."

"Where are they? Are they safe?"

"They're alive...last time I checked. They're my prisoners—along with a lot of your ex-Piecer brothers. Sadly, some put up a fight, and well...let's just say they won't be joining us."

"What do you mean, 'your prisoners'? What are you talking about? What the HELL are you doing with the Klix?"

Loose laughed again. "Don't you get it, brother? I'm Team Klix. You're Team Loser."

Chase's face turned ashen white with the realization. "You're betraying your own kind...your own family?"

"Oh please; save your sanctimonious bullshit for the pulpit. My own kind is me, period. I was hatched in a lab just like you. We have no family; it's all government orchestrated shit—merely a fantasy."

"If you have a beef with me, fine...but just let Eve and Max go."

"A beef with you? Well, sure, there's that, but this is bigger than both of us. This is planetary big—galactic big."

"Just let them go, and I'll go with you."

"You have no bargaining power. I could destroy you, your ship, everything you hold dear. I just have to order it and it's done."

"But why?"

"You still don't get it? I'm better than you. You, the super soldier. Faster, quicker, better—the Bad Batch. Always one-upping me...humiliating me, but not now, not anymore."

"I never tried to humiliate you."

"Well, you did leave me for dead in the woods. That wasn't very brotherly."

"You tried to rape Eve! I should have killed you."

"Oh, who cares, she's just a 'normie.' She is not like us. We are bred to be superior. She should have been grateful that I even tried. But you're right about that last part; you should've killed me when you had the chance."

"You sorry fuck. I won't make that mistake again."

"Even now, you don't get it. I'm smarter than you ever were. Do you think the Klix just leave ships lying around with their engines running?"

"They didn't; I killed their crew."

"Well, yes, some pawns have to be sacrificed to capture a queen. I knew you couldn't resist a damsel in distress. You're so goddamned predictable, brother. That's your problem. We snatched that hapless Quargg female and staged the station to look like she was looting it. She was bait and you fell for it...hook, line, and sinker."

"You killed all those men—just to get me?"

"Technically, you killed all those men...which I knew you would...somehow. Well done, by the way."

"You're sick, Loose. You need help."

"Hardly, I have a clarity of thought you cannot comprehend. I am not like you—with your wishy-washy, goody-two-shoes, save-the-world bullshit. I see what I want. I plan. I take it."

"Let them go and I'll come with you."

"Fuck you; this isn't a negotiation."

"Chase, I'm not letting him take me alive," said Eve. "I'll kill myself first."

"Max, check our weapons."

"Weapons are offline."

"Come on, Chase. I haven't got all day. I've got a planet to run, and I need to repopulate it. In fact, I think I'll start with Eve."

"I'll fuckin' kill you first!" yelled Chase.

Loose waved his hand, and Chase's scout ship began to vibrate. Then a loud whine started, getting louder and louder, higher and higher pitched—so loud it hurt. Chase, Eve, and Max covered their ears. Max tried to fire the ship's weapons, but they were useless.

"My head is splitting open, Chase!" Max screamed as loud as he could. "We have no weapons."

Chase checked his guns, readying for a fight. He pulled

Big Boom-Boom out of his coat pocket and slid it under the ship's console, out of sight. Then he moved to put his arms around Eve's ears. She held him tightly, trying to cover his. The sound became louder and louder until they all collapsed, blacking out from the overwhelming noise.

Chapter Twenty-One

The Belly of the Beast

When Chase woke up, he tried to cover his ears, thinking he was still being assaulted by the horrendous noise. He could not pull his hands forward. His hands were chained to a wall above and behind him. He moved slowly to stand and pulled on the chains as hard as he could, but there was no give in them. He looked around the small cell and saw nothing but stone walls and floor.

"Eve," he screamed, but there was no answer.

From a cell adjacent to his own, Max heard him. "Chase, they took her somewhere. I couldn't see where," he called out.

"Are you okay?" asked Chase.

"I'm okay. They got me chained to a wall. I can stand, but that's about it."

Footsteps approached and then fell silent. The cell lock turned, and Loose walked in.

"Loose, let Eve and Max go; I'll do anything you want."

"Oh, I don't really care what you do. If you haven't noticed, you can't do anything. You see, even with all your strength, you're impotent...bested by my superior mind."

"Just leave them out of this. Let Eve go."

Loose moved closer to Chase, just out of reach. "Um, no, I don't think so. Eve Tupi will be the first mother of my many children. It seems fitting, don't you think? General Tupi's granddaughter, my first wife. I mean, it's biblical when you think about it. Her name is 'Eve', for fuck's sake. You see, I plan to repopulate the Earth with my seed only—perfect DNA. The world will be a place of order because all orders will come from me... Big Daddy. No more fighting, no more petty bickering, no war, just peace and order. Even you should see the benefit in that."

"And the Klix?"

"I have a deal with them. I become king of Earth, and they leave us alone in exchange for all of Earth's silver...and some help getting it out of the ground. See? It's win-win!"

Chase lunged for Loose, trying to reach his neck. Loose jumped back, laughing.

"Ho ho, nice try. Nothing worse than a trapped, dumb animal."

"Loose, you don't have to do this," said Chase.

"Of course not; I want to do this. I've wanted to do this, well, ever since I can remember. I was born to do this. Oh, and Mumsy and Pops send their love. Yes, they're still alive. Mom's a little old for the smelter, but she can take care of my brats for me, don't you think? She always wanted grandchildren, well now she'll have a shitload of 'em. Pops, though? Well, he belongs in the smelter."

"They never did anything to you. They took care of you. You're crazy!"

"I assure you, I feel great. Oh, and nice six guns, by the way, Wyatt Earp—except it's not Halloween. Figures dear old Dad would give you his prized possessions; he always favored you, anyway. I prefer a nice laser rifle or stinger pistol; more bang for your buck. But you won't be needing them, so I think I'll hang on to them for a bit."

"He left his guns for both of us, asshole."

Loose's sneer melted for one second, and he looked surprised.

"You can have the guns. You wouldn't be here if it wasn't for them."

"Bullshit; if not them, then some other dumbass government foster family."

Loose paused. "It's odd how much faith they have in you, Chase. Even now, they still think you will rescue them somehow—the old fools. If they saw you like this, I think you would be a bit of a disappointment. Don't you?"

"Eve and Max have done nothing to you. They aren't a part of this."

"Oh, Max...yes, thank you for that gift! A Fixer; hard to find these days, so few survived. He's being fitted for a collar and a leash right now. He will come in handy as my mech-monkey. Did you know he can fix anything? Amazing, really. Oh, and you know my plans for Eve, so..."

"You're not going to get away with any of this. There are others who will stop you."

"Oh, your Piecer brothers and that android woman—who are all hiding behind the moon? Didn't think I knew about that, did you? We've been monitoring your ship for some time now. What are you calling it now...the Vengeance? That's hilarious, you and your feeble little crew. What do you think three men and a sex robot can do against all of us? I've sent ten cruisers to get them, dead or alive. I really don't care which, though I wouldn't mind taking a spin on that sex machine I've heard so much about. Have you?"

Chase glared at him, saying nothing.

"Nah, not you...not Chase the chaste, but then again, you did have Eve, so it's not like you were exactly celibate, were you, big brother? How was she anyway? Am I going to have as much fun as I think?"

Chase lunged at him again, the chains holding him back. He pulled forward but could not escape.

"Pathetic as usual; no thought behind your predicament—a dog on a chain."

"I'll kill you, one way or another," said Chase, straining against the chains.

Loose cocked an eyebrow. "I'm scared! Okay; this was fun, but now it's boring. I think I'll go see how Eve is doing. I'll hang a tie on my door, so nobody disturbs us." Loose laughed, grabbed his crotch and thrust his pelvis forward. "Ungh," he grunted. "Don't wait up."

Chase could hear him laughing down the hall as the cell door slammed shut.

"Leave her alone, Loose!" Chase screamed after him. "I swear to God I'll kill you."

There was no response. He pulled at his restraints, trying desperately to free himself, and then he heard Max shout from his cell, "Get away from me, you fuckers."

There was much clicking back and forth until he heard the zap of a stun gun. Max screamed and went silent.

Chase could hear the hammering of metal as a collar was affixed to Max's throat. He looked around the room for anything he could use, but the cell was bare. He summoned all his strength and pulled at the chains but could not free himself. He squeezed his hand together and tried to pull it through the steel cuffs, but his hands were too big. He screamed in anguish, thinking what might be happening to Eve down the hall.

Chapter Twenty-Two

All is Lost

"**A**lert! Seven Klix enemy vessels approaching. Update: nine Klix enemy vessels...update: ten Klix enemy vessels approaching," the Promise computer blared.

"Lone Star, this is Sheen. Klix vessels are appearing through wormholes all around us."

"We see 'em," said Gage. "Klix cruisers—a shitload of 'em."

"Weapons hot," Tripp yelled. "On your command, Sheen."

"I count ten in all, Sheen," said Gage. "You think this has anything to do with Chase not being here?"

"There is a high probability," she said. "We are being hailed."

"Piecer ship Promise, this is General Klume of the Klix Supremacy. You are surrounded by superior ships and superior numbers. We have your Piecer Chase 523 and his crew imprisoned on our home world. If you resist, they will be killed and you will be destroyed."

"Sheen, are you hearing this?"

"Affirmative, Gage 523."

"You ready to fight?"

"Negative," said Sheen. "I have analyzed their capabilities and ours. Our two ships would be ineffective against their ten. We would surely be destroyed."

"We can't just give up!" said Gage.

"They have Commander Chase and the others; unless you wish us all to die, we must capitulate."

"Fuck! How the hell did this happen?" Gage shouted in frustration.

"Tripp 523," said Sheen, "prepare yourself for surrender."

"Well, shit, I ain't never surrendered before. Not sure I know how."

"You must not oppose the overwhelming forces that will surely come for us."

"I wasn't really asking."

"This is General Klume. We are sending you coordinates to enter into your worm-drive navigation systems. Do not deceive us or try to escape. If you do, Chase 523 will die immediately."

"This is Sheen of the Piecer ship Promise. Your coordinates have been entered."

"Engage your worm drives, Piecer ships, and follow us. Remember, if you deviate, your Piecer friend and his crew will be killed."

The Klix cruisers disappeared into wormholes one by one, and the Promise and Lone Star soon followed, disappearing into the stars.

"You have any idea where we're going?" asked Tripp.

"I believe these are the coordinates for the Klix home planet, Kattar," replied Sheen.

"Oh great; from ten to millions. I need a drink."

"Prepare yourself, Tripp 523. This will be unpleasant. Max keeps whiskey in his quarters, if it will help you to cope."

Tripp left and returned with a bottle of whiskey.

"If you don't mind, I'll drink your share," he said, putting the bottle to his lips. "I know it does nothing for you."

"Do not despair, Tripp 523. I can service you, if you like."

"Thanks. Any other time I'd say yes to that, but I'm not in the mood."

Tripp took a deep swig and put the bottle down unfinished. The ships came through wormholes—surrounded once again by Klix cruisers orbiting a planet covered with thick yellow fog.

"Shit," said Gage over the com. "That's the Klix home world. I don't want to die...not here, not now."

"Me either," said Hector. "I will not be put down like a dog."

"If you see your chance, take it," said Gage. "Stay sharp."

The Klix boarded the Promise and the Lone Star, putting their men in place on the bridge and in the engine room to fly the ships to the surface. Sheen, Tripp, Gage, and Hector were searched, put in chains, and taken aboard General Klume's ship.

"You were wise to surrender, Sheen," the general clicked into his translator.

"I am Acting Captain Sheen, of the Piecer ship Promise," Sheen snapped back.

"Ah...yes, Colonel Loose told me about you. From space slut to Acting Piecer Captain—a lateral move if I ever saw one," he clicked, laughing.

"I wish to see Commander Chase," said Sheen. "Has he been hurt?"

"You will join him soon enough. Colonel Loose has plans for you all."

General Klume clicked out orders to his crew, "Set coordinates for the compound. We will transfer the prisoners there and then return to Earth."

"Yes, General; we are preparing to land. What do you want us to do with their ships?"

"Colonel Loose wants their ships. Have them follow us down to the planet and leave them there. He can do what he wants with them."

Tripp overheard the orders over Klume's translator. "Loose?" he asked. "I thought he was dead."

"I assure you he is quite alive," the general clicked in response. "How do you think we found you?"

"Fuckin traitor," screamed Hector. "I'll kill him."

"He has been useful to us," clicked Klume. "His planning has proven to be excellent thus far. We could never have found all your underground hiding places without him. Humans are like insects; always one more hiding in the dirt."

The general clicked like he was laughing.

"I'll kill that motherfucker!" said Gage. "I swear to God I will."

"I might let you," said the general, "but he is still useful to me. And his pathetic needs in no way conflict with my own." The general turned to his men. "Guards! As soon as we land, take them to the prison and put them in cells. Make sure they stay chained. Then return and rendezvous with my squadron at Earth."

"Yes, General Klume," they said, saluting him.

The ships landed on the uppermost deck of a vast military compound, and the prisoners were marched down a long corridor below ground. The compound was part of an enormous foundry where silver was smelted from ore in giant furnaces. Rivers of molten silver ran below the industrial complex—beneath a blanket of thick yellow fog. The fog surrounded the entire planet, a byproduct of the sulfur exhaust from the foundry. It made the air musty, acrid, and difficult to breathe. As the prisoners walked past Chase's cell, Gage coughed.

Chase called out to the hallway, "Gage? That you? Is everyone okay?"

"So far so good, Chief. Nice to know you're still alive."

The Klix guard hit Gage in the kidneys with his rifle butt. His knees buckled from the pain.

"No talking," he clicked into his translator. "Keep moving."

"Put the rifle down, motherfucker, and we'll see how tough you are."

"No talking," he said, again raising the butt of his rifle. Gage turned around and was led to his own cell past Chase's and Max's.

The captives were chained to the walls in the older section of the prison complex with steel chains and cuffs. They tried breaking them without success.

Sheen calculated the tensile strength of the chains holding her. These chains cannot hold me, she thought, but I must not resist until I am sure my Commander is safe.

Meanwhile, Loose had made it back down to his quarters, the old emperor Kalar Ku's throne room. The room was cold, damp, and surrounded by moss-covered stone walls. The room had been sealed until Loose found it and had taken a liking to it. He said it suited him as he was soon to be the king of Earth and should have a king's quarters. That amused the general—knowing the dead king was interred there—so he let him use it while he visited the Klix world.

Evelyn was chained to a cot by her hands and feet, pulling her chains, trying to free herself.

"We meet again," Loose said, entering the room. "Kismet?"

"Let me go, you pig," she shouted.

Loose moved closer, running his hands up and down her legs. "Oh yes, I'm going to enjoy this. God your skin is like velvet!"

Evelyn screamed, and turned away, crying.

"Oh there, there, my lovely...don't cry. You will get used to me. In time, you will grow fond of my touch. I can be a very generous lover."

"Fuck you. I could never love you."

Loose started to undress, and Eve started sobbing uncontrollably, pulling at her chains as hard as she could. Suddenly, there was a loud pounding on the door.

"What?! And it better be fucking important."

"We have captured the other Piecers, Colonel Loose."

"Oh. Well, then, excellent. For once...you didn't screw things up."

"Do you want them executed?"

"No. Not yet. I want to get a look at that sex robot."

Loose grabbed his shirt and got dressed. "Don't worry, Eve. I'll be back soon, and we can start our adventure together." Loose laughed, looking over at her. "Now don't go anywhere; I'll be right back."

He laughed again, watching Eve squirming to free herself as he closed and locked the door behind him. "Where did you put the captive Sheen?" he yelled to the guard.

"Cell seventeen," he clicked back through his translator.

"Ooh...lucky number seventeen. We have a winner!"

Eve's scream had echoed through the halls reaching Chase's cell. He could feel his rage building and started to breathe heavily. He closed his eyes and stood close against the wall, letting his arm-chains slacken. Then, as hard as he could, he began to beat his left hand against the stone wall. Each blow was harder and harder until his skin split, leaving blood-red smudges on the wall. Sweat began to pour from his face as he slammed his hand against the wall again. He held in screams of pain as he crushed the carpal bones of his hand against the stone. He could feel his hand disintegrating, the bones breaking from the repeated blows. Finally, after one last hit, he could feel his hand fold in on itself as he pulled against the cuff holding him. His hand was free.

Down the hall in cell seventeen, the guard opened Sheen's door, and Loose walked up within reach of her.

"Well, well, well, what have we here? They were right; you are a beautiful robot."

"I am Sheen. I am Courtesan. I am android, not robot."

"Not a robot, eh? What part of you is human, then?"

"Not human, Soren."

"Okay, well...what part of you is Soren, then?"

"My brain is Soren."

"I used to think Courtesans were a myth—like mermaids—but here you are." Loose ran his hand over Sheen's body. "You feel real. I understand you're some kind of cosmic whore?"

"I am Courtesan."

"I command you to have sex with me right now."

"You are not my commander. I have no commander. Chase 523 freed me."

"Fuck him. He's as good as dead. I will kill him, and then I will be your commander."

"No. I will not service you. Commander Chase said I am free and only do service if I wish it."

Loose moved in closer and grabbed Sheen by her face, squeezing her cheeks and jaw. "Nobody says no to me, princess. I will be your commander if I kill your commander."

"No. Commander Chase gave me freedom. You will not be my commander."

Loose pushed her face hard and her head hit the wall.

"You cannot force me to be your Courtesan. I have been beaten by worse than you."

"You have not known worse than me, robot. I have other ways to make you obey me."

"I will cease to function soon—as I cannot regenerate. You will not have me."

"Well then we'll find a way to plug you in."

"I do not plug in. I must regenerate."

"Colonel," said the Klix guard, clicking into his translator, "the robot has a regeneration machine on the Piecer Promise ship."

"Well, go get it, you fool...and plug this bitch in. I want full power when I take it for a ride."

"I will not service you," said Sheen.

"What is it with everyone having a mind of their own?!" Loose exclaimed angrily.

He turned back to the guards and pointed at Sheen. "Make sure she's chained while she regenerates. I don't want her getting any ideas. She will service me, or I will destroy her."

After a moment, Loose turned to the guard outside the door. "And bring me the prisoner Max-what-the-fuck—that Fixer. He'll make that robot obey me or I'll kill 'em both."

The guard clicked his response and saluted him.

Chase heard a commotion from the hall and then heard Max's cell door open. Chains clanked, and he could hear scuffling.

"Don't pull me, you alien shits!" Max screamed.

The Klix guards clicked into the translator, "Colonel Loose wants you. We will stun you again if you do not comply."

Chase heard Max cursing down the hall as he was led away.

Chapter Twenty-Three

The Fixer

Max was led to Sheen's cell, which was slightly larger than his and was mostly empty— except for her regeneration station, a table, and a tiny iron stool on wheels. Loose and several guards were waiting with their stingers drawn. Sheen was chained to the wall by long chains, allowing her to reach her regeneration station.

"Oh finally, you're here," said Loose. "Good; I have use for you."

"Fuck you, traitor," Max snarled.

"Please…save your indignation for someone who gives a shit. You'll do what I say, or I will hurt you until you do. And trust me, I can really, really hurt you."

"I won't help you," Max replied softly.

"Yeah, you will. You see your Courtesan friend over there recharging? Beautiful, isn't she?"

Loose paused and turned back to Max. "I wonder, have you? Did you?"

Max looked away and did not respond.

"Oh, you have, you randy devil! You took a ride on the robot, did you? Tell me, was she as good as they say?"

"I won't help you."

"Such a gentleman! She must have been a fabulous fuck-ing fuck. Here's the deal: you help me, or I will kill her while you watch…then I'll kill you just for fun. Whadya say?"

The regenerator chimed, indicating that regeneration was

complete.

"Oh good my Pop-Tart is ready," said Loose, smiling. He turned to Sheen as she stepped out of her regenerator. "Sheen, who is your Commander?"

"I am Sheen. I am Courtesan. I have been freed by Commander Chase. I have no Commander."

Loose turned back to Max. "You see my problem. My robot is broken. I need you to fix it, Fixer. I will be her Commander or you both die. Got it? Now, get to it. Reprogram this bitch or whatever it is you have to do."

"I don't know how she works," said Max. "I wouldn't even know where to start."

"Oh well in that case, guards, kill her...and then kill him."

The Klix guards raised their weapons, pointing them at Sheen.

"Don't! I don't how she works. I don't know how to reprogram her."

"Too bad," said Loose, "but I am a busy man, worlds to conquer and all that, so guards, if you will? Proceed."

"No; don't. Let me look at her first."

Loose smiled and waved his arm. The guards put away their weapons.

"I would have to get inside her, and I have to see if she has an access point."

"So do it."

"I don't know where it is."

"Oh, for fuck's sake, do I have to do everything? Sheen, do you have an access point?"

"It is forbidden," she replied.

"Nothing is forbidden to me."

"It is forbidden," she repeated.

Loose paused for a moment, thinking. "What if your life is in danger and you need a doctor?"

Sheen cocked her head searching her memory. "If Sheen needs repair, it is allowed."

"Well you do need repair. You are broken."

"I have performed a diagnostic following my regeneration. I am functioning within normal parameters."

"Well you won't be. Show us your access point or these guards are going to shoot Max dead in the head, then I'm going to send them to shoot Chase 523, and when they come back they're going to shoot you. Guards!"

The guards raised their weapons and pointed them at Max's head. Sheen looked at Max and forced a smile. "I do not wish to die, and I do not want him to kill you or Commander Chase. You must reprogram me and live. It is senseless for us all to die."

"Is it me or is the robot the only one making sense?" asked Loose. "Guards, take the chains off my new toy."

"I don't know how, Sheen," said Max, "and even if I did, I wouldn't want to make you subject to this a-hole."

"Hey! I'm standing right here," said Loose. "I could cut your ears off for less than that."

"Big man with weapons and guards," snapped Max.

"Oh please, Fixer...I could snap your neck before you blinked your eyes."

"I will comply," said Sheen. "Do not fear for me, Max."

The guards removed the long chains from Sheen, still attached to her and the wall. Sheen removed her top and turned around sitting on the nearby table. Leaning forward, she went quiet, and suddenly an outline of a panel formed on her back. Everyone stared in amazement.

"I do not know how to reprogram me," she said, "but you now have access."

Loose clapped and rubbed his hands together. "Excellent. Now we're getting somewhere! She better be calling me Commander by the time I get back, if you want to stay alive. Oh, and erase her memory while you're at it. I don't want her to remember you, Chase, or his motley crew. But leave all her sexual expertise intact and any useful subroutines. We don't want to lose those now do we?"

Loose headed to the door turning back over his shoulder to bark out more orders. "Guards, if he tries to leave, shoot him. I'll be right back, and I better not be disappointed."

"Yes, Colonel!" they clicked, saluting him.

Loose slammed the cell door behind him as he left. The Klix guards watched Max's every move, keeping a stinger trained on him at all times. Max walked over to Sheen and stared at the exposed outline of a panel on her back.

"I have had many commanders, Max," she said. "All have been cruel and self-serving—until Commander Chase. I did not know any other way, and I have always survived. So must you. Do what you must to live."

Max touched the outline of the panel and it opened. Inside a small screen and a keypad of alien symbols was exposed. "I don't know what any of this means," he said.

"You must hurry, Max," said Sheen, "before he returns."

Max turned to the guard closest to him. "I need one of your translators."

"Fuck you, human," clicked the guard, laughing.

"I need one of your translators, or I will tell Colonel Loose I couldn't complete my task because you refused me."

The Klix raised his stinger, pointing it at Max's head. "I could shoot you and tell him you tried to escape," clicked the guard.

"You could," said Max, "and he might believe you, but then again, he might not...and he is a crazy motherfucker."

The guards clicked back and forth until the closest guard handed over his translator. Max held it up over the symbols on the keypad, viewing the translated results. He pressed a key, and Sheen twitched. He pressed another, and she responded, saying, "I am Courtesan." Max continued to press buttons, noting each movement and expression Sheen made.

He pressed the buttons faster and faster, watching through the translator's screen. Suddenly, Sheen slumped forward as if unconscious. The Klix guards watched in wonder, and then pointed their guns at Max.

"Take it easy. I didn't kill her. Give it a minute."

The guards watched, and nothing happened for several seconds. Then her arm twitched and her eyes opened. Sheen sat up.

"I am Sheen. I am Courtesan. Are you my Commander?"

The Klix guards smiled and clicked back and forth to each other.

"No; I am not your Commander," Max replied.

Sheen turned to the guards. "Are you my Commander?"

The guards clicked into their translator, "Colonel Loose! Colonel Loose is your commander."

"Which of you is Colonel Loose?" she asked.

Max looked at Sheen and put his hand on her shoulder. "Do you remember me?"

"Are you Colonel Loose?"

"No...I'm your friend—Max."

Sheen cocked her head once more, searching her memory. "I am sorry. I have no memory of friend Max," she said.

Loose burst into the room, throwing the cell door open so hard it hit the wall with a bang.

"Well? Did you fix it?"

"Yes," Max replied somberly. "She is rebooted. She has no Commander."

"Sheen, who is your Commander?" Loose shouted.

"I have no Commander. Are you my Commander?"

"Yes! I am your Commander, Commander Loose."

"Do you wish me to service you now, Commander Loose?"

"Yes, well, no, not yet. Do you know who Commander Chase is?"

"I do not know a Commander Chase. Commander Loose is my Commander."

"Very good. Yes, very good indeed. I do not want you to use the name 'Sheen' any longer. Your name as my Courtesan is Luna."

"Yes, Commander Loose. I am Luna. I am Courtesan."

"Excellent; good job, Fixer. I knew you could do it. Guards, take him back to his cell."

"But I did what you asked," said Max.

"I said good job and you're still alive, so hey, there's an attaboy for ya. So fucking needy! Did you think I'd let you go?

Guards! Get him outta here."

The guards took Max back to his cell, chaining him to the wall again. Chase heard the commotion from Max's cell and pretended to still be chained to the wall, holding his bloodied arm up against the wall in case the Klix looked in. One of the Klix guards glanced into Chase's cell through the barred window in the door. He saw Chase with his head down as if unconscious and left. After the noise died down, he could hear the guard's footsteps head down the hall.

"You okay, Max?"

"I'm okay—chained to the fucking wall again, but okay. Chase, I have to tell you something."

"Hang tight. I'll get you out of there. You can tell me after."

"No...it's important.

"Shh! Wait."

Chase looked at his mashed hand hanging limp, still bleeding. His right hand was still chained to the wall attached to the cuff. Chase turned around and pulled the chain, climbing up the wall with his legs on either side of the ring holding it to the wall. He pulled, using his leg muscles, the cuff cutting into his wrist. He pulled more. The ring holding the chain bent—elongated by the pressure—but held. He took a deep breath and thought of Eve, the day they met and how the sun lit up her hair. He pulled harder and harder, the cuff cutting deeper into his wrist to the bone. He heard the sound of a crack, like ice breaking on a frozen pond. Finally, a chunk of rock wall gave way and he was thrown across the room on his back, still attached to the cuff and chain.

The chain had four long bolts through a metal plate still attached to the large broken chunk of rock wall. The noise from his fall brought two Klix guards running to his door. He plastered himself against the wall at the cell door. The guards stared through the barred window but could see nothing— only an empty chain and a wrist cuff hanging from the blood-streaked wall and the cavity where the other chain had been attached to the wall. They clicked back and forth frantically, and then checked the still-locked door. They argued until the one closest to the door unlocked it and stepped inside, his weapon drawn.

Chase swung his rock chain like a mace, hitting the guard in the head, decapitating him. The other guard turned to flee, clicking loudly until Chase wrapped his chain around the guard's throat and dragged him back into the cell.

"Where is he holding Eve, you piece of shit?"

He released the chain for a moment and the Klix gasped for air. "In the king's chamber, but I will not tell you where that is, human," he clicked into his translator. "I will not betray my people."

"I don't have time for games," said Chase.

Chase pulled the chain tighter until he heard the Klix's neck snap. Searching the guard's pockets, he found keys to the chain locks and cell doors and looked outside. The corridor was clear. He looked down at the chain and the now-bloodied rock hanging from his right hand and decided to keep it to use as a weapon. He crept outside and down the hall to Max's cell, unlocked the door, and slipped in.

"I knew you'd find a way," Max said, pulling on his chain. "Get me outta here."

"Shh," said Chase, holding his bloody finger to his lips "Klix."

He unlocked Max from the wall, his chain still attached to his collar.

"Get this fucking thing off me," Max whispered, grasping his collar.

"I can't. It's hammered shut. There's no key."

"I'm gonna kill your fucking brother."

"If I don't kill him first."

"I gotta tell you something...it's about Sheen. I reprogrammed her and—"

"It's gonna have to wait. We need to free the others."

"But it's impor—"

Chase held up his hand to silence him, and he and Max crept down the hall, entering each cell using the guard's keys, and freeing Tripp, Gage, and then Hector. Gage spotted Chase's bloody left hand dangling loosely at the end of his arm.

"What happened to your hand?" said Gage. "They do that?"

"I'll be fine," whispered Chase.

"We need weapons," said Hector in a low voice.

"I feel naked," whispered Tripp. "They took our knives."

"Klix weapons won't work for us," Chase whispered. "We need to get to the Promise, but first...we have to find Eve and Sheen."

"I can make the Klix weapons work," said Max, "but I'm gonna need one of those dead guards."

"Back in my cell," said Chase. "You need help?"

"No, you go get Eve. I'll catch up, but Sheen, she's—"

"Shh, someone's coming." Chase held up his hand, waving Max on to leave.

Goddammit, thought Max, nobody ever fuckin' listens. I'll have to hurry.

Max snuck back to Chase's cell—where the bodies of the dead guards lay on the floor.

This won't be pretty, he thought, searching the guards for anything that he might use to cut Klix flesh. He searched the Klix guards. They were not carrying knives, but one of the guards had a thin metal belt buckle.

This will do, he thought. Now I need something heavy or at least heavy enough.

He grabbed the guard's stinger and used it as a hammer, the buckle as an axe head, and chopped the Klix's hand off with a few quick blows.

"Now I just gotta clean out these finger bones and guts, and my new Klix glove will be ready to go." He grinned.

A few moments later, Max held up his hand with a makeshift Klix skin glove. He grabbed the Klix pistol, and it lit up in his hand.

"Disgusting, but it works," he said to himself. "I'm a frikkin' genius."

Max turned to head for the door—with his gun in hand—when a guard came in.

"Don't move, human, or I will shoot."

Max aimed the pistol at him, and the Klix laughed.

"You fool! Our weapons won't work for you," he clicked into his translator.

"Wanna bet?" Max fired the laser pistol, hitting the Klix in the chest, and he fell to the ground dead.

"Now to find the others," Max said, stepping over the Klix's body.

Chapter Twenty Four

The Kings Chamber

Chase, Tripp, Hector, and Gage made their way down the long hall of cells.

"Loose is holding Eve in the king's chamber," said Chase.

"Where the fuck is that?" asked Tripp.

"I don't know. First, we get Sheen, and then we'll get one of these guards to tell us."

"I heard them take her," said Hector. "Then I heard them drag Max in the same direction. It's this way."

They opened the doors of every cell until they came upon cell seventeen. They peeked inside and saw one Klix guard standing by Sheen's regenerator.

"Regen's here...no Sheen," whispered Gage. "One guard inside."

"I say we ask him politely if he knows where she is," said Tripp, "and if he doesn't give us the answer, we rip his fuckin' head off."

"Brute force," said Hector, "my favorite kind of force."

"Works for me," said Chase.

"I'll go high, you go low," said Tripp.

"Why do you always get to go high?"

"Fine...you go high, then, and I'll go low."

"Ladies, get on with it or get out of the way," whispered Chase, pressing himself against the wall.

"Sorry," Tripp and Hector whispered together.

Hector banged on the cell door. Inside, the Klix guard pulled his weapon and looked out through the barred cell door window.

"Don't move," the guard click-shouted into his translator.

"Oh, I'm not," said Hector, his hands raised over his head. "You got me. I surrender."

The guard unlocked the door and Tripp threw himself against it, slamming the door into the guard. The Klix fell backward and onto the floor. Hector was on him in seconds, ripping the weapon from his hand and pointing it at the guard. The guard started laughing, clicking into his translator, "You can't shoot me with our weapons, foolish human."

"You're right," said Hector, as he pistol-whipped the guard in the face until he was nearly unconscious. "What was I thinking?"

Chase walked in and stopped him. "Don't kill him yet; we need to know where Eve and Sheen are."

Hector pulled the pistol back as if to hit the Klix once more.

"No more, please," the guard clicked. "I beg you."

"Not so funny now, huh?" said Hector. "Where are our friends, Eve and the Courtesan Sheen being held?"

"They were taken to Colonel Loose's quarters, the old king's chamber."

"Where the fuck is that?"

"Below the compound."

"How do we get there?"

"Behind the door at the end of the hall, there are steps down. The chamber is there."

"What do you want us to do with him, Chief?" asked Gage.

Hector and Tripp turned to hear Chase's answer. Chase made a slashing motion across his throat.

"Sorry," said Hector, as he drew the pistol back to beat the guard to death.

"Wait!" the guard clicked into his translator. "I told you what you asked. I have a family...children."

Hector looked over at Chase, who paused hearing him. "He'll turn on us if we leave him," said Hector. "Fuckin' Klix are all alike."

"I know," said Chase.

"No; not all alike," clicked the guard. "Many of us hate Klume. I won't say anything. I don't want to die."

Hector raised the pistol to strike him again. "Your call, Boss, but I'd kill him."

"Me too," said Tripp. "Can't trust 'em."

"Are all humans like Colonel Loose?" he clicked.

Chase remembered his father's words. "Wait, Hector. Don't. We're not like them or Loose. Besides, on a whole fucking planet of Klix, one more won't make a difference. Tie him up, bind his scrapers, and lock him in here. I don't want him warning anyone."

The guard looked shocked. "Thank you, thank you, human. They told us you were all animals," he clicked. "You are not. What is your name, Piecer?"

"Chase, Chase 523."

"Chase 523, I am Katal. I promise I won't say anything. You have my word."

"We'll see," said Chase, turning back to Hector. "But just to make sure..."

Katal nodded as Hector bound him and the scrapers behind his head so he could not make any clicking sounds. He also stuffed a rag in his mouth to prevent him from bleating, a sound the Klix could make from their throat.

"We still need weapons, Hector. What's taking Max?"

"You think he bought the farm?" asked Gage.

"I doubt it. He's like a cat—got nine lives. He'll turn up."

"Should we wait?"

"No...we can't. Let's go."

Chase led his team through the hall and down the long stone winding, circular stairway to the king's chamber. The walls and floor were ancient by comparison to the upper hall and cells. A lone shaft of light from a hole in the ceiling lit a chiseled stone throne in the center and illuminated the surrounding chamber. The throne was raised above the floor on a round stone step and looked out from the center of the room.

Chase stepped onto the chamber floor first and saw Loose sitting on the carved stone throne. He was wearing Chase's black hat and had his holster and guns slung across the back of the chair. A black-haired and nearly naked woman was draped across his lap, wearing only panties, boots, black eyeshadow around her eyes, and black lipstick. To the left of the throne, Eve was chained by her wrists to the wall, wearing only her underwear.

"Chase!" Eve screamed from the wall.

"Well, well, well...the gang's all here," said Loose. "Like my new hat? You know Eve, of course, but let me introduce you to my new Courtesan, Luna."

"Luna?" asked Chase. "Is that Sheen? What have you done to her?"

"I am Luna. I am Courtesan," said the woman, standing.

"Sheen, it's me—Chase."

Luna did not respond.

"She doesn't know you, Chase...and her name is Luna. Get it through that thick head of yours. Luna."

"What did you do?"

"Oh? Didn't Max tell you? He fixed her! Much improved, don't you think?" said Loose, standing and holding her hand, displaying her as a trophy. "Will you just look at that? She's perfection—and let me tell you, very, very talented. If she could reproduce, shit, you could have Eve. She's a little too yacky for my taste, anyway. But since she can't, Eve will have to bear my children, and Luna will be my queen."

"You're insane, Loose."

"Am I? I hold all the cards."

"Not anymore."

"I got this Cha-Cha," said Tripp, moving forward.

"You're no match for me, Tripp," said Loose. "You never were."

"I will kick your crazy fucking ass!" replied Tripp.

"Luna, don't let this soldier—Tripp 523, near me," shouted Loose.

Luna moved between Tripp and Loose, blocking his way. "Sheen, it's me…Tripp, remember?"

"I am Luna. I am Courtesan. Do not proceed, Tripp 523."

"Sheen, I don't want to hurt you, step aside."

Tripp lunged right and then left to get by her. Luna mirrored his movements and punched him hard in the face. Tripp flew backward off the throne step, landing with a thud on the hard floor.

"Sheen!" Eve screamed, "don't. They're your friends."

Luna paused momentarily. "I am Luna. I am Courtesan."

"We don't want to hurt you, Sheen," said Gage, "but we will if we have to. Hector, let's do this."

Hector lunged forward, grabbing Luna's right arm while Gage grabbed her left. She threw them across the room as if they were toys. Chase ran toward her, swinging his chain rock, heading for Loose. Luna grabbed the chain, stopping the rock's motion in mid-swing. She pulled the chain hard and threw Chase off balance, throwing him back from the throne's step.

"You can't win," said Loose, laughing. "This bitch kicks ass."

Tripp got up and charged forward. Luna picked him up and tossed him behind the throne, using his own momentum to smash him against the chamber wall.

Chase, Gage, and Hector got up and advanced at the same time. Hector grabbed her legs, while Chase and Gage tried to grab and hold her arms. Luna kicked Hector back hard in the gut, and then threw Chase and Gage into opposite walls.

"Finish them," shouted Loose, pointing. "Start with that one…the one they call Chase 523," he said with a sneering grin.

"Yes, Commander," said Luna as she walked steadily toward Chase, who was still stunned from hitting the wall.

She grabbed him by his arm and under his shoulder, picked him up and threw him hard against the floor. Then she straddled him and began punching him left and right in the face, breaking his skin and drawing blood. Blood gushed from his nose as she continued to beat him.

"How do you like it?" screamed Loose. "Not so great getting your face beat in, is it?"

"Sheen, stop it—you'll kill him," screamed Eve. "Sheen, you love him!"

Luna hesitated. "I am Luna. I am Courtesan. Commander Loose has ordered me to finish him. I will finish him."

Gage, Hector, and Tripp struggled to their feet, charging her from behind. Chase lay bleeding on the floor, trying to catch his breath, trying to wipe the blood from his eyes to see. The trio jumped on Luna, knocking her off Chase, giving him a moment to breathe and clear his eyes. Luna stood up and grabbed Tripp, punching him several times in the stomach. Then she picked him up and body-slammed him to the stone floor. A loud crack was heard as his ribs gave way from the force.

"You fucking bitch," screamed Hector, grabbing Luna from behind and around the throat in a choke hold. "I'll kill you for that."

"I do not breathe," she said, elbowing him in the chest, gut, and face in rapid succession until he released her. "You cannot choke me."

Finally, Luna spun him in the air and threw him into the wall.

"Okay, psycho bitch," said Gage, "let's dance."

"I do not understand 'psycho bitch.' I must finish you."

"Finish this," said Gage, throwing all his weight into a punch that landed squarely on Luna's face.

Luna reeled from the blow, stumbling backward.

"I'm sorry, Sheen. You're not yourself. You're sick or something."

"This...this is fabulous," said Loose, clapping. "More! Finish them, Luna. I am your commander. Finish them!!"

"I am Luna. I must destroy you."

Gage motioned her forward with his fingers. "I don't

want to hurt you, Sheen, but I will stop you."

Luna ran forward, ducking her head at the last moment and throwing her head and her full weight into Gage's stomach, knocking him backward. He stumbled back, trying to regain his footing. Luna continued pushing hard and fast until he hit the wall with a loud crack, the back of his head snapping against the wall and splitting open. His eyes rolled back, and he slid down the wall unconscious, leaving a trail of blood on the wall behind him.

She's going to kill him, Chase thought. "Luna!" he screamed, staggering to his feet. "You were ordered to finish Chase 523 first. I'm Chase 523. Obey your commander."

Luna turned, narrowed her eyes, and began to run toward Chase at full speed. She ducked her head, preparing to ram him. Chase let her charge him, and as soon as she was upon him, he lay down on his back, grabbing Luna's arms and placing his foot in her stomach. He pulled her off balance toward him, flipping her across the entire length of the king's chamber. She hit the wall with a loud crash and a whimper. She appeared stunned momentarily, and then got up slowly. Locating Chase quickly, she ran toward him, arms out in front of her as before.

Chase swung his rock chain in wide circles. As Sheen came close, she smashed the rock with her fist, breaking it into pieces, ripping open her skin and exposing her metal skeletal hand. The chain fell limp, and Luna kept coming. Chase grabbed her once more, intent on flipping her again. Luna grabbed onto his spacesuit, her fingers squeezing his collar tightly. Chase flipped her over, but she did not let go. She did not fly across the room. She landed behind him—still holding on—right on her back. She then pulled him to the side and got on top of him, straddling him again.

"Oh bravo, Luna," said Loose clapping. "This is better than interplanetary wrestling."

She resumed punching Chase in the face repeatedly, opening up previous wounds and breaking his already bloodied nose.

"Stop it, Sheen!" Eve screamed. "You're killing him!"

"I am Luna. I must finish him as ordered."

"Yes, Luna...finish him—FINISH HIM!" screamed Loose. "He wants to hurt your commander."

"Don't, Loose," screamed Eve. "Stop her. I'll do anything you want."

"Anything?" asked Loose, turning to Luna. "Luna, stop."

Luna stopped hitting Chase immediately and stared straight ahead.

"Will you love me?" asked Loose, turning back to Eve.

"Yes; I'll love you."

"Like you did Chase?"

"Yes...anything—just let him live."

"Oh, now you had to go and spoil it. If you loved me, you wouldn't need Chase to live, now would you? And I don't think you're being entirely honest with me. No. As long as Chase is alive, you will still love him."

Loose turned back to Luna. "Luna, finish him."

Luna returned to beating Chase as Max entered the room, holding a Klix gun in his hand. "Sheen, stop," Said Max pointing the gun at her.

Luna ignored him.

"Fixer, those guns won't work for you," said Loose. "You should know that."

Max fired the pistol into the ceiling and Loose flinched. Max turned the pistol, pointing it at Loose's head. "Next one is through your head, Loose. Call her off. I won't miss at this range."

"Oh, you are a clever Fixer. You got the Klix pistol to work for you. Luna, stop."

Luna stopped, still straddling Chase. Chase wasn't moving. Max ran to him, holding the pistol on Loose. He bent over and checked the pulse in Chase's blood-covered throat.

"He's still alive, you fucker. But if he dies, you die."

Loose started moving around the perimeter of the chamber. Max kept his pistol trained on him.

"You know, Fixer, I had big plans for you. You could have

lived like a god! You still can. Just put down that pistol and we can talk."

"Right. I put down this pistol and you kill me."

"Why? Why would I kill you? You're no threat to me. Besides, I need you in case Luna ever needs a tune up."

"I'm not fixing anything for you ever again. You're a psychopath."

"Psychopath? Is that what you think? I will create peace on Earth as king, and you call me a psychopath?"

"Narcissism...plus killer...yep, that's pretty much the definition of a psychopath. They have your picture next to the word in the database."

Loose kept moving, and Max had to move to keep following him with the gun.

"Move any closer and you're dead," said Max. "I'm not playing."

Luna stared straight ahead while Max patted Chase's cheek to bring him around.

"C'mon, Chase, c'mon, wake up, we gotta go."

Chase moaned and coughed. Max looked down at him, taking his eyes off Loose for a moment. Loose ducked behind the king's throne—hiding—and screamed, "Luna, disarm him."

"Yes, Commander."

Luna grabbed the pistol, struggling with Max for it. Max jumped on top of her, and she fell back on the floor, his face close to her head. Max whispered into her ear, and Luna struck him hard in the face. He flew backward across the floor.

"Kill him," screamed Loose. "Kill him!"

Luna stood up, pointed the pistol at Max, and pulled the trigger. Nothing happened. Max moaned, and reflexively tried to block the coming blast with his arms. Luna cocked her head, stared at the gun, then Max.

"Luna, kill him...I command you," Loose hollered again.

Luna pointed the gun at Max, then at herself—as if wondering what the gun did. Her head started to twitch, then her

295

shoulders. She turned her head left, then right, and started walking sideways.

"Luna, kill him…kill him!" screamed Loose. "Where are you going? Kill him!"

Luna continued walking sideways into the chamber wall, backed up, and walked into the wall again, looking confused. She held out her hands, feeling the wall as if looking for an opening or exit. She turned and dropped the pistol to the floor. Max and Loose stared at the pistol momentarily before Loose ran for it.

"Fuck, I have to do everything myself," Loose said, diving for the gun.

He pointed the weapon at Max who was still lying on the floor.

"Now you pissed me off, Fixer. I was gonna let you live, but you had to be a hero. You're gonna die, right after you fix my robot."

"I'm not going to fix Sheen for you, you pathetic loser."

"It's Luna, you fucker, Luna…and you will fix her." Loose pointed the stinger pistol at Max. "If you're not going to fix her, then I have no need for you."

Loose pulled the trigger, again and again.

"Aren't you forgetting something?" said Max, holding up his Klix-gloved hand. "Klix weapons won't work for you either, dumbshit."

"Then I will kill you with my bare hands," Loose snarled.

Suddenly, a loud and hard punch came from behind Loose into the center of his back. His knees gave way, and he screamed and fell to the ground, dropping the Klix pistol. Now on all fours, he drew a deep breath, then stood up and turned around, throwing himself at his attacker, Luna.

Luna was ready and picked him up, easily throwing him against the wall. He slid down, stunned, and then charged her again.

"You will not harm my friend Max. I am Sheen. I am Courtesan and I am free. I will defend myself."

"No!" screamed Loose. "You are Luna. I am your Commander. I command you to stop."

Sheen grabbed him by his collar and threw him across the room. "You made me service you."

Loose flew, landing on his back with a thud. Sheen ran toward him, picked him up again, and threw him back to the ground hard. Loose howled.

"You enslaved me when I was free."

She picked him up once more and slammed him to the ground again. Loose groaned.

"You made me tell you that I liked servicing you—that you were the best. I did not like it. You were not the best. You are pathetic, weak," Sheen stared at his crotch, "and small. Sheen can do what Sheen wants. Sheen will destroy you."

"No. It's not true. The robot bitch lies."

Sheen slammed him to the ground again. "I am Sheen. I am Courtesan. Sheen does not lie."

Loose tried to get up again and then fell back down. "I will have you all killed," he moaned, his face turned sideways on the floor, bleeding. "Do you think you can escape Kattar? The Klix will gladly kill you for me!"

Sheen ran over to Chase who was beginning to come to. "Commander Chase. It is Sheen. I am sorry for betraying you."

Chase looked up at Sheen, squinting through bloodied eyes. "Sheen?"

Sheen concentrated for a moment, shook her head. Her face and hair changed back to her normal color.

"It is you. Are you okay?"

"I am functioning within normal parameters," she said, smiling.

Chase smiled and then coughed up blood.

"Commander, you are injured," she said, holding her arm up to scan him. "I am sorry for what I have done. You should have left me. You broke your promise."

"It wasn't you; it was Luna. Besides, I told you we don't leave people behind."

"But you promised, and I could not stop myself. I would

have killed you."

"Luna would have killed me...not Sheen. It wasn't you."

"Machines do not forget, Commander. You must not make promises you will not keep."

"You are not a machine. A soldier has a duty to his crew. You are part of my crew and more than that, you are my friend. I could never leave you behind."

"I am malfunctioning, Commander. I am leaking from my eyes."

Chase smiled. "It's okay. You'll be fine."

Loose ran up to hit Sheen from behind.

"Look out, Sheen!" Eve screamed.

Sheen hardly moved, reaching up and behind her, grabbing Loose by the throat. He gasped as she squeezed his throat closed. He struggled and kicked, trying to free himself, but her hand was a vise tightening around his windpipe.

"You hurt my friends. You would force Evelyn to service you. You are an evil being. It is time you ceased to function."

As Sheen squeezed tighter, Loose began turning blue. After a few moments, he stopped struggling and went limp.

"Sheen, don't," said Chase. "We need him."

"Yes, Commander."

Sheen released Loose, and he slumped to the floor, barely breathing. Max reached down and helped Chase sit up.

"Commander Chase is injured, Max. Can you repair him?"

"Chase, can you stand?" asked Max, putting his arm around him to help him up.

Chase sat up, holding on to Max for help.

"How," Chase asked Max, "how did you do it?"

"Do what?"

"Change Sheen back."

"Oh. She was my weapon of last resort. I programmed a keyword only she would know and stored all her memories in a part of her brain that could only be accessed by that word. I tried to tell you."

"Kinda risky, wasn't it? What if someone said it by accident?"

"Unlikely. There were only three of us who knew it. Even Loose didn't know."

"What was it?"

"Luminfleur."

Chase smiled.

"I couldn't take a chance that someone would say something and trigger her too soon," said Max. "The keyword was a last resort."

"I think you should be leading our crew," said Chase, coughing more blood. "You're good at this."

"Oh no, I'm a Fixer, not a fighter. Besides, I don't heal like the rest of you. You fight, I fix."

"But you might have said something sooner," said Chase, forcing a painful smile.

Max's eyes widened in disbelief, until he realized Chase was kidding him.

"I think you like to fuck with me," said Max, laughing.

"I kinda do, Stinky," said Chase, trying not to laugh too hard. "Ow. Shit, that hurts."

Sheen looked at Max. "I am sorry, Max. I remember all that happened now."

"It's okay; I reprogrammed you. If it's anybody's fault, it's mine."

"No. He would have killed us both. You saved us."

"Still," he said, shrugging. "I'm sorry."

"Do not feel bad, Max. Let me help you," she said, leaning over and grasping his neck manacle.

"You can't, Sheen. It's been hammered shut. I can't get it off."

"I can," she said, pulling at the hasp until the bent iron pin pulled straight.

"Oh, thank you. Thank you. God, I hated that thing," he said, throwing the neck manacle and chain to the ground.

"Your hand," said Max. "Your skin is damaged."

Sheen looked down at her skin, torn away from the exposed metal below, and her eyes narrowed. She walked over to Loose, picked him up, and slammed him into the floor again. Loose groaned loudly as he hit the ground.

"Do not worry, Commander. I did not kill him."

"We need him, Sheen. He knows where our families are."

"Yes, Commander," said Sheen, swinging her arm back and smacking Loose in the head once more.

Loose moaned.

"He is fine," said Sheen casually.

"Sheen, these keys should work on Eve's manacles. Get her out of those chains and check on Gage, Hector, and Tripp."

Chase wiped his blood off the keys and handed them to Sheen. Sheen ran to Evelyn and unlocked her manacles. Evelyn put her arms down and shook them to get her blood flowing into them again, and then pulled her arm back and punched Sheen in the face as hard as she could. Evelyn screamed in pain.

"Sonofabitch, your face is hard!" she said, shaking her hand. "You almost killed him."

"I am sorry, Evelyn. You are right to be angry with Sheen."

Evelyn ran to Chase, sobbing. "Chase, are you all right? I thought she killed you!"

Chase coughed more blood, and grabbed his broken nose, bent to the side of his face by Luna's repeated blows. He groaned as he pushed it back in place.

"I'll be all right; just need a little time to heal."

Sheen then scanned each of the Piecers—stopping at Tripp, and then called to Chase.

"I have harmed them all, but they are recovering. I will not forgive myself for hurting them."

"It wasn't your fault. They won't blame you. It was Loose."

While all attention was on Chase, Loose had crawled back to the king's throne and grabbed one of Chase's pistols from the holster. He crawled behind the throne and pulled the trigger back.

Sheen heard the click and shouted, "Commander, look out."

"I'm gonna kill you with our dear old dad's antique fucking gun!" screamed Loose.

He raised the gun, pointed it at Chase, and pulled the trigger. A loud boom echoed in the king's chamber. In an instant, Sheen jumped between Chase and the throne. The bullet hit her in the stomach, and she collapsed to the floor.

Gage jumped across the room, landing on top of Loose. Loose fired the .357 again, but the shot went wide, striking the walls. He kept firing, hoping to hit Gage to get him off. Gage struggled with the gun until he wrested it out of Loose's hand and then smacked him in the head with it repeatedly until Loose stopped moving.

Chase crawled over to Sheen and pulled her onto his lap.

"Somebody help," Eve yelled.

Chase patted Sheen's cheek. "Sheen, Sheen, can you hear me?"

Sheen didn't move.

"She's not responding," said Chase. "Max?"

Chase looked down at the hole in her stomach. A semi-clear viscous fluid was leaking from her wound on to the floor. "Max, what do I do? Do something."

Max looked at the bullet hole and rolled Sheen over to see the exit wound.

"It's a through and through, but I don't know what was damaged inside...or how to fix it."

"Can't you do something—anything?"

"I'm not sure what that is coming out of her, but we better stop it. It could be her blood."

"Stop it how?"

Max grabbed Loose's knife and cut up the leg of Loose's flight suit for a bandage.

"Tie it around her. It may slow the leaking. We need to get her back to her regen machine. It might keep her alive until we can figure out what to do."

Chase shook his head to clear it and wiped his bloody

nose on his sleeve. "We have to go, Gage," he said. "Put that collar and chain on Loose. And bind his hands behind his back."

"Roger that, Chief."

Gage placed the manacle around Loose's neck and hammered the iron pin shut, using the empty .357 for a hammer. He tossed the gun on the floor while Hector ran forward and picked up Sheen out of Chase's lap.

"I've got her, Chase."

"It's okay, Sheen; I've got you," said Hector. "Chase, her regen machine is back in her cell. I'll take her there."

"No...we have a mission."

Chase grabbed his holster from the throne and then picked up his battered pistol on the floor alongside his hat. The handle was chipped from hammering Loose's neck manacle on, but the cylinders turned easily, and it was undamaged. He then loaded the cylinders with cartridges from his belt, dusted off his hat, put it on, and adjusted it forward in front.

"But it's Sheen," said Gage.

"I know. She just saved my life. Do you think I'd leave her behind? We're not leaving anyone behind. We're going to get her regen and get her back to the Promise. I have an idea. Max, grab that stinger. You're the only one who can use it. I need you to convince my scumbag brother to assist us."

"My pleasure," said Max, picking up the stinger from the floor and watching it light up in his gloved hand. "Ready."

"Gage, wake that asshole up."

Gage slapped Loose across the face. He moaned.

"Again," said Chase.

Gage slapped Loose across the face again hard, and his eyes fluttered open. Max leaned down and pushed the Klix stinger into Loose's right nostril.

"Wakey, wakey, you piece of shit," said Max. "And please...please make a move, so I can give you a new way to sneeze out the back of your head."

Loose's eyes opened wide, and he tried to move his hand.

forward.

"Not this time, loser," said Max.

Max yanked on his chain, and Loose coughed as the manacle dug into his throat.

"Not very comfortable is it?" asked Max.

Chase stood up over Loose. "Everyone here wants to kill you, especially me. You're only alive as long as you help us. If you deviate from that, any one of us here will gladly rip your head off. Do you understand?"

Loose nodded.

"Get up."

Max pulled Loose to his feet by his neck chain. Loose winced and whimpered.

"If he makes any move at all, shoot him until he stops moving."

"Yes, sir," said Max with a smile.

"Where are our ships?" Chase asked. "Are they where we landed with Klume on the top level?"

Loose nodded again.

"Tripp, Hector, see if you can get Sheen's regen machine and load it into the Promise. Gage, we're going to find our families."

Hector handed Sheen to Gage carefully. Then he and Tripp ran back up the stairs to Sheen's former cell to retrieve the regen station.

Chase turned back to Loose. "Where are you holding our families, Loose?"

"You'll never leave here alive, brother. The Klix will stop you."

"Max, shoot my brother in the balls."

"Yes, sir," said Max, aiming.

"No—wait! All captives were either put in cells in the compound or put to work in the foundry."

"Where's Mom and Dad?"

"Our dear mother is in a cell on the same level you were on. I'm surprised you didn't run across her already. Dear old Dad is in the foundry, smelting silver."

Max aimed the stinger closer to Loose's crotch.

"No! That's where they are. I'm telling the truth."

"I don't believe him, Chase," said Max. "Shall I? Can I?"

Chase looked at Max and then at Loose.

"It's true, I swear it," cried Loose. "I swear it."

"Where's our weapons?"

"You have your guns. Your knives were taken as souvenirs by our officers."

"Where's my fucking coat?"

Loose jerked his head pointing across the room. "There, in the corner on the floor."

Evelyn walked over to Loose and stood directly in front of him. His hands were bound, and Max was holding his neck chain.

"Where's my spacesuit, you perverted piece of shit?"

"Behind the throne."

Evelyn turned as if to get her suit, then whirled around and kicked him between the legs as hard as she could. Loose buckled to his knees.

"You bitch!" he screamed in agony.

"You ever touch me again...," screamed Evelyn, "and I'll kill you and wear your tiny balls as earrings, I swear to God!"

Chase put on his coat slowly, groaning with each movement while Eve slipped into her spacesuit.

"How's Sheen doing?" asked Chase.

"Can't tell," replied Gage, cradling her. "She's mumbling but I can't make it out. I think she's saying 'leave me.'"

"Somebody has to carry her back to the Promise and meet up with Tripp and Hector."

"I can carry her," said Max.

"You're the only one armed besides me. I need you with me."

"Well, Evelyn can't carry her—not far, anyway."

"Gage, it's gotta be you. We'll find your mom, I promise. Take Eve with you."

"I know you will," he replied. "I got Sheen."

"No," said Eve. "I'm staying with you."

"You can't. Help Gage with Sheen."

Chase held out one of his guns, spinning it over grip first. "Here, take this. Know how to use it?"

"Aim and then pull trigger...duh."

"Be careful; it's got a kick."

Eve took the gun and aimed down the sights. "Easy peasy."

"You have six shots; don't waste 'em."

Gage carried Sheen closer to Chase, and she moaned quietly, "Leave me."

Chase leaned over her, stroked her hair, and whispered, "We don't leave our friends behind. Besides, where would I ever find as good a first officer as you?"

Chase looked up at Gage, Eve, and Max. "We've made it this far as a team. We're not leaving this world without each other. No matter what happens, everyone goes home."

Eve moved over to Chase and wrapped her arms around him, kissing him, not wanting to let go.

"Don't worry. We'll be fine. Stay safe, and don't take on a fight unless you have to."

Eve began to cry, but quickly wiped her tears biting her quivering lip.

"I love you," she said. "Don't you dare leave me again."

"We're right behind you," said Chase. "I promise."

Evelyn, Gage, and Sheen headed up the stairs and back to the Promise, leaving Chase, Max, and Loose alone in the room.

"You ready, Max? Grab those keys."

Max picked up the bloodied keys Sheen had dropped when she got shot.

"Got 'em. I'm ready as I'll ever be. Let's go."

Chapter Twenty-Five

Evelyn's Gambit

Cradled in his arms, Sheen opened her eyes and looked up at Gage.

"What happened?" she asked.

Eve patted her arm. "You're gonna be okay. You got shot. You saved Chase's life."

"Don't move, Sheen," said Gage. "You're bleeding."

"Where are you taking me?"

Gage stopped and looked down the hall. "We're taking you back to the Promise. Tripp and Hector are meeting us there with your regen."

"Where are Commander Chase and Max?"

"They're going to free our families. We need to get to the ship and get it ready for them."

"I need to help them," Sheen said. "I must go."

Sheen struggled to raise her head.

"Stop talking," said Evelyn. "Save your strength."

Sheen raised her arm, scanning the hallway. "Klix," she whispered, "two by two. Go. Save yourselves."

"We got our orders, Sheen—now hush," said Gage, putting his finger to her lips.

Gage put Sheen down, gently resting her against the hall wall just out of sight. Eve slipped out of her spacesuit and threw it next to Sheen. Then she cocked the trigger on the 357 and put the gun behind her back, standing there in only her panties and bra.

"What the hell you doin'?" Gage asked. "Are you crazy?"

"Stay here," she whispered. "I got this."

"There's four of 'em!" Gage whispered loudly.

"I know."

Evelyn stepped out into the hallway in her bra and panties. The Klix drew their weapons, screaming into their translators, "Halt or we'll shoot."

"Oh, don't shoot, boys," said Eve coyly. "It's just little ol' me. Colonel Loose sent me to entertain you."

Evelyn stood with her hands behind her back, shimmying up and down, and turning half around and back in one motion. As she turned, she moved her gun hand back to the front and back again to conceal it.

Three of the Klix holstered their weapons and began clicking to each other as if arguing, moving forward and pulling the others back— each trying to be first with the Earth woman. The fourth Klix lowered his weapon but held it in his hand.

"Come forward, Earth woman," he said. "What are you hiding there behind you?"

"Hiding? Why, I'm not hiding anything as you can plainly see."

The three Klix pushed forward, trying to pass him. He held them back, his arms high to both sides. His gun now pointed to the side.

"Show me your hands," he clicked.

Evelyn pulled her empty hand forward.

"The other hand," he clicked.

"You're gonna spoil your surprise," she said, unhooking her strapless bra with her free hand.

The three Klix paused in amazement as her bra fell forward and Eve caught it with her free hand. The three pushed forward and were held back yet again.

"First one to catch it gets to go first!" she said waving her bra, watching them follow it with their eyes.

"Wait, you fools," screamed the lead Klix.

Evelyn tossed her bra high into the air at the three waiting Klix, their arms held high, jockeying for position to catch it. The bra fell, and they jumped and grabbed for it until they were rolling on the deck fighting over it.

"Show me your other hand!" clicked the Klix closest to her, growing more impatient.

"Okay," said Evelyn, pulling her panty waist band down with the thumb of her free hand while watching his eyes. His eyes shifted downward, following her thumb.

She whirled her gun hand around and let loose with four shots. The first one hit the closest Klix in the head. The second and third shot caught two of the three in the chest. The fourth shot missed, and the last remaining Klix scampered down the hall after dropping her bra. Evelyn aimed slowly and deliberately as the last Klix became a smaller and smaller target farther away. She fired, and he dropped forward, hit in the back. She scrambled for her bra, grabbed it, and then turned back into the hallway by Gage and Sheen.

"Men can be such idiots," she said as she hooked her bra, "doesn't matter what kind."

Gage stared, his mouth open as Evelyn got back into her flight suit.

"What are you lookin' at? What?!"

"I woulda fallen for that," said Gage.

"No shit," said Eve. "You'd still fall for it. All men are idiots. Now let's get Sheen back to the Promise. I got one bullet left, so we better hurry."

"Yes, ma'am," said Gage, cradling Sheen. "Everybody on the whole planet probably heard those shots."

"We need to find another route to the surface," said Eve.

"There's a ladder we passed back in the hall. Leads up, but who knows where."

"Better than a hallway crawling with Klix," she replied.

They scurried back to the ladder and looked up. The ladder spanned the entire Klix complex from the flight deck down to the planet's surface. The walls of the compound were dirty yellow brown, stained from the sulfuric smog pouring from the foundry. The small ladder was dwarfed by the immensity of the wall. It seemed to narrow near the top—almost disappearing—making it appear to go on forever.

"It's a long way up," she said.

"These walls are probably forty or fifty stories high. That's a helluva climb. Think you can make it?"

"I can make it. At least we're not starting from the ground."

"Tie Sheen's hands around my neck. I'll have to carry her on my back, and I don't want her slipping off."

"Leave me," Sheen moaned, barely loud enough to be heard.

"We have a date, remember?" said Gage. "We all go or no one goes."

Gage unfastened the top of his space suit and pulled off his undershirt, exposing the yellow spots on his back and neck to Evelyn.

He ripped his shirt into long strips, wove them together and tugged, making sure it was strong enough to bind and hold Sheen's hands. Evelyn stared and Gage saw her.

"Never seen my spots before?" he asked.

Evelyn looked away quickly. "Oh...sorry."

"It's okay," he replied, "that's where God touched me."

Evelyn smiled.

"Here, take this," he said, handing his improvised rope to Evelyn. "It should do the trick."

Evelyn bound Sheen's hands in front of Gage's neck using the cloth rope, and he shifted Sheen to his back, the weight of her hanging limply behind him.

"I'll go first," said Evelyn. "I've got the gun."

"One bullet ain't gonna be much help up there."

"It's all we got. Besides, I don't want to use it—just brings more trouble."

"Your grandfather taught you well."

"He always told me to be careful, saying, 'You can't make plans if you're dead.'"

Gage laughed. "Sounds like Tupi to me. Sorry...I mean

your grandfather."

They climbed for a long time, starting and stopping to rest along the way.

"Are you okay?" asked Eve, looking down, pausing on the ladder.

"This ain't nothin'," said Gage. "Your grandfather made us carry each other up and down ladders, steps...you name it, just for drills. Sheen's a whole lot lighter than Tripp or Hector. You okay?"

"I'll be fine, just need to catch my breath."

Evelyn started back up with Gage directly behind her. She stopped just before the opening at the top of the ladder to the flight deck.

"Hang on a sec; let me see what's up here."

"Okay...but no more naked heroics."

"Pfft, I'm just gonna peek up there to see if there's any Klix."

Eve stuck her head into the floor opening above, looked around and then ducked back down. "We're on ship level!" she said excitedly. "I can see the Promise and the Lone Star from here."

"Any guards?"

"Don't see any."

"Shit."

"I said I don't see any."

"I know. I hate the ones you can't see more than the ones you can see."

"Yeah, but we got no choice. Okay, I'm going up. You follow with Sheen. When we get on top, we head straight for the Promise."

Eve climbed up and reached down to help Gage up and off the ladder with Sheen. Once on top, Gage slung Sheen to the front while Eve untied her hands.

"How's she doin'?" asked Eve.

"Not good. I haven't heard even a moan out of her for a while. I don't like it."

They checked Sheen's bandage and tightened it more,

putting pressure on her wound.

"We got to get her to the Promise fast," said Eve. "I hope Tripp and Hector got that regen machine thingy."

"Those two are knuckleheads, but they always get the job done. They'll be there."

They ran as fast as they could, Eve in front, pistol raised, with Gage carrying Sheen in his arms behind her.

Chapter Twenty-Six

Porkchop and Tubs

Hector and Tripp made their way back to the prison cells to retrieve Sheen's regeneration station.

"I think it's cell sixteen," said Hector.

"Seventeen," said Tripp.

"And I'm tellin' ya, it's sixteen...I'm sure of it."

"Okay, but I'm tellin' you it's seventeen. Go ahead; check out sixteen if it makes you happy."

Hector ran to cell sixteen and looked inside. It was empty.

"Told ya," said Tripp, grinning. "Dumbass."

"Fuck you. How'd you know?"

"Cause I lost my virginity at seventeen, so I remembered. I was pretty advanced for my age."

Hector laughed. "Seventeen? Really?"

"Yeah...what's so funny?"

"Nothin', grandpa."

"Grandpa, my ass! I was only seventeen."

Hector laughed more almost bent over.

"What? What is so funny about that? You're such a dick."

"Ha! At least mine doesn't still have training wheels on it."

"Yo, laughin' boy, we gonna do this or what? People are waitin' on us."

"Right; sorry. It's just that, well, here we are at seventeen."

Hector looked inside, stifling a laugh. "It's clear, just that Katal fucker still hogtied."

"I'll get the machine," said Tripp. "Stay sharp."

Hector bent down to Katal, who was barely breathing.

"Katal," said Hector, "you okay?"

Katal did not respond.

"I think he's suffocating on this rag," said Hector, pulling it from his mouth. Hector untied his scrapers so he could talk. Katal gasped and coughed.

"Fuck, Katal, you still with us?"

"Thank you," he clicked into his translator. "I could not breathe."

"Sorry," said Hector. "We couldn't let you call out."

"Yes, but I gave you my word. I won't call out."

"Yeah, well, you Klix ain't too good with keeping your word. A lot of my friends are dead because of your word."

"It was not my doing. I am a soldier; I follow orders—like you. No gag, please...I'll choke...I'll die. I can help you. One of your combat knives is there, under the table."

Tripp pushed the small table aside and picked up the combat knife. "Thanks. This might come in handy," he said putting the knife in his boot sheath.

Tripp broke down the regen machine, folding it and closing the latch on the regen case. "Let's go, Hector...regen's packed."

Hector looked at Katal and the rag. "Katal, on your word, you won't make a sound?"

"On my family's lives! I swear to you."

"Okay, then—no gag, but we're still gonna bind your scrapers. No clicking."

"You sure about that?" asked Tripp. "You can't trust 'em."

"Not everyone is an asshole."

"All right...whatever. Let's boogie."

Hector half saluted him and waved goodbye. He grabbed a handle on one side of the regen machine's case while Tripp grabbed the other one.

"Which way?" asked Tripp.

"I don't know," replied Hector. "Where were you when you lost your virginity?"

"You're a funny guy, you know that?"

Hector laughed. "We go up," he said, still grinning. "Ships are on top level."

"This thing is fuckin' heavy. I say we take the lift," said Tripp, pointing to the door leading to an enormous platform that looked like an elevator.

"Agreed. Maybe we'll get lucky and not run into any more Klix."

They stopped in front of the large opening with doors top and bottom, like an enormous Earth freight elevator. The massive lift could easily carry multiple pallets of silver from the foundry to the flight deck with room to spare.

"How do we call the goddamned thing?" asked Hector.

"There's buttons here on the outside, but which one? I don't read Klix. You got a translator?"

"Nope; gave it to Max."

"We could try 'em one at a time, and see what happens," said Hector.

"Fuck it. Push 'em all!"

Hector ran his hand across all the buttons on the wall, and they could hear the whine of an engine starting and the clank of gear teeth on a chain.

"That worked."

The doors opened, and they climbed into the lift with the regen machine between them. The lift started up and then stopped on the next floor.

"You had to press all the buttons, didn't you?" said Tripp with fake irritation in his voice.

"You told me to," replied Hector calmly.

"Yeah...but you don't have to listen to me."

"True, I rarely do. I plead temporary insanity."

The doors opened, then closed, and they started up again. The lift sped up then slowed at the next floor. The doors opened, then closed.

"This could take a while," said Tripp, leaning against the wall. "And it's all your fault."

"If we ever get out of here…" said Hector, sighing at every floor. "I'm not talking to you."

Tripp laughed. "I was right about cell seventeen, though!"

"You got lucky cause you couldn't get lucky."

"You seriously should consider stand-up comedy," said Tripp. "Remind me not to talk to you, either."

The elevator opened and closed again at each floor until they finally reached the top. Each grabbed a handle and lifted the regen machine, waiting for the doors to open.

"We need to hightail it back to the Promise," said Tripp. "That took forever. You ready?"

"I'm up for a good sprint," said Hector. "Besides, you need the exercise. You're getting a little fat."

Tripp laughed. "Don't fat shame me, Fatso. I was gonna say the same thing about you, but I was taught to be polite to porky people."

"Well, I appreciate your consideration, my tubby friend," said Hector. "Let's hope I don't have to carry this machine and drag your fat ass along the ground with it."

"Ready?" asked Tripp.

"Ready."

The doors opened, and standing in front of them was Katal holding a stinger pistol.

"Hey, Katal, what are you doing here?" Hector asked in surprise.

"Halt! If you move, I will shoot," clicked Katal into his translator.

"Katal, it's us, remember?" said Hector. "You hate Klume too."

"Stupid humans, you are so trusting…so simple, so stupid."

Tripp and Hector looked at each other in disbelief, then back at Katal.

"We could have killed you easily," said Hector. "What about your family?"

"I have no family. I only said those things to gain your trust."

"Wow; that's pretty cold, Katal," said Hector, "and I thought you were cool."

"But you gave me my knife back," Tripp interrupted. "Why would you do that?"

"It is the little touches that sell lies," clicked Katal. "You trust so easily. What can one knife do in a world of weapons?"

"You're kind of a dick, Katal," said Hector. "I'm sorry I didn't snap your neck."

"Oh...but my children, my poor children," Katal click-laughed, his top and bottom scrapers flipping frantically against one another, while feigning human weeping.

Katal turned back at them, glaring. "You are too stupid to live, humans."

Tripp looked at Hector, and Hector back at Tripp.

"He said you're too stupid to live," said Tripp, pointing at Hector with his free hand.

"I think he was talking to you," said Hector.

"No, he was talking to you," said Tripp.

"Nuh-uh," said Hector, shaking his head. "He was talking to you because you're the stupid one."

Katal watched each of them argue with some amusement, waiting for each to respond to the other's insult. He turned his head back and forth like watching a ping pong game, click-laughing. Katal turned his head to hear Tripp's response.

"How can you say that?" asked Tripp emphatically, dropping his part of the regen case with a loud boom. "You know I've always been smarter than you...always!"

Tripp waited for Katal's head to turn for Hector's response and reached into his boot sheath for his knife. Katal saw him, turned back quickly and pointed the stinger at him.

"What will you do with your stupid blade against my stinger, human?" said Katal laughing.

"Oh, it's not for me—this is Hector's blade," said Tripp,

tossing the knife over the regen machine and shouting, "Squirrel!"

Hector's forest training kicked in; he caught and threw the blade at Katal in one fast motion. The blade flew like an arrow, striking into the center of Katal's face above his nose—stopped only by the hilt. Katal fell back in slow motion like a tree cut down at its roots. He never made a sound.

"Nice," said Tripp.

"Thanks," replied Hector, laughing. "Nobody misses at that distance...except maybe you."

"Oh really?" asked Tripp, smiling.

"Yes...really," replied Hector. "Why'd you yell 'squirrel,' anyway? Kind of dramatic, don't you think?"

"Maybe a little; I was caught up in the moment."

"You could have said, 'look out' or 'catch.' That would have made more sense."

"Did you look out?"

"Yes."

"Did you catch?"

"Well, yes, but..."

"Did you stop the bad man from killing us?"

"Yes," said Hector with a sigh.

"Well, then, who is being dramatic now?"

Hector laughed. "I see your point, you strange man."

"He should never have given us a knife," said Tripp.

"Nope...big mistake and a little unsettling."

Hector made the sign of the cross. "The universe has a way of dealing with liars."

"I didn't think you were all that religious," said Tripp.

"Not always," replied Hector. "This was a special case. For a while there, I really liked Katal. He seemed nice. I feel badly for his family."

"He didn't have any family," said Tripp. "He made it up."

"I know, but I felt like I knew them."

Hector reached down, put his boot on Katal's face, and pulled his blade out of Katal's head. "Don't worry, Katal—your family is better off without you."

"He still doesn't have a family, ya know."

"I know, so they'll be fine."

"You're kinda crazy you know."

"I know."

They turned around, changed hands and lifted the regen machine.

"You ready, Porkchop?"

"Ready, Tubs."

"Promise is over there. Let's go."

Chapter Twenty-Seven

Into the Cell Block

Max and Chase made their way back up the winding stone stairs to the cell block, pulling Loose by his neck chain.

"Let me go first," said Max. "I've got the quieter weapon."

"Roger that," replied Chase.

The cell block was eerily empty, the guards having been sent to the vicinity of Evelyn's shots heard earlier. In the background, loud clicking alarms blasted from the tops of the foundry.

"It's clear," said Max.

"You can't get away," said Loose. "The whole planet is looking for you."

"If he speaks again..." said Chase. "Shoot him in the mouth."

Loose stifled a laugh but said nothing. Max jerked his neck chain, and Loose gagged and turned red with anger toward Max.

"What? You wanna kill me?" asked Max, pointing the stinger at Loose's face. "Try it. Please."

Loose huffed and looked down.

"I didn't think so," said Max, now peering into cell seventeen.

"See anybody?" asked Chase.

"No; it's empty. Looks like Tripp and Hector got Sheen's regen, though."

"Wonder what happened to that Klix guard we tied up," said Chase. "Never mind...we better hurry. Let's get our people and get out of here."

Max pulled Loose's chain toward the next cell, and then the next. Finally, in cell thirty-two, Chase found his mother.

"Mom, are you okay?" he asked, bursting through the door and hugging her.

Twin girls approximately seven years old quickly hid behind her.

"Oh, Chase," she said, "I knew you'd come. I just knew it. Oh God, what happened to your face?" She turned behind her to the twins, bending down to comfort them. "It's all right, girls, he's my son."

"Did they hurt you, Mom?"

"No, but your father...they took him away with the rest of the men." She glanced down, noticing he was favoring his hand. "They hurt you," she said, gently cupping his battered face. "And what happened to your hand?"

"It's nothing. It's already healing."

She saw Loose hiding behind Max and lunged at him, hitting him about the face and head. "Traitor!" she shouted, slapping at him. "What is he doing here?"

Chase held her back, pulling her away from Loose.

"I'll kill you myself," she screamed.

"It's okay, Mom," said Chase. "He's my prisoner. He's only alive if he helps us find the rest of our people."

"You can't trust him. Chase, don't trust him," she snarled. "He'll do anything—say anything."

"I know, Mom."

"Get that bitch away from me," said Loose.

Max yanked his neck chain hard and Loose gagged. "Watch your mouth; there's children in here, and I don't like you anyway."

"I loved you like a son," she said. "I took care of you. I fed you. We raised you as one of our own, and you betrayed our entire planet. I am so ashamed of you. I disown you."

Loose turned away for a moment as a brief flash of shame

crossed his face. Then, he turned back quickly with a defiant smile. "I could give two shits what you think."

Max yanked his neck leash hard, and Loose coughed.

"Son," she said, holding on to Chase's arm, "I am not fond of killing, but if anyone ever deserved it, it's Loose."

"I know, Mom. He will stand trial. No jury will forgive him for what he has done."

"Do you think the Klix would have let you live?" Loose snapped. "It's because of me that any of you are still alive!"

"It's because of you that we were taken prisoner," said his mother. "Most of our friends and their families were slaughtered because of you." Saddened, she looked away, then turned back angry. "So many people are dead because of you. These girls are orphans because of you."

The twins hid farther behind her, trembling.

"Well, you're alive, so you should be thanking me!" Loose said, raising his voice.

"How could you? How could you betray your own people?" she asked.

"Screw you, bitch..." he started to say, until Max jerked his chain so hard it brought Loose to his knees gagging.

"The next time I jerk this chain, your head is coming off," said Max. "I don't care if we need you or not. So you best mind your manners."

"We have to find Dad and anyone else we can," Chase said to his mom. "Do you know where they are? Have you seen Hector's or Gage's moms?"

"Some of the older women and children are in cells, like me. They took some Piecers, any able-bodied men, and even some children to the smelter line with your father."

"Max, here's the keys. You and Mom release everyone in the cells. I'll take Loose with me to the smelter."

"You only have one gun," said Max.

"First bullet is in Loose's head. He'll make sure I get there. Take everyone back to the ships."

"You got it."

"Chase, be careful," his mother said, hugging him, "and...

bring your father home."

"Don't worry, Mom. I'll find him."

Max handed Loose's throat leash to Chase. "Don't turn your back on him, Chase. He's a snake."

"I know. Now get going and keep that stinger handy."

"See you up top. Been a pleasure serving with you, Chase."

"Same here, Fixer Max. See you up top."

Max nodded, shook Chase's hand, and left with Chase's mother, going from cell to cell releasing any prisoners they found. Soon they had released thirty adult prisoners including Hector's mom, Catherine, and fourteen children. Max led the way—with stinger in hand—to one of the ladders leading to the surface and the ships.

"We're not going to make it up that ladder, Max," Chase's mom said. "Some of these women have been through a lot, and some are older than I am. These kids can't climb that far, either. I don't even think I can make that climb."

Max looked around the passage and spotted the lift. "Okay, Momma Chase," he said. "There's a lift. Maybe we can use it."

"Name's Gwen," she replied.

"Okay, Gwen...let's get everyone in the lift. Put the kids in back behind the adults. I've got a translator, so we can see how it works pretty quick."

The women ducked into the elevator quickly so as not to be seen. Some of the smaller children were crying.

"It's gonna be okay, kids," said Max. "We're just going for a ride—then we're going home."

Max held up the translator to the button controls and pressed the button marked flight deck. The elevator started moving up slowly, then gained speed.

"Everyone, move back and to the right," he said, directing the frightened women. "I'll be on the left with the stinger. If we run into trouble, I'll start shooting, and they'll train their fire on me."

"How did you get their gun to work for you?" Gwen

asked.

"I'm wearing a Klix-skin glove."

"Oh. Smart."

"Thanks. It works."

"We need to get more of those."

Max looked at her surprised, knowing she was serious. "If anything happens to me, just take it off my hand, put it on, and pick up the gun. It will work for you too."

"I understand," she replied. "But let's not let anything happen to you."

"Let's not!" he said, smiling.

The lift clicked loudly and stopped.

"Okay, everyone," Max shouted, "this is it—the flight deck."

Pressing the open button on the doors, Max peeked out the lift, looking for their ships. "Our ships are nearby over there. Keep your heads down and run as fast as you can. We have friends there waiting." He mumbled under his breath, "I hope."

Gwen heard him and he tried to look away. "Don't worry," she said. "Chase will come."

"Here we go, everyone," he said. "Run!"

Chapter Twenty-Eight

Into Hell

Back on the stairs, Chase pulled Loose behind him, gun drawn, making his way down to the lowest level of the complex: the smelter. The air was thick and hot.

"It doesn't have to be this way, brother," said Loose. "We could rule together—just you and me. You could have anything you want. Any woman you want. You could have Eve; I don't care. I'll trade you...for Luna."

"Shut up, Loose. You're embarrassing yourself."

Chase jerked his chain and pulled him toward the last door to the smelter.

"What should I expect to see when I open this door?" Chase asked.

Loose laughed. "A shitload of Klix and the furnaces from hell."

"How many?"

"More than your puny six-shooter can handle, that's for sure."

Chase pressed the barrel hard against Loose's temple and pulled the hammer back with a loud click. He moved his hand up the leash close to his neck ring. Loose winced.

"I only need the one," said Chase. "If anyone starts shooting, you're the first to go. If you have any control over these monsters, you better use it. Let's go."

Chase opened the door, and an intense blast of heat hit

them both. They closed their eyes for a second until the searing heat blew past. On both sides, long rivers of molten silver ran by them in V-shaped troughs. The heat was unbearable. Chase could see many men and some women pouring finely crushed ore into giant smelting pots. Sparks flared everywhere. It was difficult to breathe. He could see bodies on the floor of people who had succumbed to the heat. They were left to die and only dragged out of the way if they interfered with the silver production line; some were human, others were alien. Some appeared to have been there a long time and were merely desiccated shells of beings, dried out by the unrelenting heat. As they entered, a few guards saw them and pulled their weapons.

Chase pressed the gun harder against Loose's temple. "Tell them to put down their weapons or I make a whistle out of your skull."

Loose yelled into his translator, "Put down your weapons. I'm Colonel Loose, your commanding officer."

The Klix guards looked at each other and then at Loose but kept their weapons pointed at them.

"Better do something to convince them, or you're dead," Chase whispered.

"Drop your weapons!" Loose shouted, "or General Klume will hear that you disobeyed me."

The Klix hesitated, and then one by one put their weapons on the ground. The people tending the smelter stopped, confused, afraid to do anything, watching.

"Everyone," Chase shouted, "it's time to go. Follow me. We're leaving."

Nobody moved. They all stared, afraid to leave their stations. Chase raised his gun into the air and fired. The blast rang out throughout the smelter.

"Now!" he shouted.

Two Piecer prisoners came running from back in the smelter.

"Fynn 521 and Sung 522, reporting," said the first two Piecer soldiers to arrive in front of Chase.

"Name's Chase, of the 523s."

"We know you, Chase...from the academy. "Everyone knows the 523s."

"I'm looking for my father, Martin Chambers," he said, showing them his picture. "Have you seen him?"

Fynn and Sung looked at each other and then down.

"Is he dead?" asked Chase.

"Not sure," said Fynn, "but he couldn't take the heat."

"Where is he?"

"They dragged him off the line about an hour ago—in the back where we came from."

"You need to get these people up top and into our ships. I'm going back for my father."

"Yes, sir," said Fynn, saluting.

"Some are going to need help," said Sung. "Many are dehydrated, especially the kids."

"Organize a squad and get them up there as fast as you can," said Chase. "And get 'em some water. We're going to be swarmed by Klix. Get the injured paired with the able-bodied to help them. Those that can't walk will need to be carried."

"Don't you see it's pointless, brother...your little crusade?" said Loose with a smirk.

Chase pushed the gun barrel back up against Loose's temple. "You put fucking kids in this hell, you piece of shit. I should kill you right now for that!"

"I didn't know they would put kids in here. It was only supposed to be adults. But at least they're with their parents, right?"

"You're a sick bastard."

"We're all sick bastards, we Piecers; Sacrificium Pro Victoria, Chase. Fuck that shit. Don't you get it? We're the sacrifice for their victory...their dogs of their war. They don't give a shit about us. We're expendable, like the Sixers. It just takes longer for us to die. Why should we, the superior beings, give a shit about them? They should fucking die for us."

"It's not like that, Loose. We're still human and plenty of normies died fighting with us. They are our people. We are theirs."

"Bullshit. We are fodder. Did you think I was just going to drill, fight, and die for nothing...for Earth...for humanity? Fuck that! They made us to die, so they didn't have to. They're the monsters."

"You're crazy. They had no choice. Humanity would've been wiped out if not for the Sixers and the Piecer program."

"You're pathetic, Chase. You still believe they are your family. And tell me, what do you think is going to happen? The Klix aren't going to just let you fly away, la-la-la. And even if you could, where would you go? To Earth? Klix own the Earth now. You will die, and for what? Nothing."

"Shut up! You should be more worried about what happens to you. And you better hope that Dad is still alive."

"You're the crazy one if you think you can get away," said Loose, laughing.

"Ya know what, Loose? I'm beginning to not care if I get away. All I want to do is make sure that you pay for what you did...one way or another. You're a disgrace to our family."

Loose paused and stopped smiling. "So...we die together, brother," said Loose, the lines on his face relaxing, the anger melting, almost happy. "Together again as brothers, like before. I'll race you to the other side; only this time, I'll let you win."

"I'm not afraid to die," said Chase. "But not yet. And if you don't get these assholes to back off, I'll make sure you make it to the other side first."

The Klix guards inched forward, taking advantage of the confusion.

"Tell 'em to back off!" Chase screamed to Loose.

"Stand down!" Loose screamed into his translator. "Klume will reward you later."

The Klix guards stopped and stepped back.

"Pick up their weapons," Chase screamed to the survivors. "Toss them into the silver."

The survivors picked up the Klix stingers and tossed them—one by one—into the glowing rivers flowing by. The stingers flashed as they disappeared in the molten metal. One of the guards wrestled with one of the survivors for his stinger. Chase fired his gun, putting a bullet in his head. The children screamed, covering their ears from the sound. The adults gathered the remaining stingers and tossed them into the river of silver, flashing as they disintegrated.

Chase screamed into Loose's translator, "Don't move or Colonel Loose dies."

"That's two bullets, Chase. You only have four left."

"I only need one for you."

Chase turned to Sung and Fynn. "Load everyone into the lifts. They won't make it on the ladders."

People hurried past Chase—both hopeful and scared—heading toward the large elevators.

"There's two lifts, but I don't know if we'll all make it in one trip," said Sung. "Might have to make two trips to get everybody topside."

"Then do it," replied Chase. "Take the kids and the injured up first. Make sure they have an able-bodied adult with them to carry them, if need be. We have people waiting up top at the ships. Grab a translator from the guards so you can operate the lift controls."

The elevator doors opened, and Fynn and Sung loaded people into the lifts. Chase waited with his gun held on Loose until they filled the elevators a second time.

"Everyone that we know of is accounted for, Chase," said Fynn. "Time to go."

"How many?"

"I counted one hundred and fifty-three."

"You go ahead. We'll catch the next lift. I'll hold them off until you're safely on board."

"But sir, it's just you against all of them."

"I have my insurance card right here," he replied. "Don't , Loose? I'll take the next one; I'm going back for my father. end it back down after everyone is clear."

Chase walked Loose toward the back of the smelter. The arther they went, the more intense was the heat, and he wiped the sweat from his brow with his sleeve. The air was thick with heat and difficult to breathe. Sparks flew from the silver troughs as they changed direction and ran into assorted ingot molds of various sizes. As they trudged forward, Chase pushed Loose ahead of him. Pallet upon pallet of silver bars were stacked as far back as they could see.

"This is what you betrayed your planet for?" asked Chase.

Loose shrugged. "I could give two shits about silver," he said. "I was born to rule. The Klix want the silver, not me. They are disgusting creatures—useful idiots. They do my dirty work."

"When this is over, you will pay for what you've done."

"You're such a pussy. Can't kill me yourself?" Loose changed his voice to a mocking tone. "Oh, I'm a good guy! Wahh. You're all such useless bitches."

"Shut up, asshole," said Chase. "I'm sick of you already."

"Then pull the trigger. Do it."

Loose grabbed Chase's gun and pushed the barrel to his forehead. Chase pulled the hammer back on his pistol, his finger poised on the trigger. Then he looked forward and saw his father slumped over on the floor. He released the trigger, holding the hammer back with his thumb, slowly resting it on the chambered bullet.

"Time for you to rest that mouth of yours," said Chase, taking a full swing with his gun to Loose's head. Loose slumped to the floor, unconscious. Chase threw Loose's leash on top of him. "Stay," he said, half smiling, stepping over his brother's limp body. He bent down and turned his father over from his side, cradling him in his arms.

"Water, please," his father begged.

Chase looked around and saw a bucket and a rag. He dipped the rag in the bucket and held it to his father's lips. "Slow," he said as his father sucked the rag of its moisture.

Chase dipped the rag again and patted his father's face and cracked lips with the wet rag.

"Chase? Your mother, she...they took her...to a cell."

"She's okay, Dad. She's being moved to my ship."

"Oh, thank you, Son, thank you. Take care of her for me, will you?"

"No. You're going to take care of her yourself—after I get you out of here."

"Go. Save yourself. I'm done. I can't walk. I'll just slow you down."

"I'm not leaving you here. I promised Mom I would bring you back."

"You must. Take your mother out of this hell."

"Do you think I could ever look Mom in the eye if I left you behind? Do you think I could look myself in the mirror? No. I'm not doing this for you, Dad; I'm doing this for me. I wouldn't leave you behind any more than you'd leave one of your own men behind. That's not what honorable men do."

"But your brother...he is part of this. He is one of them."

"I know. But he's not going to hurt anyone anymore."

Chase sat his father up a little higher and pointed over his shoulder to where Loose was laid out unconscious. "Look, Dad, over there. See? He won't be hurting anyone anymore."

Martin peered through the darkness, blinking. "What, Son? I don't see anything."

Chase turned to look where he had left Loose. He was gone.

Chapter Twenty-Nine

Luminfleur

Hector and Tripp ran back to the Promise, carrying Sheen's regen machine. They could hear sirens clicking loudly and the occasional gunshot ring out.

"Sounds like Chase's .357 to me," said Hector, smiling.

"Yup," replied Tripp. "Somebody's dead. Let's get this thing up and running."

They unpacked the regen in Sheen's cabin and tapped it into the ship's power supply. The machine came to life; its lights flashed bright and welcoming.

"You see anybody?" asked Hector.

Tripp glanced out the port window. "They're coming. I see Evelyn and Gage. He's carrying Sheen."

"Lower the cargo ramp. It will be easier on Gage to get her in here."

"Roger that," said Tripp, lowering the ramp.

"Thank God you're here," said Evelyn, reaching the top of the ramp first. "I've never been so happy to see anyone in my life."

"Why, thanks, Darlin'," said Tripp. "Glad to see you too. How's Sheen?"

"Not good; where's her regen?"

"In her cabin—up and running," replied Hector. "Glad you made it. You need help, Gage?"

"No...I got her. Show me where her cabin is."

They ran Sheen into her cabin, where her regen hummed and flashed in the background. The lighting in the room changed as they entered, growing purple and brighter, the light coming from her Luminfleur.

"What's with that flower?" asked Hector. "It's glowing."

"I don't know. It got brighter when we came in," said Evelyn. "I think it's changing color too."

"How we gonna get her to stand in the regen?" asked Gage. "She's out cold."

"There's a collapsible table unit—looks like a gurney," replied Tripp. "Probably for just this sort of thing."

Gage laid Sheen carefully on the gurney. Diagnostic bands covered her chest, thighs, and feet. They rolled the gurney into the regen machine, and it flashed as if recognizing her. The long charging arms reached out from the circumference of the regen machine, grasping Sheen at her wrists. The flashing intensified, and the machine began to hum louder.

"Is it working?" asked Evelyn.

"I can't tell," said Tripp. "She looks the same."

"It's getting brighter in here," said Hector.

"It's the plant," said Gage. "It's turning red. Should I get rid of it?"

"No," said Evelyn. "It's reacting to her. It's like it knows she's hurt."

The machine hummed and flashed. The Luminfleur grew brighter and brighter red.

"Bring it closer," said Evelyn. "There's something about that plant. I can feel it."

"Did you give her another soap?" asked Gage looking sternly at Tripp.

"No! I didn't give her nothin'. You just got here, remember?"

"I'm fine," said Evelyn. "It's the plant—can't you feel it?"

"I don't feel nothin'," said Gage.

Hector pushed the Luminfleur closer to the gurney, and the plant began to pulse from red to purple. The room glowed as tiny spores shot out from the plant in Sheen's direction. The spores attached themselves to her stomach wound and the ripped skin on her hand. The wounds began to pulse color, in sync with the plant.

"What the hell is that?" said Hector.

"Ain't never seen nothin like it," said Gage.

"Me either," said Tripp, drawing his weapon. "You want me to kill it?"

"No!" Evelyn shouted. "It's helping."

"Helping?" asked Tripp. "Helping how?"

"Her wounds are closing. They're getting smaller. Those spores are repairing her."

"Well, holy shit," said Gage. "If I hadn't seen it myself, I never would've believed it."

The plant continued pulsing faster, putting out more and more spores. The wounds became so bright you could not stare at them without shielding your eyes. After several minutes, the wounds glowed red, then purple, and then stopped glowing altogether. The plant ceased putting out spores, and the Luminfleur went back to emitting a dim purple-hued light. Sheen's wounds had closed completely. The regen machine dinged, and its lights dimmed.

"Sheen, are you okay? Sheen?" Evelyn asked, patting Sheen's cheek.

Sheen opened her eyes blinking and looked around the room at everyone leaning over her around the gurney.

"Have I been ill?" she asked.

"You were shot, remember?" said Hector. "You saved Chase."

Sheen sat up immediately. "My Commander. Where is Commander Chase?"

"He's coming," said Evelyn.

"He'll be here," said Gage. "He's getting our people."

"Yeah, you need to rest, Sheen," said Tripp. "You took a bullet."

"I have no need of rest," she replied. "I am fully charged and fully functional."

"But you just got shot," said Hector. "You should rest."

"I assure you, Hector, I am repaired. I must find Commander Chase."

"You can't go out there alone, Sheen. Commander Chase ordered us all to stay here— to get ready to leave."

"Then I must follow orders and prepare the ship."

Everyone looked at each other, then at Gage.

"You heard what she said, ladies," said Gage. "We're following Chase's orders. Sheen, you have command of the Promise until Chase returns. Tripp will man the weapons, and Evelyn will prepare for survivors. Hector and I will get the Lone Star ready. Let's get these ships ready to receive passengers and get the hell out of here."

"Roger that," said Tripp.

"I'll lower the cargo ramp on the Lone Star," said Hector. "Gage, get the engines runnin'. Chase'll be comin' soon."

Chapter Thirty

Back to the Promise

Max led the women and children to the Lone Star and the Promise. Many pleaded to stay on the Klix world as some of their family members were still missing.

"More will be coming," Max said. "Please get on the ships. We'll do our best to find your families."

Eve ran down the ramp of the Promise to help.

"Hector!" Max screamed up the ramp. "Your mom is here. She's okay."

Hector ran down the ramp to find his mother.

"She's over there. She's pretty weak, so we had to carry her."

"Thank you, Max," said Hector, his voice breaking. "I can never repay you."

"No payment needed. We're all brothers—the Fixers and the Piecers. I'd do anything to help a brother."

Hector's eyes watered, and he took a deep breath to compose himself. "I am so sorry about getting mad at you before...about Sheen," replied Hector. "You are a good man, Fixer Max. I will be the flower girl at your wedding to Sheen if you like."

Max laughed. "Forget it; I was happy to help!" he replied. "Besides, you'd look pretty stupid in a frilly little dress."

Hector smiled and cocked an eyebrow. "You never know my friend, but for you, I would make it work."

Max laughed again. "Better get her on board and get some food and water in her. She's pretty dehydrated."

Hector bent down and picked up his mother gently. "Mom, it's me," he said. "You're gonna be okay."

"I knew you would come for me," she replied weakly. "Somehow...I just knew it."

"Let's get you inside," he said, climbing the ramp. "Tripp was really worried about you, too."

"Oh, how is he? Is he okay?"

"He's fine. You can talk to him. He'd like that."

Hector carried his mother up the ramp and inside the Promise.

"How's Sheen?" Max asked Evelyn.

"She's seems fine," she replied. "Between the regen machine and that plant in her cabin, she's completely healed."

"The plant?" asked Max, "the Luminfleur? The purple glowing thing?"

"Yeah, it healed her somehow. Weirdest thing I ever saw."

"That is weird...but tell me later; right now, we need to get these people on board. Some are very weak."

"I'll take care of these people, Max," she replied. "Chase wants all the ships up and running."

"All of 'em? The Vengeance too?"

"I don't know; he just said to get all the ships ready to take off."

"Chase wants a Klix ship, Chase gets a Klix ship. I'll see if I can reprogram the nav system so the damn Klix can't send us back to their world like the last time. No more surprises."

"We'll take care of the survivors; you get that ship running and wait for Chase."

As he turned to the Vengeance, he could see Fynn and Sung followed by the survivors of the smelter line. They all looked like they had been to hell. They were covered in dirt and sweat and had wide, vacant, terrified eyes.

"Get them on board one of the ships," Max called out to him. "Make sure they get plenty of water and rations. Take the sick to the infirmary. I'll have Evelyn come and look at them and see if she can do anything for them."

"Roger that," said Fynn, leading the survivors to the ramps of the ships.

"Sung, take half to the Lone Star," said Fynn, "but, let them choose the ship they want. Let's get these families re-united if we can!"

The families split up, seeing their wives, husbands, mothers or fathers standing on the ramps—waiting. Some wept and some hugged while others looked to see if more were coming, worried that they were not. Gwen Chambers looked over the crowd of men coming up the ramps, desperately searching for Martin and Chase.

"Max, have you heard anything from Chase?" she asked.

Max shook his head. "Don't worry," he said. "He'll be all right."

Tears ran down Gwen's face. She feared the worst. She ran up the ramp and through the ship, searching for anyone who could help. She found Sheen at the helm.

"Have you heard anything from Chase 523 of the Piecer Corp?" she asked.

"I have not been in contact with my Commander since we were taken prisoner," Sheen replied.

"You...you were with him? He's your Commander?"

"Yes, he is my Commander."

Gwen looked at her curiously. "You're in the Piecer Corp? But there are no women in the Corp."

"No," replied Sheen. "I am Sheen. I am Courtesan."

"I don't understand," said Gwen.

"Commander Chase—he freed me. He is my Commander."

Gwen reached out her hand to shake. "I'm Gwen, Gwen Chambers. Chase's mother."

"Ah, mother of Commander Chase. You have done well with your son. He is a good Commander. He is worthy of love."

Gwen half-smiled, shook Sheen's hand and glanced at her curiously. "Yes, he's very special...did you say you...you love him?"

Sheen cocked her head, and then turned back to her. "Evelyn Tupi loves Commander Chase. Sheen has not known love, but Evelyn Tupi says Sheen loves Commander Chase."

"General Tupi's granddaughter, Eve?" Gwen asked. "She's alive? She's here?"

"Yes, she is helping survivors."

"Does Chase know?"

"Yes, Commander Chase is aware. She has reunited with Commander Chase, and she has serviced him."

"What?"

Sheen paused for a moment. "Commander Chase is aware that Evelyn Tupi survived and is aware she is here on the Klix world."

"I need to go get my son," said Gwen, "and my husband. They need my help."

"No," said Sheen. "Commander Chase has ordered us to remain and ready the ships. We will ready the ships."

"But he could be hurt."

Sheen cocked her head several times, started to speak then stopped.

"Gwen Gwen Chambers, do you think Commander Chase is hurt?"

"Just Gwen," she said, "and I don't know. But if he needs me, I must go."

"But he is my Commander and has ordered us to stay."

"Well, he's not my Commander," said Gwen. "He's my son. And you said he freed you."

"Yes," said Sheen, stopping for a moment, thinking. "Sheen can do what Sheen wants. Commander Chase said this. I will go with you Gwen Chambers. We will need weapons. Come with me, Gwen."

Sheen and Gwen went to cabin one—Chase's quarters—and opened and closed lockers until Sheen found the black leather coat, hat, and two .45 caliber pistols Chase had brought from home.

"Commander Chase told me to use these weapons if the

shit hit the fan. Do you think the shit has hit the fan, Gwen?"

"Yes," she replied, "and then some!"

"Then we must use these weapons. But...he told me these were your weapons. Would you like to wear them?"

"Do you know how to use them?" Gwen asked.

"Yes. You aim them and pull the trigger mechanism."

"Are you a good shot?"

"My sensors do not allow me to miss once I have locked on to a target. As long as the weapon is functioning properly, I cannot miss."

"Your sensors?"

"Yes, I have sensors to assist my aim."

"You take them, then."

"Very well, Gwen. I will use these weapons."

"You can keep them, Sheen. Chase would want that, and I don't need them."

"Thank you, Gwen," she replied, strapping on the holsters and checking each gun to make sure each magazine was full. "If Commander Chase would want Sheen to keep these weapons, then Sheen will keep these weapons."

"What about your hat?" asked Gwen.

"What is the purpose of the hat?" asked Sheen.

"Keeps the sun out of your eyes—for better aim."

"Ah, targeting assistance. Sheen understands. Commander Chase is wise."

Sheen placed the hat on her head, and Gwen adjusted it. "Like this," she said. "Point first. And don't forget your coat."

"I do not get cold, Gwen. I do not need a coat."

"Oh, it's not to keep you warm. It's to conceal your weapons, hold ammo, and make you look bad ass," replied Gwen.

"Concealment, ammo storage, my Commander truly is wise," said Sheen, slipping on the coat. "I am ready, Gwen. Sheen will look bad ass. Do you know how to use a laser rifle?"

"Yes, I know how to use them."

"Very well; we have procured working laser weapons

from the Pwyll crater station. You can use one of them to defend yourself. They are below in the cargo deck. Let us go find Commander Chase and his father."

Gwen followed Sheen down to the cargo bay and picked up a laser rifle. "They are in the smelter, Sheen."

"We must hurry," said Sheen. "Can you run?"

"I can, but don't wait for me...just go!"

Sheen took off running, stopped, and held up her hand scanning the complex. Gwen caught up panting, trying to catch her breath.

"The highest level of heat is on the lowest level," she said. "I have found the smelter."

"There's a freight elevator that goes directly to the smelter, Sheen. We used it to take water to the prisoners."

"Perhaps, you should wait here," said Sheen, scanning her. "Your heart rate and respiration are very high."

"You go; I'll catch up."

Sheen took off running, and Gwen called out to her, "And Sheen, be careful."

Sheen smiled.

Chapter Thirty-One

Survivors

Chase picked up his father, cradling him in his arms, holding his gun in one hand. He surveyed the area and started to head back when he heard a moan.

"Goddammit, Dad...someone else is here. They didn't get everyone out."

"I didn't hear anything, Son."

"I did. I'm going to put you down for a second. Here, take this," he said, handing him his gun. "You know how to use it. If Loose comes back, shoot him."

He gently placed his father back on the ground, leaning him up against one of the smelter control panels. He strained to hear whatever he could over the sounds of the machinery and the sirens. He heard the sound again and quickly moved through the foundry to the back in a dark corner. There, he found Gage's mother, Karen Bielinski, lying on her back, exhausted and dying from the heat. He ran back for the water bucket and rag he had given his father.

"Here you go, Mrs. Bielinski—water."

She moaned but did not respond. Chase dunked the rag in the water and put it to her lips. She sucked the moisture out eagerly and her eyes fluttered open. "I know you," she said.

"It's me—Chase. I've been to your house. I'm Gage's friend."

"Have you seen my little Gage-baby? Is he all right?"

Chase smiled. "He's fine. He sent me to get you."

"He did? Oh, that's nice. He was always a good boy."

"Yes, yes, he was. He is."

"I think you're too late, Son."

"Nonsense; you just need some water and some rest."

"You need to go before the Klix catch you."

"I'm not leaving you here," he said, dunking the rag for another drink.

"Oh, that feels so good. I'm so thirsty. It's hot in here. Are you hot? I'm hot."

"Yes, it's hot. Go slow, but there's more."

Chase dipped the rag in the bucket and put it over her face. The coolness and the water dissipated quickly.

"Oh...that feels so good," she said. "Thank you, Chase."

"Don't you worry, Mrs. Bielinski; Gage is waiting for us at our ship. We're taking you home."

"You're a nice boy too, Chase. You've always been such a nice boy. I'm glad you and Gage are brothers."

"Me too," he said, dunking the rag again and placing it over her face. "We have to go now, so I'm just going to carry you."

Mrs. Bielinski closed her eyes as if passing out. Chase patted her cheek, and she opened her eyes again.

"I'm still here, Chase. You go...save yourself. Tell Gage I love him."

"Tell him yourself," he said, lifting her. "I promised him I'd find you and bring you to him."

He carried her out of the dark back corner to the console where his father was propped up and laid her gently beside him.

"Oh, hello, Martin," she said, sitting up. "Looks like we're both in a fix."

"Hello, Karen," he replied. "Good to see you again."

"You raised a good 'un," she said. "Stubborn, though."

"Yep; he's a real pain in the arse," he said, forcing a laugh, "just like yours."

Chase ran back for the bucket and the rag and dunked it

again—giving some to his father and then to Mrs. Bielinski.

"You can't carry both of us, Son," said Martin. "Take Karen back to the ship and get the hell out of here."

"No," said Chase. "I can carry you both."

"Son, I love you, but you can't. You know what you should do. Now take Karen and go."

"With all due respect, sir, screw you. Now give me the gun, Dad. You're not going to be facing forward for a while."

Chase picked up Martin and put him over his right shoulder. Then he bent over and picked up Karen and put her over his left shoulder. Sweat poured over his face as he steadied himself. He wrapped his left arm around their legs, holding his gun with his right hand in front of him.

"Here we go...try not to move around too much."

They stepped out of the darkness—toward the front of the smelter. The weaponless Klix guards collected in front of him.

"Halt!" they clicked into their translators. "You cannot go forward."

Chase raised his weapon and pointed it at the lead Klix. "Who wants to die first? You?"

"Where is Colonel Loose?" he clicked. "Where is your hostage?"

"One of my men is holding a gun on him," said Chase.

"You lie. Your men have all left. You are alone. You will return to your cell, and the humans you carry will return to the smelter line."

Chase took two steps forward, his gun raised and pointed at the Klix head. "These two are nearly dead. They're going home with me."

"Then why bother?" he clicked, laughing. "Nobody goes home!"

More weaponless Klix joined them, and soon a wall of more than twenty Klix stood between Chase and freedom. The sounds of the foundry roared in the background.

"You cannot kill us all," said the leader, the Klix now fanning out around him.

Chase kept his gun trained on the lead Klix. He turned around to put Karen and his father on the ground, behind a pallet lift control box to protect them. As he bent down, the Klix took advantage of his distraction and moved forward slowly.

"Son, do what you have to," Martin whispered, "to survive. Leave us. You can't fight them all."

"Not too many, Dad," he said smiling, "and they have no weapons. I do."

"More are coming—there are too many. A deer knows to flee the hunter."

Chase smiled warmly. "Dad, I'm only a deer when I run. I'm not running. I'm ready, I'm calm, and I'm focused. This is what I was born to do." Chase took a deep long breath, letting it out slowly. "I'll be back, Dad," he said standing, moving toward the Klix. "Take care of Mrs. Bielinski."

The first Klix lurched forward, and Chase shot him point-blank in the head. Other Klix rushed him from the front and the sides. In his mind, everything slowed down as he analyzed the Klix positions and his remaining shots.

Gotta make 'em count, he thought.

Chase waited a split second before seeing two of the Klix line up—one behind the other—and shot the first Klix in the head. The bullet flew through his head, hitting the other Klix in the chest; both dropped to the ground.

Two Klix jumped on top of him, and he pushed his gun barrel against the closest Klix's chest. The bullet flew through the Klix's chest and into the Klix behind him, dropping two more.

Chase jumped to his feet, letting loose with one more shot, and dropping two more Klix as they lined up perfectly— one behind the other. He was out of bullets, and more Klix were coming. The first ran at him, swinging his fist. Chase grabbed his arm, picked him and smashed him into the rock floor. Two quick punches to his face and he stopped moving. Two more ran at him, and he punched the first in the throat. The Klix grabbed his throat, gagging and staggered away clicking.

The largest Klix stood in front of Chase, his arms out, baring his claws to make himself look even larger. Chase moved into him in an eye-blink, and pummeled him in the stomach, chest, and head, his fists moving so fast they blurred. The Klix crumpled to his knees, and Chase finished him off with a roundhouse kick to the head, breaking his neck.

Chase took a step back, seeing more Klix charging him.

Too many, he thought. Going down swinging.

Chase took a deep breath and blinked. It was all he needed to focus on the Klix massing themselves in front of him. He was ready.

The horde of Klix rushed forward, clicking war cries. Suddenly, two long, loud shots rang out, and all the Klix fell to the ground—gasping. As they fell, Chase could see a cloaked figure behind them in the smoke. Suddenly, a hot wind blew from the furnace, and the smoke cleared. Sheen appeared with both .45s pulled and smoking, wearing Gwen's long black coat and cowboy hat.

"These are very effective weapons, Commander," she said, staring at the still-smoking barrels of the .45s. "The shit has hit the fan. The threat has been eliminated." She cocked her right eyebrow and smiled broadly at Chase.

Gwen caught up and came running from behind her to Chase. "Chase, are you okay?"

"Couldn't be better," he said.

"And your father...is he...?"

Chase grinned and pointed behind him, toward Martin and Karen. Gwen ran over to where Martin was sitting. "Oh my God, you're alive," she said, kissing him all over his face and hands.

"I'm alive," he said meekly, "thanks to our son."

Chase walked toward Sheen, stepping over the dead Klix bodies. "I am so glad to see you," he said.

"Thank you, Commander. And I am glad to see you as well."

"Are you okay?" he asked. "You were shot. We were all so

worried."

"I assure you, Commander, I am fully functional."

"You saved my life, Sheen. Thanks; I owe you one."

"I put you in danger; it is I who owe you, Commander."

"Nonsense. We're a team. We take care of each other."

"Thank you, Commander. What are your orders?"

"We need to get these people back to the ships."

"Would you like me to carry them?" asked Sheen.

"If you would carry Gage's mom, Mrs. Bielinski, I can carry my Dad."

"As you wish, Commander."

"Why does she always call you Commander?" Gwen whispered to Chase.

"It's a long story, Mom. I'll tell you later."

"She's a very pretty girl."

"I know, Mom."

"And an amazing fighter. I don't know how she killed all those Klix. I didn't even see her pull the trigger more than once. It was like a machine gun!"

"Yes, Sheen is amazing."

"A girl like that could make a man very happy."

Chase grinned. "You have no idea, Mom. Let's go."

"Sheen, reload and...hey, where'd you get that translator?"

"I removed it from a dead Klix, Commander—outside the freight elevator. It was fully functional."

"Great! We might run into more of them on the way up."

"Yes, Commander."

Sheen reloaded the .45 caliber magazines in a blur, slapping the magazines into her pistols and pulling the slide to load a bullet into each chamber. As she did so, she stepped over the Klix body closest to her. The Klix clicked and Sheen whirled around and shot him in the head.

"I am sorry, Commander. This one was still alive."

"It's okay, Sheen. The threat was eliminated." Chase paused and smiled. "I like the coat and hat. Looks good on you."

"Thank you, Commander," she said, smiling. "Sheen is bad ass now."

Chase laughed and picked up his dad, cradling him in his arms. "It suits you," Chase continued.

Sheen half-smiled and picked up Gage's mom, holding her twin .45s at the ready.

"Let's go. We'll take the lift. Ships are up top. Be ready for trouble."

Chapter Thirty-Two

Cosmic Karma

Chase put his father down gently at the back of the immense lift. Gwen got in and sat next to him. Sheen placed Gage's mother next to Gwen and moved to the control panel. She held up the translator to the buttons on the lift and hit the button marked flight deck. The elevator took off, and Chase and Sheen readied themselves with Sheen pointing her guns at the lift doors. The elevator rose swiftly.

In the back of the elevator, Gwen whispered to Martin, "I like her."

"Me too," he whispered back. "Are they...you know...together?"

"He is her Commander or something. She said she's a Courtesan. What's a Courtesan?"

"I have no idea," he replied.

"Chase told me it's a long story," whispered Gwen.

"That I gotta hear."

"I don't think she's entirely human; said she has sensors."

"Really?" said Martin, looking Sheen up and down. "Looks human to me. Which parts are machine?"

"I don't know, but did you see her shoot those Klix at the smelter? That's not normal. She shot twenty Klix—with twenty bullets—in less than two seconds. It was like two long shots. Probably saved his life...saved all our lives."

"I really like her," Martin whispered.

Sheen turned around to Martin and Gwen with a big smile. "I really like you too," she whispered.

Gwen's and Martin's mouths fell open.

"How could she hear us?" Gwen whispered.

"I don't know, but I'm glad she likes us," said Martin. "I wouldn't want to get on her bad side."

Sheen turned around again, still smiling. "I have no bad sides," she whispered. "I am perfectly symmetrical."

Gwen and Martin stopped whispering, stunned.

"Commander," Sheen said, "my thermal sensors detect two heat signatures at the level above us. They are armed."

"Stay down, everyone," said Chase, turning to his passengers. "Take 'em out, Sheen."

"Yes, Commander—targets are locked on."

The lift stopped with a jolt as they reached the flight deck. Sheen stood at the ready, her guns pointed at the line where the top and bottom door met in the center. The doors were less than two inches open when she let loose with four shots through the slit in the doors. The two Klix guards poised with laser rifles on the other side flew back on the deck, dead.

"Four shots, Sheen?" asked Chase, "through a slit in the doors?"

"Yes, Commander. I believe it is what your military calls a double-tapping. I did not wish to fail you again. They are both very dead, I assure you."

"Thank you, Sheen...nicely done, but you didn't fail me. Reload and save your ammo. One shot should suffice."

Sheen blushed. "Yes, Commander."

Sheen added bullets to each magazine and then holstered her weapons.

"Any more, Sheen?" asked Chase.

Sheen held out her arm, scanning the top deck. "I detect no Klix between us and the ships."

"Okay then, let's move out."

They cradled their survivors in their arms and ran as quickly as they could to their ships. Max, Gage, and Evelyn were waiting outside on the cargo ramp. Gage saw them coming and ran toward them, taking his mother from Sheen's arms.

"Thank you, Sheen," said Gage, his eyes welling with tears. "It's okay, Mom, I gotcha. Are you all right—you okay?"

Mrs. Bielinski looked up and smiled. "I'm okay," she said. "I never thought I would see you again. Your brother Chase found me."

"Get some water over here," Gage screamed. "Now!" Gage's eyes watered as he looked at Chase, trying to hold back tears. "I owe you one, Chief," he said, sniffling.

"You don't owe me anything. Thanks for taking care of everyone."

Gage nodded, wiping his eyes.

"Now, let's get these people on board and get outta here," said Chase. "Mom, Dad, you're on the Promise. Sheen, can you please carry my dad? Max, you're with me on the Vengeance. We rendezvous on the dark side of Earth's moon. Be ready to wormhole in five minutes."

"Yes, Commander."

"But we should stay with you," Gwen said. "We can help you."

"Sorry, Mom...you look after Dad. Make sure he drinks a lot, but not too fast. I have my mission; I have to end this."

She looked at him worried. "Please be careful, Son."

"Don't worry. I'll be fine."

"Sheen, you're in command of the Promise with Tripp. Please take care of my parents. And I need you to move some equipment from the Promise to the Vengeance. Can you do that for me?"

"Yes, Commander."

Chase whispered into her ear, and she jumped immediately—from the ground to the top of the cargo deck of the Promise—carrying Chase's father. A slight yelp was heard from Martin as she landed on the cargo deck with him in her arms.

Chase yelled to the cargo deck from below, "You okay,

Dad?"

"I'm all right; just scared the crap outta me. Did you see that? Did you see her jump?"

"Yeah, Dad sorry; I should have told her to take the ramp. I forget how literal Sheen can be."

Mrs. Chambers ran up the ramp to where Sheen was carrying Martin.

"Martin, are you all right?" she asked.

"I'm fine...fine. Just startled me, is all."

"Mr. Chambers' vital signs are within normal parameters," Sheen replied. "However, he is dehydrated and in need of water."

"But you jumped all the way to the cargo bay," said Gwen.

"I am sorry. I did not realize it would frighten him. It seemed the quickest way to get him to water."

"No, no—it's okay. I was just surprised, that's all. Thank you for carrying him and for saving us."

"You are most welcome, Gwen. Please take care of Martin while I perform a task for Commander Chase."

Sheen disappeared into the ship as Evelyn came running down the ramp and threw her arms around Chase, hugging him hard.

"You're all right? Are you hurt?"

"I'm fine. Would you please help my folks, on the Promise?"

"No. I'm coming with you."

"You can't...not where we're going. Please. I don't have time to explain, but I'll join you shortly."

"I can't lose you again, Chase Chambers—not again."

"I'll be fine. Please. I have to do this or nobody will ever be safe."

Eve grabbed his head and pulled him close to her, kissing him as hard and long as she could. Chase hugged her close, kissed her on the lips and face.

"I'll be right back, I promise," he said. "I will."

He turned away, and then turned back, grabbing her one more time for a last kiss.

"You be careful you...you damn amazing Piecer soldier you," she said.

Eve walked backward up the ramp, tears streaming down her face, staring at him. Sheen returned from the Vengeance and headed up the ramp, quickly catching up to Eve.

"Please don't take any chances. Be safe," Eve shouted to Chase, crying.

Eve watched from the ramp as Chase and Max entered the Klix scout ship.

I love you, she mouthed as the door closed on the Vengeance. "Come back to me," she whispered to herself.

"We must go, Evelyn," said Sheen. "Do not worry. Commander Chase is a very capable Commander."

"I'm so scared," said Eve. "I don't know what I'll do if something happens to him."

Sheen put her arm around Eve and led her up the cargo ramp. "I do not know what will happen, Evelyn. I will be without a Commander, too. I feel twitchy, but I must focus on our mission as you must as well, because Commander Chase has asked that of us."

Eve hugged Sheen until the cargo bay door closed.

"We must hurry," said Sheen. "The Lone Star has left, and we must rendezvous with them."

Sheen made her way to the helm, started the engines, and the Promise took off following the Lone Star into space.

The Vengeance engines were running, and Chase and Max were ready to go.

"Where to, Captain?" asked Max.

"Space," said Chase. "Get us out of orbit heading for Earth—engines only, no wormholes yet. And you really don't have to call me captain."

"I know," said Max, "but you earned it."

"Let's go finish this, then."

"Aye aye, Captain!"

The ship took off vertically, and they reached space in seconds. Chase reached his hand under the helm console, searching. Big Boom-Boom was still there.

"Max, take us to the nearest asteroid field, but just outside it."

"I don't know what you're up to, but there is an asteroid field starboard of us. We'll be there in sixty seconds."

"Great. Let me check to see if Sheen did what I asked."

"Just so you know, Captain, I disabled their navigation telemetry, so they can't send us trans-warping back to the Klix world like before. We can use the wormhole engines again, if you like."

"What? Put it back!"

"Put it back?"

"Yes. Re-enable the telemetry device."

"You sure?"

"I'm sure," said Chase.

"Okay; but I hope you know what you're doing."

"We'll see," said Chase. "Can you rig a timer for Big Boom-Boom, and a timer for the ship to open a wormhole?"

"Sure. But you told me to change it back the way the Klix had it."

"I know. Set the coordinates for Earth's moon just like before."

"Did you hit your head? We won't get there, ya know. With the telemetry device active, we'll head right back to the Klix world."

"I know."

"You want to tell me what's going on?"

"You'll see soon enough."

"Can you rig the com, so we can communicate through the Dragonflies?"

"The ones on the Promise? Are they here?"

"Yes; I had Sheen bring them over...along with a couple of spacesuits. They're in the cargo bay."

"Sure, I'll patch the com in from them to the main com station of the Vengeance. Piece of cake."

"Great. Now set those timers."

"How long?"

"Set the wormhole timer for three minutes and Big

Boom-Boom's timer for four minutes."

Max pressed a few buttons on the bomb and on the console of the scout ship. "Done, now what?"

The ship's alarm clicked loudly.

"What the hell is that?" asked Chase.

"Klix," said Max. "Three heavy cruisers headed our way."

"Let 'em come. Hug the asteroid belt and lead 'em away from the Promise and the Lone Star."

"They are in pursuit," said Max. "We're being hailed, Captain—from their lead ship."

"Hello, brother, did you miss me? You cannot escape, you know. It's over for you."

I wondered when he'd show up, Chase thought to himself before turning to Max.

"Ignore him and help me with these spacesuits...and I need something to write with."

"What the hell are you doing?"

"Prop them up in the pilot's and copilot's seat. Put their helmets on too."

Max propped the suit up in the copilot's chair while Chase manipulated the suit in the captain's chair.

"I need something to write on."

"What are you talking about?" asked Max.

"I'm making a sign."

"You're making a sign...for what?"

"Can you take that side panel off the console? It's about the right size."

"Sure—no problem—here...but why?"

"You got something to write with?"

"Umm, no," said Max. "I didn't think I'd be needing a pen in space."

"That stinger you're carrying one of ours?"

"Yes. I tossed the Klix glove...started to smell."

"Can I borrow it?"

"Sure. You gonna write with a stinger?"

"Yep. Gonna burn a note on this metal."

Chase laser-burned a note on the side panel, making the

letters large and dark.

"You are one crazy mutha," Max quipped. "You know that?"

"This is for Loose," he said.

"He'll know what that means?" asked Max.

"He'll know."

"Okay...hope this works."

"It'll work. I'm counting on his arrogance...and he has no shortage of arrogance. Now start those timers, and let's get to the cargo bay."

The ship continued heading away from the Promise and Lone Star, going faster as it got farther away from the Klix world.

"The telemetry device is active again, Captain," said Max. "If we warp anywhere, we'll end up back at the Klix world—same as before."

"Perfect," said Chase. "Get ready."

***

On Loose's Klix ship, the Klix captain started click-laughing. "Colonel Loose!" he said, "he has taken the same scout ship he came in. Your telemetry device is active on the ship. He has set the coordinates for Earth's moon. If he tries to use the wormhole engines, he will end up at our home world as before. Your brother is a fool."

"Yes...yes, he is," replied Loose. "He really fucked up this time."

"Chase," said Loose over the com, "surrender now or you will be destroyed. You cannot win." Loose smirked, turning off the com. "Enter those coordinates into our ships, and we will be there waiting for him!" Loose shouted to the Klix Captain.

"Yes, Colonel Loose. It is too easy."

"Sadly, it is," said Loose with a sigh. "I expected more of a challenge from him, but I have always been able to outsmart him. Oh well, every dog has his day and all that. Today is mine. Have your weapons armed and ready to fire."

"Yes, Colonel Loose."

"Chase, they're leaving. They're trans-warping away," said Max. "Where they going?"

"To meet their maker," said Chase. "Let's fly."

They headed down to the cargo bay and boarded the twin Dragonflies.

"These ready?" asked Chase.

"Yep; anything we say into the com on the Dragonflies will appear to be coming from the Vengeance's com. When did you get these on board?"

"Sheen put them here—before we took off."

"I love that girl," said Max. "I really do."

Chase laughed. "Time to go," he said. "We need to make sure we're nowhere near those Klix world coordinates."

"Aye aye, Captain. Wouldn't hurt to hide behind one of the larger asteroids, either; it's going to be a big boom."

Chase and Max flew out of the cargo bay and headed into the asteroid belt.

"Be careful," said Chase. "Stay hidden for a bit."

"Roger that."

"How much time left?" asked Chase.

"There goes the Vengeance...it just trans-warped away, right on time."

Loose's three Klix ships arrived at the coordinates originally entered in Chase's Klix scout ship. They armed their weapons, waiting for Chase's ship to appear. On cue, the Vengeance appeared from a wormhole above the Klix world, directly in front of Loose's three Klix cruisers. The ship went dark for a moment—as before—until the engines came back online and the forward hull became transparent. The two propped-up spacesuits with helmets appeared, sitting in the pilot and copilot seats draped with a sign.

"Chase, you fool. You took the same ship. You're slipping, brother."

"Sacrificium Pro Victoria, remember, Loose?" said Chase from the com in the Dragonfly.

"Colonel Loose, shall we fire?" asked the Klix captain in the starboard ship to Loose's own.

"No. Hold your fire. He is no threat to us. He can't flee and his weapons are useless. Besides, I want to see what he's up to," replied Loose. "You can't go anywhere, brother," he said over the com. "I have disabled your ship with my telemetry device, as before. Stupid mistake...even for you."

"You win," said Chase. "Just let my friends go."

"I don't think so," Loose replied. "Of course, I'll keep Eve, and maybe that robot. I'm sure I can get Max to fix her again."

"I don't think so!" Max said from his Dragonfly.

"Oh, you're on board with Chase, too? Splendid. You really are making this easy."

Loose waved his hand and initiated the loud-sound weapon on Chase's ship, attempting to render them unconscious. The ship vibrated as the sound became louder and louder. The spacesuits propped up in the pilot and copilot seats stared straight out the transparent hull, holding the sign Chase had made.

"Something's wrong," said Loose. "They're not moving. They're not covering their ears or trying to block the sound. Zoom in on the pilot. He's holding something."

Loose's ship's camera zoomed closer and closer to the pilot and copilot.

"Enlarge it, you fool!" Loose yelled. "I can't read it."

The Klix held up his translator to read the sign. "Colonel Loose, it says: 'This is for mankind and for Spot.' What does it mean?"

"What time you got?" Chase radioed to Max in the other Dragonfly.

"Five seconds to boom-boom. Four, three, two..." Max replied over the com.

"Never underestimate your opponent, Loose," Chase said through the com.

"Shields up," screamed Loose, punching his engines. "Evasive maneuvers!"

"Boom!" said Max. "Space glitter."

The Vengeance exploded in a nuclear EMP fireball, and

the three Klix cruisers were engulfed in the explosion. The EMP blast rained down on the Klix world, halting their machines, ships, and communication. The silver slowed and solidified. The smelter machinery stopped, and the Klix world was plunged into darkness. Klix ships below orbit crashed while those in orbit were damaged by the blast and stuck there.

"I'm sorry about your brother," said Max, "but not a lot."

"He had it coming," replied Chase. "He would have killed us all."

"I know, but still...he was your brother."

"He crossed the line a long time ago in the woods. I should have killed him then. A lot of people are dead because I let him live. That won't happen again."

"How we gonna get back to the Promise?" asked Max, changing the subject.

"I arranged for a ride." said Chase grinning from ear to ear.

The Promise appeared from a wormhole just outside the asteroid belt.

"Commander, this is Acting Captain Sheen of the Piecer ship Promise. We have monitored the explosion on the Klix world. Well done, Commander."

"Thank you, Sheen. If you would please open the launch bay doors, we'll come aboard and head back to Earth."

Another voice interrupted over the com. "Chase, this is Eve—are you okay?"

"I'm fine, Eve. I told you I'd be right back!"

"Commander, the launch bay doors are open and waiting for your arrival."

Chase and Max flew the Dragonflies back into the Promise cargo bay.

"Sheen!" Chase yelled over the com, "rendezvous with the Lone Star at Earth's moon."

"Yes, Commander. Coordinates have been entered. Prepare for wormhole initiation."

The wormhole opened and the Promise disappeared inside, arriving just behind Earth's moon where the Lone Star was waiting.

"Chase, you made it," said Gage over the com. "Is everyone all right? Sheen radioed us after the explosion. Nicely done, Chief."

"Thanks. I had a lot of help and we're all good here."

"We've been monitoring the Klix on Earth from behind the moon," said Gage. "There's a lot of activity and they seem to be pulling out. All their orbiting ships trans-warped outta here already."

"Roger that," said Chase. "I guess they got the word that their world was under attack."

"Hey, Cha-Cha, this is Tripp. Nice move with the EMP. Payback is a bitch. Hector wants to know what's next."

"Sheen, put this on the com to both ships. I want everyone to hear."

"Yes, Commander."

"Everyone, this is Chase 523 of the Piecer Corp. I wanted you to know that we were successful in deploying an EMP device above the Klix world. Their world has gone dark, and their machines and smelter are dead."

Everyone on both ships cheered as Chase continued. "Most of the Klix have fled Earth to return to their home world. We have weapons on both ships that we will need to get down to our families on Earth to drive off any remaining Klix..."

Chase's speech was interrupted by Sheen.

"Commander, my sensors detect ten Klix cruisers appearing through wormholes around us."

The ship's computer blared a warning: "Alert! Ten Klix cruiser-class vessels have surrounded the Promise. Alert."

Chapter Thirty-Three

A Rock and a Hard Place

"Everyone, get to your battle stations," Chase screamed through the com.

"Weapons hot, Sheen," Tripp yelled.

"Commander, our weapons are online and ready," said Sheen.

"Chief, there are ten Klix cruisers—all armed to the teeth," said Gage. "Don't look good."

"Sheen, can you put out a distress call? Maybe there are other ships in the vicinity— with people that hate the Klix as much as we do—and maybe they could assist us."

"Yes, Commander," she replied, initiating the distress call.

"Commander, we are being hailed by their lead ship."

"Chase 523, this is General Klume of the Klix Supremacy. There is no one coming to rescue you, Captain. There is no one left to come to your aid. You will surrender your vessels or be destroyed."

"It's over, Klume," Chase replied. "You lost. Go home and take care of your people."

"It's not over for me. I do not lose to humans."

"You already did. Your planet is in shambles, Klume...a little trick I learned from you, with your EMP blast. Your ships are gone. Your smelter has gone cold. Your world has gone dark."

"Our remaining ships are returning to our world to undo the damage you have done. It will be my pleasure to destroy you for the crimes against my people."

"Sheen, target Klume's ship with everything we've got."

"Yes, Commander. Ship's weapons are locked on Klume's star cruiser."

"Our sensors indicate you have targeted our ship. Your weapons are of little consequence, Piecer. Our ten cruisers are more than a match for your two inferior Piecer ships."

"Max, anything you can do to give us a better chance?"

"You want me to start throwing shit at them?"

"Got any ideas?"

Max paused, trying to think of any weapon he could come up with. "Wait; remember when we worm-holed away from the Quargg?"

"They'll destroy us the minute we initiate a wormhole," replied Chase.

"I saved the computer sequence to instantly open a wormhole and fly in with a burst of our engines. The timing was perfect and should work again. It's all controlled by the ship's computer."

"Max, I could kiss you!" said Chase.

"That's the second time you said you wanted to kiss me. I'm starting to think you love me."

"Sheen, send the computer sequence to the Lone Star."

"Yes, Commander. Sequence has been relayed to the Lone Star computers."

"Gage, this is Chase. The program sequence we just sent will allow you to wormhole away instantly. Use it and get the hell out of here. Rendezvous at Alpha-Nine."

"What about you?"

"We'll be right behind you."

"Roger that," said Gage. "I just initiated the sequence; how long does it—"

The Lone Star disappeared, cutting him off in mid-sentence.

"Do not attempt to flee!" screamed Klume. "Fire

weapons!"

The Promise was rocked with multiple blasts from Klume's ships.

"We have damage to several areas of the ship, Commander," said Sheen. "Some passengers are reporting injury. No deaths have been reported as yet."

The Promise was rocked with another blast from Klume's cruiser.

"Reactor is offline," said the computer-generated voice.

"Max, get to that reactor and get it back online—now."

"On my way, Captain."

"Surrender now, or the next blast will destroy you," said Klume. "We will find your other ship and destroy them, too."

"Sheen, do we still have weapons online?"

"Yes, Commander."

"Fire everything we have at Klume's ship."

"Yes, Commander."

The Promise bucked with the release of all her weapons. The shields held on Klume's cruiser. The Klix cruiser shook with each blast but stayed steady.

"You dare fire on me, Piecer scum?" said Klume. "When we are through with you, we will destroy your planet and every living thing on it."

Suddenly, the Lone Star appeared, firing all its weapons at Klume's ship.

"We missed you, Chase," said Gage over the com. "You were supposed to follow us."

"Sheen, evasive maneuvers...let's not make ourselves an easy target!"

"Yes, Commander."

Sheen spun the ship into a dive and then looped above the Klix cruisers.

"Gage, get the hell out of here! You have all those people on board."

"Sorry; no can do. They all voted to come back. Check this out, Chief," said Gage.

The Lone Star disappeared and reappeared behind one of

the Klix cruisers, firing a series of rockets point-blank into their rear engine. The Klix cruiser turned to fire, and the Lone Star disappeared again, reappearing behind them. Another volley of rockets hit the main engine on the Klix cruiser, sending it on fire and spinning out of control.

"Watch this, Chief."

Gage maneuvered his ship in front of one of the cruisers, waiting until it locked on and fired its weapons. He engaged the computer wormhole sequence and the Lone Star disappeared, reappearing on top of the cruiser, almost touching it. The missiles reacquired the Lone Star and hurtled toward it. Gage punched the wormhole sequence once more and disappeared. The rockets hit the cruiser he was above, blowing a hole in it. Gage reappeared behind the now-crippled ship.

"I could do this all day, Chief," Gage screamed, laughing.

The other Klix ships turned to fire on the Lone Star, but it continued popping in and out of wormholes. They could not lock on, and when they did, the Lone Star directed the missiles at the ship that fired. General Klume called out orders on the com.

"This is General Klume—all ships target the Promise. Stand down, Piecer. You have no wormhole engine."

"Chase, what's the call," said Gage still popping in and out of wormholes.

"Gage, no matter what happens...get those people home."

"No can do, Chief. They took another vote."

"Goddammit, Gage..."

Suddenly, a fleet of Quargg ships appeared, surrounding the melee.

"Alert! Thirty Quargg battle cruisers approaching. Alert!"

"Chase, we got company," said Gage. "Are you seeing this?"

"Go, Gage, get out of here. The Quargg are after me, not you. Save yourselves. Rebuild the Earth. Go!"

"I can't leave you, Chief. Nobody gets left behind. You said so yourself."

"Gage, there's thirty ships out there. They all want me.

The Quargg have no issue with you. Go, that's an order."

"I love you, Chase...we all do. We'll be nearby. I'll figure something out to help."

The Lone Star blinked out and was gone.

"Sheen, open the com to Max and Tripp only."

"Yes, Commander."

"This is Chase. I'm sorry, but with our core offline, we can't outrun the remaining Klix ships or the Quargg. If they take us prisoner, they will surely kill us. I say we fight them with everything we got and give the Lone Star time to get away."

Eve ran up to Chase and threw her arms around him. "If I'm going to die, I'm glad I'll be with you," she said.

"I'm sorry Eve. I should never have gotten you into this. Soldiers know they could die, and they do it willingly for their brothers in the Corp or for their country, but you're not a soldier. You should be home—safe—anywhere but here."

"Home safe? There is no place like that anymore. I'm as much a soldier as you are. It was my choice to be here, and we'll live or die together."

Chase hugged her close as Sheen came forward. "Commander," said Sheen, "thank you for freeing me and treating me like a person and not a machine. It has been an honor to be your first officer and your friend."

"Thank you for saving my life, Sheen. Soren would be proud of you. You have been the best first officer and friend I ever had."

Sheen blinked repeatedly, her eyes filling with tears. "Commander, I appear to be malfunctioning; my eyes are leaking fluids again."

Chase smiled. "You're not malfunctioning. You're just crying."

"I do not like this," said Sheen. "Crying does not help. Tell him, Evelyn; it does not repair the malfunction."

"It's the Soren in you, Sheen," said Chase. "It's a good thing."

"Yeah, Sheen," said Eve, "it's a good thing."

Sheen paused and then smiled slightly, wiping her eyes. "Thank you. Sheen will remember. It is Soren; it is a good thing."

Max broke in on the com as the Promise was rocked by another blast from the Klix.

"Captain, this is Max. Thanks for everything. It's been a helluva ride, sir."

"Thanks, Max. You saved the world. Who gets to say that ever in their life?"

"Wasn't exactly alone, ya know," replied Max.

"Yeah, but you did most of it. It was a pleasure knowing you, Stinky."

Max laughed. "Same here, you sonofabitch."

"Okay!" shouted Chase, "let's man those battle stations and give them something to remember us by. Those weapons still locked on Klume's ship?"

"Yes, Commander."

"Max," said Chase over the com, "do we still have engines?"

"No wormhole—core is still offline—but the engines are okay."

"Then let's go down fighting!" said Chase. "Set the coordinates for Klume's ship."

"You gonna ram him?" asked Max.

"We have one helluva missile left with a tritanium hull. I'm gonna park this bitch on Klume's bridge."

Max laughed. "You're a crazy mother. I like it. Coordinates entered. Whenever you're ready, Captain."

Sheen interrupted. "Commander, we are being hailed by the Quargg flagship. It is an Admiral Seloth."

"Piecer Chase 523, please withdraw."

"Commander, he wishes us to withdraw."

"I heard him, Sheen."

"Admiral Seloth, this is Piecer Chase 523. I do not understand your request to withdraw."

The com cut in and out with a squeal, and then another voice broke in. Some arguing could be heard in an alien dialect.

"Chase 523, this Milat Seloth—the Quargg prisoner you saved at the Pwyll crater. Admiral Seloth is my father. He has asked you to withdraw so that your ship will not be further damaged as he destroys the Klix scum. We are prepared to offer you assistance, after we deal with these vile creatures."

"Milat Seloth, this is Chase 523. Thank you, and please thank your father. We appreciate your assistance and are preparing to withdraw."

Immediately, Admiral Seloth's ship moved into position between General Klume's ship and the Promise. Over the com, they could hear arguing between Klume and Seloth.

"You will stand down or be destroyed," said Admiral Seloth. "You are no match for my fleet."

General Klume's ship fired another missile at the Promise, but Admiral Seloth's ship intercepted it, and it exploded harmlessly on their shields.

"Get us outta here, Sheen," said Chase.

"Yes, Commander...full reverse."

The Promise pulled back and away from the Klix cruisers and the Quargg fleet. They watched as the Klix launched missiles against the Quargg to no avail. The Quargg responded with their own missiles and blew up three of the remaining Klix vessels. Finally, a wormhole opened, and General Klume disappeared, fleeing back to his world. The remaining Klix vessels put up a fight but were heavily damaged. The few that remained intact trans-warped back to Kattar. The rest were destroyed by the Quargg.

Chapter Thirty-Four

Milat Seloth

Chase watched from the deck of the Promise until it was over. Suddenly, the Lone Star appeared through a wormhole and hailed the Promise.

"Chase, this is Gage—what's going on? Couldn't leave without you. We got your back. Where'd the Klix go?"

"We're okay for now," Chase replied over the com. "The Quargg are here to help."

"Here to help, huh? Better check your wallet."

Chase laughed. "No...they really are."

"Well, wonders never cease, huh, Chase?"

"One sec, Gage," said Chase. "Sheen, please invite Admiral Seloth to our ship for a drink to thank him formally."

"Commander, I have contacted Admiral Seloth's vessel, and he and his daughter have accepted your invitation."

Chase hit the ship's internal com button. "Max, do you have any of that Pappy Van Winkle's left?"

"I'm on my way, Captain—with one bottle in hand."

"Sheen, please come and meet our guests with me."

"Yes, Commander."

"Gage, I'm going to have to get back to you. We're having the Quargg over to thank them."

"You be careful," replied Gage, "and lock up the good silverware."

"Roger that," Chase replied, laughing.

Chase and Eve met the admiral, his first officer, and his

daughter in the galley. Admiral Seloth was dressed the same as Admiral Malton had been at the Blue Angel: with a yellow-orange sash, a silver-plated stinger, and a large medallion pinned to the front of the sash indicating his rank as Admiral. His skin was wrinkled, and he looked older than Admiral Malton, but fit and muscular through his black spacesuit.

His first officer never spoke, standing off to the side, near the exit with his arms crossed, a prominent silver-plated stinger hanging on the sash at his right, his hand nearby. He was taller and thinner than Seloth, and his black-almond eyes shifted back and forth suspiciously. His spacesuit was similar to Seloth's—with a green sash and smaller front medallion—indicating he was an officer, but of lower rank than Seloth.

Max arrived armed with his stinger and filled glasses for everyone, setting them down on the galley table. Sheen arrived, sliding down the galley ladder—followed by Tripp. The first officer waved off his drink as Seloth approached Chase.

"Captain, if I may have a moment of your time in private..." Seloth whispered, "before we begin?"

"Of course," said Chase, "let's just step over here, away from everyone."

They walked off to the farthest corner of the galley and Seloth leaned in close to Chase to speak. "I was called to this sector of space to investigate the loss of one of our flagships, the Malton, when I received your distress call."

Chase swallowed uneasily and instinctively felt for his guns.

"Do not worry, Captain, Admiral Malton was a drunken fool and overly fond of Bloddo. He was known for his carousing and foolish decisions. How he ever got command of his own ship is beyond me...blackmail, probably."

"Any luck finding that flagship?" asked Chase.

"We haven't found his ship or crew, but three of my cruisers reported they were in pursuit of a Piecer vessel—just like this one."

"You don't say..."

Admiral Seloth half-smiled. "Apparently, it was the Piecer ship..." Seloth paused and carefully pronounced the name of the ship, "...Province," he continued.

"The Province?" asked Chase.

"Yes, under the command of a Captain Race 532."

Chase cocked his eye. "I've heard of him," he said. "Kind of a rogue Piecer. I'll keep my eye out for him."

"Thank you, Captain. That is all I ask."

"And your cruisers...they are searching for the Province?"

"Yes, Captain. I have corrected their ships' logs to that effect."

Chase reached out his hand to shake, and Seloth shook it firmly and earnestly.

"Well, I hope they find this Captain Race," he said with a sly smile.

"I love my daughter, Captain. She is the starlight of my life. What you did for her, I will never forget. It is an honor to meet you."

"You would have done the same," replied Chase.

"Oh I doubt that," said Seloth, laughing, "but you did, and I am in your debt."

"Let's call it even," said Chase.

"As you wish, Captain," said Seloth. "Friends?"

"Friends," replied Chase. "Let's get back to the celebration. I owe you a drink."

Chase and Seloth walked back to the center of the galley where everyone had already picked up their glasses.

"I would like to propose a toast..." said Chase, "to Admiral Seloth and his brave fleet. We thank you for everything that you did."

"You are most welcome," said the admiral and downed his shot of whiskey. "Ooh, that is very good—very good, indeed. Thank you. And I would like to thank your Captain Chase 523 for saving my daughter from the Klix. Kindness is a rare commodity in a cold, uncaring universe. It is not something I come across very often."

He held out his empty shot glass, and Max filled it again.

Admiral Seloth gulped it down eagerly. "Ooh, that is so good," said the admiral. His cheeks blushed bright green, and his eyes went wide and bugged out. "We don't have anything like this on our planet. More...please."

"Careful," said Chase, "it sneaks up on you."

"I do feel warm and tingly," he replied , laughing while turning to Sheen, leering at her. "And this must be the Courtesan I have heard so much about? She is beautiful."

"Thank you, Admiral," Sheen replied curtly.

"Can I purchase time with her, Captain?"

Sheen looked surprised and then angry. She turned to Chase and then immediately turned back to the admiral. "Chase 523 is my Commander. He has freed me," she said, placing her hands on her twin .45s. "My time cannot be purchased. Sheen does what Sheen wants."

"Oh, she is fierce. I like a fierce woman. How much?"

"I'm sorry, Admiral," Chase replied, "but Sheen is not for sale. She is part of my crew as long as she wants to be. If she would like to go with you, that is her choice to make."

"Well, Sheen..." said the admiral turning to her, "would you like to go with me? I will give you whatever you want. Do you want silver? I have silver."

"Sheen is not for sale," she said. "Sheen will service who Sheen wants."

Admiral Seloth laughed. "So feisty," he said smiling, undaunted. "I can show you the stars, Sheen," he continued, gesturing to the port window.

"I have seen stars," said Sheen. "I prefer to remain with my Commander and my friends."

"Are you sure I cannot change your mind?"

"I am sure."

"You are very lucky, Captain. She is loyal to you, and I can see why. You are a good human—which is exceedingly rare in my opinion."

"Thank you," said Chase, "but there are a lot of us."

"Not in my experience," he said turning to Evelyn. "How about this yellow-haired one... Evelyn, is it? Would you like to see the stars with me?"

Eve pulled in close to Chase, holding on to his arm, moving away from the admiral.

"I don't bite," he said, laughing, "well, not too hard, anyway."

Milat moved closer to Chase and began leaning against him and rubbing herself up and down against his leg. Chase stepped back, gently holding Milat at arm's length, looking at Admiral Seloth for what to do, and not wanting to offend.

"It seems my daughter has taken a liking to you as well, Captain."

Eve turned her body, putting herself between Chase and Milat, scowling at her.

"I see you have several women desiring you," said the admiral laughing. "You are indeed a lucky man."

"Tell me about it," said Max, rolling his eyes, and pouring himself another drink.

"I don't have them..." Chase started to say. "I just—"

"Come, daughter," said the admiral, interrupting, pulling his daughter's arm.

"No," she said, "I wish to remain with Chase 523. He rescued me; I am his."

Admiral Seloth sighed. "Do not become a parent," he whispered to Chase. "You will love them completely until your early death because of them."

He smiled wistfully and sighed heavily.

"It is time to go. Come, Milat, you will have to find someone else to rub against. The Captain has enough women to keep him occupied. Besides, he is human. You will mate with Quargg and give me many grandsons. No offense, Captain."

"None taken," said Chase.

"But I love him!" Milat squealed. "And he loves me."

Admiral Seloth shook his head from side to side and looked down. "I apologize for my daughter. Milat is only sixty-seven and she has not matured past her adolescent phase."

Milat huffed and turned away from Chase, giving Eve a

threatening look.

Max handed the half-empty bottle of whiskey to Admiral Seloth. "Here, take this with our compliments and thanks. It's the last bottle."

The admiral's eyes lit up with surprise. "Thank you," he said, accepting the bottle and hugging Max close. "This will make the trip home easier on an old Quargg."

Max stood awkwardly, not hugging him back.

Seloth continued hugging him for too long.

"Okay," said Max, pulling away, "you're welcome—really—you're welcome."

The admiral turned and headed up the galley ladder with his now-weeping daughter in tow. His first officer waited until he cleared the ladder and followed silently behind him. Everyone waved to the Quargg as they left the ship.

"That was a nice gesture," Chase said to Max, "to give him the last of your whiskey."

"Yeah, well, he did save our lives... and it's not exactly..." Max stammered for a moment, looking sheepish.

"What? Not exactly what?" asked Chase.

"I kinda stole a few cases of it from Shoom. It wasn't exactly my last bottle...but it was the last bottle from the first case, so it was mostly true."

Chase laughed. "Well, it was still nice of you to give him some for the road."

"I'm a helluva guy," said Max, laughing, patting his space suit and searching the floor. "Hey, has anyone seen my stinger? I know I had it when I came in."

"I believe Admiral Malton removed it from you—while you were hugging," said Sheen. "Were you unaware of this?"

"He hugged me. I wasn't hugging him," said Max. "Chase, Seloth stole my gun."

Chase laughed. "Let him have it. We have more, besides, it's what Quargg do. Probably should check the silverware, too!"

"Here I thought he was grateful, and he was just picking my pocket," said Max.

"Thank you, Commander," Sheen interrupted.

"For what?"

"For not selling me to the Quargg."

"You are not mine to sell, Sheen."

Sheen reached out and hugged Chase, with Eve still draped around his arm. Sheen reached around them both and squeezed them hard.

"I have not known friends," she said. "Thank you for being Sheen's friends."

Chase smiled and hugged her back. Eve reached out and hugged Sheen too. The three stood in an embrace for a moment, and then Sheen's hands slid down Chase's and Eve's back, and she simultaneously squeezed their butt cheeks. Chase's and Eve's eyes went wide with surprise. Sheen smiled.

Epilogue

The Promise and Lone Star landed at the Piecer Academy Stadium where the bombs had first started to fall only a few days earlier. Weapons were distributed to everyone on board, including those children who could understand how to use them. Chase, Sheen, Eve, Tripp, and Max descended the Promise cargo ramp with weapons drawn. Gage and Hector descended the Lone Star, carrying working laser rifles. It was quiet, still, and as hot as it had been on graduation day.

"Sheen, can you scan the area?" asked Chase.

Sheen raised her arm and scanned the perimeter of the stadium. "There are numerous heat signatures in the forest side of the stadium, Commander. They are unarmed."

"Can you tell if they are Klix?"

"Negative, Commander—though they appear to be of various sizes."

"You getting anything with that nose of yours, Hector?" Gage asked.

"No, sir. Don't think they're Klix, though. Klix have a certain stink about them."

"Seein' anything, Tripp?" Gage whispered.

"No, sir; just bushes and trees. Whoever they are, they are well-hidden."

They all moved down the ramps toward the woods. Suddenly, a young boy stepped out from one of the bushes and ran toward them.

"Don't shoot!" Chase yelled.

The little boy ran up to Chase and hugged his leg. Then he waved to the bushes and trees, motioning to come forward. Little by little, more and more children and adults came out of the woods, hugging them, crying, and thanking them for coming to help.

"Have they all gone?" one elderly man asked. "Is it over?"

"It's over," Chase replied, "for now, anyway."

The old man started to cry, unable to hold back his tears, and patted Chase and Max on the back. "Thank you," he said. "We thought we were all dead."

"Do you know how to use this?" Max asked, handing him a laser rifle.

"If it works," he replied. "None of our weapons work."

"Works fine," Max said. "If you see any Klix, shoot 'em."

"All the Klix around here left," he said. "They just took off in their ships...like they were never here."

As more people emerged from the woods, Chase and his crew passed out rations, water, and weapons. Chase's mother was put in charge of food distribution while his father was getting his strength back. Soon, survivors were showing up from underground, including some Piecer Corp soldiers.

"What do we do now, Chief?" asked Gage. "Looks like it's pretty safe."

"We take care of our people and rebuild. The former Corp members can train everyone how to use weapons and fight."

"You think the Klix will come back?"

"They'll be back."

"Should we set up defenses?" asked Hector. "You want us to set up a perimeter?"

"No, not playin' defense anymore. Besides it's not necessary. It will take 'em years to rebuild their ships and machinery. We have time."

"So what do we do now?" asked Tripp.

"I can't tell you all what to do. There is no Corp anymore—not officially. You're free to do whatever you want."

"At first, all I wanted to do was to go lie on a beach," said Tripp. "Never thought much past that. And then I thought we'd all be dead by now anyways."

"Me too!" said Hector, grinning at Tripp. "I thought Tripp would be dead by now too."

Hector laughed.

"Oh, very funny," said Tripp. "Seriously, you should think about opening a comedy club."

"What are you going to do, Chief?" Gage asked.

Chase took a long deep breath. "I'm tired of holding back my anger, playing nice-nice with the monsters," he replied. "I'm tired of defending, trusting phony truces and lies. Everywhere I've ever been, there is always some scumbag taking advantage of some poor guy who just wants to be left alone to live his life. I'm sick to death of monsters preying on the weak, and it's time they feared a monster. I'm going to be that monster."

"How you gonna do that, Boss?" asked Hector.

"I'm gonna kill all the monsters," Chase replied in a calm quiet voice, "starting with Klume."

"You going after Klume?" asked Tripp.

"Klume is the first monster on the list. He's not getting away with killing our people and my friends. I have a ship, and I have weapons. I'm taking the fight to them, and I'm starting with Klume."

"All by your lonesome?" asked Tripp.

"Anyone who wants to join me is welcome. I'm going to do what I was trained to do; I'm going to rain holy hell on them."

Everyone was silent for a moment.

"I will come with you," said Sheen. "I am Sheen. I am Soren. Sheen will kill the monsters with you, Commander."

Eve looked at Sheen and then Chase. "I'm coming too," she said. "You're not going anywhere without me."

"Count me in," said Max. "You're going to need help, and I'd get bored or drunk just sitting around waiting for shit to happen."

"I'd like to come, Chief," said Gage, "but I should stay and take care of my mom. I'm all she's got now."

Mrs. Bielinski walked down the ramp slowly, holding on to Chase's father's arm for support. She heard Gage and started yelling, "Don't you dare stay here to take care of me when there are people out there needing your help! That's not how I raised you. I can take care of myself."

"But Mom, you can hardly walk by yourself."

"I'll be fine. I just need a little rest, is all."

"We'll watch out for your mom, Gage," said Martin. "You don't have to worry. But it's your decision to make."

"You get your speckled ass back on that ship and go save people," Mrs. Bielinski said, scolding him. "That's your purpose; that's why God touched you."

Gage laughed and hugged her hard with tears in his eyes. "My speckled ass?"

"You know what I mean," she said.

"Thanks, Mom, and thanks, Martin," said Gage. "I know she's in good hands."

Gage raised his hand and nodded. "I'm in too. I wasn't trained to fight just to end up sitting around and wondering what you guys are up to."

"And me," said Tripp. "I've got a little score to settle with the Klix and I'm not going to miss the fun. You'll need my eyes, anyway, Cha-Cha, and you might want these."

Tripp dug into his pocket and pulled out the Piecer Stars he had collected on the stadium field.

"Where did you get those?" asked Chase.

"On the field—thought you might want yours. I have one for everyone."

"Thanks, Tripp...I did want it. Thank you very much."

Chase reached out and hugged Tripp hard. He picked up a star from Tripp's hand and pinned it to his chest.

"I know it doesn't work, but I still want it."

"Oh no, these work!" said Tripp. "Max fixed them all for us—fixed one for himself, too. And he added Klix translator tech to it. Don't need their translators anymore."

Chase turned his head slightly toward his badge. "That guy is amazing! Can you hear me, Tripp?"

"Well, I am standing right next to you, but com works loud and clear."

Tripp pinned his star on his chest to the left of his heart as Chase had done.

"I like it," he said, holding out his hand of stars. "You guys want yours?"

"I do," said Hector.

"Me too," said Gage.

Hector and Gage followed Chase's lead, pinning the com stars on their chests.

"You got any more of those stars?" Chase asked Tripp.

"I do," he said, smiling, holding out his open hand with two stars in it, "just in case."

Chase grabbed the two remaining stars and turned to Evelyn and Sheen. "We have two more Piecer Stars, and if you would like to wear them, we would be honored."

Sheen stepped forward, with her hands at her sides. "I am not a Piecer, Commander. Is it not a requirement?"

"You earned this, Sheen—for Soren and for Earth."

Chase pinned the star to the front of her vest.

"Thank you, Commander. I will cherish it," she said, her eyes tearing. "I am malfunctioning again, Commander. I apologize. I will do a system check and—"

"You're fine just the way you are, Sheen. You are not malfunctioning." Chase saluted her and she saluted back. "Eve, would you do us the honor of wearing a Piecer Star?"

Eve stepped forward next to Sheen. "I would be happy to," she said, "if you think I should."

"You more than earned it," Chase said. "Your grandfather would be very proud of you."

"He would be very happy...he would," she replied, wiping her eyes. "I think I'm malfunctioning too."

Everyone laughed except Sheen.

Hector turned to Martin standing nearby watching them. "Can you check on my mother too," Hector asked Martin, "from time to time?"

"Absolutely," said Martin. "It would be my pleasure."

"Then I'm in," said Hector, "and we have two ships, so double holy hell."

"We have no idea what we'll find out there," said Chase. "We may not see our families for a long time."

"Are you kidding?!" said Gage, laughing. "I know how to instant-wormhole now. I can pop in on weekends to see my mom."

Chase laughed, and then the smile melted from his face.

"Seriously, if we do this...we don't know what kind of forces we'll be facing."

Eve flipped the switch on her laser rifle and the familiar whine signaled it was ready. She fired at a pinecone on a branch fifty yards away, putting a perfect pencil-sized hole through it.

"They should be worried about us," said Eve, shouldering her weapon and smiling. "It's monster killing time."

Sheen pulled her pistol in an instant and shot the branch the cone was sitting on. "It is payback time," said Sheen, spinning her .45 on her finger and slipping it back in the holster in one quick move. "The shit has gone sideways. The shit has hit the fan."

"Okay, everyone," said Chase, "if you're sure. Let's go kill some monsters!"

The End

ACKNOWLEDGEMENTS

I cannot thank my wife enough for listening to the umpteenth version of The Promise. Her patience, understanding, and encouragement through this process was incredible.

Special thanks to my Beta readers who took time out of their busy lives to make this a better book. Thank you.

Thanks too, to my Facebook cover commenters.

Special thanks to the following modelers for their great 3d art:
Sevein (ship model)
Flink (star background)
Coflek Gnorg (wormhole)

ABOUT THE AUTHOR

Maxx Powr is a husband and father, founder of two companies, web site developer, programmer, vocational specialist, child & family therapist, crisis intervention specialist, 3d illustrator / animation student, and dog lover.

Maxx holds a master's degree in Rehabilitation Counseling from Southern Illinois University in Carbondale.

Note from the Author:

Thank you for reading The Promise. I really hope you enjoyed it.
Reviews are gold to authors.

If you've enjoyed this book, please consider rating it and reviewing at your favorite retailer? Thank you!

If you would like to be included in our e-mail newsletter, opt in at:
PiecerChronicles.com

Or

Send an e-mail to Maxx at: piecerchronicles@gmail.com

You can find our Facebook page here:
Facebook.com/PiecerChronicles

CPSIA information can be obtained
at www.ICGtesting.com
Printed in the USA
LVHW011728241020
669607LV00001B/25

9 780997 007152